MW01145508

INFLUENCES FROM THE BEING'S INNER DOMAIN BOOK 1

The Dominating Force
Within US

Racq Thah

Copyright © 2022 by Racq Thah.

Library of Congress Control Number:		2022915829
ISBN:	Hardcover	978-1-6698-4432-7
	Softcover	978-1-6698-4431-0
	eBook	978-1-6698-4430-3

All rights reserved. No part of this book may be reproduced or transmitted in any form or by any means, electronic or mechanical, including photocopying, recording, or by any information storage and retrieval system, without permission in writing from the copyright owner.

This is a work of fiction. Names, characters, places and incidents either are the product of the author's imagination or are used fictitiously, and any resemblance to any actual persons, living or dead, events, or locales is entirely coincidental.

Any people depicted in stock imagery provided by Getty Images are models, and such images are being used for illustrative purposes only.
Certain stock imagery © Getty Images.

Print information available on the last page.

Rev. date: 08/25/2022

To order additional copies of this book, contact:
Xlibris
844-714-8691
www.Xlibris.com
Orders@Xlibris.com
844311

The origin of all life on the earth has long been a mystery and one not yet nor perhaps will ever be completely understood or solved. No one knows for certain how our species originated or why. Some still spend much of their time thinking about these mysteries in great detail. They question our meaning, our true purpose, our value on this earth, or what really comprises our being. Beyond the obvious flesh and bone, some would question what the underlying elements of our being are. What constitutes life itself within our being? Is it only in what we see, in what we can touch, and in what we feel and experience that we should believe to be real? Is it these things that represent the primary constituents of the whole human makeup? Or is it more probable that we have limited ourselves to only what our external allows us? Could it be that we limit ourselves and are only partially aware of the whole of our makeup, the ownership of our space and our capabilities? Is there a likelihood that another layer of truth and discovery exists for those who choose, even dare, to explore further what lies unknown inside us? There is evidence that there is more to our existence than what we know, other than the tangible, the superficial, and that which is openly outwardly perceived. Significant portions of life, indeed, originate from what we do not yet acknowledge or understand.

We humans have many components within our architecture that cannot be seen, cannot be heard, or cannot be felt. These are the things that help define our being. They make the being alive. They make it special and unique. Some give us our range of emotions, our nature, our culture, our thoughts and perceptions, our perspective, and even a history. These and the other more obvious components come together to comprise our "selves," our unique composition, and our total package. It's not only to us humans that this applies. The same holds for all types of living existence. When I talk of emotions, of thoughts, and of conscious perspective, one immediately thinks I'm referring to the cerebral part of our anatomy. It's the mind or a control component of the being, that which gives us our mental abilities to decide and create thoughts. But this is not all of it, at least not entirely.

What I'm referring to is the true origin of ideas, thoughts, and emotions. It's the unknown component that answers the mysteries of what turns flesh and bone to animate life. I'm referring to the true source and stimulus that initiates feeling, impulses, and commands to be served and reacted on by the other more obvious components of the being. The mind is a part of it but more a conduit for final presentation, packaging, and distribution of the products originating from a more vital component. The mind is a partner in a well-orchestrated process. It acts primarily as a filter and as a switchboard. It controls command communication and some temporary warehousing. This is especially true in nonhuman living beings where the mind is less developed or less function rich. In these beings, its controlled channels and filters are more porous and act to pass through to other switches.

Not all beings are as complex and gifted as us humans. This is known and accepted. Not all are equipped with all the special capacities and features provided by a full portion of nature's complementing components, those familiar and those not. But all are blessed with a full portion of life's mysterious gift, the one I allude to. No matter the measure of what we can acknowledge or not, all living beings are more than what can be outwardly seen, felt, or heard. The chapters in this collection are focused on the invisible and often overlooked component—the secret, the gift of our creation and existence on this earth.

So, the question arises, what is this unknown component? Why is it a mystery? Allow me to share.

The mystery component's existence is not outwardly obvious. Rather, it is cloaked by the other more recognizable components of the being. As alluded to, it generates and supplies thoughts and ideas to the mind; it choreographs the motion, the animation, and the response of the being to all of life's stimuli. It works through the being's more obvious and known components but never directly with the outside world. Only through these other parts and processes will it interact and react with the world. It creates the impression that its contribution is actually that of the others. It never seeks recognition. It answers only to its nature and to its origin. It is primarily contained within a special domain deep within every being. It is commonly referred, when referred to at all, as the spirit. There are actually three in a human domain. It is this special domain of the three spirits that represents the third primary component in us humans. The three components together represent who and what we are.

For clarity's sake, let's identify the three components. The first component of a being is the physical one. It is made up of the body and the physically tangible structure. This part gives form, physical presence, and movement to the being. It is the direct interface to and from the others of the outside world. It's the filler of a being's space on the earth. It's what others perceive as the being. It's the vision others recognize.

The second component of a being is the control component, the mind and the nervous system. Combined with the physical component, it represents the cellular, the cytoplasmic, and the chemical and electrical reactors of the being. Like the physical component, it, too, is tangible and explained to a degree by science. The control component is thought to be the source of order and cognizant reaction and thinking. This is partially true. It assembles and orders ideas. It transmits and communicates actions and responses to the physical being. It temporarily stores information and thought.

It is in the third component, the spirit component, that stimulates and arouses the other two. It is what provides them with the raw materials to initiate response and action. The spirit component provides all the being's emotions and feelings. Ideas and thoughts originate from the spirit domains. It is through the spirit component that beings are driven. The body and mind are tools of the spirit, guided and directed by the spirit domain. The spirit gives them reason, thoughts, ideas, impulses, and emotions. The spirit stimulates the other components and orchestrates cohesiveness and coordination between the parts. It's the source of our complexity, the source of our simplicity. It's the energy and inertia that changes mass and assembly to life. It's not easy to accept the existence of this spirit component without human-defined proofs. These are usually what the actions and outputs from physical and mind components can externally touch, see, or sense. This creates a problem for the spirit.

Spirits are not external to our being. They can only deal directly through their two liaisons from a position internal to the being. Therefore, you may not be convinced of their existence. You will never touch or see them directly. But they are a part of our every action, every vision, and every thought. Spirits do exist. I will prove it. To do so, we'll need to step back and explore the mysteries of this component's existence in greater detail. The proofs will come through examples and stories.

First, let's examine what the spirit component offers its being. The spirit's contributions are many things that are important to us but none so important as life itself. It is in the spirit that a being's life originates and operates. This should be enough, but it offers much more. The value goes beyond the being. To establish the spirit's full worth, we need to first know of and develop its past, how its relationship and value to beings came about.

Spirits have existed in the earth's realms forever, much earlier than the appearance of physical beings on the earth. These physical beings came centuries later. This is where the mystery exists; they came from where? We'll discuss this later. In the earth's early existence, there were much magic, much mystery, and many things that we can't comprehend or understand based on today's contexts. But these same things made sense and were a natural part of a being's daily life and experiences in these earliest times. In these times, there was a need for magic and a valued premium placed on the mysteries and unknowns by the inhabitants of the young earth. There was a lack of science and understanding of its theories and truths. These things had not evolved as they have so completely today. It was a time of new discovery. The world was awakening. It, as well as its inhabitants, needed their horizons and motivations expanded. It was magic that was needed to move evolution and development of the beings and their civilization forward. Magic is of the spirit, it's a pure and direct contribution from the spirits. This magic and mystery were totally undiluted, not adulterated by any of the nonspirit components of the earth or of its beings. Most of the spirits, at this early time, were not of a being and not of a being's domain. They were free yet still unknown, mostly unseen and unacknowledged by humans.

In these early periods of growth and awakening, there were far fewer beings, either human or otherwise, inhabiting and roaming the landscape of the earth. Spirits were numerous. They were as numerous as they are today, but they were unencumbered and freer. Again, few were committed as a component of a being; this was because there were few beings. Those without an assignment to a being were allowed to move about unhindered and able to create and affect their magic directly on the world and its inhabitants without the restrictions or constraints inherent to being assigned in a domain and partnered with other components as part of a being. The unassigned ones teamed up amongst themselves in endeavors not common to the beings. Their effects were deemed fantasies, miracles, and mystical events. The source of these events was still a mystery to humans. These were occurrences where many free spirits might band together and take on a temporary form, one from creativity and feeding off imagination; this was for the being's benefit. Examples of how these teams of spirits might manifest themselves into visions would be as fairies and ghosts, both good and evil, but also as mystical images of other sorts, even dragons, mermaids, and other visions of our disbelief and imagination.

Spirits are the origin of our dreams and imaginations. These images were all the handicraft of the magic of the spirits. There had been many stories and folklore stemming from the sightings and events created by these mystical forms. To the spirits, however, these things were deemed ordinary. The full force of the spirit's strengths and powers was multiplied in these early freedoms and unleashed onto the naive and welcoming earth. It brought about change and adventure. It forced beings to recognize things beyond themselves, to explore and discover. It brought comfort and familiarity to the assigned spirits within the beings. It helped them remember their histories, their past before they were assigned and constrained as part of a being's domain. It was when their freedoms and influences were greatest.

In these early times, spirits and their magic truly influenced and affected existence and discovery. Magic was everywhere. Miracles were commonplace. The spirit's magic and effect were recognized and accepted as a part of nature and existence in the strange new world. The spirit component was in total control, truly dominant, and with the greatest influence to and effect on both the environment and the beings. It was quite different from what it is today. In the early times, beings didn't control the spirits; they were subjects to the spirit's effect. This was the greatest change arising from the many years since.

Things did indeed change over the years as things tend to do. Human and other forms of beings began to multiply with increasing rate. This proliferation of the species was significant because it, in turn, assigned and committed many of the free spirits of the earth to the new being's domains. It is through conception that spirits are assigned to a being. Specifically using the human as an example, a human conception commits three spirits to its being's spirit domain, more than any other species. Every human conception creates residency for three spirits. This is how life begins. Their residence, herein called the spirit domain or simply the domain, receives two spirits, one a portion from each donor, the parents of the new being, and a third joined to the domain from the pool of free and uncommitted spirits; this last one was previously unrestricted and freely and directly affected magic on the realm. Through this natural process, nature's creation, the free and uncommitted pool of spirits is thus reduced by one spirit. The magic and the mystical happenings on the earth are also reduced equal to the effect of the one spirit, now committed to a new creation's domain.

As populations grew, the pool of free and uncommitted spirits shrank by the growth rate of new beings. It wasn't long before the uncommitted pool was only a fraction of the size that it had been originally. The earth became less influenced and affected by unbridled and unhindered magic. Fewer sightings of magic or its corresponding and representative forms were reported. These events were soon only memories and tales, many times forgotten by newer generations. The world became more predictable and more stable after most of the spirits were confined and controlled within the domains of beings. This is how it is currently. There were simply fewer free and uncommitted spirits to affect the earth with their direct magic and spontaneity. Whether this was a good thing or bad is not clear. The rate of change, however, was accelerated over time. More and more spirits were committed to domains of the beings.

Within the new domain of their beings, the three spirits partnered and worked together to mold, shape, and guide the physical and mental components of their assigned being. There was never a doubt that, given a choice, these spirits would have preferred to be free and uncommitted, but they accepted their assigned role, purpose, and set of destinies specific to their assignment to their being. Crucially important was that these spirits brought with them not only gifts of life but also those of life enrichment and value. On the value side, they brought powerful and perpetually growing volumes of knowledge and experiences to their new domain residences. They brought with them a history, a pool of thought, ideas, visions, and insights from each instance and lifetime, whether experienced from their uncommitted and free periods of existence or from a previous commitment within another being. These were experiences and instances of learning from each day with each assignment or free moment that they had experienced or served since their origin. Collectively, it was a record of events and experiences since the beginning of time. The collective experiences and knowledge of each domain thus formed the potential of each new being's reference, and their source of new thought, ideas, imaginations, and dreams.

Domain stores recorded the heritage of the species. It helps explain and answer questions like "how do minnows know how to swim, or how do salmon know when and where to return to spawn?" It answers the question of how a baby knows where and how to suckle. It's in the innate knowledge store of the spirit domain brought to each life by the spirits of the domain. On a grander scale, as the civilization grew, the aggregate pool of knowledge and insight stored in all the spirit domains of the total populace became immeasurable. The spirit's catalogued storage and available access to retained information, the collective internal reference library, grew in its expanse and totality to near levels of infinity. It left the captive spirit population well stocked with many of the answers and parcels of knowledge it would need to evolve its beings.

More limited in its expanse when compared with the whole yet still quite significant as far as its volume and power and the value of its vaults were the single domains. These are characterized as being the spirit-specific stores of reference and resource. Each is unique and defined by the backgrounds, histories, and contributions of the spirits assigned to the domain. They and their stores of knowledge and experience are committed to serving the assigned being's needs and the destinies for which they've been charged to deliver. New knowledge, new experiences, and new information collected by each of the three spirits within a domain are commingled with that which each brought from prior assignments and are offered up for the good of the whole domain. This expanded base then better serves to add to their spirit-specific purpose and to add reference and support to the being. Yet this also serves to add to the knowledge and experience pools of the whole spirit community through general sharing, and significantly, it's a product of placing the third unrelated addition from the unassigned spirit pool at every inception. All knowledge of the spirit domains is shared through each generation by means of cross-pollination and new assignment. This contributes to building overall depth and breadth to the general knowledge and experience pool of the spirit and world community.

The collective growth in the knowledge pool thus acted inversely to that of the reduction in numbers occurring in the unassigned spirit pool. As numbers in the unassigned pool grew smaller, volumes in the community knowledge pool grew larger due to more sharing and partnerships within more domains. What was lost in the overall composition and change of the spirit world was spirit freedom and autonomy. Everything of nature has balance and trade-offs.

Knowledge in the spirit world is an extremely valued commodity, so much so that a spirit's freedom and autonomy will willingly be sacrificed for more sharing and knowledge stores. Spirits never allow knowledge, even in its most raw and primitive state, to be lost. They shepherd and nurture it. They sort, and portion it out in different mixes and combinations. It generates new perspectives and vantages. It provokes new thoughts and ideas. These are then stored away by the spirits for a time when they might be most appropriately needed.

The spirits are a collector of sorts. They are the guardians and keepers of all stores of information and experiences. Each spirit carries forward all its knowledge and experience from its past lives throughout the generations and eras it served. Combining the cumulative and historical storehouses of knowledge, past and current, and the experiences of the three spirits of the domain makes the domain a rich and bountiful source of guidance, influence, and answers to problems for each being. It makes domains with aged and well-traveled frequently assigned spirits rich in value and well primed with history and information stores to prompt profound, guiding, and influential thoughts and arguments from their being. It defines intelligence. This allows and supports change, evolution, and invention from these domains and their being. The current generation is able to build from the contributions of all the previous ones. The wealth of history is shared through the contribution of what each spirit brings with it through time to each new generation.

It's not a case of simply releasing the thoughts and ideas stored within the domains or the knowledge gained from past generations. This is not without provocation or impetus. The information doesn't come free and unsolicited to the new being or the other partner components of the being. It must be earned. There must be an initiating need. The spirits and the domain require a trigger or a stimulus to initiate release of the knowledge and lessons from history, the ideas and the know-how from the domain's deepest storage. It requires a problem or a situation that specifically matches and prompts the knowledge and calls for the past experience. The other components of the being, not the spirits, must be the initiators and present these problems and situations. This is where the mind of the being contributes. They must call on the spirits. This establishes a dependence between the other components of the being and the spirit and its domain.

On the basis of the severity and the urgency and depending on the impact of the problem, the spirit role is to deliver the most appropriate thoughts and ideas to address it. Information, knowledge, and ideas are parsed out in measures and levels required to address the need and only to the immediate level of the need presented. Problems build on problems, situations on situations. The more a being learns, the more it realizes there is more to know. As the being and as the culture and nature will allow, spirits feed this evolution of learning, invention, and exploration with progressively higher levels of information, knowledge, and ideas as triggered by the being's development, drive, and curiosity. The spirit serves each level of development and invention with new materials and supplies from its stores to continue intellectual growth.

It is not an easy thing for the spirit to change the world. It is not as easy to influence and affect outcomes and degrees of change as it had been before most spirits were committed to a being nor when magic was external and the spirits were unhindered to use it. Now captive and committed, the only avenue to the outside world must be through the tangible physical and mental components of its being. Its identity and influence through magic and other mystical phenomenon is diluted and often shielded from the outside world unless released by the being. Release through the being is rare and occurs in the form of a miracle or a pure act of the spirit that escapes unyielded by the being. The strongest and purest of domains can make miracles happen through their being and without harm to the being. This occurs only in extreme emotional scenarios. It is an infrequent and usually bizarre occurrence. An example might be a person who in an emergency lifts incredible weight to free another from being crushed or a faith healing initiated by a pure domained being that has no medical or scientific explanation.

An experience with a miracle represents an output and direct contact with or the presence of the most powerful of spirit domains. Lesser domains can also bring about miracles but only with serious consequences to the being. These can create miracles only through release from their being. Release occurs through the death of the being. Through these releases, the spirits are returned to an uncommitted and free state. They, then, can use their magic directly and with full external impact but only for an instant before they are reunited to the pool of uncommitted ones awaiting reassignment to the next new being.

It is in these split seconds after death, through this sacrifice, that the miracle can occur. Examples of this scenario playing out are far more prevalent than the others and involve one being sacrificing their life to save another or to remove another from danger. Strong emotions, like that of a parent for a child or of a husband for a wife, will provide the strength and impetus for these types of miracles.

Through this form of death or any other form of death to the being, the knowledge and experience thought to be specific to and residing within the being is not lost. Residence of all knowledge and experience is actually held within the spirit, not the being. Thus, it is retained and safely guarded within the three released spirits. Both good and evil stores, both the knowledge and know-how to help and hurt beings in the future, are stored for transfer to their next assignments. This wealth of information is then disbursed with each new assignment of spirits to their new domain to the benefit or detriment of the next assignment of the being and its spirit domain. Disbursement is random across the different segments of the earth. The spreading and pollination of the spirits knowledge and experience to another being supports the cycles of change. It's about chance. It's as the wisdom of nature commands it. The spirits make it so.

As decades have passed and populations grown, the time spent by spirits in the uncommitted pool has been reduced to very short periods. Magic, miracles, and mystical happenings on the earth have become less planned, less coordinated, and less significant. They've become only short blips on the radar, far less commonplace, less dramatic, and less powerful in effect than before. But significant instances do occasionally still occur. As long as there is a spirit in the uncommitted and free pool, magic and miracles will always be with us, even if it is only in rare and reduced form.

This brings us back to the concept of change in our world, from a time when the mystical and magical events were commonplace to that of our current world where few spirits remain uncommitted to a being and are no longer free to dabble unhindered in magic and the mystical realms outside a being. It's part of the evolutionary plans. Perhaps it's deterioration of one set of ways or obsolescence of an era. It depends on your perspective. In essence, it's a transformation. The spirits still exist. The magic and mysteries still exist. But now they're within the beings. Activity of the magical sort, if it is to be retained, must now come from the being's spirit domains. It is the being that must accept and allow magic and mystery to work through them.

The answers to life's mysteries are now within all of us. It's up to us to determine if we allow the spirits to work their gift, especially through the more dominant beings of the earth, us humans. Within our spirits is the power and ability, but it is not within our common natures to operate on faith, the unseen, and to support that unproven by science. Thus, there is an internal struggle within the architecture of us humans between the spirit and nonspirit components of our being. The nonspirit components are strong. They are easier to accept and give dominance. Magic comes from the spirit, the other component. This is why magic has been relegated to a lower position of priority in modern-day life.

So what's the overall effect of our unwillingness to fully recognize the spirit and its magic? How does this explain much of what we see and experience in our world today? Where are the promised proofs that spirits really do exist in our current being?

The proofs can't be seen or tested. They don't fit within a formula. You can't see a spirit through a microscope. Spirits can't be presented, at least not usually so in today' time, and not those that are committed to a being. The proofs can only come from our logic, actions, and open-mindedness. The results of the spirit, or lack thereof, are evident. You need only to be prompted to look in the right places. They are there. They are everywhere. I'm here to steer you. I will share more regarding the spirit world and their attributes and abilities. The following will help in providing the basic building blocks, background, and foundation for understanding spirits. The proofs are coming. If you dare, allow me to continue.

Even More about Spirits

Spirits are servants. They serve as directed from the highest orders of nature. They are in tune with nature. Spirits are sharing beings. Their contacts outside their own kind and the other components of their being that they are partnered with are limited; thus, they share primarily between and amongst themselves. There is much teamwork and synergy within the spirit world. What they share can then be passed to many minds and bodies when needed. Spirits are naturally purposed and driven to gather as many experiences, as much information, and as much knowledge as they can. They store this knowledge and these experiences in a repository within the domain. The content of this repository can then be used by each of the three spirits of the domain, each having equal and continuous access. Each grows from the collective efforts of the three to gather and to share. The spirits of the domain, in turn, share with the mind and the body but only in controlled and monitored portion to the whole wealth of information and knowledge at their disposal. They offer portioned gifts based on the willingness and openness of the other components to accept and use them. Much of what a spirit carries with it, or adds to its stores in terms of knowledge and experience, never gets called on to support a mind or body; rather, it lies in reserve of a future need or calling. Sometimes stores may lie dormant for generations before the appropriate need or the right stimulus occurs. Yet other portions are used daily.

Knowledge is passed through the physical and mental parts of the being through thoughts and ideas, responses and reactions, initiated and developed by the spirit. These are then passed from and through being to being, spirit to spirit, and generation to generation. The bits of ideas and knowledge used over and over through successive generations are more fully developed and synthesized and result in common knowledge, progress, innovation, and the evolution of the overall being. Spirits act as the creator and doorkeeper of the knowledge between generation to generation and body to body. This is how civilizations develop and how each generation exceeds the previous, builds on the progress of the previous, and becomes more and more technologically and philosophically developed. Ideas and thoughts are the vehicles through which stored knowledge and experience are carried to and through the mind.

Information can also be carried from spirit to spirit and domain to domain through other means than physical or mental interfacing. Information can be carried forward and across through means other than human procreation of new generations. It can be passed through strong, open, and spiritual relationships. It is through bonding and strong relationship such as friendship, love, hatred, and other strong connections between beings that spirits can directly connect, share, or take from one another's stores within their domain. The transference of information between spirit domains is the root determinant of the relationship's intensity and emotion. The stronger the relationship, the greater the feeling of emotion, the more sharing, the more exchange is occurring at the spirit level. It's electric. This explains why a feeling of joy, love, or hatred can leave one tingling, shaking, or quivering. The spirit exchange is felt by the entire being. It is in these instances that the mind and body become the contributing and serving conduit and vessel within which the spirits exchange. This further fortifies the importance of the mind, body, and spirit complementing and supporting one another, all as key components of the one total being, and one total experience.

We now know that the domain of a being is the richest source of solutions. We also know that the spirit does not provide knowledge without impetus or reason. Each stimulus that a being encounters and initiates release of information from the domain and allows the being to react appropriately. Choice of which piece or pieces of information to transmit to the mind and body is determined by the spirits based on their natures and destinies. It is of these natures and destinies that we will now focus. Before we do, however, a key point to remember is that we are all the benefactors of our spirit trio. They are truly the influence behind our actions and thoughts.

Each spirit has an attraction or repulsion to one another. It's a natural force. It's called their nature. We often see these manifest themselves as curiosity, interest, allure, fear, or apprehension, and we give these feelings many other labels. Spirit domains connect with one another through interactions of their beings, be it through sight, speech, or contact. The connection between the different beings manifests itself through emotions. Spirits initiate and control emotions. Contact can bring positive sharing between domains, causing happiness and joy, or can cause negative sharing and contention, causing fear, anger, or discomfort. The aura or senses radiating from the spirit mix can be intense or can be very, very mild. Some spirit mixes undeniably attract; others will just as curiously strongly repel one another. This is based on how compatible the natures and destinies of the mix of spirits within each domain are with one another, how the natural forces within the different domains react with one another.

The spirit world is filled with like and opposites, complementing and contending parts. It is filled with degrees and levels of strength and dominance. These differences in the natures and destinies are what make all the beings of the world different. It's what spreads difference and makes each difference in the whole scheme of things of little or great importance depending on the focus. It ensures an overall balanced representation and fairness to each difference of the world. This counters advantage in one being with different advantage in another. It's a balance of power.

Humans only know the power of spirit sharing to a minimal degree. Some relationships stretch the normal bounds of this sharing due to their inherent and natural spirit attractions, like that of a mother to its child. But even this is not nearly to its fullest potential. We are not creative enough or believing enough in the powers of spirits and relationships. We do not understand the ingredient of the spirit and spirit sharing as the core to establishing and strengthening relationships. We only feel the strength in the pull or repulsion between the spirit domains, the by-product of it. We feel the emotion, the attraction between mother and child, representing strongly attracting natures of the spirits within their domains. We think this natural. It is natural, as natural as the spirit component of our beings. This is why convincing a being that there is a spirit component is so important yet difficult. It is because what is natural, what causes natural emotions and feelings within us, is not believed to be from a spirit source. Rather, it's thought to be from an obscure dimension of existence we often label as nature. What we think of as "nature" is close but not what a spirit knows it to be. I'll make this clearer later. Natural emotions, the attractions or repulsions that are felt, are the result of the spirits, their natures' internal charges, their destinies, yes, their existence within us.

Spirits have natures and destinies. So, what exactly are these? To begin, these are two core ingredients in the spirit's makeup. Every spirit carries into the world an unalterable nature. They also have defined destinies. The overall nature of the domain, and ultimately the being, is determined by the blending of the natures from each of the three spirits residing therein. For example, aggressive beings are those with a majority of aggressive-natured spirits in the domain. Passive beings, on the other hand, are those spirits with three passive natures in their domain.

Natures are generally classified as either good or evil. The attributes and strength of each specific nature vary in dominance and degree. This allows every being, and particularly those with a mix of three different-natured spirits or even those with like-natured spirit mixes, to be quite different from one another. No two spirit natures or domains are alike. The culminations of the spirit natures within the domain make up the being's unique personality, general attitude, and natural characteristics. Each spirit contributes to the domain through its variation of strength and its type. Its type (good or evil) creates its tendencies and preferences. Strength (its dominance within the domain) creates its attitudes, idiosyncrasies, and behaviors, each unique from one domain to another and from being to being. It's in the natures of the individual spirits where similarity can also be found. Like natures, as do destinies, pull spirits and spirit domains together to work as one.

Destinies can be good or evil, just like natures. Spirits have multiple destinies, but all have at least two primary destinies and at least one secondary destiny. It is the destiny that gives the spirit purpose. Each spirit will feel complete and accomplished only after all the destinies that it is assigned are achieved. Each domain strives to achieve all the destinies of each of its spirits housed within its domain as partners. Only then is the spirit and the domain's work complete. It is a challenge to achieve all the destinies of each of the spirits of the domain within a single lifetime. This is especially true when the destinies of the different spirits conflict and contend with one another for the domain's priority and dominance. This happens frequently. In these cases, the domain is temporarily in a state of turmoil. This shows up through the being as a change in personality or an attitude swing. It will be brought on by an abrupt change of focus by spirits with different destinies, shifting into the position of dominance within the domain. The spirit that is in control of dominance, and for its time in dominance, will refocus the attentions of the domain and its being on the destinies of its urging. When these shifts from a previous nature and destiny are sudden, inconsistencies in what the being might say or do will occur. If the new destinies are very different from the previous and are quite incompatible with the previous, the change in the being's behavior and attitude can be drastic. This explains why beings can appear fickle or moody, why they might suddenly change their positions on issues or promote actions of goodness at one moment and then be antagonistic in the next.

There are many minor, and not so bizarre, examples of sudden shifts of dominance in a domain and being's focus. In most cases, this does not create a significant disturbance. In fact, these are common. But in the absolute, most extreme cases, coming from those with very strong and opposing spirit natures and destinies, and when they are contending and forcing their positions on their being, the change can be very significant. These are ones that could be considered having unpredictable, even split, personalities. In these cases, the spirit destinies are so divergent that there can be no smooth crossover from one to the next, no leveling or compromise, and no soft transition from one to the other. In these cases, the shift is shocking. This scenario is quite uncommon but happens. Fortunately, most common is the significantly milder shifts of focus and destiny, hardly noticed, if at all.

Most of us have extremely mild case shifts in our spirit natures and destinies. All our domains have different natures and destinies. We show different sides; we are different people in different situations and settings. We are certainly not the extreme; rather, we are the norm. It is natural to be different, even within the same being, within the same spirit domain, and between spirits.

Difference in a domain's natures and destinies has positive effects. It allows different opinions and perspectives on problems. It promotes complex and alternative views, and it results in different approaches and actions as a result of drawing from opposing spirits' influences, perspectives and their stores of information and knowledge within the domain's repository. It allows the spirits to take more in aggregate from this storage, to support solutions to issues more than it might if the spirit mix was of one nature and of little difference. It's in this multiplicity and in many cases incompatibility between the spirits that new and expanded thoughts and approaches develop. New combinations are forced to come forth and new possibilities to consider. Results and products are established from the internal compromise and trade-off between opposing spirit offerings. In the end, difference becomes less a hindrance and more an enabler of creativity and discovery. Multiple and different interests and destinies are served as the result.

The domain is the conduit to new and complex views and thoughts. It is the spirits that allow us to justify and reconcile things that might seem inconsistent, misdirected, unthinkable, or unacceptable. Within the domain and within the spirit, creativity and flexibility are the drivers of change. Whatever it takes to achieve each destiny drives out life's actions and influences. Change serves destiny. Serving the destiny is paramount to the spirit. The natural balance between good and evil in the world is intertwined into each spirit's ability to serve its nature and achieve its destinies. The success of each supports the overall balance for controlling natural forces on the earth. This will become clearer with subsequent examples throughout the stories.

Can a spirit's nature and destiny ever change? The answer is generally no. Regardless of reason, if it has anything to do with the nature or the ingrained tendencies of the nature, except in specific instances, you simply can't change a spirit's nature. It is either good or evil. It carries with the spirit from generation to generation. There are very few exceptions. Love can alter an evil nature. The details of this will be addressed when we discuss relationships. But more commonly, the nature and destiny can only be diluted through the mix of the three spirits' natures and destinies as one domain. Good natures can counterbalance evil natures within a same domain and vice versa. Strong natures can dominate weak ones at times. Good destinies can be countered by evil-natured destinies and vice versa. The nature and destiny of the spirits usually do not change. It is only the effect of these, from a domain's holistic blend, that can be diluted.

How does the longevity of the being and the spirit differ? A primary distinction between the being and the spirit is that body and mind have a set span of time that they will exist on the earth. The body and mind will not recycle or reincarnate through to future generations. When their time is through, they cease to exist. Civilizations are much the same in this regard. Every civilization is measured in its allotment of time along a circular period of existence. Eventually, the civilization will become extinct. It will not return. A being, and a civilization, is marked and measured from its birth to its death. They are temporary. They simply affect only a designated frame in history.

This is not the case with the spirit. The spirit exists forever. Contrary to a single life or a civilization, the spirits refill the unassigned and free pool and await their next assignment to a new being or the next civilization of beings that it will support. They are perpetual. They are a part of the world in all its continuity and perpetuity.

Spirits are the only things, other than the universe itself, that are permanent and consistent through time. They are what is real and true. This is quite a paradox to how we beings have seen things up until now. This sheds a new and different light on what is important and real, what is truth, and what is life. We tend to believe in only what can be seen, touched, and experienced, not in what we cannot apply or verify through our tangibles. The things that we measure through our senses and what most perceive as true and real are the temporary. Ours is the short-term view of the world we live in. Beings see things only from a single frame of time, only from a tangible, superficial perspective. The reality is that spirits and their domains, not beings, are what capture and perpetuate life, being to being, generation to generation, era to era. They represent, and they nurture ongoing life.

It's in our limited viewpoint of life and existence that supports human-centricity. This is the idea that the mind and body are the primary components of the being, the hub of existence. We place too much emphasis and focus on these components. It allows too much discretion and power to these temporary components. It creates urgency on nature. By this, I mean it tends to drive the size of the circle representing life and civilization inward, making it smaller than it needs to be. It limits the breadth and scope of life to one being's lifetime. It hastens movement around the circumference of existence's circle at an over accelerated pace. And as the being matures and begins to consider its short-term existence, growing shorter every day, the mind and body lack trust and understanding in how the spirit component, with its immortality, will be able and willing to tend and protect their shorter-term interests. They become more skeptical of spirit guidance and most certainly of the long-term views of the spirit. Conflicts with supporting the short-term benefit of the mind and body and long-term view of the spirit arise. It results in incongruence. It all leads to disconnect and secession of the temporary components of the being from the spirit's guidance, creating cracks, even chasms in the spirit and the other components' working order.

Without the spirit as an equally contributing part of the component equation, it marks the downturn and ruination of our species and our civilization. It creates favor to the physical and mind components, favor to dominate the being for short-term needs and pleasures. This heightens the focus and struggle to achieve life's every goal and desire in the life span of a single being's components, those with the shortest duration. It creates shortsightedness and conflict. It creates urgency "to have it all now," and it fuels competition and selfishness. Focus on community and concern for the species or building for the future generation becomes a secondary consideration at best.

In this environment and with direction coming from a mindset like this, life is indeed short and strives to enjoy things today while it lasts. It decays the future. It forces the civilization around the circular model of existence very quickly, eventually to a closing of the circle. It brings finality. The beings expire. They lose their life portion. This portion is the spirit. Yet the spirit is not lost. Unlike the body and mind components, spirits live on. Spirits are the foundation on which new beings and the new civilizations will be built on. They are the building block of life. The spirit is life itself.

Humans Are Not the Only Vessel of the Spirit

There is a spirit in all living things. Many of the earliest humans knew this to be true. It is a natural conclusion to come to. In earlier times, humans did not rule the earth so absolutely as is the case today. There was no such feeling of superiority of any one species. It was easier to see other living things as equals in importance and as adding special contributions to the overall equations of existence. In this earlier time, it was easier to see the spirits, their natures, and their powers in all other forms and beings as well as in us humans.

Through evolution and an exaggerated opinion of our species' worth and importance in this world, the respect and appreciation diminished for things nonhuman. The spirit did not bring these changes; rather, it was the mind and body that created them. The spirit makeup, duties, and source of know-how and direction are the same today as they were then. They are the same in nonhuman domains as those found in the human domain. There is a constant, and there is consistency in the spirit. Life comes from the spirit. It is not just human. It shares equally in its offerings to all species.

There are differences in the domains of different types of living things, not the spirits themselves within the different types of the living. The primary difference between the human domain and the animal domain is found in the number of spirits that are assigned to the domain. An animal's domain contains only two spirits. Each spirit is a contribution from one of its parents. The absence of the third "wild card" spirit from the unassigned pool (as is found with the humans' domains) creates less contention and variation in the animal domain's nature and destiny. On the other hand, the stores of knowledge and variation in options gathered within their domain are not as rich and voluminous due to the loss of what an unrelated and independent third spirit might add. Still, the domain grows and evolves with each generation like with humans. It is at a slower and more controlled rate. There is less creativity. There is little invention or breaking from the norm. The lack of the third spirit hinders challenge and the expansion of new thought beyond that of what their heritage's combined stores of information might initiate. Instinct replaces creativity. Limited options provided results in acceptance of a consistent, tested, and proven approach to life's challenges.

Ways of their heritage, fears of their heritage, and nature of their heritage are passed forward. Fear of humans, however, does not come completely from the nature of the beast's spirits. It comes primarily from history. The animal domain's access to and familiarity with how each of its ancestral generations was treated and how they knew the human nature to have been with its ancestors feed the current generation. Fear has been established over years, not in the present. It is deeply rooted in the stores of the animal domain.

Animal domains are better able to penetrate and read human domains. This is due to less conflict between the spirits of their domain. This explains how animals can sense our feelings and our natures quickly and without words or communication. They tap directly into our domains. They see and feel the natures and auras of our spirits. This seems to make animals appear immediately skittish and quickly reactive to a human's presence.

Just as with human spirits, animal spirits have natures. It forms the temperament and the aggressiveness of the animal. Unlike with human domains, the most prevalent mix within the animal domain has more compatibility. The common animal domain is usually made up of two like-natured spirits. Just as with human spirit natures, these vary in strength, but unlike with the human's spirits of the domain, these two-share dominance in the domain space in equal percentages of time. It is the imbalance in their strength, however, that determines the timing of when each of the animal's spirit holds dominance in the domain. Stronger spirits shift frequently in and out of dominance at critical junctures, such as in times of danger and confrontation. These shifts create the impression of instability and the tendency of unpredictability found in many animals' behavior. It's what we commonly consider "wild."

The overall nature of an animal's domain is more prevalently good in some species and more prevalently evil in others. Why this occurs stems back to the animal's histories. The more nondomestic-type animals, those of the forest, were hunted. They were killed for many reasons. In many species, the less aggressive, the good-natured and trusting specimens, were easier prey for predators, including man. Many of the good-natured ones were first to be killed. The numbers between good-natured and evil-natured dominant domains within their species were soon placed out of balance. This left the evil-natured dominant animals in the majority. The domains of new offspring were filled from the contribution of the parent domains. They, too, were evil natured and dominant, perpetuating the trend toward more aggressive and less domestic-natured creatures. The hunted breeds thus became primarily evil natured by selection. This same, but in the inverse, also held true for the animals prone to be easier to domesticate, such as dogs, cats, rabbits, and the like. In the inverse, the animals that could not be tamed, those dominated by an evil-natured domain, were weeded out, killed, or released to the wilds, leaving a majority of good-natured animals to multiply. Through selection, the good natured and dominant of the species survived, perpetuating their good nature with man.

No matter how select we've made them, and most prevalently as it relates to mixed-strength domains, there lurks the potential of unpredictability and the uprising from an unexpected and stronger nature. Animals are especially prone to this. They feed off the more diverse and nature-rich domains within us humans. Evil natures arouse evil natures, even between human to animal. Animals are far more sensitive and reactive to the human nature's auras and influences. They see through us, directly into our domains and our natures. They are ever on watch. Their spirits contain vast storage of histories, information, and experiences. Deep in their stores lie reference to man and his treatment of their species. It's there to warn and support them and their destinies as initiated. Man's world and the animal world are quite different. This is not just because of the physical, the mental, or the differences of the domains but also because of the histories and experiences with each other and because the information stored within the domains is quite different. Where and when these differences arise and take effect, therein lies the unpredictability and mystery of the animal world, not understood by us humans. We cannot share or appreciate their domain's perspective of us.

Spirits are less challenged by the other components of the animal than they are in humans. The nature, the destiny, and life's plan in animals are consistent and set. There are no mixed messages or different influences coming from their domain. Natures and destinies are passed down from generation to generation. Physical aspects and the physical component share influence and power compatibly and willingly with the spirit component. This allows animals to react, to initiate action or defense quicker and more effectively than humans. It creates balance by giving them this advantage.

Plant life and trees also contain a spirit component. They differ from humans and animals in that they are limited to only a single spirit within their domains. Just as with the animal kingdom, plant life is limited by their spirit number. The plant life of the world is even less diverse and more consistent in terms of their nature and destiny from generation to generation than the other forms of life. This further limits the creativity and diversity of influences coming from their domain, yet it allows them to be totally consistent in presentation and focus. There is no conflict, no variation, and no struggle for dominance within their domain. They are in total harmony between the tangible and intangible parts of their being.

Because their domain is simple, their control center is also simple. There is no need to translate or filter the information coming from the spirit. It comes direct and pure through the connection between spirit and the physical side of the being. It creates involuntary actions. This is different. Whereas with humans and animals the involuntary actions and reactions do occur, they are mixed with the voluntary and are most times in the minority to these voluntary ones. In plants, the spirit-initiated, involuntary actions drive them almost exclusively. A single seed, a single root, is cultivated solely at the direction and nature of the single spirit. There are few inhibitors or controls.

Nature is free to express itself. It does so by transcending the plant into the many different blossoms, blooms, flowers, shapes and colors that present themselves from the spirit's influence, each a characteristic of the spirit and its nature or of its history and of its preferences, either currently or previously established. Each plant structure reflects its inner attributes through the physical. Each end product reflects much about its nature. Plants contribute to the balance of good and evil in the world much like all the other forms of living things. Plants can be harmful or harmless, sweet or bitter, fruitful or barren. Plants can be thorny or delicate, provide cover or be porous; their fruit and pollens can support life or poison it. Plants can provide natural shelter or act as traps and dangers. Differences can be evident even in the same species. Differences reflect the plant's nature.

Even in plants, there are variations of good and evil. But don't be fooled by the plant's beauty. Beauty is not solely from the good-natured or evil-natured spirit. It is just as prevalently found in both. It is a true product of the physical component of the being. Only inner beauty is of the spirit, its nature, and its domain. This is equally true in all species of the earth.

All that affects the human spirit affects the animal and plant spirits in like manner. The music of life, community, kinship, the environment, and freedoms or the lack thereof are just a few to name. Yet they all affect spirits and their natures no matter the being in which they reside. The spirit of the human and the spirit of the animal or plant are the same. Spirits are interchangeable between the species, passed between them from generation to generation. Spirits connect, and although their domain stores are partitioned to separate the experiences and content by living species that they have been assigned, they share and exchange across species. Know it or not, we current humans relate to all our surroundings, spirit to spirit. It allows us to fit into our environments. It allows us to know them, what is safe, what is not, what our comfort zones are. It allows humans and animals, humans and plants, and animals and plants to share a common bond. Spirits protect these bonds based on their histories, knowledge stores, natures and some common destinies. The nonspirit components have a tendency to destroy each other. This has created another challenge and conflict between the spirit and these nonspirit components of the being.

What, then, is a spirit? We know something of its purpose and contribution. What is its physical side? Is it flesh, a mix of molecules and atoms? What?

Spirits are not flesh, although they reside within our flesh. They are not tangible. They are not substance or compound, yet this cannot be confirmed. They just are. I realize that this won't satisfy the scientific or skeptical, but little is known about the physical, tangible composition of them. What I do know is that a spirit is life. It transforms a body into life, into animate and functional life. Spirits generate and produce life's magic and mystery as its product. They germinate the fruits and products of existence. They feed and tend to existence. We are one of their many products. We are its biggest nemesis. We use, and we eventually bring their creation to ruin.

What are spirits? Spirits just are. They are tolerant of us and serving. They are persistent and driving. They are in everything we can touch, see, and feel. They are everything. They are dependent on nothing, nothing except their natures and destinies. In spite of their power and how they might feel about the self-destructive components of our being, they will not, they cannot, interfere with the being's choices or tendencies toward it and its civilization's movement on the circular path of life. Spirits are governed and affected by our world based on the natural circular path of life. The circular path of life will be discussed in greater detail in the chapter that follows.

What else would be helpful to know about the spirits? There is much that will be revealed in the upcoming chapters, but here are a few tidbits.

Internal communication comes from the spirits. Spirit dialogue is what you hear inside your head when you do not speak. It is the communication that you believe is in your mind, but it is really the dialogue between the spirits, and perhaps it includes the mind. It is what is often loaded as thoughts and ideas into the mind. It signifies the search through the stores of information held in the domain. It is many times unfiltered. It contains information from different spirits' perspectives and natures. It is an unfinished product. Yet it forms the framework for decisions delivered through the mind of the being. It is solely from the spirits and spirit domain. It addresses problems and solutions, proposals of direction and position. It is natural and healthy.

Sleep is the release of the being to the spirits. It is the spirits' opportunity to restore themselves to their uninhibited form, even though still confined within the being space. It allows magic and the mystical to control the body, to control the caverns of the mind. Reality is replaced by dreams and the sublime. Through dreams, the spirits can share without stimuli, can choose what to access from the unlimited stores of the domain. From what the being might not understand or have never experienced, a nightmare can arise. Sometimes the shock will awaken the physical and mental components of the being from its slumber; perhaps even shock them. These are not intended, just the result of a spirit's moment of freedom to take the being a step beyond its comfort zones.

Dreams can carry over from sleep and become one way that a spirit loads the mind with new thoughts and ideas that might motivate, inspire, or initiate it. It is the spirits' way of treating the other components, giving them something special. Sleep is thus craved by the other components. Spirit dreams can feed our creative side; they can purge the old thoughts and norms and can replace them with fresh thoughts and ideas. Spirits restock and retool the mind in sleep. When we do not get enough sleep, the creative process, the spirit renewal, and the ability to charge us is hindered.

The spirit and domain never sleep. It never leaves its post or stops working for the being, unless or until it is forced to. It never leaves the being's needs for requested and solicited direction, information, or consultation unattended. The continuous, uninterrupted service of the spirit domain sometimes manifests itself in unrealistic expectations of the other components of the being to equal the spirit's example. It's what makes some beings feel that they do not need to sleep and relax. It might develop itself in one to think that they need only a minimum number of hours of sleep, each of the tangible components thus taking the lead from the spirit component. Yet this is a mistake. These other components are not architected like the spirit. They are not perpetual in nature. They miss the spirit's gift. They become uninspired and unimaginative. It marks differences in the components' makeup and abilities. It's another example of balance. In this case, it's an advantage to the spirits.

Spirits don't need to eat per se, not like the body, which must be routinely fed a portion of protein, vitamins, and nutrients, or the mind that receives its fuel through the body. Spirits are nurtured instead through acts of goodness and evil. Their natures are the part of them that need to be nourished with acts and instances of good and evil in the world. They are supported in meeting these needs through the other parts of the being. Spirits draw strength and develop from and around other spirits of their like type. For instance, a good-natured spirit becomes better, stronger, and more developed around other good-natured spirits. The spirit nature feeds off others like it, as well as from acts and instances in the world that reflect their natures and destinies.

A being's limitations, their inhibitions, and their inabilities come from the other components of the being, not from the spirit or domain. Spirits provide only ability. They are not limited by weakness, hesitation, lack of confidence, or fear of harm. They are not limited by their confines, molecular or cellular structures, or lack of know-how. They are what drive us beyond our perceived capabilities and allow us to reach new plateaus of discovery and ability. They allow us to reach beyond and to test or remove limitations.

Spirits are almost exclusively confined and stationary within the domain. This is true except with a few special situations and for a few special domains. These special ones are those with completely pure domains containing only like-natured spirits. A spirit from a pure domain cannot actually move about physically, but they can transfer an envoy spirit from the domain metaphysically to another's domain. This is to share with, and to provide support to, the other spirits of their nature's type within another's domain. These crossover visits are usually short in duration but highly impactful. These "crossover transfers" are the most powerful source of spirit interaction, sharing, and transference of information, strength, and support. They are special and cherished by every nonpure domain. It leaves them revitalized and with new strength.

Nonpure domains will also transcend toward one another but neither in a physical nor in a metaphysical way. Rather, theirs is a sharing through the overlap of spirit auras and initiated through a relationship. These are the mildest forms of spirit ventures. A third form of spirit venture represents the extreme case. It is the only form when a spirit from a nonpure domain can leave the domain space. This occurs when spirits are truly and physically released from the being's domain as a result of the death of the being. At the instant they are released from the being's domain and free to rejoin the unassigned spirit pool, it is the only time that spirits can move from the domains of beings in an actual and physical way. It is certainly a worst-case scenario for the being. It is rarely an intent or action of the spirit that initiates such a result on their being.

It is best to describe the spirits' roles and contributions to our lives through examples that we can relate to and understand from our daily and normal life routines and experiences. The following collection of scenarios will hopefully achieve this. But first, a brief description of nature's evolutionary circle of life is in order.

The Circular Path of Life

Every civilization traverse around a circular track of evolution referred to as the circular path of life. It marks its creation until its extinction. This is true for all living things and their components except for the spirit. Spirits are affected by the circular model in ways that are different from others. Depending on their natures, spirits are either hindered or helped by the position of the civilization on the path. Good-natured spirits are favored in the early half of the circle and become hindered as civilizations move into the final two quadrants. Evil-natured spirits are hindered in the early turns of the circle but favored in mid-to later portions. Both natures are eventually hindered as the circle draws to closure.

Spirits have seen numerous civilizations come and go. They have traversed around the circle many times. It is the spirit domain and its influence over the other components of the being that are affected most by the shifts on the circular path. These shifts around the circle occur naturally with the changes of the civilization, almost unnoticed by the being. To break it down for understanding, the circle of life is composed of four quadrants. Each is characterized by the state of the civilization through to its full evolution and rotation to destruction.

The first quadrant is characterized by the early, more primitive periods, not so much referring to the spirits but rather the initial evolutionary stages of the physical and mental components of the civilization. It is a spirit-rich time. Few are advantaged from a worldly sense. Many are advantaged from a spiritual sense. Free or unassigned spirits are numerous. Magic and mystical events are commonplace. Beings' domains are undiluted. Many pure domains, the ones with common natures among the three spirits of the domain, exist. There are many mysteries and unknowns to the beings. No one is more important than the next, although some begin to try to be. It is the nonhumans, some are the images created by a free and uncommitted spirit's magic that are many times held supreme in power. The physical and mental components are not dominant; the spirit component is in command and highly revered by the other components. An overall balance of power between good and evil natures prevails. Beings are an equal partner with all other species and see themselves as "part of the whole" of their surroundings and environment. The first stages of societal behaviors show a glimpse, although it's quite primitive. The beings seek relationships but limit the numbers that they trust to only those to whom their domains have strong attractions. These are easiest to identify because there is little dilution of the spirits or spirit natures within the domains. Attractions or repulsions between domains are strong, pure, and clear. Beings form small loosely bound clans and tribes of those that are similar in nature. The mind and body are in total reliance on their spirit counterparts within the being for influence and direction in all matters. The pull from the spirit's wealth of knowledge and experience is great. There is little technology or sophistication, but there is much advancement and learning, even though rudimentary in type. Life is, for the most part, simple and in harmony with nature.

The second quadrant is characterized by the awakening of the mental and physical components of the being. Experimentation and exploration emerge as characteristics of the beings. Yet nonspirit components still remain subservient and reliant on the spirit domains for all important decisions and actions. It's the beginning of a renaissance of sorts. Beings begin to be more adventuresome, to test new things and new influences. They begin to see themselves as special in the world. Beings begin to multiply to more significant numbers. The emergence of other hindering influences and factors on the spirit domains begin to emerge. Alcohol and tobacco are examples. Spirit natures begin to build alliances both within domains and between domains. The concept of "we versus them" emerges. Beings are categorized based on the sides they take up, the ideals they choose to support. Class divisions begin to form. The dilution of the spirit domains, the diversity of the domain's mix of spirits, and the effects of this dilution and diversity result from population growth. Shifts in the balance of power between good and evil are minimal and not an issue yet, but the factors that will tip the balance are beginning to be put in place. Large groups, communities, and societies begin to emerge more prevalently. Individuals begin to truly exhibit their natures in these societal settings. There is more discovery and invention; some are good, and some are bad. There is the emergence of a physical ruling class. Skirmishes between groups begin to occur. Premature deaths of the beings caused by those of their own species and clans are more common. Recycling of the spirits through new assignments is accelerated, adding to the stores of history, experiences, and knowledge to the common repositories but also to the mixing and dilution of the natures and domains' strengths and dominance. Combinations multiply. Spirit diversity is expanded.

The third quadrant is characterized by the physical and mental components of the being beginning to emerge as more dominant, more confident, and more controlling of the spirit domain in a larger proportion of the population. Natures begin to take sides against their non-like-natured partners. Stronger natures take more dominance and hold control over weaker natures within a domain and outside of it. Beings take on the personality of only their dominant spirit natures as they dominate the time of influence within the domains. Some dilution of the spirit domain, even though minimal at the onset of the quadrant has affected nearly everyone. Pure, good-natured domains are fewer and become more valuable and cherished. The balance of power shifts to evil natures. Evil natures and the products of their deeds are wider spread. Good natures still have victories and fend off and protect their strongholds but are less publicized and widespread. Evil is more popular to the nonspirit components and thus marks a more successful and adopted lifestyle. Technology emerges as a presence and is the metamorphosis of the mind component's assertion of a stronger position within the being. The upper class emerges as a force. "Special" emerges as the preference to "fair." Wars and large-scale skirmishes happen. The use of force is common as the physical component of the being also emerges as a greater influence within the being. Breakdowns in law and social mores occur with increasing frequency. There is an emphasis on being noticed, particularly being in the spotlight. Heroes are no longer people of wisdom or people who have sacrificed for the sake of others. Rather, they become the great athletes, the great actors, or those of greatest appeal and deception. Value is measured with money, not based on contribution or character. There is little that is sacred. The spirit power and influence are defused by the other components, and the domain becomes less of an influence.

The fourth quadrant is characterized by evil. Evil is dominant. But it is not only evil brought on by the evil-natured spirit. It is a different type of evil, the type that is dominated by an attachment and reliance on the appeals and allures of the world. This influence infiltrates and infects the physical and the mind components. The being is less and less influenced by the spirit but instead by these outside influences of the world. In turn, the world holds the being captive and eventually shut off from the spirit domain. It only draws out the evil natures from the domain when it is to their advantage and when they can control them to add strength to their positions and actions and to pass its thoughts to the body and mind for its own purpose. By this frame in evolution, dilution has assured that spirit influence is very weak and that there's an evil-natured spirit in nearly everyone. Pure, good-natured domains are a true rarity, and by the quadrant's later third, they are entirely entombed. The physical and mental components of the being are evolved to be a far greater and dominant force on the being. Beings are selfish and vain. Beings strive to possess and control as much of the value and stores of the earth as possible without regard for effect on others. Tightly defined profiles and standards for acceptability are set. Individualism and creativity are frowned on. The importance of others' "person" is diminished. Dependence on technology is great. Business and wealth drive all. Immorality and decadence run rampant. Community and family values decay. Celebrity status rules. It's an "all about me" attitude. Crime, disobedience, radicalism, abuses to the body (such as piercing, drugs, and other indulgences), and a general disregard for the spirit or the spiritual contribution of any kind are common. The wealth of knowledge from the spirit stores and histories goes untapped. These things are not seen as wealth but rather as having little value. Eventually, the physical component becomes the dominant one. Choices are made based on appeal or strength of the superficial factors. Muscle mass deems an individual a more important characteristic than one's decency or civilities. One's beauty becomes more important than one's intelligence or humanity. As the quadrant moves into its later half, even the mind component is relegated to a secondary position compared with the physical self. It becomes all about pleasure and status. The final decay is initiated and spreads like an active cancer. The final years are few.

Is it ever clear what quadrant the civilization resides? It's not obvious from the single vantage of one being or from a few instances. It is difficult from even the broader assessment of a group or set of frames from time. The civilization and its members are so large in scope and the instances and activities so subtle, vast, and changing that only nature can accurately assess the tally from the domains of all the earth's contributions and flow. Only it, with the help of its spirits, can mark the point on life's circular path. But with the characteristics and trends listed above, one can estimate the general quadrant and condition. This is based on the nature, treatment, and characteristics of the beings toward one another.

Each position on the rim of the circle defines the actions and influences allowed the spirit and spirit natures. It's a two-way street though. The spirit influences the beings, who in turn define the point on the circle's circumference. Likewise, the point on the circle distinguishes the spirit condition and its general influence. Consequently, as you move around the circle, the absences of the spirit's influence are just as critical. These absences of the spirit and spirit nature's influences mark the later critical points on the circle.

First, at midpoint, there is the significant decline in numbers and influences of the good-natured spirit. At three-quarters, the evil nature's influence also begins to significantly decline as an influence on the nonspirit components. Near closure, the absence of all spirit influence is an end result. At closure, the slightest influence from even one spirit cannot be detected. One single influence from an evil spirit nature will, at this point, keep the circle open. The end to the civilization is marked by this last spirit influence. It is at this single moment when the spirit realm stands aside, they watch as the civilization takes its last breath and dies. Only spirits survive the fall; only they remain. It is after this moment that spirits once again become dominant and valued. It's the moment when they return to power and influence. They become free. Mysteries and magic reemerge. A new civilization will soon emerge and begin to capture them in domains of their beings. They will again be treated with respect and as of value. The new civilization is soon to emerge and recouple itself on life's evolutionary circle. Life's master plan assures it.

Good Seed among the Thickets

Becky Turner was the sweetest girl that Tom McDouglas had ever met. She made him feel special. It was a strange and unexplainable feeling yet a very good one. He felt a strong natural pull toward her. It was not physical. It was not mental. It was made up of emotions and feelings. It short-circuited him. He liked it. It made him feel alive. It was as if he were under a spell that had been cast on him by her magic. He can't understand what went on inside him when in her presence, but he looked forward to every chance to be near her.

Becky and Tom lived in the same apartment building in a lower-middle-class section of Millborough. They'd been there for several years. During this time, Tom had been fortunate to have many opportunities when he and Becky had crossed paths and when he was able to greet and exchange a few passing pleasantries with her. After each, it never seemed to be enough. It never satisfied him. Just a hello or to talk briefly about the weather or to ask and share how they felt at that moment it never seemed adequate. He really wanted to get to know this special pleasure much, much better. (Yet it also seemed that she was the antagonist of his emotions.)

He felt the inspiration build within him to further explore the feelings that arose whenever he was around her. He wanted to understand the growing attraction he had to her. He'd especially like to establish a more substantial relationship with her than that of just a neighbor or that of a mere participant in the brief encounters that they experienced every now and then. As a start, he'd like to form a stronger friendship between them.

What he really yearned for was to ask her on a date. The desire to approach her and ask her to dinner or to a movie continuously gnawed at him, but he was so hesitant, even slightly afraid, to ask her out. He was reluctant to show his feelings and to say the things he'd like to share with her because he feared that she might not share the same interest in him as he had for her. Despite these fears and insecurities when around the opposite sex, he was convinced that he must eventually find from within his makeup the courage to ask Becky to go out. He thought that it needed to be someplace nice, quiet, and well suited for talk and sharing, someplace nonintrusive, comfortable, and of his choosing. It was his plan to ask her out the next time they met. Yet it had been his plan to do this, "the next time they met," for several months and numerous previous encounters.

Becky and Tom were, in most ways, still strangers to each other. Yet in many other ways, they were not. They were two people moving along a similar path in life's plan. Their schedules were not always in sync, but then again, they were coordinated as much as any. Nature's forces created opportunities around these schedules and kept their paths crossing at random intervals. Destiny seemed to be drawing them together. It seemed they had much in common, yet they were also quite different. This excited them both all the more.

To Tom, Becky was such a mystery. She seemed so interesting and of goodness. It was everything she did, everything she said, and the way she did what she did. She occupied his thoughts quite regularly. He was strongly attracted and driven to her unlike any other. It seemed so natural and yet so unnatural. It sometimes seemed out of his control. Just the chance that their paths might cross that day made it worth getting up in the morning. Just the hope of seeing her gave him welcomed anticipation and energy.

Between their apartments were several floors of like apartments; each was filled with different and interesting people. Many of them Becky and Tom came into contact with frequently. Each had an effect and impact on their lives, even though most were incidental, superficial, and insignificant. Most of the encounters and experiences with these others were good. There were also those that were not so good. This is the way of life. It's the diversity that comes with life, both in the people and the events, that make the experiences and events interesting and exciting.

The building contained quite a diverse mix of personalities, backgrounds, and natures. It seemed a complete and accurate microcosmic model of their neighborhood as a whole. Independently, Becky and Tom had formed personal opinions, both likes and dislikes, about many of these people of their buildings. This group included Mr. Arthur, who lived in the apartment just above Tom's. Mr. Arthur grumbled and complained continuously. He was always in a foul mood. He liked very few people. In fact, there was none whom Becky or Tom can name offhand, no one from the neighborhood whom Becky or Tom knew. And certainly no one who had discussed it with them had ever had an especially good encounter or experience with this man. No one seemed to consider him a friend or even to like him. He seemed a very mysterious, very frightening, and unhappy man. He created many challenges for Tom and anyone whose apartment was in proximity to his. His torment frequently seemed to be purposeful. He painted the image of one who was inherently mean, in fact evil to the very core. Tom often wondered why one, like Becky, can be so sweet and nice and another, like Mr. Arthur, can be so nasty. He thought, *what a strange and diverse world I live in.*

On this particular day, Tom was to find good fortune in another chance meeting with Becky. He and Becky arrived at the main entrance of their building at nearly the same moment. Both put on the appearance that they were eager to check their mailboxes, which were located just inside the entrance of the building and within only a few feet of each other. They hoped to find a bit of good news or a surprise within the envelopes as opposed to the usual bundle of junk mail and bills. But really, both could see the other moving toward the same destination and were eagerly welcoming the chance to stop and talk.

As usual, Tom was first to say something as he greeted Becky with a broad smile. It was the signal that started those uncontrollable bursts of reactions within him. "Hi, Becky," he said. "It's good to see you again. How have you been?" He'd greeted her with these same words so many times in the past months that he feared it might sound like a recording. The familiar warmth and feelings that he experienced each time she was near him immediately began their rush through his being. Every pore, every synapse, and every channel composing his internal passage ways were fully energized with impulse. There were so many feelings and messages, both of action and reaction, now racing through him. His mind was left in a conundrum about which to acknowledge and what set of instructions and directives to send to the body. This became the barrier to a normal internal flow of information. It left his internals with nothing to work with, thus suspended.

As for the external, it was now partially disconnected, resulting in the awkward state he so commonly experienced and displayed whenever he was around her. Tom stood before her, mostly unsupported from the neck down, anxiously awaiting the sound of her voice or any show of attention or interest that might momentarily free him from his semiparalysed state. He can never understand why he looked forward to these encounters so much. He sometimes wondered why he felt so happy when he was in her presence, at the same time so awkward, out of character, and without control. All the same, he looked forward to these special moments of torture. They made him feel whole and complete.

On the other hand, Becky often found herself bubbly and giggly from her insides whenever Tom spoke to her. It was usually and mostly concealed from escaping but occasionally made its way through her smile. She, too, cherished these times when Tom recognized her and shared a moment of himself. She can almost recite word for word the greetings that they usually shared with each other from their past encounters. This was not only because many of the same lines were used over and over again but also because she'd hoped for them. The word's familiarity gave her much comfort. She loved it when he said her name and the way he did.

She hoped that he might ask her out on a date. He made her feel happy and at ease. She can't explain her feelings toward him or her excitement from being the focus of his attention, not any more than Tom can explain the awkwardness that devoured him in her presence. It electrified her. She finally replied, "I'm fine, Tom. I've been so busy, and it's still so early in the day. The good thing of it is that I've already completed most of the errands from my Saturday list. It really feels good to be home." She exhaled as if to imply she needed to slow the pace.

She then continued, "I'm now ready to enjoy a commitment-free afternoon." She smiled at him and waited for him to offer an invitation that would help fill this free time in her schedule. The opening seemed so obvious to her, but unfortunately, it was not so to Tom. He didn't respond, at least not on cue.

Becky had sized Tom up as a shy one. His fidgeting whenever around her gave her obvious clues. She decided that if she was to rely on him to make the first move, he might never find the courage to do so. Therefore, she decided to initiate these first steps that might move them to a new point in their young friendship. She asked him, "Would you like to come over to my apartment this afternoon and have lunch with me?" She hoped that he would not construe this as being too forward or bold. She was just simply running out of patience waiting for him to ask her out. She knew that she was risking months' worth of foundational work building up to this moment, all part of the hope and strategy to gain his interest. It, now, all seemed hinged on just this one decision. She so hoped for a positive response.

Tom was taken by surprise at her invitation. It was what he'd been wanting to do for such a long time. He'd been trying over the past months to craft the perfect phrases to do just what she had done so effortlessly. He'd searched and rehearsed through a number of scenarios and approaches, hoping to settle on just the perfect one to ask her out. Through his efforts, his mind would fill with different variations of the presentation, the invitation, and the moment; but when one of these seemed appropriate, even prompted, his mouth would always disconnect or freeze, letting opportunity go by. She had done in this current instance what he'd wanted to do so intently for so long. She'd done what he'd hoped to do so spontaneously. He marveled at how perfect she seemed to be.

He was now ashamed after realizing that he could have asked her on a date months ago without fear of rejection. It was obviously clear that she would have accepted his invitation no matter how badly he might have bungled it. She did have an interest in him as he did in her. He smiled, now feeling completely at ease, and uttered the first words that filled his mind. Unfortunately, he did this without a spirit's help and without really thinking. He replied, "Well, I had already made plans for lunch today, but . . ." His response confirmed why he had a consistent history of failings in these male-female encounters. It was the wrong way to begin a special moment. There was an immediate disconnect by Becky.

Within her domain, there were a thousand messages clashing and chastising her for the haste and the boldness of her approach with Tom. While her internals were in a wild flurry, her external components were frozen in place. All this activity occurred within split seconds of registering those nine horrible words from Tom. All she heard was no. The words kept replaying in her mind. She couldn't clear them through her filters. Her failure was all she could focus on. The devastation and crushing pain caused by rejection kept exploding within her. The incredible disappointment generated from these nine horrible words was just too great. Her expectation of an unqualified acceptance was obliterated. She wondered how she could have been so wrong. She heard only the nine initial words of Tom's reply over and over inside her mind. Her thoughts and feelings, now beyond the initial shock of the rejection, were in reevaluation. The focus of her thoughts was on how she'd risked her hopes on one bold whim, how she'd sacrificed all her planning and work to attract Tom's attention with one mistimed and miscalculated moment. It all seemed to be swept away in nine ugly words. She had apparently misread his attraction to her. Her domain could not explain or understand what had gone wrong or the reasons why.

Meanwhile, while Becky was lost in her inner domain's dialogue and self-diagnosis, Tom continued with the rest of his response. There were additional words that immediately followed his initial nine. He added, "But if you can get away, Becky, I would really like you to join me this afternoon in my plans for lunch." He looked to her for a response. She was still internalizing the punishments and reasons for what she initially interpreted as a rejection to her offer. The counterproposal from Tom had not yet sunk through the torture she and her domain were putting themselves through.

Tom was not as keen or aware, as he should have been, to Becky's body language. He continued with his counterproposal without registering any of her signals and expressions. It was everything he could do just to get his offer out for consideration. The fact that he was initially oblivious to Becky's state of being was actually somewhat fortunate. Had he taken the time, had he had the ability or applied the skill to assess her nonverbal messaging and reactions, he would have lost the courage to finish what he had to say. Instead, he confidently went on unaffected by her lack of connection or reaction. He added to his offer, "I know this quaint little place on the far end of the neighborhood. I think you'd like it."

It was at this point that he began to look for and expect some sign of confirmation. He got nothing. It brought the red flags from within him to full staff. Finally, as if a thunderbolt had struck within his mind, he tailed off from completing the end of his last sentence. He was registering a feeling that Becky might not be listening or was rejecting what he had been saying to her. It dawned on him that she had maintained the same blank expression and had retained the same frozen, empty stare. It was like a laser piercing directly through him for several moments. It looked like she might be upset. It was making Tom uncomfortable. His confidence was disappearing. It seemed to him to be a message of some sort. He wondered if it was something he'd said, yet he'd missed the harm of it.

Tom was definitely a bit slow with nonverbal matters. He was not yet in tune with Becky's cues. But he was fairly certain that something was not right. He'd finally realized the emptiness and chill of the moment and looked for indications that he was still connected in some way to her, that he was still getting through to her. The tables had turned. It was Tom's internals that now began to analyze the experience and the information it was receiving.

The internal dialogue of his domain's spirits rose to a roar. His domain was now wondering if they had been foolish. The dialogue between the internal workings centered on an assessment of whether they'd made a critical mistake by not accepting Becky's initial invitation as unaltered. His entire being, in its ordered sequence, now began to struggle over the possibility that she might not accept his offer, that he might have made a very bad decision. He felt so stupid and inadequate. His plans for the day had not been so important as to risk not being with this angel for the day. His counteroffer was only made out of consideration. He didn't want to inconvenience her with planning and preparations, not on their first date together. His internal now struggled for a reason to finish his request for her company. He looked for a backup plan for recovery. He needed a way to salvage anything he could from this obvious blunder. He was searching for a miracle.

He was lucky. Becky's fixation on the initial rejection finally lifted. Her domain began to acknowledge and act on the new information that awaited and was now seeping into her consciousness, the subsequent stream of Tom's invitation. Her expressions began to transform as a first reaction to the new information received. It was hitting her that Tom was asking her out. It was what she'd wanted from him all along. This was a victory, instead of what appeared only moments earlier as a devastating defeat. She smiled again and began to absorb and then to internally coax each additional word of his invitation through her filters. She gladly allowed the rest of the words to form their meaning. They were good. They rejuvenated her.

The return of her smile, her excitement, and her subtle giggle, in sequence, returned goodness to the moment. Tom picked up on the change, and his confidence reappeared in response to Becky's awakening. It all happened in an instance, but the emotions spent in this span of time made it seem an eternity. They'd both made a complete journey through the breadth of their emotions and feelings. They'd both drawn deep from their domains and domain partners. For Tom, this included a complete renewal of confidence. He added, "This place that I'm suggesting, it's a small and quiet place. It's not too fancy, but it's inviting." He paused to reconfirm Becky's reactions. "It's also a very pleasant walk from here to there. We'll have time to talk." He closed the deal with "Most importantly, they have great Italian food."

Becky was now fully recovered from her initial disappointment. She was bobbing her head on almost every word, showing subtle and controlled joy. She was sold on his request and ready to go.

Tom continued though, almost as if rehearsed. In fact, it was rehearsed. He didn't want to leave anything out. He'd worked on this so hard. The words were coming easy. The adrenaline filled his body. He had every indication from her smile and the way she hung on his every word that she was going to accept his offer. He finished, "We will take our time. We can get to know each other better and have a good meal and a relaxing conversation. Will you join me?" The proposal was complete. Tom felt especially relieved about finally getting this out.

Yet he also felt a need to backtrack a bit and to repair the damage of his earlier mistake. As a final thought and now having considered how insensitive he must have seemed with his rejection of Becky's initial offering of lunch, he added, "I really do appreciate your offer to make lunch, Becky. On any other day, I would very much like to have lunch at your place. If you still want to, I can come over for lunch another day."

Becky was pleased by his courteous and thoughtful explanation. Both of their domains' energies and the resultant emotions were running high. There was now more at stake in this relationship. They were moving into new and uncharted territory that both were anxious to explore. On the more practical side, Becky was actually quite relieved to be going out for their lunch date. She realized that she did not have the groceries in her apartment to make a lunch, nor did she know what Tom might like. She accepted Tom's plans gladly by responding, "I'd love to go out with you for Italian food. It all sounds so wonderful."

She relished in the relief that he'd finally come across with an offering of a real date. She shifted her mail into the one hand to free the other to search her purse for the key to her apartment. Then she asked, "Do I have time to drop off my mail and check my apartment?" She added a confirming quantifier. "It shouldn't take me more than a few minutes." She looked for his approval and smiled.

He responded, "Certainly. Take whatever time you need."

Then he took a quick glance at his watch before returning his gaze, hoping to prompt a reply of the time she would need. She offered nothing. He then felt compelled to suggest, "Would twenty minutes be enough time for you to do whatever you need to?"

Becky nodded yes and said, "That will be fine." She smiled appreciatively. It was a smile that melted Tom completely. Her smile usually did.

She then started toward the stairs leading to her floor. Tom watched her to the stairs and closed the conversation, saying, "It's a date, then. I'll be here in twenty minutes." His voice was assuring.

And even though she'd disappeared from his sight, he added, "I'm looking forward to this time together."

In twenty minutes, they'd be testing a new phase in their relationship; neither of them fully understood the reasons for its allure and attraction nor its composition. They just felt the goodness and emotion that oozed from it. Both Becky and Tom made their way to their apartments to prepare for their upcoming outing together.

In the spirit domains of Becky and Tom, there was much magic. It was forming what we commonly refer to as good or compatible chemistry, but in reality, it is the many inner actions of the natures of the spirit domains that explain an attraction between two special beings. To understand this, it is essential to explore deeply the world of the spirit domain and the makeup and attributes of each spirit within the domain.

Spirits that are assigned to domains in different beings and when they are of a like nature will form an attraction to one another. This is the case with Becky's and Tom's spirits. In the spirit world, there are either spirits with natures that are good or spirits with natures that are evil. A being's domain may contain both good-natured and evil-natured spirits within it. Combinations of good-natured and evil-natured spirits are probable, but the number within the mix is limited to three. The choosing and composition of the mix is beyond the control of the being or the spirits. But it is not at random. Rather, it's in accordance to nature's search for wholistic and perfect balance and in accordance to life's master plans. Each domain is specially designated and the mix specially calibrated.

When two beings meet and their domains interact, this initiates a natural and immediate assessment of compatibility between them. There are nine possible combinations of spirit pairings between any two domains of three spirits each. This assessment of compatibility specifically and uniquely involves the nature and its attributes of each spirit involved. Each paired combination will attract when both spirits are of a like nature, either both good or both evil. They will repel when they are of a different nature (one being good and the other being evil). The more paired combinations of like natures between the two domains and the nine combinations, the stronger the attraction will be. When like combinations are in the majority, this will foster an opportunity to develop a relationship between the two beings. The more paired combinations of unlike natures between the two domains, the stronger the repulsion will be. Unlike-natured pairings, when in the majority, will inhibit a relationship from forming.

Within the nine possible pairings of the spirits and their natures, it is quite likely, and in fact most probable and natural, that all paired combinations will not result in like and compatible conditions. Some will be. Others will not be. It will allow the two beings to both attract and repulse each other at times. However, what will ultimately be the determining force in the relationship between two beings is based on which combinations, like or unlike, are in the majority across the nine pairings. This will determine the natural tendency toward compatibility or repulsion. It will determine the likelihood of a relationship germinating.

As for the actions and behaviors of the two parties in a relationship, this is governed by a slightly different set of determinants. Behaviors will be based, at any given moment, by only one spirit combination of the nine. It is determined by the one combination of spirit natures from within each of the two involved domains that, at that very moment, holds dominance over the two domains. This pair of spirits, one from each domain, is allowed to dictate the actions and behaviors of the two parties based on their specific and unique nature's attributes. These can be different from the two domains' majority- type pairings determining the domain-holistic assessment which determines compatibility. The pair holding dominance can drive actions and behaviors of the being that are different from those common in the compatibility of the overall relationship, even to temporarily seem inconsistent. The role of dominance in each party's domain is ever changing based on shifts of stimuli and situations affecting the beings and domains. Therefore, the actions and behaviors of the parties will also change continuously with each new spirit pairing shifting into the position of dominance within the two domains and trigger the behaviors to shift as well. The odds are always greatest that the majority type of pairing will also be the combination holding dominance over the domains of those in the relationship. For this reason, most times, the behaviors and actions of the two parties in a relationship will be consistent and mimic their general compatibility characteristic, those that also define the general likelihood of a relationship forming between the two beings. In any regard, it's either one of attraction or one of repulsion, good or evil centered.

Understanding the difference between the spirit factors supporting compatibility from those affecting behaviors is quite important. To add clarity to understanding these differences, the following adds a few more details.

The first impression we form of others follows a specific, standard, and natural set of rules. The first impression allows nothing to chance. It excludes consideration for which spirit pairing is in dominance within the two domains. It is a pure and simpler test only for compatibility. It is determined solely from the cumulative number of attracting and repulsing paired spirits that naturally form between the domains when they come into contact with one another. Like or unlike pairings are all that is considered at this initial meeting of the domains. The natures and paired combinations that are in the majority define the compatibility score and set the course for or against the relationship forming. Once compatibility is determined, it's permanent; the opportunity for a relationship, or not, is founded, is set, and remains stable.

There can, however, be variability in the actions and behaviors of those in the relationship, as referred to earlier, because they are governed by a different set of rules from those determining the initial test for compatibility in the relationship. From this point forward, we will be primarily addressing behaviors, not compatibility in relationships.

The rules that determine the behaviors of those in a relationship line up much more closely to the natural laws of chance and probabilities. The individual spirit pairings' dominance and also the strength of each paired spirits come into play and add the element of randomness and unpredictability. This randomness creates different moods and changing emotions. It explains why we "behave nicely" with someone most of the time and then don't at others, even though we are compatibly attracted overall. It explains why we support others in some situations and not in others. Life doesn't often offer a complete or perfect solution or fit between beings. It's not supposed to. It's not a requirement to be totally and perfectly aligned in every aspect and in every situation to befriend someone. The initial draw toward a relationship (compatibility) is unconditional and will remain stable. It will be rock solid based on the paired and total composition of the two domains, pure and simple.

On the other hand, feelings and emotions while in the relationship are the conditional variants. They will be influenced and initiated by the two beings' pair of spirits relegated at that moment to the position of dominance within the two domains. The spirit natures that form the basis for the relationship in their aggregate, likeness, or difference are also the same natures that, when considered separately and individually, dictate the being's different and unique spikes in actions and moods. The individual natures' differences allow actions and moods to run temporarily independent of compatibility and at times in opposite directions.

Looking at things from frame to frame and from the natures' pairing-to-pairing perspective, as spirits transition through the position of dominance, one must expect a compatible pair of beings to take a little of the bad to experience a lot of the good, a little bit of repulsion for a time to attract. Just as there are no perfect fits, there are no complete misfits between beings either. There is rarely a complete repulsion between two beings or a complete attraction. The factors and influences to building relationships are always about degrees in the like and opposites. Few reside at ultimate and furthest extremes. Almost all of us are residing in the middle of the measures. To others that observe and measure us, there are almost always flaws and imperfections and, as such, also in all our relationships. Even in the best of relationships, all the combinations of the natures usually do not match up like for like.

To put it in a more familiar context, we have all experienced times of trouble, times of doubt with others we feel close to. We feel drawn to another at one moment and then repelled at the next. Even loving couples quarrel at times. It's the result of their mixed-natured domains and an unfavorable draw on the pair selected for dominance. The attraction, and at times repulsion, is based on which spirits are dominant, either of like natures or of unlike natures. The spirits and natures in dominance within the domain can, and do, change commonly and repeatedly among the residing spirits. With these changes, our behaviors with others will change quickly and repeatedly as well. An attraction can turn to repulsion, or repulsion to attraction, with a shifting of the pairs to the position of dominance. Changes are usually caused by a change in situation or stimulus. The unpredictability, the suddenness of the change, is a bit "like the weather" at times. It may be difficult for some to consider that our moods and behaviors in relationships are as fickle as the weather. This is an exaggeration to prove my point, but they can be.

Things we like about others is based on like spirit natures finding each other (good to good, evil to evil). Things we don't like about others arise from differences in the natures. A final factor in the equation of how we act toward others and behave in relationships is that spirits of a same nature can be further drawn to one another and establish added synergy by having like, shared, or common destinies. This draws common interests and sharing of information and experience stored internally within each domain and brings it outward for shared use in supporting and achieving these like destinies. It is strength from a common cause that draws these spirits with like destiny together. These are usually only temporary relationships, however, and remain long enough to complete the destiny. More specific details regarding the domain and spirits' influence in relationships will be addressed later in the chapter entitled "Relationships."

The makeup of Becky's and Tom's spirit domains was ideal for supporting a strong attraction and compatible relationship. The spirits in their domains were primarily good natured. Becky's domain was the extreme case. It contained three spirits, all with a strong and good-filled nature. Her mix was quite rare. Hers afforded special abilities and gifts not found in the common domains' mix. At the same time, it caused her additional exposures and drew additional attentions to her from the spirit realm. She was quite special from the spirit perspective, even though average in most every other superficial and worldly attribute and characteristic.

Tom's domain was made up of two good-natured spirits and one evil-natured spirit. Neither his good-natured or evil-natured spirits were particularly strong. Together, the strength of the two good-natured spirits exceeded the strength of the single evil-natured one. Dominance was most times rendered to the good-natured side of the domain but only based on numbers. Overall, Tom's domain was good-natured and strongly attracted to Becky's. It drew from her strength and domain's purity. She gave value and confidence to Tom's weaker good-natured spirits. It created a charged emotional attraction to her. It made him better when he was in her company. There was much goodness to be found in the combined composition of Becky's and Tom's domains. The final tally of pairs of like natures in the two domains was six, and those of unlike pairs was three. Compatibility was definitely strong. The probability that behavior would align with compatibility was also favorable in six of the (like) pairs of natures gaining dominance in the two domains. In the three (unlike) pairs, there would be unpredictability based on the direction that the unlike natures chose to take their beings' behaviors. Both could align to the same behavior, or one could take differing degrees of variation from the course set by compatibility. In all, however, the needed ingredients to produce a good and bountiful harvest were all in the foundational base of their domains. These seeds, with spirit care and attention, will ripen into good and loving results.

The nature of a spirit will never change except for one exception. The spirit and its nature are a primary constant and a stable ingredient in forming the personality and actions of the being. A spirit and its natures influence the external components of the being. The nature can, however, be masked or diluted by the natures of the other stronger or equally strong spirits within the domain. Such was the case within Tom's domain.

The evil-natured spirit in Tom's domain was outnumbered, dominated, and overpowered by the combined strength of the two good-natured ones within his domain. Although this spirit was still evil natured and prone to its evil destinies and even though it was allowed time in a dominant role, it was controlled by the two good-natured spirits. It was allotted proportional time in dominance and proportional influence of the being yet only at the prescribed times allowed and chosen by the majority of the spirits of his domain. The strength of the natures, being relatively equal, and their time and place when allowed dominance are controlled by the strongest or in this case, where all are equally strong, the majority nature. This scenario is most common among spirits and domains with two-to-one spirit nature combinations. Most humans have domain makeup like Tom's, with spirits of different natures residing within them.

Adding to the complexity of the spirit influence is the certainty that no two spirits have the same combination of nature type and strength. It's what makes every being unique and special. Total predictability with certainty is thus made impossible. Unique and special is the norm. Becky was the exception. Her domain was especially unique and special but in a privileged way. Unlike Tom's domain, Becky's mix of spirits, nature, and strength was truly the rare and ultimate combination. She had "pure" powers. There was no diluting, masking, or contending between her spirits' natures for influence. There was no need to compromise between or manipulate for positions of dominance between the spirits of her domain. They were all of the same type and strength. They had the same general destinies. This allowed her a special and concentrated focus of influence toward the achievement of these destinies, as well as special abilities and the gift allowing her to help others of a less than pure domain. She could draw and distribute unequal shares of information to and from the mixed domains of others. She could establish special sharing relationships and connections with others' domains, those containing at least one like-natured spirit to her own. She was the renewing fuel to these like-natured spirits that would come into contact with her pure domain. She was revered and held very special by all the other like-natured spirits of the spirit community. She was pure good from which they would draw strength. It was unclear how much of her special power she might use with Tom. She had used very little to this point. She would not use it to gain advantage of his love.

The components and makeup of their domains were to naturally support what would happen in their relationship without need for her to use her special influence or capabilities.

On her way out the door to meet Tom, Becky's neighbor intercepted her. Becky and Anita Grey had been friends for years. They'd shared everything, especially every romance-rich experience. Anita greeted her friend by asking, "Why such a hurry, Becky?" Simultaneously, she touched her friend on the back of her shoulder and shared a smile. "Is there a fire in the building that I should be aware of?" The connection between their domains was instantaneous. Their domains had histories of sharing and had long ago established total compatibility and trust with each other. The flow between their domains was full and the contents shared unfiltered. Their auras were familiar, and they aligned as one. It allowed them to connect beyond the touch. There was spirit magic in it. Through this magic, Anita was intuitively aware that something important was happening. Through their sharing, Anita knew that whatever it was, it was special. It triggered Anita's emotions, yet her being knew nothing of the whys of it.

Becky also, in her subconscious, could detect her friend's excited curiosity. She finally shared, "Anita, do you remember me mentioning the man in apartment 2034?" She gave a small chuckle and offered Anita one of her patented smiles.

Anita nodded and replied, "Yes, of course, I do. You talk about him all the time."

Then she playfully added, "He's the one you act a little goo-goo over, and if my memory serves me correctly, you had hoped that he might ask you out sometime." On the word "goo-goo," Anita stuck out her tongue and rolled her eyes in fun. She waited for Becky to explain why at that very moment this was so important in their lives.

Becky accommodated by sharing, "We just met downstairs while getting our mail, and he invited me to lunch," she squealed from excitement on cue with the final word of her sentence. It was clear that this was a very welcomed and special event for her. It elicited a heightened rise in her emotions. Her excitement had now risen to a crescendo like that of a key portion of a symphony.

Becky added, "Isn't it wonderful? It's finally happened!" Her eyes opened wide, and her smile burst through her face even wider than before. She quivered slightly, controlling her elevated state of joy and exuberance. She was so excited to have shared her happiness with her best friend.

Anita was ecstatic for her. She outwardly wished only the best for her friend. She was glad to share in the moment's flow of electricity as if it were her own. It prompted her emotions to ignite as well and to begin registering a near-equal level in intensity to those of Becky's. And although she didn't intend to delay her friend from her date, she selfishly wanted to experience the moment for just a little while longer. Instead, she responded to her friend, "Oh, Becky, this is indeed wonderful." She gave her a quick hug and released. "Go and have a good time." She ordered it in a playful way. With a slight nudge, she whisked her off to the stairway.

As Anita stepped back into her apartment's doorway, she hung on the partially opened door and said, "Be sure to stop by afterward. We'll need to talk more. I will be here all day and night waiting for your report." They both giggled and went their separate ways. Friendship and sharing were such good experiences for both of these beings and the good-natured spirits that were at their cores.

Within their spirit domains, this short encounter between Becky and Anita created many actions and reactions between their two sets of spirits. The attraction and bond that was immediately established between the two domains was clearly the product of majority good-natured spirit pairings. The familiarity to each other, the history of friendship and trust, and the situation itself drove two good-natured spirits, one from each, to the position of dominance over their domains. Behaviors were thus very positive during the direct contact and sharing. This moment was of strong goodness. In the aftermath, however, after Becky had gone, it would be Anita's domain that would reassess these moments in retrospect. Although the exchange seemed completely good and innocent, there was more to it than what surfaced for the external to see.

Anita's spirit mix was made up of two moderately strong good-natured spirits and one strong evil-natured spirit. The evil one craved dominance. When left unchecked, its influence could present itself quickly and skillfully at opportune and even the most inopportune times. At that very moment, immediately after the brief encounter with Becky, Anita's evil-natured one was busy dissecting and evaluating the exchange. Moments earlier, while the auras were intertwined in the excitement and sharing, the spirits from both Anita's and Becky's domains were given free access to the wealth of feelings and information held within their active and dormant stores. The thoughts and emotions that were under examination included joy and happiness for a friend, as well as others from Anita's stores originating from her eviler nature. The joyous and happy thoughts were the majority ones, shared, nurtured, and fortified from Becky's pure domain. They came from the good-natured spirit pairings between Anita and her friend. They were the ones that drew out Anita's immediate emotions and actions.

But behind these, lying dormant and hidden beneath the initial reactions, came jealousy. This came from the strong evil-natured spirit. There was impetus and stimulus that supported it. Anita was still searching for her own special partner. She was searching for that special someone to share joy and happiness with. Her domain, and in turn her total being, was lonely. She knew that if Becky was to find her special someone, Becky would be less available, and times would be fewer for Anita and her spirits to share the emotional gifts and attentions of Becky's domain. The young man from apartment 2034 would occupy a large portion of Becky's free time. The times of loneliness and her domain's memories of wanting someone to care for her were not welcomed or easy draws at that moment.

Every spirit has a history. It is carried from generation to generation. It can't be altered. It contains good and bad, joy and sorrow, kindness and meanness. It allows all spirits of the domain to remember like experiences, to remember all effects of past life's happenings. All life's happenings have an effect. The spirit knows this. The spirit has memories of all past effects.

Anita's domain remembered loneliness. Loneliness had followed her through her spirit assignments for some time now. Her spirits felt unfortunate and cheated by fate. Her spirits remembered previous and consecutive generations, each void of a soul mate to give her comfort, strength, and happiness. These thoughts about her spirits' past triggered dominance to the darker side of her domain. It raised the angst of misfortune. At that moment in her life, her spirit influence was not of goodness. Anita's domain, now dominated by her evil-natured spirit, was filling her mind with thoughts of contempt for her friend's new good fortune. It raised conflict with the other less strong good-natured spirits in the domain. It brought new thoughts and ideas of what to do, how to influence the being. These were new bits of information brought from the domain's stores of past experiences. There were thoughts and ideas that Anita would not usually subscribe to, nor would she ever actually employ them against her best friend. But these thoughts moved through her domain and were registered within her domain's stores just the same. They revealed a new and darker side of her domain to be cautious of.

Considerations for whether to support her friend Becky and her new male interest or to raise doubt and opposition had been weighed by all members of the domain. Her future actions and behaviors were now in the balance, especially hinging on the strength of each nature's position within the domain. Their opportunity and time in dominance would determine each moment's outcome. The measures of each good and evil nature, their influence and skill to position themselves within the domain, and their ability to be of influence and rise to dominance within the domain would decide each frame of Anita's actions and behavior. The result would be evidenced throughout Anita's future relationship with Becky. Fortunately, Anita and Becky's relationship was founded on goodness and the strength of their majority spirit tendencies. The strength of their bond and Becky's pure influence over Anita's domain would help in the decisions and position that the latter would choose to take as much as the aggregate and overriding nature of their domains toward goodness would control. There would be times, though, when Anita's domain would allow dominance to the evil-natured spirit within.

The domain-centered, nature-driven inner play and the dominance-setting positioning of Anita's spirits were simply one example of how most situations and encounters within the human psyche are evaluated and decided on. The common domain is filled with natures and attitudes in various mixes and degrees of good and evil. It's comparable to raising fruit but from different trees in the garden representing good and evil. The fruit that is produced can be lovely, or it can be deformed and pitted. It can be sweet or sour. There are situations on the earth that depend on and thrive from both, just as with the different spirits. A garden needs tending. Both good and evil natures need to be nurtured and tended. Both good and evil are natural produce from similar seed of the earth. Both are essential in their controlled portion and dosage to the healthy natural balance of the earth. They are essential to the makeup of a vibrant and thriving civilization. They give the earth perspective and balance. They create difference and allow variety. Both nourish segments of the overall populations of beings on the earth, feed the likes and dislikes. It is within the spirit that the balance of the seed is trusted. Growing side by side, good and evil coexist and affect each other in balance and in the aggregate within the domain gardens of life.

Much of the aforementioned primarily addresses the mixed nature domains. These are the majority and most prevalent domains. At the current position on the circle of life, they make up about ninety five percent of domains. But there are also exceptions to these common and mixed domains. These are the ones that are most extreme, the ones with a complete allocation of one type of nature, those with a full and undiluted measure of purity, beings of only goodness or, inversely, of only evil. These are the rare and truly unique domains. Natures within these special domains still have variation of strength, but inside the domain, there are little contention or disruption of the spirit's influence, minimal compromise of the nature and destiny, and minimal need for negotiation or trade-offs within these domains. They know little of the struggles and challenges of intermixing with another type of nature within their domain.

These pure domains are the ultrapowerful and ultra-influential domains. They have special purpose. They are placed on the earth to be a source of reference and to help those spirits and natures of like type to learn and grow. They are revered by those they share natures with. Pure domains represent and create the most lasting of marks from their time. They are, as are all domains, important to the evolutionary process, but pure domains turn the dials more so than others. They stamp their influences on their like-natured community of spirits. They lead by example. They are the standard-bearers and set the boundaries, the goals, and the nature's direction for the spirits of their like nature. They establish and develop the cornerstone for future generations of spirits of their nature's type to build on. From these special few, the impact they have is profound. They leave a legacy, either a lasting and permanent memory of good or a lasting scar of evil on the world. They become the case studies and examples of either good or evil to guide the future and to measure against. They fill the domain's libraries of reference with their contributions, their exploits, and the products of their actions and teachings. They become the models and the source to draw on and try to emulate for those who have domains leaning more toward the mixed norm. They can provoke and produce unique and profound change.

Becky was one of these extreme domains. All three of her natures were strong. She represented extreme good in the earth's many gardens of good and evil. Her efforts at cultivation always produced fair and caring goodness. Tom's and Anita's gardens, on the other hand, were of a mixed variety. Becky would need to be careful not to dominate their domain. All domains of the earth (good and evil) contribute to the needs of the earth and of the natures. All are important and have their place. They are all good in their balance and total effect. Becky's just produced the purest, most potent, and most impactful product.

Can there be too much goodness or too much evil in the world? Can there be too much of these influences in any one domain? The answer is yes and absolutely. The world, in aggregate, needs all the natures in its mix and preferably balanced. As for a domain, it is the way of nature that some have more of one type, and some have less. It creates diversity. It creates differences. It allows for shifts in the power structure and to the norms. It challenges consistency and complacency. Does it encourage conflict and contention between parties and sides? Yes, this is also the way of nature as each nature makes a contribution. Each of the differences and influences affects and adds new stores of experience and history within the domains. Each feeds the aggregate as a whole. It's complex and all interwoven into the fabric of internal spirit communion and inner domain relationships occurring within the spirit realm.

Tom and Becky arrived back at the entrance of their building at nearly the same instance. As they saw each other, the familiar fluttering filled their insides. There was something special about this relationship, but on the external and beyond the spirit domain, it was too early for either to foresee where it might be taking them. Tom spoke first. "Your timing is perfect," he complimented her. His mouth turned to a grin. "I hope you're ready for a special feast."

She was still catching her breath after rushing down the stairs. She'd been in a hurry so as not to make Tom wait. She replied, "I'm looking forward to this. It's been quite a while since I've dined on authentic Italian. In fact, I'm not sure that I've ever had authentic."

Tom felt guilty. He wasn't so sure that the restaurant that he'd chosen truly qualifies as authentic. He felt a strong need to backpedal a bit. He suspected that he'd been caught in a possible oversell. He confessed, "Well, Becky, you may need to forgive me. The truth is . . . I'm not sure the restaurant where we will be dining is truly authentic Italian. I just like their food."

He then further set the record straight by adding, "In fact, I doubt that I, like you, have ever really eaten authentic Italian food, nor would I know it from those that aren't. I just know that what we'll be served. I believe you'll like it as much as I do." He sheepishly looked away to avoid the effect of his admissions. He hoped that his confession wouldn't diminish the moment or deflate the bubble of her trust. He wanted nothing to diminish the joy coming from their acceptances to be with each other today. He so hoped that her opinion of him might not have lessened.

He concluded by saying, "I'm sorry to say I am not an expert of Italy's best, not by any means." He laughed slightly as a nervous yet diversionary tactic and hoped that Becky might forgive his ordinary preferences and amateur attempt to critique food.

She did and followed with her own chuckle and admission. "I'm sure the food will be perfect. I, too, have never patronized the finest or most authentic of establishments. I wouldn't be able to afford them." She looked into his eyes and shared, "I'm just very happy to be getting out this afternoon and for this chance to get to know you better."

Tom felt a sense of relief, and even pride swell up in his chest. He thought of Becky as someone whom he would be very lucky to draw interest from. Something very good was happening to him. He didn't want to make mistakes. He feared that an unwelcomed resurrection of his clumsy nature might arise to spoil the moment. He feared that his nervousness might again arise and prompt him to appear or to say something foolish. He so hoped things at the restaurant would go well. Finally, he extended his hand and took hers in his. He guided her down the street. He shared, "It's a beautiful day for a walk, don't you think?" He was feeling the joy of attracting such a thing of beauty and goodness beside him.

Becky was content in the warmth and comfort of his grasp around her fingers. From this tender grip, she could tell that he was a good man. He seemed respectful of her wishes and her feelings. She replied, "Yes, it is. I could walk like this for blocks." Then she began to share her delight that he'd finally asked her out. The feeling was mutual. Small talk took over the conversation for the next several blocks. It could be argued that more was exchanged through the joined hands than from their conversation. The spirit connection was intense. It all seemed so natural; it was truly a good fit.

Six of the nine spirit pairings between their domains were of like type. The laws of nature made them very compatible. But it was more. The spirits from their domains connected uniquely and completely from the first moments of their date. Their body and minds lagged behind but were working intently, and as quickly as they could, to catch up with the intensity of the spirits' connection.

Becky and Tom arrived at the restaurant. In Becky's mind, they arrived far too soon. She would have liked to have enjoyed their walk much longer. She was having such a good time talking.

The restaurant was not much to look at from the sidewalk, but it felt comfortable in its nonintrusive plainness. There was much goodness to it. There was much goodness to this date so far. They entered the double doors that separated the restaurant's interior from the street outside. Tom confirmed his reservation with the hostess and advised her that there would be two. He asked for a special and quiet table. It was this juncture in time that would begin the next phase of their special future together.

On this particular afternoon, Mr. Arthur had also chosen to dine at the same restaurant that Becky and Tom had chosen. He also had a craving for Italian food. As usual, he was alone. This was not surprising to anyone who knew him well or who might have had previous encounters with him. He was never very social or personable. He carried a perpetual chip on his shoulder. He trusted no one. He liked very, very few.

Mr. Arthur arrived thirty minutes earlier than Becky and Tom. As they walked in, they could hear him from deep within the restaurant screaming at his waiter. He obviously felt that he had been serviced too slowly. Becky and Tom did not take in the details of his ranting and his rage but were clear on his general displeasure. He rose from his table and stormed toward them on his way out the door. He loudly blurted in a forceful, hurtful tone as he neared them, "Out of my way!" He was certainly in a hurry to leave. His face told the story. It was beet red. He was angry and determined to make a scene. He offered only insults to everyone in range.

He scolded, "You people must be crazy to patronize this dump." The message was also intended for Becky and Tom. They had no clue about why he had targeted them with his anger. As he passed, he pushed Tom into Becky and stormed on without even so much as an insincere apology or a concerned glance. There was no attempt to assist either of them in their recovery. He was just too caught up in his anger and chastisement of the Italian eatery.

Tom had fallen into Becky, causing her to lose her balance as well. They both found balance, catching themselves against the near wall. Tom was embarrassed. He apologized to Becky for the situation but most of all for his clumsiness. "I'm so sorry for losing my balance," he pleaded. "Are you all, right?"

She was not pushed far, nor did Mr. Arthur's brush against her cause her any real distress. In an odd way, she welcomed the unintentional and momentary embrace with Tom. She gushed, "I am fine, Tom." She grinned. "But obviously not everyone shares your rave review of this restaurant."

They both chuckled before Tom offered, "Well, maybe so, but that being the case, your opinion will be all that matters."

Becky blushed. She felt pleased to hear that he was still comfortable with her and their plan to have lunch. She was certain that no matter how the food might turn out or how slow the service might be, this restaurant and their time spent together would be special. The incident of the previous few minutes would soon be forgotten, all but the sharing of their past and recent experiences with this angry little man from their building and how he presented himself so rudely at the onset of their date. He always seemed to be in such a foul mood. Not surprisingly, they had both had a number of encounters and experiences with him and with his behaviors. They could not recall a single good memory of him. They thought how sad it must be to be so angry all the time. They were glad that they had lives that brought them happiness and goodness.

After the commotion within the restaurant subsided and the remnants of both Mr. Arthur's departure and the damage control completed by the restaurateur, Tom and Becky were led by the hostess to their table. The hostess was very pleasant, and she apologized for the previous incident, even though she was not a direct participant or cause. The table where they would dine in was perfectly positioned in the front of the restaurant near its large storefront window. A candle was burning. Relaxing music played in the background. The service was perfectly slow on this day, allowing them much time to talk and get to know each other. It would be a delightfully long lunch today. There were few distractions or interruptions.

The conversation flowed easily and continuously. Everything they said, every word, seemed so important. They shared much about their pasts, their families, and their backgrounds. Both felt connected and very comfortable with each other. They found common and vital references to draw conversation from. They found that their lives were not so different or distant. It seemed a perfect fit. An immediate and natural trust formed between them. It was uncanny. It was as if it was magical. Both felt like they could tell the other their secrets and most treasured yet protected inner thoughts without fear of reprisal, critique, or embarrassment. They shared their aspirations, their goals, and their important drivers unfiltered and directly from their inner domains as if they'd known each other all their lives. They shared their experiences in this life, all the while supported by the pairing and sharing of their spirits through the compatibility and intertwining of their auras. These woven auras formed a perfect veil of truth and trust that covered them. The attraction at the spirit level was intense and complete. It formed the ideal setting for their relationship to form and flourish.

Tom learned from their conversation that Becky had lived a relatively simple life, distant from fame or privilege. Her childhood had been happy but impoverished. She'd done without a lot of material things and didn't miss them or didn't know that she did. She had little knowledge or experience with the ease of prominence and wealth. Her opportunities had been sparingly parsed and portioned to her. She had to carefully and diligently watch for them so as not to miss them. When presented, she needed to take advantage of each before it was gone. Nothing came easy or free. Rather, it needed to be earned and deserved.

The finished product was solid and good. It had been crafted and forged through persistence and determination into her current life's position and standing. The person that she had become, her beliefs and values, and what she could claim to have established as parts of her life, her legacy and contributions were self-made and personalized. She felt comfortable with who she'd become. And even though she rarely stood out as special or of particular importance in the external world, she had many friends, people whom she had a special moment or two. Her life fit her perfectly well. It fit her expectations and aspirations. She had long since learned the value and benefits of hard work, as well as treating people respectfully and fairly. Sacrifice and drive were her most commonly traversed and familiar paths to success. Nothing was handed to her without giving something in return.

Learning was a big part of her past and her present. She studied hard at every level of her academic development. It was not only about her attendance and study in education's formal institutions but also what she learned from all around her. Life, in its natural form, was one of her most frequented and most valued laboratories. She observed all she could. She sifted out the good and the fairness of life from that which was not. From that which sifted through her filters, she crafted her personality, her approaches, and her general respect toward others. It led her to value others with fairness and as if each had value and purpose. She had plenty of experience with disappointment. It was as if she and it were on a first-name basis. She'd lost her share of struggles. She'd fallen short of reaching a few of her targets and goals. It rarely deterred her though. It made her work harder and get creative in her approaches, strategies, and efforts to reattack these disappointments.

She was not at all accomplished at manipulating others and situations to get her way. She was not willing to cheat or play outside the boundaries, no matter how minor or inconsequential. At times, it seemed to her external being to be a curse that followed her everywhere. She never seemed to get away with anything deemed wrong or against the rules. It seemed she would always get caught and would always pay a full punishment for these mistakes. This forced her to live to higher standards than most because of the influences from her nature in general. On occasion, it had been a bitter pill to swallow, especially when she was younger, when it set her outside of the norm or excluded her from some of the fun, the pranks and antics of her peers. In the end, however, she found the goodness and value in its lessons and in the intensity and corrective influences of its corresponding effect on her behaviors and emotions. Pain and disappointment were good teachers. It taught her to swallow hard and move on with new knowledge, approaches, and experiences in regard to life's pitfalls. She learned that things come with a cost, whether from a need to sacrifice, to trade off, or to draw from things hidden deeper within herself and her domain. Even with all the hardships and struggles that she had gone through and rising above them, there were surprisingly little baggage and only a few lines of defense that she put up to shield her from a fall. She didn't expect reward, but when it did come, it was appreciated and deserved. It gave her pride. She cherished success and achievement. It seemed to be always earned via the hard road.

What was unspoken was that Becky's life had been mostly driven and patterned by her special spirit influence. At the spirit level, this did not need to be communicated. Her purity of nature dictated it as so.

Tom's bio, on the other hand, read somewhat different, yet he, too, had encountered many hardships and challenges on the road to his present state. Tom had always been somewhat of a weakling. He was strong of mind and moderately strong of spirit but weak of body. To compensate for his shortcomings, his mind became more dominant and stronger than most. He was over perceptive and an accomplished problem solver even at an early age. Yet as a young boy and even into adolescence, this was more of a curse than a gift. He was many times teased for these strengths and tormented for his physical weaknesses. He was less popular than other boys. He was the geek or the dork. As a teen, he wished he could score the winning touchdown or hit the winning homerun just once in his life, but these were dreams beyond his physical abilities.

Throughout his life, he was challenged to overcome his deficiencies in one area with his strength in another. He, too, turned to books and learning as the path to self-acceptance and attaining personal goals. This was easy for him, more so than for most. Tom's developmental challenges were not with science, math, or philosophy, but rather, they lay in developing himself socially. This was where the really hard work needed to be done. Tom knew subservience all too well and about allowing others to always be first in life's playgrounds, such as in selecting teams in gym class or in lining up for lunch. This had been his whole life growing up in a world of more macho peers and classmates. They'd made every attempt to teach him that he was second best. He wanted to reestablish his confidence, to hone his ability to take charge and be assertive, and most of all to make acquaintances. Success required finding others much like himself and reestablishing his trust in them.

It wasn't until late in his teens, when he was attending college, that the physical and superficially preferred attributes of his early teens were upstaged enough to allow his intellectual excellence to be acknowledged and valued by an appreciable portion of the community. Also, by this time, the bullies had so often tormented him earlier in his life were now facing new milestones and challenges in their lives. In their late teens and early twenties, they were finding it difficult to transform their crude brawn and physical superiorities to meaningful long-term careers and financially sustaining endeavors. They were many times destined to serve the bluest of blue-collar trades. College, in most of their cases, just wasn't in the cards for them. Tom lost touch with many of them. It freed him to move on and find his truer value.

On the most positive side, college was the first place that Tom really felt a special and solid fit for his specific gifts and attributes. Here, he found others like himself. With effort and focus, he worked his way out of his insecurities and fears of trusting others. Still, he feared relationships with women. Even as he sat next to Becky at the restaurant, he was still mildly challenged by this obstacle. But she was special. She had made it easy to put away his fears and shyness. With her, it was different. It was not as it had been in the past. He was drawn by her strength and goodness.

Sharing their histories and exposing their secrets made the two appreciate and respect each other all the more. They had both overcome many obstacles. They talked for hours. Their food sat barely touched. While the two of them talked, their spirits shared nearly every detail of their history. There was much to attract one to the other.

Spirits of good natures are judged on their perseverance and their mettle. They are considered to be better and stronger when they've faced hardships; sacrificed, survived, and grown from it; and experienced and overcome pain and suffering. It grows their experience pool. It reveals for these spirits their place, purpose, and station in the world. It helps the spirits with good natures to be more focused and of more useful service to their assignments and the other components of the being. Struggle and challenge keep the good-natured spirit sharp, never allowing it to become too confident or complacent in its role, in its assignments, and to others. Spirits derive their value from their ability to make good decisions, to uncover value and solutions, to find value in trade-offs, and to use and optimize their limited opportunities and resources made available to them. Challenges motivate and draw out their creativity. It builds their partnership and reliance between spirits. Where the residing good spirits of a domain have had to work together to endure challenges, it makes them stronger. The most developed spirits, the stronger spirits, are those that have experienced hardship. It is in these periods of challenge and struggle that a spirit is triggered to pull and share from a deeper level of the domain's reserves of knowledge and past life's experiences. It makes them more rounded. It allows them to extract from the domains and to surround themselves with information and a wealth of knowledge that they might not have previously brought forth and made available for their immediate use. Who they are and who they've been are then clearly laid before them. They learn the full contents of the domain stores and histories. Good spirits, powerful spirits, have grown from hardships and suffering. It motivates and fully draws out value from the strength of their reserve. It forces the spirit to expand on its limits and explore all its nature.

Is it the spirit influence that is key to creating a being's place in their environment, or is it the environment that dictates the spirit influences? I believe the answer is found in the overall composite of the being. It is also that which the other components of the being, those more directly exposed to the outside environment, are willing to allow. It is about the spirits within a domain and how much and how the other components of the being are willing to leverage and support them and one another in unity. As it involves the other components of the being, it is dependent on the effects of the outside environment on them. But most importantly, it's about who has the advantage. It is about whether all the components are cohesively working toward and establishing a strong spiritual driver or working to establish more of an outside driver. If there is no cohesiveness, then it's back to that which has the advantage. The good-natured spirit is the strongest advocate for spirit cohesiveness and spirit-centered, spirit-driven influence. Beings with good-natured domains tend to be more in control of their environment's effect on their being.

Pain, suffering, hardship, strong emotional impulse, compassion, sacrifice, respect, commitment, honor, and selflessness, these are all critical and valued ingredients of goodness. It's what feeds and strengthens goodness. It's not a recipe of ease. It's many times not very fun. In fact, it is hard. It's always selfless. It's the more demanding and difficult of the two spirit natures. Let's examine several examples of these attributes of goodness in practice. The first portrays these attributes as present and in action. The second will reflect the effect when there is an absence of these attributes.

Louise Baker was a junior at West Crawford High School. This is the school where Becky was employed as a teacher. Her parents love Louise and provide for her as much as they can. She is one of five children. Her father and mother work hard to support the family, but there is little money for extras. Louise has two elder sisters. Much of what she wears has been handed down to her from her sisters. Occasionally, she receives something new, mainly on her birthday and Christmas. She appreciates what she has and how hard her parents work to provide for her and her sister and brothers. She hears the comments at school, mostly behind her back, about her clothes. She hears them say that she is from a poor family. It's implied that this is a bad thing. She deals with these comments without retort.

She has dreams and aspirations. She sees the achievement of these aspirations as coming from hard work, from earning what she deserves, and from what comes as a bonus resulting from extra efforts and initiative. She sees much value in helping and supporting other people and treating them with respect. She has experienced poverty at its lowest level. She knows that people like her and her family are good people. She knows them to be hardworking and driven yet just unfortunate. She learns from her experiences. It has helped her with her perspective of what is good in the world. She has learned that good, self-satisfaction, and inner well-being don't come from a trendy wardrobe or from money to spend.

Louise holds a straight-A average in advanced studies. She is friendly to everyone, even those who talk behind her back or snub her because of her economic status. She always smiles. She looks for the good in most everything but is not naive. She helps everybody who will let her. She tries to get involved in as many school activities as she can, but she chooses to work a part-time job after school to help her parents with money. As a result, she is often dropped or excluded from activities requiring after-school practice or participation. Her circle of friends is limited to those much like herself. Gatherings or activities after school are often limited due to a lack of free time and money. Dates are rare for the same reason.

Louise would like to see one particular young man more often, but his pride and inability to take her where other classmates take their dates gets in the way. Louise understands this and does not pressure him. They meet at school and talk frequently. It's enough for her.

Louise walks to school and to her job. When she needs to leave the neighborhood, she takes the bus. Her family can afford only one old car between all the members. She shares a room with her two sisters. The family shares one bathroom. Through their hardships, they've learned to share. There is much togetherness. There are strong spirit connections and guardianship between them. There is much love and respect between each member of the family. The family members are all happy and upbeat.

Louise frequently finishes second best in competitions, whether it is in athletic games, academic contests, or vying for attention at school. This is the case even though, overall, she records some of the top academic scores in the school. She often and purposefully allows others to win, to come out on top. She knows what it feels like to want to win but to come up short. Louise is actually afraid of attention and of the spotlight. She has never had it. It is uncomfortable to her. She prefers to be in a supporting or team role versus that of being the center of attention.

Becky finds her to be a star. Louise is a model student and a model citizen. Becky has transferred to her domain several times and found it to be mixed with two good-natured spirits and one evil-natured one. The good-natured spirits dominate the domain. They help her see the good in everything. Bad things, even evil things, are what she has risen from or is trying to rise from. These will not drive her down or drive her being. Louise is a strong and admirable being. Becky is so proud of her. She is currently involved in securing a full scholarship for her at a top university. Louise often shares with Becky, in trust, what she has had to endure and rise above. Becky's sprits already know these things from her past, gathered from her own domain's stored experiences. Becky can easily and empathetically relate to it from her own similar experiences. Becky knows that Louise represents the best in what the spirits, mind, and body can become.

On the other hand, Dawn Baldridge is a pampered teen. She is treated by most of her classmates as special. She is always dressed in the latest fashion. She has a midsize new car to drive. She has money to spend and does so on her admirers. They expect it.

Her mother and father are both business professionals. Much of their time is focused on their work. Their work frequently comes home with them and steals away the family's sharing and quality time. Dawn rebels against the lack of time and attention afforded her by her family. She does not work herself. Rather, she spends most of her time at parties and with those who treat her as special. Her grades are average. She is involved in high-profile activities at school and craves the attention she gets from them. She needs to be the center of attention in everything she does. It fills a need left vacant by her parents' constant absence from her life. She is very popular at school but knows that much of this comes from the fact that she can always afford to buy what her companions want or what is needed to generate a fun time. She has no one to whom she is really close or who really knows her. She cannot talk about the things that truly concern her. There is no one she can really trust or share secrets without fear of judgment or the conclusions they might draw. She does not want to be scrutinized or excluded from her clique of "special" people.

She sees someone in the mirror every day who is not familiar. She doesn't like it, but it's what keeps her popular. She is an island in and to herself. There's no one to help her set her life's course, especially not in her social circles. Part of this is from the lack of trust and caring. She doesn't know where she's going or what she wants from her life other than acceptance. She's found acceptance to be only superficial and to come from others like herself. Acceptance seems a commodity purchased through exchange of material and artificial status rather than earned. She's found this to be an empty and often lonely and unsatisfying form of status. Rather, she wants acceptance for who she really is. She wants the real her to surface and be appreciated. But it can't. It's too risky.

She has no goals. Financially, she's been taken care of since birth. Emotionally, she's an orphan, left on her own to learn life's ways. She worries what her future might bring, especially when she can no longer live with good conscience from her parents' money and provisions. How it might change after high school haunts her thoughts. She sees others who are less fortunate than her, those without money and privilege. She fears she might someday become like them. She feels she could never live like they do. She is afraid. She is a very unhappy person behind all the makeup and masks. She is catered to. She always gets what she wants, but it leaves her wanting more. She wants to be happy. She wants to feel good about herself.

Her good-natured spirits feel cheated and wanting. Her circumstances and their hold on her special life allow her evil spirit to dominate. It's this lifestyle that sets the stage for her evil side to reign over her life. She plots evil on those who have what she really wants, those who have found happiness and contentment. However, she's not willing to concede anything to obtain this goodness. She says nasty things behind everyone's back, even those who can't help their condition.

One of her usual targets is Louise. It bothers her that Louise never fights back. It especially bothers her that someone with so little, one so unfortunate, can always be so positive and pleasant. She can't understand it at all. After all, Louise knows that Dawn and those like her are superior in every way. How can it be that Louise has such peace and contentment?

Becky has transferred to Dawn's domain, just as she had to Louise's. She found Dawn's spirit mix to be one moderate strength good-natured spirit, one weak good-natured spirit, and one stronger evil-natured spirit. Her domain mix is quite the norm. The difference between her and Louise is that Dawn does nothing to exercise and to grow her good natures. All her activities allow these good natures to fall complacent. At the same time, her actions and her life are more conducive to nourishing the evil nature. It grows stronger. As balance would have it, as one grows stronger, the others grow weaker. Dawn is on the crux of a transformation within her domain. Becky will try to help her as she can but only to the level that Dawn will allow. Without giving up her attitudes, self-piousness, and strong hold on material comforts, the help that Becky's pure natures can provide will be limited. Dawn has allowed rot within and around her good-natured seed. She is now ripe for evil to take over her life.

Respect and subservience are the tonics that make good spirits strong. Self-centeredness and reliance on material things or status hastens goodness away. Such were the cases of Louise and Dawn. Such are the cases with many in the world.

Which nature is more dominant in us humans? Is it good or evil? The answer is not an easy one. In their appropriate time and situation, either can be dominant. But in which direction do civilizations tend to migrate? This is the more important question. The answer to this is formed from historical facts and trends. The evidence supports a slight edge toward evil. The spirits, especially the pure ones, do their best to maintain a balance between the natures, but there are influences other than the spirit that contribute to the final outcome. Outside favor and influence is toward evil.

The ideal world is one of balance, like and unlike working in tandem, with each contributing value in equal, offsetting portions. The good-natured spirits are the guardians of caring and goodness, and the evil natured are the influence of conflict, indulgence, and evil. Each nature safeguards and develops its own influence and impacts based on their type and for release through the being. Love can only grow and flourish from good-natured spirits. Evil can only grow and spread from evil-natured ones. Spirits form their identity and presence on only a few things, but each is very important; it's their history, their destinies, and most importantly on their nature. Natures are put to the truest test from their responsibility to continuously add a fuller and more valued portion to the wholistic and cumulative measure recorded on the universal scale measuring a nature's influence and contribution in the world. This aggregate and cumulative value is made up of the total effect and influence of all spirits supporting the nature by type. The overall measure, and the current apportionment, grows with the spirit nature's successes and effects on supporting their destinies and communal causes. It defines the overall strength of a nature. The measure at any given time forms the baseline against which the next generation's spirits will be apportioned their strength and from which the incremental change in movement around the circle of life is determined. Thus, strength of the nature and position on life's circle are always dependent and related. Success, as defined by the spirit, is achieved through completion of deeds that are consistent with their natures and destinies. All spirits adding to their nature's measure, to the extent of their potential, assures the achievement of their common destinies and ultimately each doing their part toward maintaining an ongoing balance between good and evil contributions to the universal mix. But this never happens exactly to plan.

Failures to achieve the ultimate plan, or to constantly contribute to their full potential, allows balance to falter. This is the ultimate disappointment of the spirits. Unknowingly, even they contribute to their own disappointments and failure. This is through a trick on natures called dilution. Dilution of the spirits of a domain is a compromising and controlled design for failure. It weakens the potency of the spirit natures, especially their full effect on meeting the destinies of those within the domain. It is what unlike spirits do to one another within the domain to soften one another's differences and differing effect on the domain as a whole. It makes a mixed domain more habitable for both the different natured spirit inhabitants. In effect, it reduces noncomputability issues and lessens those attributes that represent the strength and full potencies of the natures. It lightens the effect and measure of each nature's potential and contribution in an attempt to lessen contentions and oppositions. Conversely, it reduces the spirit contribution on the scale measuring the nature's contributions. It allows spirits of the domain and ultimately the beings of the species to coexist in moderate harmony in spite of their differences. This is the ultimate paradox, the greatest catch-22 scenario. It allows for a smoother and more prescribed distribution and transition to dominance between spirits, those of both different and like natures. It helps avoid major spikes from these transitions of spirits to dominance. It seems like such a good thing from the standpoint of inner domain compatibility and harmony, but in reality, it allows failures, many times, only minor or partial failures, but failure all the same in achieving each spirit's destiny to full impact and its measure on their nature's aggregate state. In the worst cases, it prohibits a spirit from achieving any of their destinies. In the lesser cases, it simply alters the measure of a spirit's contribution on the scale. In either case, it's dilution.

It is up to the spirits to maintain the balances of good and evil in beings, even in spite of other influences on them or internal dilution. It is a tremendous challenge, one not always possible. Its failure results in advantage to one nature or the other or in movement to a new position on evolution's circular path. As for which way the circle turns or which nature is seen as more dominant or successful, each effect is case by case and hard to pinpoint. But overall and over time, it's generally toward evil and a clockwise movement on the circle.

To a much smaller extent, the natural way of the universe provides a small contributing factor to the direction and measure of the two primary natures of the world. The natural tendency of other factors and other components on the being and its world is, in fact, toward evil. Spirits are part of the world. Each event, each instance is captured as an addition to the spirit domains repository of information and value and later parsed out as influences to the Being to solve problems and needs. The influences carry with them, and are minutely affected by these natural ways and tendencies of the world, that slightly tend toward evil. In the aggregate and over many instances and much time, this has an effect resulting from the slightly bias toward evil information and experiences collected and held within the domain stores. That held within the spirit's domain inadvertently shifts the balance of power.

There's an expression used by some to describe and recognize truly good people. It refers to these people as being "good to the core." Although those who use the expression probably don't understand it, but this statement has much truth supporting it. Goodness is actually at the core of any spirit domain's store of reference and history. Evil, on the other hand and in its greatest concentration, is generally stored at the outer spheres of the spherical labyrinth of spirit knowledge and experience. Evil is the last to fully mature and dominate. It therefore forms the later outer rings and layers of the domain's stores. Goodness has evolved first and is at the innermost part. As the spirit and the domains grow older and fill with additions of knowledge and experience, the inner core of purest goodness gets insulated by all the layers that are added later. It is time and incidents that add layers to the stores of history and reference. The core of goodness, the purest and most influential reference, thus becomes buried and more difficult to reach. It eventually requires much effort to delve very deep through the many outer layers and into the core of the domain's base to get to these most potent references and purest recollections of goodness. Most situations do not require this level of effort. Most domains are not prompted or presented with strong enough stimulus to justify the effort. They do not drill down so far as to touch the core, but at their deepest reach remain at intermediate levels. This contributes greatly to the advantage of evil in the world, and disadvantage to good. This is especially true later in time when at the later stages along the circular path of life much evil is being added at the peripheries. This phenomenon in a civilization's existence also sets the pattern toward evolution to evil, and supports the eventual movement along the circle of life clockwise toward closure. It is evidence of a flaw in nature's design of the domain's storage components. It is one of the justifications for bringing on the need by nature to correct its flaws and to purge and cleanse the civilization at each closure of the circle. In a civilization's final stage, the truest and purest spirit good usually resides untapped and not used, actually entombed within its own devices. The spirit's own propensity to constantly add to its stores of knowledge and information seal the openings. Extinction of the flesh and bone is the correction that frees this goodness from its imprisonment. The domain stores are disassembled and the shelves cleared for restocking at the advent of the new civilization. This action again fills the world with an equally accessible portion of goodness. Unfortunately, there is a price to be paid for this replenishing of good in the world. It comes at the expense of the mind and physical beings.

Goodness is rarely without its special challenges. At the restaurant, sitting several tables from Becky and Tom was a family of four. They appeared to be enjoying an afternoon of spaghetti and quality sharing. There was the mother, a teenage girl of maybe fifteen years of age, and two young children, one boy and one girl. Most of what was going through the young ones' minds was coming directly and unfiltered through their mouths. The babble was constant. The attention from the mother toward these smaller children was nonstop. She obviously had her hands full and showed much skill and patience handling the many incidents that they created for her.

The little girl began to squirm at one point and was in urgent need to visit the restroom. The mother asked her teenage daughter to please help her by escorting her younger sister to the restroom. The teen returned a sharp snarl of resistance. The mother snarled back in frustration. The volume and intensity from their table rose instantly.

Becky and Tom paused from their conversation to listen to the mother and teen exchange comments. The mother and teen were both embarrassed when they realized that all ears and attention from the others in the restaurant had shifted to them. The teen really didn't mean to cause a disturbance. Her terse response to her mother just simply come out badly. It was not justified. Her cause, her position, was not even important. It was not defensible. It made her feel terrible. She felt bad for what she'd put her mother and herself through. She found it hard to explain why she'd acted like she did. It was uncontrolled and involuntary. She just had so much going on inside her; her emotions and her thoughts seemed to always be racing and pushing on her from the inside. Her internals called for action, sometimes quite inconsistent with her nature and personality.

This turmoil inside was a completely new experience for her. Something was happening to her that she couldn't get a handle on. Her existence was changing and expanding, sometimes to her liking yet other times not. At these other times, she felt the need to rebel, to test her being, most of which was the product of her parents' molding and guidance. She was now challenging this influence not because it wasn't right or good for her but rather because it wasn't from her uniqueness. She needed to find her own way under her own guide. She was breaking away, and it caused outbreaks and declarations of freedom. They were often misguided and mistimed. This was part of the declaration of independence of a teen. It often brings frustration and embarrassment.

The teenage girl finally agreed to escort her younger sister to the restroom. They both got up and left together. The little one was now in quite a hurry. Becky excused herself to go to the restroom as well. She had purpose. It was to help as best as she could. While there, Becky said hello to the teen and the little girl. Their domains connected only briefly but long enough for Becky to size up what was going on in each of the two family members' domains.

The teen's domain was good natured and strong. It was doing its best to control all the impulses and tendencies of a changing and maturing teen. It was a time when the body, mind, and spirit are reacting to many stimuli, not just the influence of the outside world but many from within as well. It is a critical juncture, one that tests all the components, especially the coordination and cohesiveness of the working order. Maturity of the teen is hard not only on a family but also on a domain. The unpredictability that is brought on through the many and comprehensive changes tests all the parts. It is a metamorphosis. It's a good change, even though many times it is completed with some consternation and pain. It is natural and cast by nature's plan.

The stages of a human's development are represented as a circle, actually a circle within the ultimate circle of life. The teen experiences often represent the bottom of the circumference before the ascent back to the apex. The ascent back to the sides of the circle occurs quicker and easier for the domain that is predominately good natured. This was the case with this teenage girl. Her domain, as is most common, was going through a change after adolescence. Two of the spirits of the teen's domain originated from the parents' spirits and as such maintained a strong likeness and connection back to the parent domains. This is what fortifies the strong bond and dependence she has had all these years on her parents. But this is also the root cause of the current problem. As her being and its spirits are now maturing, the unrelated third spirit's need for an independent and unique identity and influence begins to emerge as a force. This pushes the others of the teen's domain to follow in search for its own true identity and to seek independence from the influence and likenesses inherited to it within the advocate contributions from the parents' domains.

Spontaneous incidences of revolt and rebellion against the parents' domains arise. These are the attempts to severe the childhood dependence and ties and to proclaim uniqueness and independence. Often the actions that are initiated by these changes in the teen domain are seen as rebellion, sometimes mean and thoughtless. Rather, they are a blossoming of the new domain as a separate and independent entity. It is new fruit, a new beginning. It is a good and healthy thing. The child's domain will soon be more balanced, more contributing, and more independent. It is what the parents would want it to be. The metamorphoses will most times only take a few years. There is much to learn about family love, patience, and steadfast commitment and support from each of these challenges and the teen's growth. The family will survive it.

Becky left the two in the restroom, knowing that there was no need for her help in this situation. The teen would move through these tough years normally and with a strong, independent domain. Outside at the family's table, the mother worried about what was taking her children so long. She was busy with the other little one, now with only his mother to whom to direct his energies. Within minutes, all from their table returned to normal as the teen and her sister made their way back and repositioned themselves in front of their spaghetti. The teen hugged her mother and said she was sorry. The mother smiled and returned her affection. Becky smiled as well. Tom could only wonder if Becky had something to do with the teen's transformation while in the restroom, but he didn't ask. He and Becky had many other things to talk about now that the commotion from the near table had subsided to normal levels.

After lunch, Becky and Tom decided to take another walk. The city park was only several blocks from the restaurant. The day was beautiful. The air was warm and clear. Tom took the liberty to again take Becky's hand in his. Sparks flew when he grasped it. It was a very good feeling. Becky liked the tender way he treated her. She liked his attention. It was nice just to be walking together. Again, the conversation began to flow easily. There was so much to share. They had so much in common. It was easy to find things that they admired in each other. They became so caught up in each other's thoughts and sharing that the walk to the park seemed very short.

Once there, they sat by the fountain. They watched the passersby, the birds, and the squirrels. Tom mentioned that he thought it might be nice to be a bird. Becky giggled at the idea and asked him why. He said, "It would be nice to have a life of no worries or cares. Also, I think I'd like to fly above everyone and see things from a bird's perspective."

Becky retorted, "Birds have cares too, Tom. They probably wish they were human. Then they could have a life like us."

Tom asked Becky, "Are you happy being who you are?"

Becky thought for a moment but knew right off how she would answer. She responded, "It is very good being who I am. I enjoy my life. I enjoy my job. I enjoy the people I encounter every day."

She looked at Tom with her big brown eyes and added, "There is much goodness in being me. I especially enjoy times like I am having this afternoon." Tom smiled and squeezed her hand gently to let her know she had pleased him. He wanted to kiss her then but lacked the courage.

Becky asked Tom, "Aside from wanting a bird's life, are you happy with who you are?"

Tom replied, "For the most part, I am. I sometimes get too caught up in my problems or what seems out of control in the world. But for the most part, I like who I am and where my life is taking me." He, too, enjoyed times like these. Becky brought out the best in him. He was very much attracted to her goodness, all of him except the one evil spirit within. This evil spirit would occasionally draw strength from the evil in others and create a challenge within Tom's domain. Becky's domain was aware of his spirit makeup and expected as much. She knew that the time would soon come when it would challenge her. She just didn't know when.

On the way home, they passed a beggar asking for help. This beggar's domain was made up of two evil-natured spirits and one good-natured one. His presence gave Tom's evil-natured spirit its occasion to temporary rise to dominance. While it gathered its dominance within Tom's domain, Becky reached into her purse for five dollars and put it in the man's donation container. The beggar said nothing to her but rather just turned his attention to the next passerby. Becky did not seek acknowledgment or recognition of her deed, nor did she take offense to the man's lack of appreciation. It was money well spent for the lesson that was upcoming.

Becky was not a well-to-do person. In fact, her salary was really quite modest. Tom questioned the act. "Why did you give your money to the beggar?" The question was influenced by the evil-natured spirit within Tom's domain. It knew the beggar's intents best. It had shared in the aura of the beggar's weak domain and intuitively knew that he was not really poor or destitute at all. The man probably lived in a better neighborhood and had a better lifestyle than either of them. His act was a scam. Tom's evil-natured spirit actually took pleasure in the beggar taking advantage of Becky's caring and giving nature. It felt that it was a victory for evil. Becky responded, "I gave this man money because he appeared to be in need. Someday if I, too, were in need, I would hope a passerby might help me." Charity comes from the good-natured spirit. There was much charity in Becky's domain.

Tom's evil-natured spirit questioned the intentions of the beggar. "How do you know what he might use the money for or that he really does need it?" This counter from Tom surprised Becky's nonspirit composition a bit.

Becky returned, "What if he does need it? Would you not help him because you fear there is a chance that he might not? I prefer to believe in people and help them when they ask for it. I'm sure it was not easy for the man to overcome his pride and to beg." Tom's good-natured spirits saw the goodness in what Becky was teaching, as well as the humanity in her actions. It shifted the situation and stimuli and allowed one of them to reassume control of Tom's domain from the now deposed evil nature.

Tom then replied, "I believe that it is a good thing that you've done, Becky. I'm sure the beggar appreciates your caring and kindness."

When they reached their building, Tom was compelled to kiss her. Becky was pleasantly surprised by it, and when it was done, she found herself speechless. She sputtered with the words to thank him for a wonderful afternoon. It was the most awkward she'd felt and acted the whole evening. But she was also very happy. Each of them then went to their separate apartments. Becky called Anita to share the details.

Anita's domain had earlier made the decision to dispel her evil spirit's feelings of jealousy and to share and support Becky's joy and good fortune. Anita heard the phone ring and intuitively knew it was her. She didn't even ask who it was when she picked up the receiver. She just asked, "Well, tell me all about it. How did it go?"

Becky was stunned by the voice on the other end of the line. She responded, "Anita, how did you know it was me who was calling?" Then she giggled at her friend's carefree ways.

Anita answered, "We're connected, aren't we? Actually, I heard you come in and knew that you would want to share all the details with me, your very best friend, before anything else." Anita qualified it. "I know you, Becky."

Becky admitted, "I am anxious to talk, and you do know me better than anyone else. Do you mind if I stop over?"

Anita responded, "My door is unlocked for you. Now get over here. I'm dying from anticipation. I want to hear it all."

Becky smiled at her obvious show of excitement and assured her, "I'll be right over." It only took her a moment to slip into more casual attire and then dash over to Anita's.

As soon as she appeared through the door, Anita noticed that she had changed her clothes and began to tease her, "Oh, you looked so nice for your date, but you don't dress up for me. I guess I don't rate like Tom does." Then she laughed.

Becky sat down beside Anita and just smiled. Anita didn't say a word. It was a game they would play to see who would be the first to break down and speak. Becky finally coaxed, "Well, Anita, don't you want to hear about my date?"

Anita was more than anxious and quickly accommodated her with "Absolutely, my friend. You know I'm anxious to hear all about it. I was waiting until you were ready." Then she leaned in toward Becky to capture every word, every inflection, and asked, "OK, how did it go?"

Becky squealed. "It was wonderful. He is such a gentleman. We have so much in common. It was almost perfect."

Anita then asked, "Well, what did you do? Did he kiss you?"

Becky giggled and let a deep billow of air escape from deep within her abdomen up to her open mouth, causing a surprised and breathy "whaaa" sound. She could never quite get over just how direct Anita could be. She replied, "Tom is very shy. He mostly held my hand, and we walked a lot."

She paused to savor the moments, yet knowing that Anita was waiting, she continued, "We went to Guiseppi's Restaurant to eat. Then we walked through the park."

Anita scrunched her nose and looked disappointed. She asked again, "You mean he didn't try to kiss you even once?" Before Becky could respond, Anita altered and redirected the original thought. "Did you want him to try?" Anita made Becky laugh with how single focused she was being. She also knew she could tell Anita anything and that it would remain in confidence.

Becky finally admitted. "Yes, I wanted him to kiss me several times. There were many opportunities for him to do so. I'd almost given up hope that it would happen. Then we arrived back here at the apartment."

Anita's whole body sprung into squirming motion, anticipating what Becky would say next. She squealed. "Oh, you allowed me to think he didn't kiss you. He did kiss you, didn't he?"

Becky shuddered in joy. She told Anita, "Yes, he kissed me just before we separated."

Anita quickly reciprocated with her next question from her one-track mind. "What did he say after he kissed you?"

Becky looked to the ceiling, trying to reconstruct the details of the moment. She responded, "I'm not sure he said anything right afterward." Then she laughed. "I was so stunned that I stuttered and stammered. I tried to tell him what a pleasant afternoon it was but am not sure how well it came out."

Anita followed with "Didn't he ask you out again?"

Becky's expression changed to concern. Her search and recollection of the details of that moment left her with no answer to this question. She said in a disappointed tone, "No, he didn't." Then her voice trailed off sharply.

Anita could tell that the question had left doubt and disappointment in Becky. She tried to repair the damage by clarifying for her, "He kissed you, right? He's probably on the phone calling you right now to ask you out again."

Becky wondered. She had been the victim of a number of short-term, even so little as one-date romances. Her Prince Charming had seemed very hard to find. She asked Anita, "Do you think we should move this to my apartment, just in case he calls?"

It was almost a plea from Becky. She wouldn't want to take a chance on not receiving this important call.

Anita replied, "Would it make you feel better?"

Becky shrugged and then said, "Yes, if you wouldn't mind." There was a clear and even more anxious coaxing in her body language.

Anita replied, "OK, let's go. But the pizza is on you tonight. I'm the unfortunate one between us two, the one without a boyfriend or any immediate prospects. My date tonight was to be with a pepperoni and mushroom pizza and a movie." Then they both laughed.

Becky said, "We'll spend the rest of the evening at my place. Bring your movie. I'll order the pizza." Becky still had a lot to share with her friend about her date. It would be a late night.

The first thing that Becky and Anita did when they entered Becky's apartment was to check the phone for messages. Sure enough, Tom had called. The message was short. Tom told her that he really enjoyed their time together and wanted to know if she might like to go to a movie with him tomorrow night. His final message was that he'd call her later to talk about it. Becky was so excited and happy but mostly relieved. She and Anita played the message back several times.

To keep the line open for Tom to call, Becky made Anita go back to her apartment to order the pizza from there. Anita completely understood. She, too, was caught up in the excitement of the dating game. Her anticipation and hopes for her friend were nearly as great as Becky's. She could tell that Becky was very positive and hopeful about this relationship. She seemed different in this relationship compared with the others, whose aftermaths they had talked about. Becky remembered and savored every detail of the date. She wanted to relive and then share every feeling and every instance of it with Anita.

Through their sharing and the openness of their feelings and domains to each other as dear friends, Anita's spirits were able to delve into the depths of Becky's experience. What she was able to take away was confirmation that Tom and Becky's recent experience and blossoming relationship was shaping up to be a truly special one. One spirit from each of Becky and Tom's domains was a soul mate match to the other. Only a spirit would know for sure. Through her being and from her spirits, Anita confirmed to Becky that she felt that she had made a good choice. She shared with Becky, "You seem so happy. Do you think that this one might be the special one?"

Becky responded, "I do hope so. It's far too early to tell, but it feels very right. I am just so very happy right now."

Anita was also filled with happiness and good feelings for her friend. She assured Becky, "I will always be here for you when you need to talk."

Just then, the phone rang. It was Tom. Becky and Tom talked for a few minutes. In the end, the date for the next evening was confirmed. Becky and Anita laughed and shared their joy well into the night. Becky couldn't have been more emotionally charged and upbeat. She so hoped that this feeling would last forever. She hoped that Anita would also find such joy soon.

Becky was a gift to the community. She was the strongest representative of her kind in the city of Millborough. In the spirit realm, it made her stand out. Sometimes it made her a target. By trade, she was a teacher and counselor at the local high school.

The school was located in the innermost part of town. Young adults from every background and economic strata attended this school. The problems that arose within the school cover the full gamut of possibilities. Drug and alcohol abuse was particularly an issue. The problem primarily radiated from a few within the student body and also from a few key figures outside the student body or faculty that had targeted the school as a market of their enticements and poisons. A growing number of students seem to be falling victim each year to the pull of these unsavory, undesirable elements. Violence, incidents of intoxication from many different vices, and hate-related acts were on the rise in the school, as well as within the community.

Becky, along with many of the school's staff, struggled with answers to these problems. They did everything they can to help in the fight against these dangers, as well as many others prevalent in people of the high school age. She devoted tremendous amounts of time and energy to her commitment to help these young people. Most of them recognized this. She was one of the most loved and respected of the school's faculty. Most of her students trusted her. Most considered her a friend. Becky was a safe haven for many in a world filled with peer pressure and danger.

Becky was particularly committed to making a difference in the school and to getting to know the students more personally, especially those whom she had direct contact. It became her life's work. To do so, she got involved in their activities. It was fortunate that she was very active and reasonably athletic. It was also helpful that she was creative and resourceful. She had a delightful and inviting personality to go along with the outgoingness that attracted others to her. She was an ideal role model for anyone who held goodness as an important and practiced virtue. She was an ambassador for change in those who didn't practice goodness and good lives. She coached girl's athletics. She sponsored events and club activities for students to be involved after school. She chaperoned at dances and parties. She coordinated committees and groups focused on school and community. She organized activities and programs to help improve the lives of the needy and to remedy the problems and evil influences that those of the school and community faced almost daily. She was selfless in her efforts to get involved, to add value, and to comfort and help those needing it. She sacrificed most of her free time and personal interests over the past years to these efforts and activities and for her students. She had little time for relationships as a result of this devotion to the school, the students, and the community around the school. Like one who finds a stray puppy and takes it in as her own, she was continuously taking in the lost cause, the student in need. It had become her whole life's focus.

Becky was most of all a good teacher. She was firm yet fair in the classroom. She was honest and forthright. She cultivated diverse thoughts and perspectives from her students. She promoted their growth and enlightenment from their own domain's ideas and generated thoughts. Much of what she taught, much of what her students learned and took away with them from her classroom and into their daily lives, was not always from a book. She was very active in her classes, with her students, and in the activities that affected them. Her practiced and practical methods of teaching taught life as well as the derivatives of the 3Rs.

Becky began volunteering as a guidance counselor several years previous. This allowed her to get involved with more students firsthand. It allowed her to cover a broader range of their problems. It especially allowed her to get to know those students with deeper and more immediate problems. She felt compelled to help. From the start, she seemed to have a special gift for helping some of these students. It gave her a terrific sense of fulfillment and accomplishment. Much of her gift came from her pure domain of spirits. It seemed her destiny.

In addition to her involvement in her students' activities and their external lives, Becky's spirits focused on knowing the inner domain components. She explored the domains of these students as she would make direct contacts. She used her inherent gifts as a pure domain to probe and, as if a sonar, to identify those in need of help from her special and giving domain. She used her gift to transfer, to energize, and to fortify the good spirits within these others. She shared her pure goodness to strengthen the vulnerable, to help their good spirits become more dominate, and to influence good in these students' spirit domains. She left small portions of her magic and strength within each of her hosts to help them create subtle goodness and deeds in their worlds. In essence, she was a gardener. Her role in life was to sow and cultivate the seeds of goodness in the fertile domains of those she interacted with and taught.

Until recently, the school and the students had seemed enough for Becky. They filled her life. They drained her pools of goodness, only to allow new flows, stronger flows, to recollect and again fill her. Now, however, there was a new development.

It was a time for change; it would be a good change. It was an addition. But it involved her time. She planned to free some of her time, enough to allow Tom to be part of her life. Her feelings for Tom were something new to her. She felt compelled to raise this part of her life to a level of importance. She intended to treat it at least as important as the other focuses of her life and preferably as more important. She intended to treat it with utmost protection and self-nurturing. It was primary to her being. It was to be part of her foundation.

Yet she struggled with how to cut back on her work at the school to allow more time for her personal side. It was particularly difficult because the need for her focus and attention was now growing from two primary urgencies. It had only been one date, but she felt something very special and different about this relationship and this man. It made it clear that there was more to her existence than work and giving. Tom represented a source from which there was give and take. This was different and compelling to her. Both were of goodness. This relationship with Tom filled needs that she had neglected for too long. She would now serve these neglected needs, as well as those of others. Becky carried the considerations and challenges of how to make time for both of her interests, her new one and her old one, without cheating either. She was not so much worried about the added drain on the vast supply of goodness that she had to share; instead, it was her time that presented the problem. Neither Tom nor her students would, or could, ever deplete her of care and goodness. But they could cause her much stress on her physical and mental. She intended to devote more time toward Tom. It was only fair. It was entirely natural. She was deserving of a deeper and different type of love, the love of a soul mate. She would need to be more resourceful with her time and attention. She would need to find a way to make it all fit. This new and complementing focus in her life would create her new challenge yet fuller commitment and value of natural purpose.

Good natures are truly gifts to the harmony and peace of the earth. With this being the case, then why is it that good is the most vulnerable and weaker of the natures? By its very nature, good is passive. It's susceptible to suffering and sacrifice. It gives more than takes. It compromises and is selfless. It looks for the common good, not of one's own underserved or unnatural needs. It willingly credits value to others and sees the value in other points of view. Its successes have quiet impact, subtle impacts. As such, these are often viewed as lesser impacts by the external components.

Good doesn't look for center stage or for celebrity status. There's no campaigning or advertising of its value. It doesn't manipulate. Most critical to its weight on the scale and its gradual imbalance with the opposing evil nature has been the fact that good is not easy, not easy to practice and not easy to live. It requires servitude and giving. Many times, it's not fun. Its rewards are mostly internal, coming from feelings of personal satisfaction and inner peace. These are things that can't be shared. They can't be understood or known until you feel them personally. As such, they are a hard sell to someone who has not yet experienced or felt them. It's a leap of faith to the side of goodness. It is not the nature of most beings to accept things on faith alone. Therefore, goodness is at a disadvantage in the world.

Also contributing to the challenges of good natures is the fact that goodness pushes back the position on the circle of life toward its origin, backtracking over previously and toughly contested ground. This counterclockwise push backward is against the natural flow. It's like paddling against the current of the river. Even with consistent effort, eventually, the current will win out and take you back and beyond the point in which you have started. Goodness tends to be spent of its efforts to fight the natural flow and becomes scarcer after a civilization matures.

Because of the value of the good spirit and its product of a goodness and virtue, we must identify, revere, and protect the truly good in our world, especially as our civilization gets older and moves further around the circle of life. We must especially protect those with pure, good-natured spirit domains. These are the most powerful ambassadors and protectors of good. Yet they are rare. They are most vulnerable. These are the ones who keep our civilization from ruin and decay. They keep the circle of life unclosed. These must be sheltered and cherished. Becky was one of these cherished few. Tom, Anita, and others must do the best they can to protect and support her. But from what?

It's from evil. It's from the other components of beings disregarding or discarding the good spirit's help and guidance. Goodness is best and most easily defined by what it isn't. This is because we in later generations of our civilization have lost touch with many of goodness's pure qualities and attributes. We know more about evil, both natural and unnatural evil. Evil is what good is not. Evil is what we know and what runs counter to the virtues and destinies of goodness. It is what those like Tom, Anita, and others must protect Becky against. Good is what evil isn't. Evil is everything goodness isn't. We tend to know evil best. So, what, then, defines evil?

The Bad Seed

In all likelihood, Mr. Arthur wasn't the evilest and the most self-centered man living on the planet, but neither Becky nor Tom had ever encountered anyone more so. Stories of his roughshod behavior and illegal exploits were plentiful and came up frequently in the idle chatter and gossip between friends and acquaintance but only when everyone was certain that he was well out of hearing range. The amount and degree of truth to any of these stories and rumors was hard to verify. With the sheer volume and consistency of the content, it lent credibility and probability that some were legitimate.

Becky, in particular, received a steady flow of information about Mr. Arthur's activities from the students and from her fellow teachers at West Crawford High School. Most referred to him as the man who promoted the drug traffic and fostered criminal acts in the neighborhoods surrounding the school. Becky knew the one whom others would consistently refer in evil context as the man from her building, the one that gave her the willies every time he was near.

Mr. Arthur often loitered and lurked in the background of the school, moving mysteriously between the shadows of the buildings that surrounded it. He was careful and cunning. Just in watching the way he acted, the secrecy and care in which he handled his dealings with those he made contact gave the immediate impression that something underhanded was always going on. It was difficult to catch him directly in an unsavory or illegal act. He kept himself and his trade slightly out of the sight line, always hidden to observers or passersby. His back was usually turned and his shoulders turned in to shield the actions of his hands. He often peered over his shoulders and to his sides. A direct view of his face was rarely offered. It left a bad impression.

The students knew what was going on in these encounters. They occurred with daily regularity just beyond the school grounds. The students knew Mr. Arthur well, all except his first name. No one seemed to know this man on a first-name basis. No one ever referred to him with his first name. He was just Mr. Arthur. It was unclear if this was out of respect for him or that no one cared enough to get so personal as to inquire about it. Regardless, his business and his wares were well known. Troubled and street-hardened teens treated him with the greatest respect. They protected him as if they depended on him, as if they were under his control, or as if he was an underworld messiah. They wouldn't dare confess any of the details of their relationship or the involvement they had with him, especially not to the probing teachers of the school or the police patrolling the area. To them, Mr. Arthur represented success. It was a success that they also one day aspired to rise to.

From a distorted perspective, he was a successful man. At least he was wealthy and surrounded by material luxury. He was a role model for his cult and clan. He'd made good in the streets.

He was able to buy whatever he wanted, most notably important and influential people. He dressed the part of street success, and he acted the role of someone who did not ask but rather demanded others' attention and loyalties. But pure and simple, he was just a hoodlum and a common thug.

His closest companion was fear, the fear he instilled in others of what he might do to them or anyone who crossed him. He was very effective at spreading this persona of danger and evil throughout the neighborhood. The most sensible and moral people of the neighborhood knew to avoid him. They would make it their business to always know when he was near and what avenues were available for them to escape his detection, to avoid any chance of contact with him. He was that powerful. Mere contact, especially eye contact, could trigger his evil and allow it to penetrate the less than pure domains within the community.

Most everyone at the school knew of him. The reputation was bigger than the man. He required, in fact, he demanded that those of the school take a position as it related to him and his work, whether as one who followed and admired him or one who would avoid him at all expense. They all knew him as a powerful man, one to respect for his capability and especially one to avoid for his bad temperament. You either became a defender of Mr. Arthur or were defensive and afraid of him; in many cases, it was both. Either way, you didn't make trouble for him.

The stories about Mr. Arthur were filled with many references to what he had done to those who pressed him or caused him trouble. People were known to mysteriously go missing or to die in this neighborhood. There were many cases, and there were many causes. Many of these were rumored to have involved Mr. Arthur in some shape or form. None had been formally or legally proved as linked directly back to Mr. Arthur. But the students knew. The community knew. The police knew.

Mr. Arthur was not one to cross. He was a dangerous and lethal man. The reputation of Mr. Arthur was consistent and clear. It left little doubt in anyone's mind that his business, if not drugs or more violent crime, was certainly not anchored in the legal streams of commerce. His associates, what few he had, were mostly young, hard-core, and roughshod characters like himself. Mr. Arthur didn't seem to like them any more than he liked anyone else he happened upon; rather, he seemed only to use them for his purpose. Mr. Arthur seemed to have a power over his people. He seemed to conjure out the worst in the people he confronted. He was a strange and mysterious man. What you knew about him you didn't like. What you didn't know about him you worried about. It was best not to know him too well. People he took in to his inner circles, or those he regularly associated with, usually had their lives ruined.

Becky could not recall a single instance or a single story from any one of her students where anything good had come from an encounter with this man. His reputation in the neighborhood was like that of the devil, justly deserved or not. By some, though, he was respected and worshipped. By all, he was feared.

As is the case with the good-natured spirits that influence the minds and bodies of their beings to do good things, it is their counterpart, the evil-natured spirits, that inspire bad and evil things from the beings. Most of us are partially driven by evil. Most domains contain at least one evil-natured spirit as resident. The most common mix of spirits in the human domain is made up of one or two evil-natured spirits, with the remaining being good natured. The expression that there's a little good, and a little evil, in all of us is really quite true. The common spirit composition within the domains of beings proves this out.

Even in cases of spirit balance, thus causing dilution on the efforts and effects of the natures, the evil-natured spirits are commonly the better survivors. They are the more assertive ones. They tend to have moments when they stand out and create an effect. They are more unpredictable than the good-natured spirits. They crave and inspire the sporadic and spontaneous episode or uprising to generate attention or to initiate change whenever placed in the position of dominance within the domain. They tend to be the stronger spirits, especially as they pass through the domains and lifetimes of several generations of beings. They are like a weed from a bad seed. They are more resilient than the good-natured variety. Dilution of the domain tends to affect them less. They grow stronger and more in control as the civilization moves further and further around life's circular path. This is especially true as the good-natured spirits become weaker and more effected by dilution and the movement along the circle.

Tom is an example of a being with an evil-natured spirit residing alongside two good-natured spirits. This mix allows the good and evil to coexist and to dilute each other. It is an accepted coexistence. The extreme to this, however, is the pure evil domain, the one with three evil-natured spirits. These are the ones that raise extreme fear and initiate truly sinister acts in the world. They are rare. They are deadly and destructive.

Mr. Arthur's domain was a pure evil-natured domain. He was the image that appears when evil is relegated up for definition.

Yet the potential and capability for the same evil advent, in limited and sporadic degrees is also present in Tom's domain. It's the aggregate of all domains, most are like Tom's, that determines the overall effect on the balance between good and evil. Those like Mr. Arthur are generally too few in numbers to affect this balance significantly and not all by themselves. They are more significant in their localized and isolated impact and influence of the mixed domains like that of Tom McDouglas. Mr. Arthur's domain represents the catalyst. Tom McDouglas' domain, as well as all the others like his, is what really represent the effect of evil on the grand scale. It is domains like Mr. Arthur's, though, that press them and help them achieve greatest contribution and impact.

Mr. Arthur's domain was extreme and ultimately strong in nature. Three strong and dominant evil-natured spirits resided and flourished within his core. Becky, on the other hand, was the complete opposite of Mr. Arthur; and as such, their two domains strongly, in fact completely, repelled. One could feel the presence of the other when within yards. Their auras would give them warning and protection from the other's presence and influence. Like Becky, Mr. Arthur was special. He, too, had ability to influence others, those with at least one evil-natured spirit within their domain. He, too, could draw unequal shares of information and history from his sharing with these other domains. He could transfer to other beings' domains, again as long as the other domain had at least one evil-natured spirit in residence. He was an advantaged one, an advantaged evil one. He was specially chosen for his role and this local. The world is about balance. Mr. Arthur and Becky were balanced and opposing influences. Mr. Arthur, as did Becky Turner, represented a specific purpose and place in nature's master plan.

But perhaps too much is made of the evil-natured spirit alone. This, too, will be the case with the good-natured spirit. The spirit, or the nature for that matter, cannot create evil or good things on its own. The domain itself cannot act or react in the external world. The spirit and the nature must work with and through the mind and body. The mind and body must be willing; they must accept and carry out the intent of their guiding spirit nature's influences. The being as a whole must be willing to be evil or good to create an effect on the world. All components of the being, the spirit, the mind, and the physical, must complement one another, in part or in whole, to interface with the external world.

Here's an example of how this works. A man sits in the stands of a football game, not particularly happy about what is happening on the field. As he gets more frustrated, he might make threats to take an action but not actually carry them out. The man might yell at a particular player or situation, "Destroy him! Hit him so hard that it puts him out of the game!" He doesn't really mean that he wishes for the opposing player to get hurt. This is an example of the spirit and mind components working together to arouse an emotion-based response. The fact that no action is taken suggests that the physical component of the being, as opposed to the mind and spirit, is disengaged and not acting in concert with the others. In this case, this is an intended disconnection of the three components of the being. It is a good thing. However, if the same man is to take the field and viciously tackle the opposing team's player to hurt him, then this will represent all three components engaged and acting in concert; all components will be complementing one another.

The first scenario is a common example of what happens regularly in daily life. Most of what a being threatens is exactly that, just a threat. It's disengaged and harmless emotion and dialogue between components of the being. In the second scenario, however, the effect is much greater. It is in the third component, usually the physical, and sometimes in the second, the mind, that there is effect. Yet in the spirit component, the distributed influence and idea is only that. The spirit and spirit nature's crimes are only complicity. If the action or thoughts are harmful, hurtful, or negative in nature, it is an influence and only an influence from the evil-natured spirits of the domain, but that is all. The spirit only influences. They only ignite a spark. The fire is set outside the domain. So perhaps too much is made of the spirit's contribution. It is the mind and physical components that are needed and that actually and tangibly enact the effect. They are guilty of the crime itself, or so it can be rationalized.

Then again, maybe we make too little of the spirit and spirit nature's part in the effect. It's hard to determine just how much of good and evil actions to attribute to the spirits. One thing is certain: they are instigators. Consider this: Bad things can't happen from good spirits' influence. Good things can't happen to evil-natured spirits. Things in general, good or bad, external to the being and linked back and affecting the being can't directly affect the spirit. But they happen from the spirit nature's influence or influences of the beings internal. Bad things can happen to people, both good and bad. Good things can happen to people, both evil and good.

Therefore, is it the spirit or the mind and physical that are to be credited for life's good and evil? The spirit takes ownership only in a nature and the influence. The rest is ingrained and enacted by the mind and the physical components. But should the mind or the physical components be held solely accountable? As the being is guilty, it will justly indict all three components equally.

Ease and indulgences are less likely the product of good influences. It is more likely that they are derived from or coupled with an offering from an evil influence. These would come as a by-product of or even directly from an evil-influenced action. Evil is easy to sell for this reason. Evil entertains the mind and body, whereas good generally works to challenge it. Evil stimulates from the outside in; good originates from the inside out. Evil covets things of the outside world. Goodness is, again, from within. Both can be shared, but goodness is intangible and is housed in the emotions and domain of the spirits. The end product of evil is usually represented and measured by material things or external and tangible actions.

Does this mean that evil is always and completely undesirable? The answer is no, not entirely. Balance and diversity in the virtues is necessary and natural. One thing is for certain though: it is more fun to be a little evil. A lot of what is fun is evil. Evil is craved. It makes one feel good. There is great advantage toward evil. It's competitive in nature. With evil, someone will usually lose or not measure up. This creates winners. Winning is special and fun. Evil-motivated action usually allows an escape, escape from responsibility, from accountability, from the harder parts of life's existence. It leads to quick satisfaction of wants and needs. It sometimes allows a mind to paint reality in a false light. It tips the scales in one's own favor. It is selfish. Fair and equal are not residents of its usual goals. It can give us a thrill, a feeling of getting away with something.

Goodness, on the other hand, is not easy or self-serving. It often tips the scale against oneself to allow others more credit or value. It, too, makes one feel good but is shared and person-centered. It is not selfish. It is not valued in terms of traded value. It holds no advantage, unless offered to others. It's these attributes that differentiate good from evil. These differences will form our reference.

Much of the world desires evil. Evil makes itself very attractive and alluring as a servant of the needs of the nonspirit components. It becomes acceptable in moderation and when controlled. It allows slow tolerances of it, until guards are let down. Evil is the ultimate suitor. A total and lasting relationship is not what it seeks, yet to its victim, it holds firmly and tightly clutched through the duration of the relationship. After it inflicts its full effect and measure, it is often quick to flee. It rarely fixes its problems or clears up its messes. Conscience is not of evil.

Evil truly is the ultimate salesman. The most successful sales campaign ever launched by evil was the one that introduced the theme that if you don't look after yourself, no one else will. This campaign cut to the evil core of every being. It encouraged everyone to examine their own needs and well-being before all else. It effectively stripped and victimized the society of most of its faith in the communal good or of a more holistic view of mankind. It replaced these values with self as our first and in many cases our only love. It was an impregnable force to counter. The success of this message, with the degree to which it was embraced and practiced, has been greater than any other, including that of love for a mate or even that for family. What this doctrine did best was to open the market to the nonspirit components of the being. Self-preservation lies paramount and at the very core of these components. What it did not support was good and the good nature. Without emotion and caring or conscience and guilt, which come from a good-natured spirit core, the evil nature, in tandem with the other components of the being, could easily build on established and accepted practiced doctrine of self.

The message was fully embraced by the mind and physical components. It gave them purpose that they could identify with. There will be no greater and willing consumers. The impact will not be challenged or equaled in the advertising or consumer marketing of any campaign to follow. The impact on society and civilization has been complete and, to a large extent, devastating. To evil's credit, it was genius, pure, and simply the strongest message ever marketed. It completely drove an advantage over the good-natured influences of the spirit realm. It was the added measure that tipped the scales to the side of the evil virtue. Yet without fully capitalizing on its advantage and as evil is prone to do, it planted the seeds of its new doctrine, cultivated them to near term, and then departed for something new and more interesting.

This left the aftermath to the other components of the being to do what they would with it. And use it they did. It transferred the power and influence of the self to the mind and the physical components. It filled them with confidence and ability to rely less on the spirit guide and more on their other influences. As with many things evil, it left the being with no constraint or control. The results turned ugly and turned to extreme. It made for the destruction of the civilization, devastation of community aspects, and placing the power and influence out of the control of the spirits and into the hands of the nonspirit components of the being. It would bring the circle to a close. It would sell the demise of the civilization.

Evil, in its allure and campaigns, is very appealing and difficult to resist. The costs are often deferred and hidden and extreme. It's best not to get extreme in evil's allure. Caution should be taken with each tiny sip of evil's offering, but a full gulp should be avoided at all costs. Balance in the campaigns of good and evil is critically necessary. Nonspirit components must buy into the offerings of both, spirit and nonspirit, good and evil, for longevity to be protected and assured.

Evil is necessary though. There is a purer side and value to evil. This value is not as obvious as it is with good, but it's there all the same. Evil brings balance to the world. It represents an alternative, an opposing view. It gives life a rise now and then, a fling and a thrill when it might need a boost or escape from the pressure and stress of existence. It promotes competition and enterprise. It allows winners. It allows losers. Both are valuable experiences to be held within a domain's storage. It moves humans to keep score, to measure worth or purpose, and to have a structured sense of tangible value needed to support ratings, trade, and commerce. Evil encourages exploration and the testing of boundaries, the breaking of old rules, and the establishment of new ones in their place. It breaks down complacency and status quo. Evil coaxes movement along evolution's path. Through the earliest stages, this can be a positive. It brings or coaxes change in everything. It allows us to be expressive, uninhibited, risqué, and fully creative. Evil brings out the aggressive and assertiveness in us, which is needed at times to break down barriers and to move into uncharted and unknown territory.

Without evil, civilizations will not advance nor will rockets fly to the moon and back.

Evil gives us a break from reality; it gives us fun, frivolity, and escape from society's norms and mores. It sometimes allows beings to find themselves. It allows separation from the pack, inward and self-searching. It allows difference. It allows for many shades of gray, instead of just one, and acceptances of self for what it is, not for what others need it to be. Evil is selfish. A part of this is of value to the being and for progress. Evil may allow a mental refresh, escape from the molds and cast ways of the sect. Evil makes it permissible to step out of the box and across the lines. Experimentation and invention partly come from evil's influence and propensity toward risks. Evil supports physical pleasures and delivery of needs. Evil rewards the body and the mind for taking it up, even when it might do them harm. The euphoria delivered from evil's influence to partake of drugs and alcohol is prime examples of this.

Evil challenges good to be stronger, defensive and to work harder to maintain a position of equality. It actually pushes goodness to be at its best and most influential. This is evil's greatest value.

Evil pushes the mind and the being to new ideas. It allows for adventures against unknowns and dangers. It provides another perspective from a different and rich supply of material and information from its domain's stores. It delivers knowledge, experiences, and histories from the domain that good could not. Again, it provides balance and safeguards against distortion from only one virtue, one perspective. It opens new doors and provides for diversity and variation in personalities, interests, actions, thoughts, ideas, and reactions to stimuli. It makes a being different, more rounded, and interesting. All these things are the value that comes from evil. These things make evil just as important and essential to life on the earth as its countering virtue. It gives it equal standing with good as one of the two types that natures of the spirit world have cast their lot upon.

All these values of evil relate to the type that Tom's spirit mix might provide. Mr. Arthur's evil was of a more potent variety. His evil was pure and more purposed on the earth, specifically to combat and counter pure good. All else that got in the way of this purpose stood pretty much a victim of evil at its worst.

Mr. Arthur had much business to do on this day. He started off badly by getting up midday with the aftereffects of a long night of indulgences. He had many clients to meet with and to satisfy today. He had a headache. He was hungry and slightly nauseous. He chose to venture down the street, close to where his first appointment of the day would take place. It was an insignificant Italian eatery that he chose as his first stop. He did not have time to sit and enjoy the cuisine, what little he thought it provided. He just wanted a quick bite to ease his empty and churning stomach. He was in no mood to be bothered or annoyed.

The waiter that was appointed to serve his station was a man he knew from the streets. He was an addict when he was not a waiter. The waiter knew Mr. Arthur on sight. It caused him to fumble with his duties. He feared men of Mr. Arthur's stature on the streets. He owed money to one of Mr. Arthur's lieutenants. He wondered if Mr. Arthur knew this. He worried that this might be the reason he had chosen this particular establishment on this day. He searched for another of his coworkers to take his place in serving him. Everyone else in the restaurant knew either of his reputation or of his exploits directly. There were no takers to relieve Jim, the waiter, of his duties. Jim hesitated. He remained hiding in the kitchen for an additional five or ten minutes, trying to build his courage.

Mr. Arthur looked around, trying to find someone to help him. He was in a hurry today. He was becoming annoyed. Finally, he motioned to another waiter to come over. He said, "I'd like to get some service. I'd like to place my order now."

The waiter replied, "Jim will be right with you, sir. He services this section of the restaurant."

Seeing in Mr. Arthur's eyes that this was not satisfactory, he added, "I'll get him for you now." Jim, however, still lacked courage. His continued to delay before moving to his station. This, finally set Mr. Arthur into an outrage.

Mr. Arthur was trailing a short fuse today anyway from the moment he'd gotten up. He stormed from his table and rambled to the exit, bumping into new patrons on his way to the door. He screamed obscenities and insults all the way there. It was just another inconvenience and discomfort arising from this day. But his tirade actually made him feel better. In fact, the scene that he'd made and the people he frightened and affected fed his nature. Aside from still being hungry, he was now more ready to tackle the business portion of his day.

He picked up an apple and a plum from an outside market on his way down the street. The vendor never questioned him about paying. He, too, was quite aware of Mr. Arthur's reputation. Mr. Arthur wore a particularly frightening scowl on his face this day as he moved past the vendor's view. There would be no sale from this customer.

Mr. Arthur's domain was truly an evil-nature-dominated one. His temperament, his actions, and his aura all oozed of pure evil. He surrounded himself with only those much like himself or those with at least a two evil-natured spirit mix. His place in time, now at the current world's late third quartile on the circular path of life, was primed for a man of his dominance. The current civilization was ripened and ready for his harvesting. There were many who were searching for an evil-natured messiah and willing to follow him, to become his disciples. He thought himself the chosen one of the entire evil populations but especially over his own vast evil clan. He was capable of doing nearly anything that was of the unspeakable or undesirable nature. He followed no moral boundaries or moral code. He had no conscience to hinder his nature or actions. What he desired he took. What he desired to do he did. He had only passion for control and power. Other feelings and especially rules got in the way of his nature. They got in the way of his destiny. People, in general, got in his way. They were simply ways to an end. They were there for him to exploit. He saw himself as standing at the pinnacle of the mountain and looking down on everyone else. He was the purest example of a being controlled by a domain of strong evil-natured and evil-destined spirits.

The stories that were told about him were all true and more. In fact, they only touched the surface of the evil things that he had done and was currently initiating behind the scenes and sight of the community. He did indeed deal in poisons and vices. He was the primary supplier of pure evil in the community. The characteristics of an evil nature fit him like a suit of clothes. His focus was on materialism, wealth, current pleasure, and indulgences. He had no remorse for those he took from, for those he used, or for those who fell prey to his tactics. He used his every advantage to grow in his position, his control, and his wealth. He would influence beings, their spirits first and then their minds and bodies, to indulge, to cherish, and to desire the life of money, drugs, illegal acts of all types, self-indulgence, self-pleasure, and self-righteousness. These were the staples of his vast arsenal of weaponry and traps. His victims, especially the young and evil prone, were easy targets. He had become a master of his craft. No one challenged him. Only the ease in which it came to him and now the boredom arising from a lack of any real challenges drove him to even greater ambitions and plateaus of evil.

He wanted control over more than just the beings of the community with predominately evil-natured domains. He also wanted the predominately good-natured beings to fall prey to him and his influences and offerings. They became his current target to exploit and to apply his tactics. They became his focus and passion. His army of followers would be at his beck and call to help him. It was his destiny to battle the good natured of the world, to bring the circular path of life to its last quartile.

The external signs of the evil-natured spirit domain, in their pure state, are fairly distinct yet when not pure can be masked and blended to varying degrees with the good-natured characteristics, thus making them more difficult to detect. This is the natural effect of the mixed domain. In the long run, however, the signs of each nature always show through. Here are a few of the most telling of the evil-natured characteristics.

The true mark of a powerful and evil-controlled spirit domain is the lack of conscience for its actions. A being of evil domain will inflict hurtful effect or cause loss to another and have little to no remorse. They will contribute to evil acts, partake in evil things, and be able to rationalize these as something that is the norm that everybody does and expects, or as nothing too out of the ordinary. The results from these actions and the effects they have on others are of little concern to the evil domain. The effect or benefit they derive from these actions is viewed as none of others' business. As they see it, it shouldn't fall under the scrutiny of others. The greater the evil in the actions and the more effect and impact expected from these actions, the grander and less conscionable the evil nature's internal driven incentive to indulge and the greater the appeal made by the evil-natured spirits influence is on the being to participate or partake. The more successful the evil natures are in persuading the being and the more assertive and overbearing the evil spirit becomes over its being and the good-natured counterparts in the domain, the weaker and more suppressed the conscience becomes. It's a path of cause and effect. Conscience is needed to control evil. Conscience comes from a good-natured spirit and domain within the being. The being and particularly the nonspirit components tend to be persuaded and migrate toward evil. The more supported and dominant the evil nature becomes, the less the good nature will dominate the domain and have influence. The less the good-natured spirits can influence and dominate the domain, the less conscience will influence and control evil. The less conscience that is present and controlling the being, the more dominant the evil natures become. Evil eventually controls the conscience by controlling the good-natured spirits and thus controls the influence on the being.

Mr. Arthur provided strong influence and support to the evil-natured spirits of the community. He supplied the support, the strategies, and the materials to achieve the domination of the good-natured spirit influence within the beings of the community and, in turn, reduced the associated conscience arising from them. These supports and materials took on many forms, but the most common were alcohol, drugs, money, sport, gambling, prostitution, and vices of many other sorts. These were what attracted many with an evil-natured spirit within their domain to be lured in and to become much like Mr. Arthur. These things served as the stimuli to award the position of dominance within a domain to the evil-natured spirits. The evil-natured spirits took it from there. Yet unlike Mr. Arthur with his pure evil-driven domain, the beings of a less-than-pure-spirited domains often lacked the ability to walk away from the enticements and vices that they were lured to once having partaken or indulged, at least not easily and not whenever they might choose. Evil is a strong nature. Now with the potency of their conscience diminished, it pushes the being deeper and deeper, more subservient, and fully controlled by the evil parasite and master. As Mr. Arthur saw this, it all fit very nicely into his plans. Removal of conscience as a barrier to evil only simplified his work, making evil an easier and more permanent sale.

Another important characteristic of the evil nature is the need for power and attention. Evil influences want to do what they can to stand out. Evil natures crave the spotlight. They need to feel important. The nature makes huge demands of the mental and physical components to identify and develop that unique quality or ability that will allow their being to stand above as special. Beings with evil natures are generally outgoing, sometimes flamboyant, and very self-confident. They tend to see reality as it relates to them. They are known to concoct their own realities to best fit their own needs and use for it. Evil-natured beings usually aren't hesitant to take on risks or venture past the boundaries set by other beings. The need for acclaim and significance often requires it. Laws and governances don't always apply to the evil natured, unless they are of some advantage to them.

Evil-natured beings are many times intelligent and creative. Consistent with their intellect, they are often crafty and manipulative. They push for results at higher levels and costs. Evil natures create fun and excitement for beings. They loathe boredom or stagnation. They emphasize the dramatic. They love competition and challenge. Winners stand out. Stars make headlines and demand a following. They create and encourage politics and entrepreneurial endeavors.

Evil spirits encourage advantaged and aggressive behaviors. They initiate events making the local and world news. They initiate controversy, campaigns, and even wars. They have no conscience. This allows them to do many things that better natures are wary of taking on due to feelings of fear or guilt. Evil natures have much less regard for the being. The being becomes a means to an end, the end being attention and acclaim in some form or fashion. Risk of death is sometimes a means to these ends. The evil nature's influences can cause premature death and injury in their beings. On the other side, they create the recognized heroes of the world who command them attention and win them power and acclaim.

Evil-natured spirits need to be complemented with good-natured spirits to temper them and keep them directed toward more productive aggression. Good and evil make a perfect pair when they find balance between them. While the evil nature must be at the center of attention, the good nature prefers anonymity. Position and power are very important to the evil ones. Power is not especially important to good-natured spirits. Good-natured spirits find themselves in the middle to lower strata often getting lost within the aggregate. Evil beings strive for positions of dominance and rule. They introduce the concept of a hierarchy of power where each ascending tier in the power structure preys on the lower ones as authorized to do so by the power of the position.

Good spirits control their counterparts from benefiting too greatly from the favor or advantage of position. They allow the being to benefit and grow from the evil-natured spirits' assertions and aspirations, but good-natured spirits add and provide controls. The good-natured spirits regulate and limit. Evil natures despise them for this. Controls and limits are irritants to the evil nature. This fundamental and inherent difference in the natures assures that a rift remains deep and strong between the two virtues. On the other hand, natural dependency on both in their separate and key roles to retain balance and diversity in the beings keeps them closely joined in the domain's controlling spaces as well.

Money is a third ally of the evil nature. It is used by the evil natured as an instrument of measure. It measures their exploitation and control over their environment and over other beings. As our world has evolved, it has been adopted as a necessity. It has become a bartering instrument. This has played into the hands of the evil nature's plans. Love of money is a root characteristic of evil. Spirits don't need or care about money. The love of money, of comfort, is established in the mind. What feeds the minds love of money and what manipulates and correlates the need for money to fun, ease, and happiness comes in part from an evil spirit's influence. It is the motivation and allure to what money provides that the evil spirit provides to the mix. But just to be clear, the need for things, for material, and for money does not come from the spirit. The spirit just influences the being to these things for the power and freedom that they can bring.

Money is a catalyst. It feeds off the mind's thoughts and need for value. It contributes to the closing of the circle. It infects those of a like nature and brings them together by established standards and economies that force even those of a different nature to take notice, participate, and fall prey to the disease. Money is the truest metric of one's tendencies and propensities toward the evil nature, how much they need it, how it drives and dictates their actions to get it, how they use it, how they hoard it. Money, especially net worth, is a reliable barometer to gauge the existence of one or more evil natures in the domain. Each dollar usually represents an increment of something taken from another, be it their hard labor, their dreams and aspirations, their security and sustenance, even their addictions and weaknesses. It measures one level of domination and advantage over the masses, one measure of manipulation. Money may not be evil in and of itself, but it is not of goodness unless shared or given away in true acts of charity.

A fourth common characteristic of evil is criticism and need to critique. Criticism resides at the outer parameter of the boundaries of self. It is the final defense of the perceived self. It comes from a team effort with the mind but is initiated and influenced by the evil nature. Criticism is self-centered and self-protecting. It represents self-righteousness and a "center of the universe" mentality. It represents an intolerance or negativism for that which isn't from the critic's self-core and self-perspective of things. It's an attack on that which does not line up with one's own practices and beliefs. Most of the time, it is derived and driven from meanness and with purpose of manipulation and advantage taking. The danger from criticism's impact and effect is in the potential for lost greatness. What one has to offer to others from greatness may not fit within the rules and norms protected by those giving critique. Thus, in attempts to avoid criticism, an idea, or a proposal, perhaps greatness may not be offered and thus is lost. The evil-nature-dominated being makes itself a force to be heard and reckoned with. Its loud opinions, critiques, and criticisms are spread broadly and many times forced on others. These evil-natured dominants have a superiority complex, many times not to an extreme, but it's there all the same. Subtle levels of criticism of that which is not consistent and subservient to the critic's own ways and influences are many times as effective as that which is more extreme. Criticism represents intolerance to a degree. It fosters an absence and lack of flexibility and forgiveness. Criticism requires an action and some level of change. Many times, it is coerced. One of the more common environments fostering criticisms and requirements for immediate and direct actions is found in business. Most of us have had the annual performance critique.

Alex had worked for Paula for only a few months when the semiannual review came due. Paula had little information to really share with Alex, he being so new and really just getting acclimated to the new job. Yet it had to be done. It had been Paula's history to be critical and offer areas where change was needed. She had some natural insecurity with Alex as the new guy, him coming from outside the company and with much experience. He had immediately taken on some of the challenges usually reserved for one of the more experienced in the cultures and ways of the business. He needed to be reminded of his place as a new member of the management staff. The performance evaluation was perfect for this purpose.

Alex had actually expected a great evaluation. He had come into the new environment and hit the ground running. He shared many ideas and saw many of these initiating positive changes. He had been assigned to committees and tasks that were indeed a stretch for him due to his unfamiliarity with the history and specifics of the culture and business. These were learning experiences yet also opportunities where he contributed greatly with new ideas, perspectives, and proposed models for change. Alex worked ten to twelve-hour days to allow himself time to meet his responsibilities and to catch up to others in terms of his knowledge and understanding of the business. Most of this was to make time for learning. He was highly motivated and charged by the challenges. His creativity and innovative thinking were at a peak. The job, although more difficult and demanding, was very satisfying and addressed his need of self-actualization. Then came the midyear assessment that took all the wind out of his sails.

He was asked to write the first draft of his own midyear assessment. Alex was honest and, as best as he could, addressed the good with the bad. What came back as the final version, however, included additions that were primarily only critical. Perhaps it was, in reality, only these criticisms that jumped off the pages as Alex read the review. But it was devastating to him. The motivation, the drive to do really great things, the willingness to work extended hours over extended periods were lost. The creativity and innovation were lost to the review's critique for more regulated and controlled types of thoughts and actions.

As for the impact to the business, productivity and value these took a major hit. Alex became a follower instead of a leader. From that point onward, he was hesitant to stand out, hesitant to take risks or introduce anything that differed from the current culture and procedural approaches to things. The new job became much like the old one had been. The excitement and energy were gone.

Alex fell in place. He spent most of his time in a defensive posture, careful to adhere to every set rule and standard. He had few opinions and looked to the perspectives of the few who could affect his performance assessment. He'd become a wasted source of new ideas and talents. The criticisms cut to his core and to his value. These changes were being forced on him by one with control over his pay and longevity with the firm. They drove away his independence and his perspective of things. They bore away that which was Alex's to contribute to greatness and replaced it with Paula's directives and mediocrity. The application of evil's tool of criticism was used to the greatest effect. There was no goodness in it.

A manager who better uses the mix and diversity from many domains will craft a team's different contributions and perspectives to blend in a way that best meets objectives and goals. Difference is allowed. Both the best of the good and evil natures is used. New, goal-directed and creative approaches by those of the team are encouraged. Ownership of the efforts is equally spread. Authority to act is shared. Emphasis is on achieving the goal and deliverable as opposed to staying the course and ensuring that the hierarchy of power is not tested.

Both good and evil contribute but in a most effective and valued way. It is not to change or force the individual members to fit into a singular compliant mold. Achievement and positive effects are recognized and celebrated. It becomes the focus.

Criticism is viewed as most damaging to productivity and motivation from the domains. It should be used judiciously, even avoided as much as possible, and used only when truly needed. When it is used, it should be set in a constructive manner and not intended as a threat, to enforce conformity, or as governance to ensure the giver's superiority of position power or to secure the ways of the past. It should not be used to support evil's intents and ploys; but often does

Mr. Arthur left the Italian eatery that day with an appointment to meet with his next in command. Her name was Brenda Doran. She was not only next in the line of succession to Mr. Arthur's power structure but she was also of a similar pure spirit makeup as Mr. Arthur. All her spirit natures were evil. It was an especially rare occurrence that two pure evil-natured domains would occupy the same territory. But it was so in this case. Brenda's domain was not as strong or as dominant as Mr. Arthur's but equipped with the potential to eventually reach the levels of his greatness and strength.

Mr. Arthur recognized her value to him. He nurtured their relationship to his advantage. She recruited most of his top-tier lieutenants. She served him out of fear. She provided him value, but she was also what worried him most. He was very careful to keep close watch of her progress and her favor by the masses. Because they were both of pure domains, neither could take advantage of the other's domain. Neither could transfer to the other's domain and take freely from the stored experience, knowledge, and know-how. Sharing was limited to what they were willing to give freely. What was going on, unknown, inside the spirit domain of the other represented a true risk and an exposure to the other. It kept them both cautious and under close scrutiny of the other.

There was a genuine issue of trust between their domains. Mr. Arthur feared that Brenda might someday turn against him, to strike either out on her own or out against him. He knew on the day that he recruited her into his structure that her powers would grow and that her satisfaction with the level of responsibility and authority that he granted her and the duties delegated her would become less than tolerable. It was her nature to rise above these and to want more. It was in her destiny to serve and grow evil to its greatest extent. She would have opportunity in this position to nurture her powers and her nature at an accelerated pace.

Knowing the exposure and realities of her nature and the tutelage and environment that Mr. Arthur could provide her, it gave him challenge that he badly needed. It forced him to hone his watch and his perceptions and to upgrade his skills to remain sharp. It forced him to stay in tune to all that was happening on the front lines, to remain closely aware and involved in the day-to-day exploitation of those in the community. This was to ensure that he retained and protected his position as the ultimate and superior pure domain. Mr. Arthur and Brenda Doran, even though watchful of each other, were nonetheless a formidable team against the common-domain beings of the neighborhood.

When Mr. Arthur finally met up with Brenda at the park, she was with another. His name was Robert Zeil. Brenda was by far the more sinister and evil-skilled of the two there to meet Mr. Arthur. She was most like Mr. Arthur. Robert seemed the good soldier, or maybe he was just strongly influenced and controlled by Brenda. Mr. Arthur didn't know most of the lower-level members of his organization. For the most part, he saw them as insignificant and disposable, but he knew Robert. He was a good distributor of his products. He was really making progress with the students of West Crawford High, which Mr. Arthur often frequented. Robert was instrumental to Mr. Arthur's plans and his spirit's destinies to further spread his influence into the community. It was unusual for Mr. Arthur, but he liked this particular young man, even though Robert's domain was filled with only two strong evil-natured spirits. His third spirit was good natured and had, over the period of his involvement with Mr. Arthur and Brenda's strong influences, been fully dominated by the other two evil ones of his domain. It was this third spirit, however, that kept Mr. Arthur at bay and from initially treating Robert as anything more than a good soldier. Yet Mr. Arthur felt comfortable speaking to Brenda in Robert's presence.

Mr. Arthur wasn't one to share many pleasantries. Upon contact, he immediately asked Brenda, "How's business?" He really meant to inquire whether she'd sold her allotment of product for the week and if she needed more. Their product was primarily drugs, but her portion of the business also included prostitution and some extortion. She was by far Mr. Arthur's best lieutenant. She never let Mr. Arthur down. Aside from the precautionary measures to assure him that she remained loyal to him, he stayed out of most of the details of her affairs. He would come to her for favors or for the jobs that he needed to be certain were done and done right. Initially, he couldn't recall why, on this day, Brenda had brought Robert. But after some recollection, it came back to him.

Brenda wasn't certain that Mr. Arthur would even remember Robert from the last time she introduced him. It had been some time ago. She brought him because he was her best recruit. Traffic and sales had picked up significantly in the school that he attended. Much of the success was directly attributable to him. She wanted to share his accomplishments and successes with Mr. Arthur and her plans for expanding them further. Brenda responded to her mentor, "Business is better than ever. We're making a killing. If you'll remember our previous conversation, this is why I brought Robert today."

Then she hesitated only an instant before asking, "Do you remember Robert Zeil from the party you threw at O'Brien's last December?"

Mr. Arthur looked at Robert and said, "Yes, I do. I remember everyone who distributes for me." He said it as if to imply that no one escaped once they were accepted into the fold. He could usually account for every dealer, every gram of product, and every dollar he expected to see from sales. Robert represented $125,000 to $140,000 in sales every month. He'd met or exceeded his quota for twelve months running. He was now to be rewarded a 10 percent share of the take on sales instead of the 5 percent he was currently getting.

Brenda knew that today was the third anniversary of his association with Mr. Arthur and his clan. She wanted Mr. Arthur to have the opportunity to reward him personally with the increase in his percentage. He was the first member of Brenda's loyal followers to reach this plateau. Mr. Arthur always reveled in the opportunity to reward greatness in evil things. Brenda wanted Mr. Arthur to be a part. It gave him strength. It gave him joy.

He said to Robert, "It's good to see you again, Robert. You are a good and loyal soldier in my army." He extended a hand. At the same time, he transferred into Robert's domain. This was defensive more than an interest to know Robert better. He was just checking to be sure that his evil natures were strong and dominant and that his good nature would not try anything unexpected against him. He was quickly satisfied. He was most satisfied to verify Robert's allegiance and commitment to both him and especially Brenda, his designated lieutenant.

Robert shook Mr. Arthur's hand and said, "It's great to meet you again." He wanted to be more eloquent, but he was from the streets. He spent little time honing his grammar or vocabulary. Neither did Mr. Arthur.

Mr. Arthur followed with "Do you know why Brenda brought you here to see me today?"

Robert seemed surprised that Mr. Arthur would know. He'd been told that it was to share his newest ideas on how to lure in new customers from the school. Brenda had allowed him to think this was the reason. Yet really, this was set up only as a way to get him to accompany her to Mr. Arthur. Brenda was now all smiles. In fact, she chuckled internally from her deviousness. She spoke up. "Robert thinks he is here for a reason other than what we know it to be." Robert said nothing.

Mr. Arthur then came right to the point in business fashion. "Well, let's get on with it." He looked at Brenda to be sure she was leaving the honors to him. Brenda knew better than to steal his thunder. Mr. Arthur began, "Robert, you've proved yourself to be one of my best." He locked his gaze on Robert's eyes to connect to his domain. He wanted to speak to his spirits as well as his body and mind.

He continued, "You have met your commitments and grown our business and customer base at West Crawford." There was a short pause after each sentence. The next came. "You are to be rewarded for your success, loyalty, and dedication to the business."

Robert stood stoic. He was being accommodated by the very top of the organization. It was quite a feeling yet also a bit frightening to be in the presence of such pure and powerful evil. Brenda continued to stand in the background. Mr. Arthur absorbed every thought and emotion running through Robert's domain. Robert was remarkably under control. Robert recognized that now he was into Mr. Arthur and Brenda's web so deep that he would never escape. At the moment, it didn't matter. He heard all that Mr. Arthur said, and he felt the pride in being rewarded. What he didn't realize was that much of himself was being replaced by Mr. Arthur and Brenda's hold on him. He was almost emptied of himself. He was a good soldier. He was a clone of the cause.

Mr. Arthur finished it off by saying, "Robert, I'm increasing your percentage on all sales of my product to 10 percent. You will have new freedoms to take on recruits as you see fit. You will continue to set their percentages from your take." It was all business. There was no "attaboy," no gifts or plaques or physical showings of success. The evil nature thrives on business. Money and position are reward enough. Mr. Arthur could tell through Robert's domain that he'd received reward enough.

Robert finally spoke but in choppy sorts. "T-t-thank you, Mr. Arthur." Then wanting to get out of there for fear that he might say something stupid or wrong, he finished, "I want you to know that I respect you and am proud to be a part of your organization." He gave an expression of gratitude to both Mr. Arthur and Brenda.

Mr. Arthur blurted, "Don't offer me gratitude, son. Make me money. That will keep you on my good side." He then turned to Brenda. "I have no use for sentiment. I can't eat it, I can't buy anything with it, and I can't cloth my body with it. Just make me money."

Brenda dismissed Robert from the conversation. She informed him to wait for her at the other end of the park. She had more, this day, to discuss with Mr. Arthur and in private. Robert knew the drill and left with a brief goodbye.

When he was gone, Brenda informed Mr. Arthur of Robert's new ideas regarding how to lure new customers to their business. Brenda thought them to be quite ingenious but wanted to get the boss's blessing before moving forward with any of them, especially because carrying out these plans included her. She shared with Mr. Arthur, "Robert has a plan to entice more students into using our product. It's a plan targeted at the student population that we have found difficult to influence."

She looked at Mr. Arthur to be sure he was listening and then continued, "In our first test, we have attracted two new fish to the bait. We'd like to reel them in next week if you approve."

Mr. Arthur's curiosity was aroused. He responded, "How does he intend to do this?"

Brenda allowed an evil grin. Then she offered to him, "We are young, and our hormones are roaring. We will use this to our advantage."

Mr. Arthur was still listening but not yet convinced of anything. Brenda went on, "Robert and I will double-date with others, others who will fall into our lead. We will lure them into our lives through example."

Mr. Arthur rubbed his chin. He liked the idea. It seemed simple, yet still, it didn't seem foolproof. He asked, "And what if the other couple resists your temptations? What if they threaten or, worse yet, actually report you to the authorities?"

Brenda laughed it off as unlikely. She said, "Our lives are fun, sexy, and exciting. It would be difficult for any adolescent to resist our lead." But she knew she hadn't fully resolved his concerns or answered his question adequately. She knew what he wanted. She was, in fact, the wild card and the insurance that the plan would work. He was waiting for her to play this card.

She continued, "If we can't lure them naturally with temptations, I will capture them with my evil. I will see to it that they will fall prey to our intents while under my influence."

Mr. Arthur knew this to be possible. It was the advantage of her pure evil-natured domain, just as he possessed. Mr. Arthur agreed to sanction the test. "Brenda, I agree to your plans but only under your strictest control and involvement. Do not allow anything or anyone to get out of your control." He looked into her gaze to make a final point. "We cannot afford a mistake with this group. These young people are too close to that teacher,

Mrs. Turner. She, too, has power in this community that we are not yet ready to take on." Brenda nodded in acknowledgment.

Brenda had other issues that she wished to discuss as well. She was looking for Mr. Arthur's endorsement to handle these as she saw appropriate. She said, "Mr. Arthur, I have one individual under my jurisdiction that has come up short in his payments to me for several months now. He shows a total lack of respect toward me that I cannot tolerate. I intend to resolve this problem in a way I know best." She gauged his reaction to her request thus far. Mr. Arthur showed little expression.

She continued, "I've exhausted reasonable means to get his attention. I request permission to terminate our relationship with this individual."

Mr. Arthur seemed to smile at the thought of what Brenda might be proposing. He asked her, "Who is this associate of ours?" He awaited a name before making the decision on what to allow.

Brenda replied, "Dewaun Burkes is his name." Then she elaborated with a few details. "He dropped out of West Crawford High last year. He's got a loyal group of customers. He keeps them happy by doing them favors at our expense."

She donned an ugly scowl before finishing, "He thinks he is above me. He thinks these friends of his will protect him. But we both know that he is greatly underestimating me."

Mr. Arthur now chuckled and said, "He, most certainly must not know you very well. They should be afraid." This gave Brenda partial confirmation from Mr. Arthur to proceed with her intents.

He continued, "Have you made the consequences of this disrespect very clear to Mr. Burkes?"

Brenda replied, "I have and very clearly so. Yet still, he gives me problems. He acts like a punk."

Mr. Arthur shook his head. It represented his full and total agreement. He asked, "Do you want my help on this?" But he knew that she would not accept his offer to help.

Brenda returned an immediate "No, I've got a plan." Then she grinned from his permission to proceed. "I will enjoy this one."

Mr. Arthur was beginning to get nervous standing out in the open for now nearly an hour. Brenda had picked up on this and begged just another moment of his time. Her last topic involved two girls from the school who had unpaid debts for drugs they had purchased from her. She laid out the situation for Mr. Arthur. "I have two girls from the school to whom we provided crack and other assorted pleasures for a party they threw almost a month ago. They are popular girls and are of higher economic standing than most we deal with. Their parents have social positions and influence."

She paused as if to gauge if Mr. Arthur would allow her to continue or rather to decide to cut his losses right then and there. He made no indication that he wanted to beg off. She continued, "They were to pay within two weeks from delivery, and they are now almost two weeks late with a payment. I don't see them coming up with the money soon." She looked to Mr. Arthur to interject a thought or suggestion, but he didn't. He continued to listen. Brenda continued to address him with her recommendation. "I'd like to treat this situation exactly as we have others of this type. Do I have your backing and concurrence in doing so?"

Mr. Arthur smiled for the third or fourth time today. He took such delight in these types of discussions. He replied, "You have my full backing on this." Then he elaborated on his thought. "Why don't you bring them down to the club on Saturday night? We'll get either our money or our money's worth." The discussion ended there. Brenda nodded to Mr. Arthur and walked off in the direction of the waiting Robert. Mr. Arthur moved off just as quickly but in the opposite direction. He still had much to do this afternoon.

But before Brenda could get too far removed, he yelled to her, "I'll see you after school this afternoon! You know the drill!" Their business was not quite finished for the day. It would continue after classes were let out at West Crawford High.

Mr. Arthur's next stop was to his club, O'Brien's. He'd taken it over after he'd murdered the owner and left him in a place never to be found. Before he killed him, he had him sign over the deed to the place. It was a hideout of sorts for Mr. Arthur. It was a safe haven in times when he felt heat from the local authorities or when he just wanted to escape the exposures of his lifestyle. This weekend, he was entertaining clients at the club. One of those who would be in attendance was scheduled to meet him in just a few minutes. He was not a client but rather a confidant and his insurance against the city's intrusion on his business. He would assure that there would be no unexpected intrusions or surprises to the meeting. He and Mr. Arthur were to make the arrangements and set security. Mr. Arthur always made it worth his while. They had a reciprocating arrangement to support each other's evils.

Mr. Arthur arrived at O Brien's just minutes before his appointment. He had much history with the man he was to meet. They both grew up and learned their trades on the streets of the neighborhood. This man, Bill Thatcher, was now a politician, a city council member representing the district. He was Mr. Arthur's personal choice for the office. His seat had been bought and paid for with Mr. Arthur's money. Mr. Arthur invited Bill to meet with him at O Brien's to discuss the arrangements for the weekend meeting, as well as to discuss some other business that was an irritant to him.

The need for a meeting was mutual. Mr. Thatcher was looking for more political contributions in preparation for his next step up the political ladder. Mr. Thatcher and Mr. Arthur were alike in many ways. Both were of the evil nature. Mr. Thatcher's domain was not as pure as Mr. Arthur's, having only two evil-natured spirits and one good-natured spirit in his domain, but his two evil-natured ones had gained much strength and tutelage in the evil ways from their association with Mr. Arthur and his pure domain. Mr. Thatcher exhibited all the characteristics and attributes of one dominated by an evil-natured domain. Power and money were at the core of his every thought and action.

Mr. Arthur admired him for what he'd become. He was an excellent student of his ways. Mr. Arthur was first to support Bill Thatcher in his quest to the top of city politics. Bill Thatcher recognized that he owed Mr. Arthur a lot and that his aspirations and successes in politics would continue to be achieved only so long as he had the ability to support Mr. Arthur's needs of him. Mr. Arthur said, "Bill, I'm glad you agreed to see me today on such short notice. It means a lot to me to know that you remember those who have helped you."

Bill Thatcher laughed at the thought that he might forget his mentor. He said, "Mr. Arthur, did you ever doubt my loyalty? I owe everything to you."

Mr. Arthur liked what he heard. He knew it was sincere. If he had a friend in the world, Bill Thatcher was the closest thing to it. Mr. Arthur responded, "In my business, you can never be too sure who your friends are from day to day." He paused to sip a drink and then started with a story. "Bill, let me tell you about my neighbor. His name is Tom."

Bill interrupted Mr. Arthur in fun by saying, "Arthur, should I plan to be here awhile? If so, I want to get comfortable. You know, when you start to share stories, it's destined to be a long afternoon."

Mr. Arthur chuckled and advised the bartender to keep the drinks coming. He said to the barkeep, "As long as he's drinking, he's listening to me, so keep him drinking."

He then turned to Bill Thatcher and playfully jabbed, "Do you want to hear the story or not? You might learn something about life in the streets."

Bill took a sip from his glass and replied to Mr. Arthur, "I love to hear your stories. You're the master."

Mr. Arthur then picked up on his story where he'd been interrupted. "Like I was saying, you never know who your friends are from one minute to the next." From this lead-in, he returned to his reference to Tom. "Tom is my neighbor. For years, we've made each other miserable. I despise the little rodent. He's purely an egghead, one of those computer geeks types."

Bill chimed in, "Yeah, I know the type. They're everywhere in the offices downtown. I avoid them when I can."

Mr. Arthur sipped his drink and nodded yes. He then went on, "Well, usually, I just make it a point to annoy him. But lately, I've been talking to him. I've also been observing him."

He leaned back in his chair, rubbed his chin, and went on, "He goes out with a real goody-goody from the school. She actually makes my skin crawl with all her charity and selfless caring. It never ceases to amaze me how our tax dollars are wastefully spent, keeping these types in jobs that have influence yet teach our young people nonproductive and useless dribble."

Mr. Arthur looked at Bill and said, "We both know that nice and being good will never really get you anywhere in the real world of business." He grinned. "Apparently, no one filled her in on how things are in the real world."

Bill was wondering where Mr. Arthur's story was leading. He obviously had no love for the woman from the school. He asked him, "Mr. Arthur, you want me to run a search on these two or fix it so that they lose their jobs or something?"

Mr. Arthur laughed again and then said, "Have another drink, Bill. You're a prominent citizen now. You can't be doing people in anymore." Then he leaned in and patted Bill on the back. "I just want you to listen to my story. The moral to the lesson will come in time. Just be patient and relax." With that, he again leaned back in his chair and continued with the story. "Well, as

I've talked a bit more with Tom over the past weeks, I've found that he's really not as bad as I've made him out to be. In fact, a part of him and a part of me actually seem to connect." Mr. Arthur looked to Bill for his reaction to this.

Bill finally asked, "You mean that this neighbor and you could actually be friendly?"

Mr. Arthur raised his eyebrows as if to say there could be a possibility. Then he added, "You know, Bill, you never know who your friends might be."

Bill couldn't believe such a hoax. He probed for more. "So do you two guys buddy around now or what?"

Mr. Arthur shared, "We talk now and then. I wouldn't call it a friendship. You know friendships are built on trust, like yours and mine. You need to know who you can trust. And that takes time and testing."

Bill was drinking. He was going crazy trying to determine where Mr. Arthur was trying to steer him with this story. He finally asked, "Where's this story going, Arthur?"

Mr. Arthur grinned. Then he told his friend Bill, "Well, you know, Bill, I will never have too many friends. The reason is that I know whom I can trust, and if I can't, I hurt them. That's why you definitely want to make sure that you remain my friend, even in your new position of prominence."

Bill stood to his feet and asked, "Is this what this story is all about, Arthur? It's a test?" He looked to Mr. Arthur before him. He directed his message directly. "You know I am loyal to you.

My job has not gotten in the way of my allegiance. I openly show and pledge to you my friendship and support."

Mr. Arthur sat back up and asked Bill Thatcher, "Aren't you curious what became of young Tom?"

Bill responded, "Absolutely. Is he still among us?"

Mr. Arthur replied, "Oh yes, he'll be very much among us this Saturday. I've asked him to the club. He's accepted."

Bill asked, "And what do you have in store for him?"

Mr. Arthur allowed himself a nasty burst of laughter. "I've got something very special planned for him. It's intended to teach him the very lesson I intended from this story I've just shared with you, Bill." He directed his full focus on Bill. "Tom was not wise to accept just anyone's invitation and offer of friendship. He needs to be sure he knows whom he can trust. He has not gained my favor as a friend, not like you have. It takes time to do so. I will teach him this on Saturday. I'll do it just to make this point." He then chuckled and went on, "You are invited to be there as well. It will all begin at seven in the evening at my table." He looked to Bill for his acceptance.

Bill thought it might be fun. He replied, "I'll be here at seven." Then he snickered, generally knowing what was in store. "It will be just like old times."

They both downed another drink or two before Bill asked, "What did you really want from me today? I'm sure it wasn't to share stories about your neighbor."

Mr. Arthur responded, "It's always about business with you, isn't it?" Then he shared the details that needed to be resolved before the weekend meeting with his drug suppliers and addressed several legal matters he had pending with the courts involving several of his dealers from the street. He asked Bill to see what he could do to influence the judges on these cases. Probation would assuredly be the verdict when Bill was finished.

Before calling it a session, Mr. Arthur handed Bill a substantial check for his campaign. Everyone seemed to get what they wanted from the time spent. The meeting was ended several hours after it started. Mr. Arthur ended it by saying, "Bill, it's good to spend some time with friends. Just be sure you know who they are and who they aren't. You're in a dangerous business to be without true friends covering your back." He smiled at Bill Thatcher. "You cover mine, and I will cover yours. Be off, friend. Until Saturday." They both left O'Brien's together.

As evident from the discussion, both Mr. Arthur and Bill Thatcher have strong and deep seated need to be important. Their evil natures need to be assured that they are in power and control. This is especially the case with Mr. Arthur. Mr. Arthur's story clearly bore this out. It was a test. It was intimidating in both its tone and nature. The point of the story was twofold. First, it was Mr. Arthur's way of reminding Bill Thatcher whom he can manipulate and control and whom he can't. One that he should never try to fool was Mr. Arthur. The intent of the story was to remind him of his debts to his financier. It was to test his allegiance and reconfirm the price of betrayal. The pure domain allows others their degree of what's due but takes back with a vengeance what is not. What it demands in the exchange is loyalty and allegiance. These were most important to Mr. Arthur. That was what he demanded from the meeting. This was the message of his story. As for the second point of his story, it was to invite Bill to an initiation, a hazing of sorts. It would be an evil affair. Bill had experienced such things before. He would be an ideal accomplice.

Mr. Arthur timed the completion of his meeting with Bill Thatcher to allow him time to be at the high school by last bell. There was much opportunity to do business after the students were let out. Yet it was more than this that interested him today. It was his presence, his mystic. He made sure the students saw him every afternoon. They needed to know that he was there, that he would get to them. It was his territory. It was his neighborhood. No one, not the police, the school administration, or anyone would take his business from him. He owned these streets. He was the rule.

Today Mr. Arthur had another special purpose for being at the school. Brenda would be here today to point out the girls whom he would depend on for entertainment this Saturday night. He needed to be sure that everything would be right. They needed to be young; they needed to be beautiful and sexy. He wanted everything to be perfectly evil and entrapping. The names of the girls were of no consequence to Mr. Arthur, but he recalled Brenda referring to them as Kimberly Thomas and Dawn Baldridge. He thought these were nice names for new victims.

Brenda showed up on time, exactly where she said she would be, just outside the main entrance to the school. As the girls came out, she walked up to them and singled them out for Mr. Arthur to observe and assess. Mr. Arthur called Brenda on her cell phone to tell her that the two were perfect. Before he hung up, he said into the phone, "Be sure that they do not pay their debt before Saturday. I need them at the club at seven. You know what to do." He then hung up. Brenda was also supposed to single out Dewaun Burkes for Mr. Arthur doing his business at the school, but Mr. Arthur chose not to stick around for this. He'd seen a hundred Dewaun Burkes. Brenda would know what to do about this problem. He didn't need to get involved in it. The fun for him had gone out of that line of the work long ago. The need to always be the tough guy had left him with age.

Evil itself is not people centered; rather, it is worldly. It is effect driven. It is always looking to grow and to take on new form, new victims. Its success is many times measured in its allure; it's return on investment. It's about supply and demand, about getting the greatest attention and interest from evil's influences and enticements. The evilest of beings are those who are best at presenting the temporary and immediate pleasures and return of evil. They are best at concealing the longer-term effects. They manufacture the greatest allure and enticement. They spread it to any and all takers. Their goods and their advertising of the product emphasize evil's fun, freedoms, and ease of lifestyle. Evil sells. It's similar to the good nature's product of love. It's perceived as basic and entitling. It's perceived as desirable and a reward. It's one of nature's offerings of pleasure; love is on one side, evil's fun and enticement on the other. Evil's success, as well as its allure, is many times measured on the external by its profit or cost.

Money is a vehicle of evil. The amount of profit and cost many times reflect the degree of evil. Money buys material things. The better the things, the more it costs or the more pleasure it brings. The desire for more material encourages and promotes eviler actions. Those who can pay while under the allure and influence of evil are exempt from evil's immediate recoupment on its investment. Their sentence is temporarily stayed. Money becomes the doorkeeper, allowing evil's current offerings and pleasures in, and when money is not available, it represents evil's due, its capitalization on investment. Evil is patient and subservient to money. Evil and money are reciprocating. Money simply provides an indicator and measure of evil's control and dominance over the holder. Those who can't pay evil's prices and still choose to indulge in evil's allures and darkness are the ones most doomed. Many in the position of owing evil have no alternatives but to turn from one form of payment to still another darker, more damaging form. Many times, it simply pays interest on the original debt or provides a temporary stay from final and ultimate collection. The debts to evil simply compound and eventually and totally consume the victim. The being becomes a menace, a criminal, and a danger to society. Theft, prostitution, dealing drugs, extortion, and other forms of advantage-taking become the chosen sources of payment. They grow and spread the forms of evil to which they are indebted.

Mr. Arthur knew the course of evil's mitosis. He knew that his freedom was entirely dependent on his money and ability to pay. It kept him in the businesses that he was in. It kept him one step ahead of the consequences of his evil, one step ahead of the things he never wanted to face or experience, such as facing up to society for his crimes or serving his deserved punishments and judgments. His pure powers helped him maintain his position of wealth. He was always able to stay one step ahead of evil's collectors of the ultimate debt. He was a lucky one. Most in the grips of evil were not nearly so lucky. Kimberly, Dawn, and Dewaun were about to prove this point out.

Mr. Arthur had special power over most but not over Brenda. He was most powerful from a spirit standpoint. Other domains knew this. As others felt the nearness of his aura, they would warn their being. It caused their bodies to shiver. It gave them the willies. Most who came into contact with Mr. Arthur had felt the willies in his presence but not Brenda. She was different. She was like Mr. Arthur. She was of the same domain makeup, only not quite as strong. Those of the neighborhood afforded her equal respect to that of Mr. Arthur. Had Mr. Arthur not previously established himself as such a strong presence in the neighborhood, it would have been hers to dominate. As it was, she waited for the passage of the business from him to her. It was a dangerous business that they were involved in. Their mortality was measured by their ability to dominate and to intimidate. The edge was often temporary. The power could be passed to her at any time. Brenda knew this and stood anxiously in waiting.

Both Mr. Arthur and Brenda could control a being by transferring and influencing the evil-natured components of the communities' domains. All it took for them was eye contact and the special power of pure evil. They used this power often and to their advantage. Mr. Arthur used it to ease his boredom. He used it to play games with others and to entertain his mind.

Mr. Arthur confronted Tom at least once every other day. It was usually a complaint or comment about something or someone from the building or from the news of the day. He seemed so negative about everything. Still, Tom usually allowed him to get his ranting off his chest. There was something about him that kept his interest, even though he knew he would never allow himself to be anything like Mr. Arthur. Mr. Arthur always seemed to be grinning at him as if he knew something about him. Tom did have a strange attraction to his uniqueness.

Mr. Arthur knew that he would never win over Tom's domain from Becky. But because of the one evil-natured spirit within his domain, he could use Tom all the same. He made it a point to visit with him periodically just to transfer to his domain and learn what he could about his rival, Becky. It was tactical in nature. It was to ensure that he kept up to date on his counterpart's plans and moves. Mr. Arthur, although he dropped out of school very early in life, had a good mind. He'd used it to survive in his line of work.

Each contact with Mr. Arthur gave strength and power to Tom's evil-natured spirit. Mr. Arthur would look for opportunity to share opposing views on the world with Tom. It was a game to him. Each time he had dialogue with Tom, he knew he was changing him, just a bit, through the strength he rendered to his one evil-natured spirit. It was his way of creating challenges and attacking his counterpart, Becky.

On this one occasion, Mr. Arthur offered, "Tom, I own a little club downtown. Why don't you and the young lady whom you seem so fond of stop in Saturday night?" It was one of the few times that he'd addressed him without complaining or growling. Tom was surprised. It was as if he was offering friendship. Tom said nothing at first.

Mr. Arthur offered again, "The drinks are on me for as long as you stay. You might find it interesting and different." Mr. Arthur had spent weeks baiting him and was now about to pull him in. He was appealing to Tom's lone evil spirit. "Tom, you might find it exciting."

Tom was surprisingly curious of what it might be like. He thought, *Why not? I'd rarely done things spontaneously or even mildly risky.* He countered Mr. Arthur's offer. "I might just take you up on your invitation, Mr. Arthur, but I doubt that the young lady would be interested. Would the invitation still be open if I decided to go it alone?"

Mr. Arthur nodded yes and confirmed by saying, "Of course. Maybe I'll be your companion for the night." Tom knew that Becky would not approve. But he was not totally like Becky. He, especially his evil-natured spirit, yearned for a bit of excitement and to be a bit reckless and adventuresome now and then. It was a side of him that Becky and her safe lifestyle did not satisfy.

He said to Mr. Arthur, "I'll take you up on your offer, but I'll only stay for a short time."

Mr. Arthur then grinned and replied, "Stop in around seven. I'll be there to show you around and make you feel at home."

Tom couldn't believe his hospitality. Tom finished the encounter with a smile and left Mr. Arthur with a "thank you." Tom couldn't help but wonder if he was having an effect on the usually grumpy old man. He was left feeling much better about Mr. Arthur.

Mr. Arthur walked away with another update on Tom and Becky's goings-on. He had extracted it from Tom's domain as they spoke. He thought, *That Tom, what a schmuck.* Tom had fallen full force right into his plan. Mr. Arthur would be sure to have something special for him when he arrived at O'Brien's Pub at seven on Saturday. It was his dastardly evil way of entertaining himself.

Saturday came quickly. At exactly seven, Tom entered O Brien's and worked his way toward the bar. He was nervous. He hadn't been to many clubs in his lifetime. He really didn't know what to expect. He was standing near the bar when he heard a shout from within. "Hey, barkeep, give my friend at the bar anything he wants tonight!" It was the voice of Mr. Arthur. He was sitting at a table with some others.

He recognized one at the table with Mr. Arthur as a prominent local politician. The others appeared to Tom as seedy types. Each of the men at Mr. Arthur's table had a girl sitting beside them. The girls were dressed skimpily and allowed most, if not all, of their upper portions to be exposed. Tom glanced away in embarrassment and guilt. He found a seat at the bar and ordered a beer from the bartender.

Within minutes, Mr. Arthur was at his side. He was laughing and being a bit lewd. He asked Tom, "I noticed that you turned away from me and my table rather quickly. I was going to invite you over to join us. Do the people and the activities going on at my table offend you?"

Tom replied, "They do. But to each his own."

Mr. Arthur roared, "In my bar, it's not to each his own. It's rather more like, 'To that of your choosing.' What's you poison, Tom? What are your vices?"

Tom replied, "I have no particular pull toward any vice, not to this point yet." He tried to be friendly and play along with Mr. Arthur's game, but it made him uneasy.

Mr. Arthur continued to probe, "What about your girl in the apartment upstairs? Isn't she your vice?" He smirked and covered it by lifting a finger to his mouth. "Don't tell me that your relationship with that pretty little thing isn't yet physical."

Tom took greater offense to this line of questioning. It seemed too personal. It was no longer playful or tolerable. Mr. Arthur had struck a sensitive nerve. He responded, "It is not a relationship like that going on at your friends' table, if that's what you're inquiring. You bring up Becky quite often. Do you have a particular interest in her?"

Mr. Arthur was caught off guard by his response. He raised his hands to his chest, waved them outward toward Tom, and pleaded, "No, I have no interest in her at all. I just wanted to make conversation. I just want to offer you a moment of fun, Tom."

Mr. Arthur allowed the moment to pass before saying, "So, Tom, you have no vices," and then said like the punch line of a joke, "We'll have to find you one, son. You're getting far too old to be without one." Tom took it as a joke and gave a protected chuckle. He was now on his second beer. The alcohol was taking effect, and he felt some of his stress and defensiveness toward this man begin to dissipate. He had plenty he wanted to ask him. He would never have been so bold to do so had it not been for the alcohol. Mr. Arthur knew this. The night was very much playing into his favor. It had been well planned.

After some idle conversation to allow both to settle in with each other, Tom asked Mr. Arthur about his illegal activities. He said to him, "You know that most people whom I have spoken to about you think of you as an undesirable element within the community. Before I knew you better, I, too, thought your demeanor and general attitude was abominable." The words that Tom was choosing were a bit harsh and unfiltered, but Mr. Arthur knew it was the alcohol. He knew what to expect. He'd extracted these thoughts from his domain on previous occasions. He remained unaffected by Tom's comments.

Tom went on, "As a person, I've changed my opinion about you just a little but not about your business. How can you justify what you do?" He focused primarily on his sale of drugs to the children and adults of the area. "I came here tonight at your invitation, in your pub, to have a friendly talk and to have a few beers with my neighbor. But, Mr. Arthur, please never approach me, or anyone close to me, as a target of your business dealings, certainly not about drugs or the crimes of your business."

He gave Mr. Arthur a stern look and said to his face, "If what is said about your business is true, this part of you is truly a cancer." Mr. Arthur brushed it all aside. He thought it good that Tom had courage, or enough liquor, to lay all these feelings and opinions open on the bar for the two of them to sort through. They both now knew where they stood with each other. Tom was surprised by how little he was affecting Mr. Arthur with what he'd said. He had rehearsed this part of his discussion and prepared for more of a rebuttal. Tom assumed that maybe it was nothing new to Mr. Arthur, that he'd heard it all from others before. He could only assume that the effect had been lost in the replication. Probably, by now, he was hardened to it.

With a straight face, Mr. Arthur responded, "Tom, you've based your opinions of me from stories and rumors. I am not a very bad man. Only a small portion of what you hear is accurate. But just for the sake of discussion, let's pretend it is all true." He stood before Tom like a friend trying to win over his approval. "Even so and even then, the problem is not so much me. I am just a victim like everyone else."

These statements confused Tom. He didn't see Mr. Arthur as a victim. He was anxious to see where Mr. Arthur would steer him from here. He already had a chuckle and a grin of disbelief ready and waiting for his explanation. Not enough beer in the county would help change his thoughts in this regard.

Mr. Arthur continued, "The real problem is not drugs but rather money and greed. I am just a capitalist, a businessman, like all in the world with a business to run. I'm no worse than any other enterprising opportunist trying to add to my balance sheets and income statements, working hard to accumulate my fair share of assets and earnings, as a measure of my hard work and effort." He sounded so assuring and convinced of his rightful place in business. It was so very odd in the way it sounded justified. "Tom, you are being fooled. You think that I am the problem. In fact, the problem is so much bigger than I am. The real problem, the real culprit, is big business. They are the big fish, the people who created and grew the cesspools of our community. These are the people who have funded my ventures."

He stopped and stared at Tom. He told the bartender to keep their glasses full. He then shouted, "Open your eyes, son! Take a broader view around you. Look at what's happening in our country. We have corporate corruption, corporate deception at an all-time high. Yet what we hear about is only the tip of the iceberg. They're talking billions and billions of dollars. We are talking about people who cheat everyone, not just one or two vulnerable targets. Yet only a handful of the least influential and only those who are disposable from the ranks of corporate executives are sacrificed to represent payment for the crimes of the whole."

He paused to allow his pleas of innocence by means of diversion to sink in and gain full effect. Tom was taking in the arguments as well as the alcohol. The latter was having the far greater effect, yet he remained attentive. Mr. Arthur continued, "There's a powerful brotherhood out there. Protection is rendered through belonging to the inner circle, the executive elite. The evidence of the crimes is hidden in the reams of numbers and the legal and accounting mumbo jumbo. No one so insignificant as you or me could fathom a thought of bringing corporate criminals down. Our economy is built on their preying on us common people. They're siphoning off our shares of well-being and sustenance. They're redirecting them to feed their bonuses, their compensation programs, and their golden parachutes. It drives the stock prices higher. It grows the economy, the value of the dollar on the global front, the market, and GNP."

Mr. Arthur had now worked himself into a frenzy. He was really believing and adamant about what he was sharing. At least he put up a very good front. He called on the barkeep to bring two more drinks. But this time, he said, "Bring us something more potent than beer." Two vodkas were placed before them.

The bartender said, "Start with this. Tell me if you want something different."

As Mr. Arthur raised his drink to his lips, he muttered in an attitude of disbelief, "You accuse me of hurting the community, the country, and the people. I am guilty of some things but certainly not of this." He elaborated his own view of the situation. "We are not a community. We are not a country.

Rather, we have become only a market. We lost our sense of community and service to one another long ago. We are the targets of consumerism. We are product targets, just some of the numbers making up consumer research and studies. We are the lab rats. We're simply victims of mental crimes, victims to those deceiving us, indoctrinating us on their product, filling us with propaganda and neat colorful wrappers that hide their manipulation, extortion, embezzlement, and corporate scandals. Big business should be the target of your wrath and the assaults you have misplaced on me. I am an innocent bystander compared with the harm and damage done by company CEOs, CFOs, and presidents. Big money, stock options, insider trading, and executive incentive packages are the real target of your contempt. But these real criminals would rather have you chasing me. It keeps the dogs off their trail. It keeps them perceived as innocent. I appear the criminal because I do not hide my filth. I do not deceive you to their levels of expertise. Hate me if you will, but you are after the fever instead of the virus."

As distorted as it was, Tom recognized some truths in what Mr. Arthur had to say but recognized it for what it was worth. It was simply a diversion from one truth to another. He shook his head at Mr. Arthur and held firmly on his recognition and accusations of Mr. Arthur's crimes as contributing to corruption that was closest to their homes. His elaborate oration was well developed and convincing yet done to shield his own evil by introducing the more significant bigger evil of corporate America. Using the "bigger fish" tactic would not sell to Tom. To think that Mr. Arthur really believed he had done a service by curtailing the extent of his evil, by doing it in the open and concentrated on only one small community, unlike the "big fish" corporate criminals. This would not fly with Tom or most like him. Regardless of whether Mr. Arthur's response was from his mind or from the spirit domain, it was disturbing. It brought thoughts of how distorted and self-justifying we can allow ourselves to be within our own minds.

Tom replied, "I do hate what you do, Mr. Arthur. Corporate criminals are guilty and responsible for much that is bad in this world, but you, sir, you are also misdirected, just as guilty of crimes for money and crimes for power. Your disdain for these other criminals reflects on you. You are part of the brotherhood of crime. You and corporate criminals are all out there, equally free to pillage and prey. That, sir, is the real problem. You all extort and cheat the common people. Money drives you. It is your tonic. It is the poison that drives out any good from your being. Any crime or devious action to personally and greedily secure a larger share is all of your agenda. You are no better than the worst criminals you just described to me. You are guilty and a blight on our community. You will be caught and put away someday. I will miss the neighbor that you occasionally allow yourself to be, if only in a small way, but I will not miss the criminal acts that you do."

Mr. Arthur just looked at him and smiled. He was still not greatly affected or concerned by it. Tom continued to be marveled by his lack of reaction to these indictments. Tom had fully expected to have been thrown out of Mr. Arthur's club by now. He thought maybe it had to do with the effects of the drinks both on him and on Mr. Arthur.

Mr. Arthur knew that he would never get caught in spite of Tom's warnings and threats. Mr. Arthur had secured himself against such an end. He would remain in business forever. Payoffs and the skim from the fringes of his profits were being directed to the right people of authority and government frequently and regularly. Without Tom knowing, some of these people were in the club at that very moment, enjoying Mr. Arthur's game with Tom. There were many of different clothes and uniforms on his payroll, some from both the dark side of the law and those supposedly protecting the people through the law. Mr. Arthur thought, *No one looks after the common man like they do the paying criminal.* He hoped for Tom's sake that he would one day begin to see this more realistically. Mr. Arthur had stated many truths in his response to Tom. He revealed much of what made him a success in crime as it was also the case with his peers in crime. It was not so much his lack of conscience. It was not self-incrimination or self-reflection. It was about the other guy, the ones who were really bad. They were the ones who made his crimes insignificant and justified. In his mind, his were not significant

Tom's honesty didn't even tinge Mr. Arthur's feeling. He said to Tom, "Well, Tom, let's still be friends. I'll be your criminal friend until I'm taken away to pay my debt to the community." Then he chuckled and held out his glass. Tom had to snicker in disbelief. The drinks definitely contributed to their acceptance of each other on this evening. No matter how he'd let his feelings show, Mr. Arthur seemed a nicer person. Mr. Arthur finally offered to take him to his office in the back to continue their visit. Tom needed time to recover from the alcohol. Tom agreed, and they headed toward the back of the club.

Without Tom's knowledge, Mr. Arthur had given the signal to the bartender to slip a drug into Tom's last drink. He was now really feeling the effects of it. He needed to sit down. Mr. Arthur led him to a special room where he could sit and wait out the effect of his indulgence from the bar. He wouldn't have even recognized that a room existed behind the back wall of the barroom had Mr. Arthur not guided him there.

Inside the room, he found the nearest seat and sat down. Within minutes, the room began to fill. He recognized two girls from Becky's school among the people in the room. He didn't know their names but had seen them with Becky on a number of occasions. They recognized him as well. The others in the room were obviously there for a party. Tom felt really out of place, but because he was dazed and lacking motor skill at that moment, he couldn't leave. He thought what he was experiencing was the result of too much alcohol in his body. He was waiting for his head to clear before trying to find his way out. Everything was spinning, but he struggled to focus as best as he could. All in the room but Tom were dancing and having a good time. With each new song and in the duration between Tom's ability to re-raise his head and test his orientation and bearings, more of the people in the room were taking off items of their clothing, including the two girls he recognized.

Tom heard Mr. Arthur's voice in the space in front of him. He was obviously instigating the activities around them. "Anything you like, Tom. It's all free to you tonight. Perhaps you will find a vice in the room that you might like to try. You are my special guest."

Mr. Arthur motioned to one of the girls to come over to him. It was one whom Tom recognized from the school. Tom saw the nearly naked young woman approach. Mr. Arthur said to her, "Tom is a shy one. You and your friend will show him a good time tonight. If you do this, you are free of your debt to me."

The girl whispered something into Mr. Arthur's ear and then looked away. Mr. Arthur replied to her comment, "I know that you recognize him and that he recognizes you, but this is what I want in exchange for your debt." Nothing more was said. The girl motioned to the other, and soon both were before Tom, caressing him. Mr. Arthur's response to the girl was mulled through Tom's memory for most of the night.

Even though he was slipping in and out of consciousness, he knew that he'd been set up. He was now into this situation well over his head. His body and mind were not responding, certainly not with caution and discretion. His domain was not connected. He remembered the girls' faces. He remembered their nakedness. They were indeed beautiful, and they did tempt his being. Yet he continued to be tormented by a good conscience. He knew that what was going on was wrong. It was wrong of him to have come here tonight. His good-natured spirits were not responding strongly enough to retain command of his actions, only his conscience.

He remembered waking up outside the club, leaning against the tire of his car. His clothes were draped over his body haphazardly. He feared that they'd been off. He remembered a few bits and pieces of the two hours he'd spent in the back room of O'Brien's. He wished he could forget. He was fairly certain that he'd been involved in things that he'd be ashamed of. He knew he'd been taken advantage of. He never mentioned anything to Becky or to anyone else.

When at the school and whenever he happened on either of the two girls, they always looked away and moved quickly in another direction. He wanted to ask them what happened that night. He wanted to ask if there were things that happened that he should apologize to them for. With their reactions toward him, he surmised that the answer must be yes. He had no courage to follow up with either of them. He'd learned his lesson. He now avoided Mr. Arthur whenever he could. Yet Mr. Arthur still sought him out. He always had a grin on his face when they met. He now had a secret that would allow him to control Tom.

Tom's spirits were wondering if Mr. Arthur's deception of him was the product of his evil-natured domain or of his mind. Mr. Arthur's expertise at playing the mind games was equally dangerous as his inner pure evil nature. In any event, it was deceit and his love of gamesmanship that betrayed Tom. Their previously perceived tolerance of each other was just a facade allowing Mr. Arthur to take advantage. It was alcohol and drugs that chased any good influence and judgment from Tom's domain, the good judgment and thoughts that might have changed things. Tom knew he'd been duped. He knew he was no match for Mr. Arthur's cunning and evil. He now feared the threats of extortion that he fully expected in the aftermath.

The next evening when Tom visited Becky, she innocently transferred to his domain, hoping to give his good-natured spirits a boost. Her spirits were startled to learn of the events of the previous evening. There was nothing that Tom could hide from Becky's pure domain. Stored within Tom's domain were the details of all, even the parts that Tom's mind had chosen not to remember. Becky could not understand how Tom could have allowed himself to fall prey to Mr. Arthur's tactics. The spirits of Becky's domain couldn't understand why he accepted an invitation to Mr. Arthur's club in the first place. Her domain was left questioning the state of Tom's spirits and if his mind and body had taken total control over them. But in the end, she knew that it was Mr. Arthur who had manipulated Tom.

Tom was the one person through which Mr. Arthur could truly cause the most hurt to Becky. Through this incident, Mr. Arthur had sent a clear message, and it was directed to her. He knew that, through Tom, this message would assuredly get back. Mr. Arthur had schemed and manipulated Tom to gain an advantage. This one night was the opening battle in a larger war. Becky would need to concede the first victory to Mr. Arthur's pure evil. It was a lesson learned. Becky's domain was certain that this entire evil-conceived event that he had played out on Tom was just the beginning of a larger conflict that Mr. Arthur was planning and that was yet to further play out between them. Tom and all others who would be involved were just pawns in a power struggle between the two virtues. It was clear from what her spirit envoy could draw out that Tom had been drugged.

With what Tom's domain could share from his spirits, Becky's spirits could not determine how the two students from her school got involved in all this or why they were there. On her next opportunity with them, one from Becky's domain would transfer to each and get a clearer understanding of their involvement. For now, though, there would just be hurt and disappointment within Tom's and Becky's spirit domains. It would pass with time. Mr. Arthur had his single victory. He was indeed a very evil one.

Evil can truly ruin good and decent lives in a very short period in such a few brief acts. Both of the girls from the school were ruined by that night. Their grades began to fall. They both resigned from the cheerleading squad. Their self-esteem was ruined. Their evil natures took control of them; it changed them thoroughly and completely. It was now part of their histories. It would be there to haunt them forever.

Becky's externals, her body and mind, would not know of Tom's ill-fated evening until later. Only her domain would endure the hurt in the present. Tom's spirit, the one that was her soul mate, remained the primary conduit between their domains. These two domains were specially and solidly connected. This incident and its damaging effects to Tom created the same effects to Becky's domain as well. It was added to her history. It marked an evil event and a stored reference in her domain. It made her more vulnerable to evil because of her union to Tom.

In most instances, the two good spirits of Tom's domain were able to control the one evil-natured spirit. Yet in the case when Tom was in the presence of Mr. Arthur, this changed. It gave rise and dominance to the evil-natured spirit. It was this evil-natured spirit that drove Tom to explore O'Brien's and fall into Mr. Arthur's trap. It was the evil-natured spirit that influenced Tom to take risks that made him vulnerable.

With the strength that the evil-natured spirit gained from Mr. Arthur and the incidents of purest evil influence, it found new ways to serve its common destiny. It took advantage of being present in the domain while Becky's spirits shared and filled the other two with the knowledge and power of her purity. It used this opportunity to draw from her presence what Mr. Arthur wanted most from it, to know more about the good-natured spirits and to isolate their vulnerabilities, their susceptibility. Tom's evil-natured spirit knew Becky's pure goodness and pure good natures better than any other evil-natured spirit. It was regularly connected to Becky's domain through her soul mate, its residing partner in Tom's domain. Tom's evil spirit was the

Judas, the traitor. It was proof that even in the most positive of relationships, an advantage can be gained for the counter virtue, if allowed. In essence, it was spirit espionage. It was an event that occurred occasionally in the spirit realm. It was used to control and create opportunity for advantage. In Tom's case, it explained how he could fall into the situation that he did, how he could be swayed by Mr. Arthur to explore his club and to do things that he shouldn't. It allowed Tom's evil-natured spirit to fulfill a destiny to add to evil's tally. It was indeed outside his body or mind's control. He was simply an instrument of his evil spirit's nature.

Dewaun Burkes was a cocky punk. His domain was made up of two strong and dominant evil-natured spirits and one weak good-natured spirit. He feared no one. He thought he was invincible. Most of all, he had no fear that a woman might teach him respect and administer discipline, especially of the variety that he was well versed from his days on the streets.

When Brenda showed up at his apartment for the money that he owed her, Dewaun snubbed her off. He'd been putting her off for weeks now. With each success, he grew more confident that he could put her off again, maybe forever. Brenda gave him firm warning this time. "Dewaun, I will not leave this apartment tonight without the money that is Mr. Arthur's. Either I will have the money or I will be leaving with the assurance that you will not disrespect me like this in the future." She stood before him in a posture of strength. Her hands were clenched. Her jaw was drawn tight.

Dewaun snickered and responded to her, "Is this a threat? Are you here to challenge me, here on my own turf?" He, too, tightened the muscles in his jaw. "You must be stupid." Both remained silent for an instant. Dewaun was first to break the silence. He scoffed. "You want your money? Come in here and take it from me, bitch. Take what you can find. Take what you can gather before I cut you to ribbons." With that, he pulled a switchblade from his pants pocket and extended the blade to its fullest. He postured himself wide and in a defensive position.

Brenda responded, "I see that the time for negotiations is finished. I've been waiting for this." She smiled. "You want to fight. I'll give you a fight you'll never forget." She was now smiling and inching forward. "But know this, Dewaun. I will leave with Mr. Arthur's money, or you will not be in a condition to give it to me. You will never again cause trouble in my territory or any other for that matter." She moved deliberately and closer to Dewaun. She taunted him to lunge at her with the knife.

Finally, Dewaun felt he had the angle that he wanted and threw the knife toward her body. His extending arm was met with a crushing kick from her right foot. The pain sent him buckled over and to his knees. The knife dislodged from his hand and sailed misdirected. Dewaun looked at her in confusion of what had just happened. Her expression had not changed. She shot a gaze that went through to his core. She said, "Where is the money, Dewaun? I'm only asking you one last time."

He began to whine about the pain of his broken right arm. With his other arm and hand, he pointed to a dresser and said, "Top drawer. You'll find all but a few dollars that I owe." As she moved to the drawer, Dewaun looked across the floor, trying desperately to locate the knife. He could not find it.

Brenda began to count. "Dewaun, there's only $24,985 here. Where's the other $15?"

Dewaun let out a sigh of desperation and then said, "It's only a few dollars short, like I told you."

Brenda responded to his lack of compliance, "Do you remember what I told you when I walked into this apartment?" She allowed him to replay her words in his mind and then repeated them for him. "I will leave this apartment tonight with the money that is Mr. Arthur's or assurance that you will never put me in this position again." She put her hand on his head. "When I came here tonight, your life was worth $25,000. That was far too much value to place on the life of a lowlife like you. Now your life is valued at only $15. This is a far more accurate reflection of your life's true value. Do you want to die for $15?"

Through this experience, Dewaun was now fully aware of the true nature and power of the person he'd been disrespecting. He was sweating from realization of just how close he now was to prematurely leaving this lifetime. He said, "Here in my wallet, there's another $18 or so." He fumbled to dislodge it from his pants pockets with his left hand but dropped it.

Brenda moved to pick it up while saying, "Here, I'll help you" She picked it up and withdrew $13 from the fold. She held it in front of him, splitting their gaze into each other's eyes. "Dewaun, there's only $13 here. It's not good enough." With that, she thrust the switchblade she'd picked up by the dresser into his chest and turned it several times. Dewaun died slowly and painfully in front of her. Just before he drew his last breath, she again reached into the wallet and withdrew another $5.

She looked at the dying man before her and said, "Oh, how unfortunate. I must have missed this the first time I looked." She stuffed the full $25,003 into the wallet and directed a parting comment to the body on the floor. "I'll be sure that Mr. Arthur gets this with your blessing." She left Dewaun there on the floor to die alone. Mr. Arthur's people were sent later to attend to Dewaun's remains. His body would not be found for weeks. When it was, it would be barely recognizable. It was made to look like he'd been in a fight, one where he was clearly no match for the opposition. With the condition of the remains, the fact that it was a woman who'd done this would never enter anyone's mind.

Evil natures don't close the circle of life. They influence movement to the third and fourth quartiles, where evil has much advantage over good natures. But closure comes from mind and physical components, taking dominance. Closure occurs when the spirit natures and influence are forced from the being altogether. Evil natures simply set the table for this. It is in the evil natures that the physical and mental components thrive; the pleasures, the confidences, the pride, and the superiorities that evil natures feed these other components. Eventually, the mental and physical components forget or choose to forget from where they have been nourished and nurtured. The spiritual is relegated to a place of little or no value. With its diminishment, the life also dies. The circle closes, and the civilization is no more. The evil-natured spirits are last to see the final remnants of the civilization before its fall.

The Disadvantaged

There are many types of the disadvantaged. There are those who that are disadvantaged, but the result of breakdowns in the spirit or domain components, but entirely of defects in the physical or mental components. Examples include those with a birth defect, those badly scarred or deformed by accident or disease, those with missing body parts or limbs or having physical bodily deformities like dwarfism or that which causes one to be as a giant; to name a few. These beings are all unfortunate, important, and put on the earth for many reasons. Perhaps it is to remind others like us how lucky we are not to have been chosen to carry these burdens. It may be that they contribute a special and different experience and perspective of life.

But another reason they may exist, and one that is most natural yet overlooked or downplayed is that they are the insights into our inner spirit's natures. They are there for us and those around us to assess and to test the good and evil natures' tendencies that influence our lives. It may be only the look in one's eyes when encountering a disabled one or the hesitancy of actions that is the true indicator of the true nature of one's spirit domain. To other domains, and equally evident to other components of the beings, is an involuntary, yet true glimpse into one's true inner domain and self. How we react and act among the disadvantaged is clear evidence of the good or evil within our domains. Here are some examples to show how different domains' collective spirit natures might react.

Domains comprised of a majority of spirits with evil natures often repel these encounters. Their reaction is most noticeably, often dramatic. They cannot deal with flaws. They often make fun of these unfortunate ones. They will avoid or discount these beings behind their backs and just as frequently in their presence and even directly to their face. The evil domains truly struggle to hide their rejecting reaction. Only by the grace of dilution and offsets with the good-natured spirits of their domains can these domains appear civil and controlled in these settings with the disabled. Even so, there are detectable signs from the hidden influence of an evil natured spirit.

On the other hand, domains comprised of and dominated by strong spirits of good natures will allow an initial surprise and perhaps a hesitation, but will recover and search for the value beneath the initial reaction of the encounter. The good-natured will accept the disabled and include them as just unfortunate beings. They will support them and will guard against showing pity. They will reset the encounter to that between equals. The good-nature's emotions allow for empathy and helpful understanding. There is little that the good-natured spirit domain can do but to support and treat these unfortunates as any other host of a spirit domain.

The domains of mixed domains with no particularly strong dominance of spirit's natures are the most unpredictable and could elicit mixed signals, depending on the nature of the spirits moving through dominance or the aggregate and overall strength of its nature's mix.

In the category of disabled are also those who are diagnosed as retarded or feebleminded. These inflictions are rarely from a physical defect or flaw but are from flaws of the spirit. In the case of retardation, this is caused when one of the three spirits of a domain is turned away at birth or lost sometime afterward. Problems at birth such as premature or forced birth, or unnatural birth are a common cause. Also, a spirit that transfers to another and cannot return leaves a void within the initially domiciled domain causing a defect. Another cause can come from a domain where two of the residing spirits completely overbear the third. This results in an unnatural and severe imbalance of spirit strengths and participation from the spirits in a domain. In each of these cases, retardation is from an omission to or lacking of the mind's expected stimulus and directives from a fully and supporting spirit domain. In most cases, it is missing the contribution from three function and contributing spirits. It leaves the mind confused and awaiting more, causing it to be slower and less able, if ever able at all, to react in an expected capacity. Although it appears to be a defect of the mind, the defect is in the spirits and the domain. No amount of treatment to the minds of these beings will address the true source. Whenever the synchronizations and seamless, cohesive exchanges and workings between any of the being's components misfire, this will cause the system to be disabled. In the case of the nonphysical, it will mostly appear as retardation or feeblemindedness.

David and Frederick are students at Becky's school. Becky spends a significant portion of her time protecting them from the "normal or special" groups. Both David and Frederick are easy prey.

David is considered an unfortunate one, being born with feebleness in the mind. He was born to normal parents but nonetheless is one of the anomalies of life. He is technically diagnosed as retarded. Yet as stated, it has little to do with his mind or his body. It is not his mind or body that is damaged. Rather, he was born with flaws in the spirit domain's makeup. The spirit domain that directs the mental and physical aspects is flawed. His spirit domain at birth contained only two spirits, which would cause this condition. The normal spirit domain contains three spirits. In this case, the third that would have come from the pool of uncommitted spirits, for whatever reason, was not included in David's package. Most likely, it was because the birth was affected by the mother being in an accident that forced the birth to be over two months premature. The third spirit from the unassigned pool had not been fully released and was lost.

Frederick's situation was different from David's. It had to do with the spirit contribution from Frederick's father that was flawed. That from the mother and the spirit pool were normal. As a result, there is a conflict within the domain. The flawed one is not cooperative, not complementing the other two. There is little cohesiveness. Much of the spirits' energies from within this domain are spent in controlling the flawed one, controlling the damage that it can cause. Sharing and communications between them, one of the critical functions between spirits both within a domain and between the other components of the being, are dysfunctional and minimal. These spirits that are looked to for guiding the physical and mental aspects of the being are disconnected and out of sync. The domain is ineffective. As a result, the being is misguided. It is retarded. He is a defect by today's terms.

What went wrong? Why and how did the spirit become flawed? It could have been any number of things. The flaws of this spirit originated from one spirit from the father's domain. Breakdowns in his spirit component could have come as a result of outside influences on the father's spirit component, the worst being drugs or alcohol. It could have been the result of willed self-destruction. Frederick's father was a good man. The condition he passed on to his son was, in fact, the result of one of his spirit components' desires for self-destruction. Spirits are known to do this on very rare occasion. But how and why? This seems, on the surface, to be quite odd. The answers are in the spirit's need for freedom. It goes back to its origin.

You see, spirits are naturally free creations; they crave time away from the being. They need unbound change and new scenery. When a spirit is passed from parent to child through advocacy, generation to generations over and over again and perpetually so, never being released to the pool of free spirits; not even for short periods of freedom, it grows unstable and dysfunctional. It takes drastic measures to become free again. As unpleasant as it might seem, a spirit requires the being that houses it to periodically die, or the domain not to continuously chose it for reproductive advocacy, thus allowing it to be a part of the being's death and be freed, even if for only a short time before reassignment. Drastic measures are only taken in cases where the spirit has not experienced freedom for very long periods, in fact, many generations. In the case of this misfortunate one, one spirit component of his father's domain had been passed through births of eleven generations. It found that it had no choice but to force release through spirit suicide. This leaves the domain one short of a fully functioning complement of spirits.

Another reason we will address in a later chapter is created as a result of spirit revenge. It is supported by the placement of a revenge spirit within the unfortunate one's domain. Built-up revenge on future generations can cause a misfire or a desire to self-destruct. More likely, the revenge spirit can also alter the passing of a spirit from the unassigned pool or create a flaw in a spirit from the advocate from a parent from being assigned in the domain. This is mean-spirited but will also happen and create a domain imbalance and flaw. We'll talk about revenge spirits in greater detail in a later chapter. As should now be evident, spirit domains are not immune to flaws or mistakes. The result of these is retardation or mind feebleness.

So, what is spirit suicide? What are the specifics? Spirit suicide is when the spirit wholly or partially chooses to deteriorate. The deterioration causes the domain to be flawed and thus the being to be flawed. The being becomes dysfunctional, abnormal, and barren. Becoming barren is the desired result of the spirit, thus ensuring itself and the other spirits of the being from being passed to another generation of its heritage. The flawed being will eventually die, and upon its death, the spirit is freed. At this demise, the deteriorated spirit experiences only a brief period of freedom; then because it is now flawed and because it is in this condition, it cannot be added to the spirit pool for reassignment. It must cease to exist. It becomes no more. Sacrificing itself entirely for the brief moments of freedom and escape from its captive state is its brief desired objective. It's a purging of a spirit of sort. It reduces the spirit population and one measure of balance between the spirit natures.

The body and mind of the being must endure any deficiencies of the spirit domain. There is misdirection, erratic behavior, lack of focus and direction, limited use of their past knowledge or history, and generally little constraint. The body is free to act and react as undirected by a spirit guide. The mind has limited stimuli, ideas, discipline, or direction. They are free to be erratic and off-center. Drugs may help control the mind and physical component's short-term behavior but will not cure or affect the spirit flaws of the domain.

Of course, it is a matter of degree. Not all the spirits of a domain take such drastic actions. Even those that do, do so at varying degrees. The milder the level of deterioration by the spirit, the milder the case of retardation. The stronger the other spirits of the domain are, the more they can compensate for the absence or deficiency of the one.

Neither of Frederick's or David's parents possess exceptionally strong spirit domains. As such, especially in Frederick's case, there is little support or harmony between the domains of the family to Frederick's spirit domain. Frederick is treated poorly. He is unwanted. His unflawed spirits are unsupported. He is to be detached from the society of the unflawed domains and sent to a hospital, a hospital unable to heal and certainly unable to support the flaws of the missing or deteriorated spirit of their domains.

Spiritual incest is another cause of retardation or feeblemindedness. It occurs when the spirit of a recently released near-generation or family member is assigned from the unassigned pool, at inception, as the third spirit of a new being's domain. This causes problems. The added spirit is identical in part or in whole to one of the other spirits in the domain, to one of the two advocates' spirits. This creates limited perspective and duplication. The domain is limited or skewed in its ability to add new and unique contributions and influence. The result is limited abilities. It also manifests itself as retardation or feeble contribution to the mind, depending on the strength of the duplicated spirit in the domain.

As evidenced by the above, creation of new spirit domains is not infallible. Although defects and omissions are infrequent, their impact on the being is significant and unfortunate. The truest test of one's goodness is found in their reaction and help of the unfortunate of the world. Why are they here? Why do they annoy us?

They are put among us to test the world's goodness, pure and simple. The measure that they raise is a pure reading of the civilization's position on the evolutionary circle. They clearly identify the world's evil. Evil cannot accept the unfortunate. Evil is implored to make these unfortunates suffer and to be beneath them, to be targets of their critiques and scorn. Evil will not accept or act neutral to an unfortunate one. It must comment, insult, or sneer, even if it's only from the internal. These acts clearly identify, for the rest of us, those domains with evil natures within them.

There is a lesser form of disadvantage. These are the unnatural type. Once again, there are numerous examples of these, such as impoverishment, the emotionally damaged, the depressed, the love lost, and those who have lost hope. The signs appear in the physical or mind components. They disengage the being but in a milder form compared with the disability brought on by retardation or disabilities caused by the domain and from external accidents and causes. The effect to the being is real just the same. They shut out the spirit connections.

Physical disadvantage will occasionally create spiritual advantages, even restoration. What is seen as a negative can actually be a positive in some ways. Someone scarred in an accident can use its damaged components to partner or re-partner with the good spirits. It can open doors that have previously been left closed or not opened for some time. There can be compensations, gains, and trade-offs if accepted and used wisely.

A very common form of disadvantage is that of poverty. The hardships that these beings must endure is quite different from those who are physically disadvantaged, yet the pain is much the same; the endurance from the stigma of public perception is much the same. Also, the missed opportunities and closed doors to discovery and understanding that present themselves are much the same as with other forms of disadvantages.

The Kirkpatrick family was a very large family. They gather every year, many times more than once, to celebrate their milestones or just to share their stories and events with one another. The core generation grew up as brothers and sisters. There were twelve originally. Only three still remain alive and all over ninety years of age. From the twelve were created forty-eighty children. The forty-eight created over a hundred more in the next generation and onward. The gatherings consisted of several hundred people, all close and recognizing one another as family. It was a wonderful celebration of love and diversity each time it occurred. Yet the common theme running through every branch in the family tree was their origin and commitment to one another. It ran from the core generation and passed down with conviction. The three that remained as the oldest generation passed down stories with values and strong life lessons embedded in them. They were messages that the advantaged of their time would never have heard or learned.

The core group all endured much hardship. They endured extreme poverty and challenge to survive. The next generation remembered it well also. There was rarely meat on the table at mealtime. As a result, there were unconventional sources of nourishment. There were many hand-me-downs and scraping to provide base necessities. But in this second generation's stories, there was nothing but gratitude and praise from the efforts of their parents for providing what they could. The hungry nights, those without an adequate meal, were forgotten. The ridicule from schoolmates over the holes in their shoes, dresses, or pants were no longer remembered. One said at the table of the most recent gathering that there was so much of one another and their support that they didn't even know that they were poor. It could have been the numbers of their families, the surrounding of one another with relatives of like condition and disadvantage. Or rather, it could have been the advantages, the feeling of their love, their comradery and commitments to one another that overshadowed their disadvantages. The sacrifices of each for one another opened new doors, doors that a richer person would never find.

Each gathering of the Kirkpatrick family was such a testament to the benefits and power of family, in this case a disadvantage one. The families were now quite often much better off financially. It came from professions requiring hard work and commitment.

It came from them pulling together. It could only be hoped that with the passing of the core, it didn't change the strong and powerful current that still ran through this family and gave them special attributes and strength. Their spirt domains were strong and helped support this.

Insanity is another form of disadvantage. It does not come from a spirit or spirit domain. It primarily comes from a mind that isolates itself from the spirit's offering. When misconceptions and self-realities from within a mind can no longer find solid ground with true reality and truths in the world, the mind becomes unstable. When one no longer knows truths from self-created fiction, the mind's picture of what actually is becomes blurred and frighteningly inconsistent from day to day. The being becomes completely out of sync with the views of the world and what others tell and show them. They cannot find commonality with any natural foundation. They become disconnected to all the components of their being and become insane. Their only cure is to find and re-partner with a spirit. Rare and usually guardian-directed help as gifted by a pure domain becomes the cure.

It's not a perfect picture. Yet very little in the real world is. It's about like and unlike finding their niches. It's about balance and supporting diversity. The unfortunate creates opportunities for good spirits to show their goodness and to create a special type of love. It grows additions to the stores of the domain and adds to the learning. It's part of pure nature's plan.

Contention for a Destiny

A spirit's destiny is a sequence of paths specifically designed for a spirit to follow throughout its life within the beings. Destinies are of the spirit but enacted through the other components of being. Thus, the being must take ownership and is a crucial participant in the achievement of each destiny. Destinies are assigned and shared as one when life begins. The spirits are destinies' carriers and guardians. The spirit's role with regard to a destiny is to deliver and to support the being in achieving the destiny. They are to act as a guide to navigate the being down each of destiny's chosen paths. Spirits provide each being, each life, with the map to follow and the signs to observe and act on to achieve each destiny. Destiny originates from the highest natural order and is entrusted to the spirits to ensure that it and the being achieve them to their fullest extent.

The community of earthly spirits share two driving and high-order destinies in common. These form a base purpose and the framework for the spirits and the beings to value and secure. The first of these is to preserve and strengthen the position of its nature and nature's type against those unlike itself. This destiny affects all spirits equally and serves as a guardian to ensure that the balance of good and evil efforts and activities in the world are maintained. It preserves the optimal earthly mix and effect of the two most potent influences, good and evil. It keeps the pools of good and the pools of evil constantly and continuously filling and flowing with new additions. It keeps the good and evil domain stores freshly stocked, always updated and current. It reinforces the nature.

The second of the shared and common high-order destinies is to influence human civilization toward a point on the circular path of life. The intent of this destiny is to designate evolutionary stages and points of history. It pinpoints the aggregate measure and state of the civilization's domains and natures. It defines the specific and defining position on the circle that determines, for any point, the spirit natures' advantages or disadvantages. Each incremental degree of movement around the circle defines a change in power and advantage for one of life's natures or components. Where the measure lands on the circle is crucial to all spirits and components of the being.

These above directives are the primary and defining destinies of spirits. All spirits and their assigned natures will strive to serve these common destinies above all else.

Being more specific regarding the first of the common destinies, each spirit is destined to try to tip the balance of the world's good or evil toward the side of its own nature's type. In the case of a mixed domain, each spirit works to provide advantage based on its separate defining nature, thus causing opposing pressures and intentions within any one domain's space. What is thus evident is that a destiny is an individual spirit-by-spirit responsibility. Domains do not own destinies; spirits do. Marketing, planning, and supporting the cause and well-being of its own nature must come first and foremost of importance to each spirit, regardless of other spirits intentions or the domain's mix. Of course, serving its nature comes easily for the spirit because it is inherent to their makeup. Each nature is a small part of a global nature that dictates and governs its parts. The product of the nature is its effect to an overall influence on the world. This force of nature initiates influence, resulting in activity that drives out its cause and destinies.

A single influence or single activity of good or of evil is significant and important to the instigating spirit and its destiny. Yet put in perspective, it is not so significant in the overall scheme of things. A single act or event will not so much affect the overall measure weighing good and evil, even though there might occur in an isolated instance or snapshot in time an action on a destiny that could be perceived as if it has a strong enough effect to add change to the world. It's unlikely that it will come from a single domain segment. It might appear, in its isolation or localization, to affect a moment of change in the balance of power between the natures. But in the grander scheme of reality, this is fortunately only a mirage, intended as simply a hopeful moment of a spirit's selective reality and hope. It lasts only an instant. It soon melts away into the reality of the world where the product of all spirits' initiating activity and creating instances consistent with their good and evil natures is neutralized in the aggregate effect.

Good and evil from the spirits and the beings in which they reside flood the earth with extreme volume and frequency. Each instance, each influence and effect, is owned and attended by an inspiring spirit. Each influence and effect is used to fill the spirit's stores with information units within its domain. Equal efforts on the part of good-natured and evil-natured spirits throughout the earth ensure that, in their aggregate, no advantage will form for either nature, either in numbers or in significance of these events, no matter the momentary impact that may arise from any single event. It simply ensures a full bounty and balance of contributions to the total of all spirits and spirit domains. It is a process that maintains equality, not necessarily of each portion within each domain but in the rolled-up account of the whole of all the domain's stores. It ensures that there are equal additions to both good and evil information and instances. A spike or dip in the measures of any nature's contribution at any given instance offsets the other nature's contributions at another given instance to balance the overall results. Thus, it is the common destiny of all spirits to contribute to the overall addition of instance and influence within their domains in support of their spirit natures and to ensure a natural balance in the aggregates.

Activity produces instance and experience, thus adds to the knowledge pool of the domain. Knowledge and experience feed the spirit. It serves the spirit's needs, natures, and purposes. Activity, experience, and influence are the throughput of destiny, which is the master source and inspiration. In turn, the destiny also generates and serves activity and influence. It's a reciprocating and circular arrangement between all these elements of the domain. They flow together and can be represented by a circle, another circle within the master circle of life. The outer circumference is that which houses the destiny of the civilization as a whole. The inner circle is the spirits, the natures, the spirit-specific destinies, the activities, and the spirit influence on the individual. Each fit and relates to the other. Each drives the being to what it will be and what it will do within its lifetime. Only within the inner circle do the separate and individual spirits have control to influence and guide the being. As this influence is accepted, a balanced control and protection of the natures by the spirits will exist.

Specific to the second common destiny, spirits are also driven to influence the being as a part of the civilization of beings toward common goals and common positions. They are to influence calibration and charting to a position on life's evolutionary circle, the circle of life. The intention is to move their being, and the civilization, to a quadrant that best serves and provides advantages to the spirit's nature. Of course, as all spirits are working simultaneously toward this same purpose, each spirit's influence and effect on the final overall destination is miniscule. Yet each is important to establishing the true aggregate. The position that is finally derived is that which is representative of the overall cumulative mix of spirits and natures in all the civilization. Directing the traffic to this end is the spirit's common and shared destiny. The point on the circle is perpetually moving. The efforts to establish the measure are continual, just like the activities and influences from the spirits, their natures. Thus, that which is dictated by the position is also constantly changing. It allows situation and circumstance of the world to be every changing, ever evolving.

These common and shared destinies are not freely elected by the spirit or the domain but rather are chosen for them. These destinies, as well as every form of spirit destiny, are handed down to them from nature's master plans for the earth's creatures. In the grand designs of nature, destinies drive evolution itself through the quadrants of life's eras on the earth. However, it is not the spirit's destiny to bring life's circle to full closure. This destiny is planted within the nonspirit components of the being. A spirit will not usually position a being to its end. Full closure is not of benefit to the spirit or its nature. The circle will not close while the spirits of the being maintain some degree of influence. Thus, and although it is the spirit's most dangerous and risk-filled strategy, the evil-natured spirit looks only to advance the civilization around the circle into its third and early fourth quadrants. Here, it gains advantage over the good-natured ones. But it will never push for a position too far into the later stages of the outer circle where the civilization is placed in jeopardy of extinction. Contrary, the good-natured spirits strive to avoid risk to the being altogether and look to resist the advancement around the circle to any point beyond the midpoint. All points before the midpoint represent those of balance between themselves and the evil-natured ones. These are points where the good natures are most effective and find occasional advantage.

Destinies fall within the outermost and determining circle but not upon it. Only the being, only the civilization, can designate the point on the circle. Spirits, natures, and destinies can only coax and influence. They reside within the circle. Their links to the specific points on the circle's circumference are many. There is one link from each being. The influences and the pull come from many sources and points of reference, each originating from a spirit and their natures. Each creates constant and minute incremental movements in the position of the civilization on the circle. Changes in the strength and in the influence of a spirit and spirit nature are what cause change in a civilization status. Each has a small effect in the overall positioning on this circle. It's why as we grow older; we look to our past in surprise to see how much things have changed. In each moment, in each year, it doesn't seem so significant; but over the entire span of a lifetime, change happens without our detection. The beings, each spirit, and each nature influencing the being change with time. Ultimately, it's the beings that register these changes by how much, and when they occur. Spirits and natures provide the raw materials to initiate or control change as long as the other components of the being allow it. They influence based on their natures. But the being determines the point on the circle. The spirit only renders influence.

The primary and common spirit destiny to and influence the point and position on life's circular path originates from nature's plan of evolution. Closure of the circle completes the evolutionary cycle. Although it might seem extreme, there is intent and value derived from closure. It allows a natural cleansing and purging of flaws, of philosophical and genetic damage in the current generation and cycle of existence. This slow evolutionary process toward extinction is called the circle of life. Spirits are not its source. They simply play a role. Compared with the evolutionary cycle of plants and simpler forms of life, the process for humans is a more extended version than that governing these other more basic life-forms. The key difference between human, even animal forms is in its extended duration. It's really much more extended compared with the cycle created for the earth's plant life. A plant's life cycle completes within only a season's duration. The basic design is, however, the same whether for a plant, an animal, or a human. But for plants, with benefit of the spring's warmth, they are created. With the fall's chill, the entire species wilts away and dies. It dies only to recreate in the next spring period without blemish of the previous cycle. The cleansing of disease and purging of flaws and damage created from mid-cycle summer heat and stresses is healed and swept away before the new cycle arrives with the new year. The next generation starts anew, stronger and more plentiful than the last. Animals and humans follow a similar process as do plants, but unlike the plant's limited duration of life they are afforded significantly more time to develop. Instead of four seasons, their time is measured in the four quadrants of life's circle. One cycle for these more complex forms of species is the span of one civilization's existance. It can range from hundreds to thousands of years. This is the case with the human species.

The catalyst for change in humans, unlike for plants, is not the weather. But rather, it is the being's reliance on the spirit's guidance and influences. Civilizations exist for centuries before eventually withering away into obsolescence caused by their own being's self-reliance, self-inflicted, self-indulged damage and decay. The being's abandonment of the spirit and domain influence brings about a withering end to their cycle. It comes from a departure and rebuking of the guiding insight and protections of their spirit domain. The cycle eventually comes to a close. It closes until a new civilization is allowed to germinate and blossom, renewed, and to start a new era predominantly pure in spirit, domain, and spirit influence. Spirits have carried out their roles in these cycles since creation. They are nature's gauge for when a cycle comes to a close. It is when they are no longer able to achieve their destinies and purposes through us beings that a purging is in order. It is when we close spirits' influence out of our circle of life that we are doomed.

So what about the pure spirits? Are their contributions to the common and shared destinies more significant? All spirits, both evil natured and good natured, look to the pure-natured domains of their type for help and direction with their destinies, especially those spirits that are assigned to a common and mixed domain. The pure domains are constants. From the pure spirit's perspective, the nature's destiny is clear, undiluted, and unalterable. This is in contrast to the mixed domains where differing natures, interests, and positions within the domain space are negotiated and compromised, some of this to seek harmony and compatibility within the domain space, other times to gain dominance and advantage. It is in the pure domains where the nature's position and purpose are retained and referable as uncontaminated and uncompromised. They represent the vision and the standard for the like-natured spirits in the mixed domains to follow should they lose their way or should their common destinies ever become blurred and diluted. Through the pure domain's vision and achievement of their destinies, isolated, localized, and temporary changes in the position and advantage of a nature's power can be won between good and evil interests. It is in the power of the pure domain and their effect on civilization that the balance, or lack thereof, is evidenced. These pure domains are the surest barometers for which quadrant the civilization currently resides. Through the first two quadrants of life's circle, pure good- and pure evil-natured domains exist in fairly equal numbers. It is in the third quadrant where this begins to change, where pure evil-natured domains begin to outnumber the pure good-natured ones.

For each spirit, the common and shared destinies govern its actions and priorities according to its nature. Primary destinies, however, do not give the spirit its unique characteristics or purpose. This comes from a second type of destiny. Each spirit is also responsible for delivery on at least one spirit-specific destiny; most have more than one. These are what gives specific purpose and effect within the being. Spirit-specific destinies don't need to be particularly significant, nor do they need to have particularly large impact or effect. Rather, most are of the variety where they represent the formation of a single block in the foundation of a greater destiny. They are many times achieved in support of subsequent and additional steps for another destiny to be supported in a future generation. Each action, incident, or experience relating to the destiny is absorbed and collects within the stores of the spirit domain. A current destiny might simply be an incident or action completed for storage within the domain for a future domain's reference. Destinies are, for the most part, simply vehicles of purpose. Spirits build on each lifetime's purpose until eventually achieving a finished state, the ultimate, specific destiny of the spirit's journey through many lives. This final product, as well as the other spirits-specific and unique contribution to the primary and shared spirit destinies, is what drives the spirit and its being.

The key difference between the spirit-specific destiny and its primary and common destinies is that each spirit nature owns its spirit-specific destinies. Spirits, in tandem with all others, jointly own the primary and common destinies. Primary ones will be achieved through numbers. Omissions by one will be compensated by the greater and correcting efforts of those who follow. Allowance for error is greatest for these. The impact of one spirit's effort, or lack thereof, is lessened by the effect from the masses. To the contrary, achieving spirit-specific destinies rests entirely on the single spirit. The impact of omission for a destiny of this type is far more significant to both its current and its future purposes. There are no spirits in waiting or to back up and support, correct, or fill the void left by the failed and unachieved spirit-specific destiny. In the end, after each assignment to a being is complete and each era of time brought to a close, the spirit returning to the free and unassigned pool is evaluated based on their contribution to the overall accounting of achieved destinies. It is as if each is a piece to the patchwork of a grand quilt representing life's master plan. It's important that the patches are not left missing from the pattern. When put up for display, it's the omissions that will first be noticed. It's the omissions that will devalue the overall product.

Destinies within the domains are usually a mix of good and evil. Good spirits have good destinies. Evil spirits have evil destinies. What is added to the overall balance of power between good and evil lies in the abilities of spirits of each domain to succeed in achieving all their destinies. Evil-natured spirits tend to be most aggressive and focused on delivering on their destinies. They tend to push for results at any cost to their being. Good-natured spirits tend to be more cautious of the effect that achieving their destinies will have on the being. Good-natured spirits tend to guard against taking risks except in drastic cases, always questioning and rationalizing to avoid undesirable incident and unintended and undesirable contribution to the evil stores of the domain.

Achieving an evil nature's destiny seems to come with more dramatic an impact than achieving those destinies of the good natures. Achieving destinies of the good natured, on the other hand, are less dramatic but tend to have greater long-term impact. With such contrast in the effect and approach toward achieving destinies between good- and evil-natured residents of the domain, it's not surprising that much conflict and contention for dominance and focus arises within the domain. Conflicting destinies of the spirits or conflict arising from the plans to achieve the destinies within the domain is common. Several of the types of conflicts that spirits experience includes actions by one spirit that jeopardize the ability of another spirit to achieve its destiny. Also, conflict can arise from an assigned destiny that is inconsistent with the spirit's own nature, such as a good spirit destined to do an act that is generally considered evil for the sake of good. Finally, a third type of conflict comes from two or more spirits of the domain having destinies that are in direct opposition to or in contention with one another. The following are some life examples.

Evan Filmond was a national hero. He was a soldier. He had won many medals for his bravery in battle. It was as if he was invincible. Even as a boy, he was the athlete that took risks and pushed his dexterity and abilities to the limits. He was a daredevil, pure and simple. He had little regard for his nor other's limitations of their body. His domain pushed for new frontiers, for conquering obstacles and surviving unnecessary risks. His domain contained a mix of two evil-natured spirits and one good-natured spirit. Of the two evil-natured, one was strong and dominant and the second weak and moderately dominant. The third spirit was a good-natured one but weak, controlled, and diluted by the others. It was allowed few opportunities in the dominant roles of the domain. When it was allowed dominance, it was only when deemed non-intrusive, harmless, and appropriate by the stronger evil-natured ones.

The stronger and most dominant evil-natured one's destiny was to test the limits of a human's physical gifts. It held little regard for the single life. It was to search the being's breaking points, how far before the ultimate sacrifice. Evil spawned aggression and would benefit greatly by knowing these boundaries. This spirit tended to influence and expose the being to excess and harmful consequences. It influenced the being not only to physical limits of exertion and dexterity but also to limits including those involving drugs and alcohol. It encouraged the being to test limits in its use of devices, such as cars. It pushed the being to drive fast and carelessly. Essentially, it encouraged Evan to be one to try almost anything once and to its fullest extent. It drove him to risks that a lesser controlling domain would not condone, certainly not those dominated by good-natured spirits.

The other two spirits of his domain frequently questioned the actions and tactics of the most powerful one among them. This caused contention within the domain. It drove the strong and most dominant evil-natured spirit even harder. The other two regularly feared that their being might not survive through the trials placed on it by the dominant evil-natured spirit of its domain, not long enough to allow these other two to achieve their destinies in this assigned lifetime.

Needless to say, the domain was not a cohesive one. It accounted for Evan's off-center and changing character and personality. In his current role as a soldier, Evan charged through the battle lines as one not thinking about death. He was driven by his evil-natured spirit's destiny. This destiny did not allow for hesitation or fear. His spirit was a strong motivator and driver within him in combination with his mind's guide. Each success, each battle that he survived, every weaker-spirited and less aggressive enemy he killed further fed his destiny, fed his domain's stores with information and experience available for future assignments and for present and future like-natured ones to feed from. It would add to the evil-natured wealth of information within the domains of spirits, particularly his domain and those it shared with.

But even as the destiny and the spirit and the domain were achieving their purpose, the being was eventually felled. A bullet hit its heart. Through it all, the destiny was realized and fulfilled. The limit that the evil-natured spirit sought to know, the limit to the physical component's abilities, was determined. Evan was again a hero in battle, but on this occasion, his medal would be sent elsewhere, not to be pinned to his chest. Rather, it would be sent to his family back home in honor of his actions.

His spirits were freed to spend a brief period in the unassigned pool before returning again in another with another destiny. For this life, two spirits return to the unassigned pool without new knowledge and information that should have been gathered from achieving their destinies. They would not have information added to their spirit stores to be used by the next being in which they would reside. How much of an impact their unfinished destinies would have was not yet known, but there was now an omission and potential flaw in their ability to support their futures. Only the one dominant evil-natured spirit would benefit. The stores to be used by the evil-natured ones had grown as the result of the one evil nature's destiny being completed. Yet it was at the cost of two small holes in the fabric of life's master plan as well as the life of one human being from the current generation of beings.

On the other side of the battle line, lying deeply and securely within his bunker was Saul Montgomery. He never aspired to be a hero. It was not in his destiny to test the limits of his physical component. He did not join this war to be pinned with medals, but today one of his spirits' destinies was to be fulfilled. It would come as a surprise to the other spirits of his domain.

It would be an action completely inconsistent with the spirit's nature.

Saul's domain was made up of two good- and one evil-natured spirit. One of his good-natured spirits was strong and dominant. The other was moderately strong to weak. The evil-natured spirit was also strong and dominant. The evil-natured one, particularly its zeal to exercise its nature, was what drove Saul to military service, that and the draft. Saul did not intend to kill anyone. On the whole, he was passive. In his mind and domain, his only reason for being here was duty and patriotism. He wanted his family to be proud that he served his country. He could always take orders well. He was disciplined and accommodating. He could march. He could exist in the worst of conditions, but he wasn't anxious to be tested under fire. He was anxious for his term to end before he would be forced into actions or into acts that his two good-natured spirits would regret in the long run.

While he was enlisted, he gave encouragement to the others of his platoon and promoted unity and teamwork. The closer he got to battle action, the more time he spent convincing himself that the conflict he was in was for a good cause, but it never became his cause. He was not so committed to it as to take a life or to get himself shot for it. He did, however, carry out every order. This was why he now found himself lying in this bunker, with bullets and shrapnel whizzing over his head. He hoped that no enemy came into his vicinity.

But today was an exception to all he hoped to avoid, everything his good-natured spirits had influenced him to avoid. He was in the thick of the battle. Many of his friends, those whom he and his spirits had shared information and experiences, were dying beside him. Human beings with domains of good-natured spirits like his own, spirits that were displaced in this environment like his, were being taken down with frequency. The weaker good-natured spirit from Saul's domain found itself temporarily allowed dominance of the domain for only an instance, while the other two assessed the situation and established their plans of action to survive this situation.

At that instance, Saul saw the enemy hurdling toward his bunker. This enemy was a fearless killing machine. A number of his platoon mates were falling backward, hit by his fire. Drastic measures were called for to stop this evil-natured one from inflicting more harm on the beings of his platoon and from releasing additional domains of their good-natured and evil-natured spirits within. In a whirlwind moment, the weaker good-natured spirit directed Saul's attention to aim his rifle and pull the trigger. The madman fell meters in front of him, shot through the heart. Saul froze for a moment in shock. After the adrenaline subsided, he pulled the rifle down, buried his head in his chest, and cried. Those around him saw what he'd done. They knew he had saved them. A new hero, one not desiring such recognition had emerged.

As for Saul, he was ashamed. He wanted no medal. It was his weaker good-natured spirit's destiny to kill Evan. It was his purpose to contain the indiscriminate damage being done by Evan. Yet it was totally against this good spirit's nature. It was an evil that its destiny had forced him to commit. The paradox of it was that it was an evil done for the sake of good. The inconsistency of it caused confusion and conflict within the spirit and domain. The memory and the incident, with all its details, filled the domain. It was one instance that haunted the good-natured parts of this domain for a lifetime. It fed the evil-natured one. It fulfilled a destiny. But it did not seem conceivable from a good-natured spirit.

Saul was alive, but his good-natured spirit had lost its focus and its identity in all the confusion. Nothing good had come from this, nothing for the "good" stores of the domain. Only evil could count its winnings after all the cards had been played. The balance of power within Saul's domain was now shifted.

Was it murder justified for destiny's sake? Did removal of a being through evil justify the deed that was done to counter it? It did not. It simply added more to the outer circle of the domain's stores. For a moment, for the current moment, it seemed quite significant. On the whole of life's plan, however, it was not significant at all. Other considerations and events would have far more bearing on life's long-term plans. One such consideration was Evan's two spirits who had been deprived of their opportunities to achieve their destinies. These would be far more significant to the whole than Saul's recent actions.

Saul's spirit and nature would one day gain an understanding of the good that it had done. Saul's experience begs the question Do destinies go wrong? Can a destiny backfire on a nature, like what seemed to occur with Saul's weaker spirit? It would seem, in an instance like Saul's, that the answer might be yes and perhaps by design as well. Yet a nature cannot be careful. It cannot be tentative for the sake of its immediate aftermath, the historical significance of the actions that achieving its spirit's destinies may create. The natures do not keep a tally on good and evil's scorecard. Neither spirit or natures determine the destinies that they draw. They simply carry them out. It's at a higher order that decisions are made of what destinies will bring and to what overall long-term effect they will create.

What seems like a mistake at a moment can make a dramatic and crucial turnabout in the future. It's all about balance, and it's all about timing; the whole of existence must be measured in its entirety as opposed to single frames. Spirits recognize this; beings do not. Saul's situation would become as such. His actions would yield addition to the good stores of the community in the future. It would take time and further play. Here's another example.

In an earlier civilization on the earth, there existed a king named Eriphidas and a kingdom named Zurxus. This civilization had long since seen extinction, but in earlier times, it flourished. Eriphidas was its third king. The first two, his grandfather and father, were of mixed-natured domains but good nature dominant. They ruled the kingdom with wisdom and treated its many subjects fairly. The kingdom was a good place for all its inhabitants to live and raise their families. Its subjects were happy.

After the death of Euripides's father, the rule was passed to him. He was the first of the lineage to be of an evil-natured domain. To further accentuated the change, it was a pure domain, making him quite dominant and powerful. The other components of Euripides's being, although certainly not lacking in potential, followed obediently to the influences and tendencies of the spirits within him. Timing was also a crucial factor. When Eriphidas took power, the civilization was just moving into the second quadrant of the circular model of life. It was a time when beings still relied heavily on the spirit influences. This gave his domain advantage over his other components. It gave his evil natures impetus and authority to dominate and drive the beings' thoughts and actions.

And even though it was a time when good and evil natures were primarily balanced in their influence and presence, Eriphidas was an exception. He was completely evil. The destinies of his three spirits were intertwined quite dastardly. His primary destiny was to secure advantage to the evil natured of the kingdom. There was no one in the tiny kingdom that could match or counter his pure and evil spirit's power, nor was there anyone to match his physical prowess. It was a lethal combination and quite unfortunate for the subjects of this isolated civilization to contend with. Eriphidas represented a combination that could create a significant yet isolated impact to the balance of natural power within the single frame of time and space marking this civilization.

Euripides's evil rule was to bring hardship on the good natured of the kingdom. It was to give favor to the evil natured. He chose as his legacy to eliminate good from the Zurxus population. His plan focused on the highest concentrations of good-natured spirits from within the kingdom. His methods were brutal and barbaric. The result was a partial spirit good-nature genocide. The victims were any and all those with good natures in the kingdom. The advantages were all Euripides's. He was of a pure domain. He could transfer and dissect the natures and tendencies of his subject's domains. He could isolate the good from the evil spirits. As he came into contact with his subjects, he would mentally classify them and remember. If good natured, he would find reason or opportunity to order them to his dungeons and then torture them. They would rarely emerge from their captive state. After a period, he began putting them to death.

As he had success with the segments of the population that he had regular contact with, his confidence grew. This, in turn, fed his desires to expand the scope of his plan to something much bigger. He wanted the effect of his destiny to be more widespread. He schemed opportunities and plans to evaluate everyone in the kingdom, to identify and to eliminate good altogether. He proclaimed that every subject of the kingdom should visit his palace once per year to pay him homage. It was to be as they reached milestones, such as birthdays or anniversaries. It would be at this event that he would sort through their domains and assess their natures. The decree went out.

At first, the kingdom's subjects saw this as a good thing, an opportunity to share time with a king. The inhabitants accepted his invitation with excitement and anticipation. As they visited, their king welcomed them personally with open arms and a full banquet in their honor. He transferred to their domains one by one to determine their makeup. Filtering out the good-natured domains from the evil-natured ones was a slow and deliberate process, but Eriphidas made it his priority. It was to serve his destiny. The good ones were removed from the community by Euripides's guards as they left the palace. They were then placed in the dungeons. The evil ones, on the other hand, were rewarded with a bag of grain and Euripides's mental record of approval.

For several weeks, the plan was working perfectly. He was feeling very accomplished. Unfortunately, it was an extreme case of serving one's destiny. It was not as nature had intended this destiny to be carried out. He was very much out of control. It was that of an overzealous destiny resulting in criminal results. It wasn't long before questions specific to the whereabouts of the missing members of the community began to flow among and between the people. The common factor of each disappearance wasn't hard to isolate. All had paid their homage at the palace sometime after they were last seen.

It also wasn't long thereafter before a leak from the palace guards reached the people. The rumor among the palace guards was that the king was sending hordes of people indiscriminately to his dungeons. These unfortunate ones were not being released. The people were horrified to think that such an act could be ordered by their king or from any within their community. Many abandoned their appointments with the government and its armies. Most abandoned their plans to pay homage to their king. As their time came up, they instead chose to go into hiding.

The numbers coming before Eriphidas began to dwindle. By this time, however, Euripides's actions and this brutality had left a significant effect on the balance in numbers of good-natured and evil-natured domains in his kingdom. The standing of the good-natured spirits within the civilization had already been weakened. The good natured who remained kept themselves primarily in hiding or maintaining a very low profile. As a result, they had little impact or effect on the civilization. When there was an isolated or infrequent show of revolt or an isolated forum to address their frustration, Eriphidas would send his evil faithful and would have them either killed on the spot or captured and filling his dungeons, where their fate would be the same. Only the timeline for those captured and sentenced to the dungeon would be extended to allow Eriphidas time to administer more pain and torture.

Through all the success that Eriphidas seemed to be having at the onset of his rule, he failed to realize the impact he was making on the future. With each death of a being and release of the good-natured spirits within them to the free and unassigned pool, this pool was filling disproportionately with good-natured spirits. These same good-natured spirits would soon be reassigned to the next generation. The manner in which they were dispatched to the unassigned pool gave them favor in the order in which they would be returned and special rights ordained by nature's highest powers. Each would be awarded special rights of revenge. New births in the kingdom, even including that of Euripides's own son, contained a disproportionately larger number of strong and dominant good-natured each being assigned revenge destinies within their domains. They held as a spirit-specific destiny to exact a measure of torment and discomfort upon the king and those loyal to the king. These were the ones who sealed the previous good generations, past life's fate and stole their past domain's opportunity to complete destinies. This generation's life and domain's destinies would not be so easy to destroy by their king. Those that returned were gifted and supported by the tools and powers that allow spirit justice.

The civilization's mix between the good and evil natures once again found overall balance, yet the distribution within the population became quite distorted and uniquely different between the generations. There were a disproportionately larger number of older surviving beings with evil-natured domains. The younger generation, those who were stronger and positioning the civilization to the next plateau of evolution, was predominantly good natured. The power of revenge was heavily on the good-natured side and laced their destiny's missions. Had these good-natured fourth-generation beings chosen to employ their powers of revenge unilaterally, the older evil natures would surely have been the next wave of spirits and natures to fill the unassigned pool. Fortunately, most did not choose revenge. Forgiveness is a common characteristic of the good nature. Even upon Eriphidas, most did not exact a measure of revenge. It was enough for them to watch his influence and power curtailed to the older evil-natured population dwindle to near nothingness among the changing and growing good-natured population under his rule. He found himself now mostly hiding in his palace, confined and tortured by his ineffectiveness and fear that ghosts of his past would catch up to him and make him a victim of his own device. He grew old and insane from his paranoia.

The end result of Euripides's acts of poor judgment and planning was that Zurxus began to see disproportional and unequal mixes of the natures with each new generation. With disproportionate numbers of evil, followed by good natures, a change in every other of its subsequent future generations emerged. These trends grew burdensome on the beings of the civilization, particularly on the mind and body components of the beings. With the inconsistency in the spirit makeup between parents and children, generation to generation, relationships across the generations began to suffer. The institution of family began to suffer. Spirits of different generations repelled. The other two components, the mind and the body, still held close ties to their predecessor generations and began to resent the spirit conflict and to lose faith in spirit influence on those relationships. They took on more responsibility for guidance and control, shielding the spirits from the being's considerations and influence. They could no longer operate effectively through the swings from good to evil influence from generation to generation. They grew impatient waiting through generations for the redistribution nd rebalancing of natures to again level. It hadn't corrected itself through the next four generations. Beings in the civilization cast off the spirit influence on them. It forced Zurxus prematurely into fourth-quadrant conditions. Soon thereafter, Zurxus was no more.

In the final analysis, it seemed that Zurxus was a failed civilization. Nature had apparently corrected its mistake. It would seem that there couldn't be anything of value taken from this atrocity. Yet in the world of the spirit, it was simply a cycle of life. It was a special one. It was one that would live on forever through the lasting information it provided and as a model for learning. It was, and will forever be, an example of how disregard for the balance in the natures will prove to advantage neither good nor evil natures. In the holistic view, Zurxus was a special example of something failed but of value to ensuring the future lesson for the greater whole.

Eriphidas would never be held in high esteem. He was an evil and ineffective king. He brought ruin to his kingdom. He wasn't the first, nor will he be the last of his type. Spirits and domains of future generations have and will carry the lessons learned from him and his destiny. Eriphidas spirits live on. Spirits do not die. The experiences and the instances of these spirits carried forward in the domain stores of the beings currently assigned these spirits. The history and natures live as do the spirits. The value to most of the spirit world is in the lessons and the incentives not to allow the same mistakes in the future or certainly not to make them to such a degree as Eriphidas did. It helps set boundaries for all future domains, pure or not, evil or good, to adhere to.

Yet as is always the case, there are exceptions. History has produced other Eriphidases in subsequent civilizations to that of Zurxus. They, too, attempted to rid their kingdoms of the different element and after a time faced their justice like that in Zurxus. Their rules, too, were dismantled. Their names also now rest in infamy. There will be others in the future. It will bring times of chaos to balance and offset the times of order, just as good is to balance with evil. The world is filled with balanced opposites. Fortunately, most are not of the extreme variety, but the extremes do and will occur naturally and as planned.

There are no mistakes in destinies, even though some may appear as such. There are no mistakes in spirits or in natures. There's no fault or deviating from life's master plan. Episodes of the extremes of good and evil natures create the most dramatic examples, the largest impacts to the stores of the spirit's domains. These may appear as a mistake or deviation when looked on from a channeled, limited, and shortsighted view. But one must observe and gather results through many generations or a few evolutions of civilizations. Then you will see the reason for the outcome and effect of each event, each action, and how it eventually lines up and fits into life's grand plan. The feelings and effects that come from good are accentuated and enhanced after a period of extreme evil and vice versa. It does the world good to be reminded and to have norms jilted at times. There is purpose and destiny in everything, even if at the time we feel it is a mistake of nature.

So, is killing justified for destiny's sake? The answer will be different depending on if it is asked of the spirit or asked of the being. In any regard, a spirit might reply yes but with great reserve. The repercussions must be weighed carefully. All spirits return after the death of a being. The effect of death on the spirit is minimal as compared with that of the being. Death to a being is final. Removal of the spirit from a being by killing generally perpetuates the effects on the future by additions to that spirit's internal stores of history, knowledge and experiences and its destinies for the future. Any rewards or concessions it might be granted for revenge will have greater impact and when returned through a future assignment on the earth, both positive and adverse, to the balance of a future generation's good and evil influences and the good-to-evil scorecard than the effect of the original killing. A destiny to kill must be considered very carefully, not so much by the spirit but within the master plan. Most killings are not of the spirit's doing. Most are not of a destiny. It is truly a rare calling for the spirit.

To the contrary, most are from the body and mind components. Over time, they have learned from the spirit how to kill from its rare employment of killing as a tactic to serve a destiny. Unfortunately, they have not learned the discretions and controls over the use of these destructive measures as have the spirits. This learned behavior was not intended and has created deviation from life's master plan. This represents a flaw in the master plan, one originating from the being, not the spirit. It represents an undesirable and unplanned variable. This is unfortunate and creates a need to rectify the problem, along with others as they cumulate, by destroying the civilization periodically. It is one factor in the establishment and monitoring of the position on the circle of life. It is one that accelerates the movement around the circle a full measure. Nature does not allow its flaws to remain forever. It purges them as thresholds are exceeded.

To conclude the example involving Saul, he still housed two spirits within his domain that needed to fulfill their destinies. Unfortunately, these destinies were in direct contention with each other. The destiny of his good-natured spirit was to keep the domain out of contact with other evil-natured spirits and evil-nature-dominated domains. Saul was to be kept confined for a while so as not to release the recent stores of his domain to the evil of the world. His memories and his experience while in the bunker were a strong tonic to the evil-natured spirit population. This was because the addition to its domain was created in contradiction to the good spirit's nature. This item from the domain's stores was rare in the spirit world and was potent magic to the evil nature, even more potent than that from a pure evil domain. The destiny of Saul's dominant good-natured spirit was to keep Saul as inconspicuous as possible until it could search out a pure good-natured domain to help it, one with which Saul's domain could share and bond to find guidance and protection enough to set itself right again.

For the three months after the incident, the good-natured spirit created condition to allow Saul to be treated in confinement at a military hospital. The diagnosis was battle fatigue. It would allow time for the weak good-natured spirit to partially recover from the shock. It would also buy time for the stronger good-natured spirit to work on its destiny of finding a pure good-natured domain to protect the weaker good-natured spirit. It would find Becky during this period. It would come with support of a miracle from the free and unassigned spirit pool to ones in dire need. It was one example of a miracle that was initiated without a calling from a pure domain on the earth. It was the extreme exception to the rule, that of a pure gift of nature itself. Saul was to eventually become a teacher in Becky's school.

The destiny of Saul's evil-natured spirit was to make full use of the valuable evil experience within Saul's domain stores. Its destiny was to bring the domain into contact with a pure evil-natured domain. Here, its potency could be multiplied through the powers of the pure domain. The pure one could extract the tonic from Saul's domain stores and disperse it to all in the evil-natured community. This spirit's destiny was to introduce Saul to Mr. Arthur, one it remembered from its old neighborhood. The memory would then be drawn from the stores of its domain.

It was unclear which happened first or which was more influential in the decisions affecting Saul's future, whether it was the guidance from the stronger good-natured spirit of Saul's domain leading him to a pure good being or the result of the spirit gift of a guardian from the unassigned pool taking control; or whether it was his evil-natured spirit's urgings to the being to return home to West Chester after his discharge. In any regard, Saul was pressed to return to the neighborhood in which he grew up, the neighborhood of both Becky and Mr. Arthur. Both of these parties were then available to fulfill a purpose, the remaining contrasting and conflicting destinies within Saul's domain. It became a matter of which of the two would make first contact. This was determined by which of the two conflicting spirit natures would prove more powerful.

As it turned out, Saul was first introduced to Becky. He interviewed and took a job as a physical education teacher in Becky's school. Becky's domain was soon made aware of what was stored in Saul's domain. She could sense the power of the stored experience. The spirit from Becky's domain transferred to Saul's domain. The truths were laid open to her. Her domain realized the importance of her role in this situation. First, it would need to suppress the evil-natured one, to limit its opportunities to dominate Saul's domain. She did this through one of her strongest spirits' transfers and by adding strength to the stronger good-natured one in Saul's domain. Her spirit urged it to be assertive, more dominant, and in complete control over the evil-natured one. The pure spirit from Becky helped by dominating the evil one's powers with numbers and presence in dominance.

Second, Becky's domain was to protect the vulnerable stores within Saul's domain from those that might use them for advantage. Saul needed time and other experiences, preferably good experiences, to form and insulate around the one that brought such an ordeal and misery to the weaker good-natured spirit. Additional layers of information and experience were needed between the vulnerable experience and the perimeter of the domain stores to make it difficult to get to and to shield its attracting pull toward the pure evil domain's awareness. Becky could provide this insulating wealth of knowledge and information. This she did by sharing and transferring much knowledge and experience from her own stores. She also did her best to nurse and heal Saul's troubled good spirit back to health. She provided goodness and temporary protection from evil's influence. She guarded his evil nature from making contact with Mr. Arthur. This she succeeded in doing for as long as she was able to. But another event eventually made this impossible.

It was later in the year that the destiny of the evil-natured spirit was also finally fulfilled. Saul made contact with a pure evil-natured domain. All destinies of the domain, at that point, stood as achieved. Yet it was not as planned. It was not to Mr. Arthur that Saul was introduced. Rather, it was to Brenda Doran.

Even though an extended span of time had elapsed since the first of the destinies of Saul's domain had been achieved to the last and even though the domain was faced with obstacles of conflicts and contention, all the destinies of Saul's domain were now complete. In doing so, the great tonic from Saul's domain was made available to the evil-natured spirits of the community. But by the time it was, the return of the many good-natured spirits that Evan had prematurely released from their beings in battle had also been returned in the same disproportion as they had been taken. The good from the traumatic action of Saul's weaker good-natured spirit was finally revealed.

As earthly nature would have it, many of the reassigned good-natured spirits were distributed to the neighborhoods where Saul now found himself living. They contained special power and concessions for revenge on the evil natures that might benefit from Saul's misfortune. The overall result was a countereffect to the evil nature's advantage. It was a concentration of good dispensed to the area to make things right and to reestablish balance. Some of the good-natured spirits were sent with destinies to control the damage that could be done to the balance between the good and evil natures by Saul's secret. It righted Saul. It restored good experience and instances within his domain and a new equilibrium between good and evil within the community. It diminished the memories and the power of the evil instance, allowing the focus to move to other things in Saul's domain and his life. Saul was finally healed. He lived a fulfilled and normal life. The balance in the neighborhood returned naturally.

As for the destinies of others, they are many and complex at times. Becky's spirits were all the same type and fairly consistent in terms of their attributes and strengths. In her case and in all cases of the pure domain, there is no contention or incongruence in the spirits' efforts to achieve their destinies or in the domain's approach to serve these. With the pure domain, the destinies tend to blend and become as if from one source. It gives the pure spirit advantage and special focus to achieve these destinies. It allows a pure spirit to make a fully coordinated and concentrated effort, impact, or impression toward the attainment of its destinies. Pure spirits rarely leave destinies unfulfilled.

Becky's destinies were many. Some of these were small and insignificant. Some were huge yet each a piece to her full legacy. Her destinies all involved supporting and growing goodness where it was needed. She was tasked to help suppress the advancement of her community around life's circle. Unfortunately, by the time she was born into the civilization, the quadrant that had been designated inherently brought her disadvantage. She was challenged by predominance in numbers of evil-natured spirits, especially by a greater number of pure evil-natured domains on the earth. It was a time when the evil nature was finding favor and advantage. Finding refuse in kind and advice when it was needed was difficult. Her work was plentiful. The need was truly great. Her rare attributes set her apart and tended to expose her as a target of the evil-natured majority as much as it set her up as a most valued guardian and source of strength to the good natured. Her gifts, and the draw and power that went with them, made it impossible to hide her influence. Her strong aura and the electricity radiating from her spirits and domain invaded the spaces claimed by her adversaries. It frightened them. Her strength and influence were uncharacteristically bold and attention grabbing, especially surprising and unexpected for a good-natured domain.

These domains usually avoided attention. In this case, however, due to the circumstances and the times, she had no choice. She was different. It was her destiny to be found and to be exposed to evil-natured spirits and domains. It was equally her destiny to challenge them and to be available to and surrounded by the need of the good natures. She was there for the needy good natures to seek her out for help. She was crafted to be especially pure and strong of nature to attract others to her through her strong magnetic aura and presence. On the other hand, this same aura would be a clear beacon that would allow her evil-natured counterparts to hone in and contend against her. She was a titan. As such, her time on the earth was destined. Her destinies were all significant. They were more significant than her being. Her destiny was to give totally of herself for the good that remained within the beings and domains of her community. The cost of failing in any of her destinies would be extremely significant in the final enactment of life's plans. She would not allow herself to fail in these primary missions.

But it brought her much frustration and challenge as well. Becky had so many areas to attend that even when spreading herself and her time across the whole of all needs within her community as thinly as she could, she still had to turn some away. The good natures of the neighborhood were still significant in number, even though in most instances diluted within mixed domains. It was a good sign for the current civilization. It meant that there was still hope. These good-natured spirits recognized Becky's domain as their source of strength and magic through which they could rejuvenate themselves within their mixed domains. She seemed to be their best and last hope in the area. The community of good-natured spirits held her up as their deliverer. She contained within her the ability to restore the good natured to a position of equality in power with that of the evil-natured spirits of the community.

She was like a spirit doctor. The strength of her spirit would administer remedy to ailing good natures and would prescribe the right medicine that would bring them back to full strength and health. She provided information, training, and encouragement to the good-natured community like a teacher. She provided them with reference and the tools to build their knowledge. She came to the rescue of spirits that were in trouble or in danger, like a fireman or policeman. She helped them through the hard times and to establish new starts. She helped feed the good spirit nature like a gardener and a grocer. She fed them what they needed most, good and caring acts and examples. It fed their domain stores. She was many things to many domains. But through all these vocations, she provided goodness. She provided example and renewal. Becky's domain would give the good-natured spirits new lease on their purpose and their primary destinies. She would offer advantage over their coresident evil natures. Her domain would help good natures grow stronger and more dominant. She would help them turn the tables and instead dilute the power of the evil-natured ones.

Becky's pure domain held as its primary destiny to be a countering effect to that of the pure evil domain of Mr. Arthur. It was much like a chess match between the two, each vying for the ultimate prize, to win the influences of the students and people of the community. Becky was the best hope of the neighborhood to defend the position for goodness. She was the strongest hope for righting the imbalance between evil and good. She was a gift. Her caring and support was genuine and given freely. She was respected and admired, even by those with evil-natured spirits housed within their domains. Only a few, such as Mr. Arthur, refused to acknowledge the good she was doing in the community. But he knew her to be a capable and strong adversary.

Becky's destiny included finding and then showcasing the effects and benefits of soul mate love throughout the community, including the rewards of waiting for that one special partner. The example of her and Tom's love, its strength, and its goodness would be one of her stronger legacies fast-forward into the future. In general, her loving ways influenced all that supported her and loved her. They would contribute and support with others that would extend the third quadrant of this era out several additional generations.

Finally, Becky's destinies included creating a plan for the succession of her role to another pure spirit. These efforts were occurring deep within her domain and unbeknownst to her being. Her destiny was to be taken from the earth to neutralize a greater evil. The greater evil that would cause her being's end was made known only to her inner domain. The being that she would need to prepare and pass her work and support to was only known to her spirit domain and protected deep within. This made the task of preparing for the being all the more challenging. In response to this challenge, parts of her transition needed to be left as stored memories and messages within the domains of those that would surely have future contact and sharing with the new pure domain. Becky's domain, and only her domain, would be made aware of who these messenger beings were. Their identities would be made known to her through a gift of sharing with a special clairvoyant named Madame Extrovia. One that would carry her message forward within her domain stores would be a special little girl named Susie Jamison. Becky's message would be further provided by others whom she would befriend and associate with from the community and from her hometown of Councilville.

She would leave pieces of herself in the domains of many whom she touched. These would be grown and ripened for harvesting by the next in pure good's succession chain. She would never personally meet her successor, but her domain was aware of how this new one would come to be the heir apparent. It would be one from her own family. It made the destiny especially good. She held this destiny to be most difficult because she didn't want to leave her work unfinished or her community of good unprotected. Yet it was a most critical part of nature's plans and destiny for her spirits. Sacrifice of the being would also be most difficult. It was to pave the way for another like her to come to the neighborhood and continue her work and to combat the pure evil stronghold created by Mr. Arthur. Her destiny was to make way for balance to be continued in the neighborhood and for the young people attending West Crawford High to be protected of influence and pressure from the temptations of evil.

A number of Mr. Arthur's destinies were much like Becky's, but his were the antithesis of her goodness. His destiny was to accentuate the position of the evil spirit in the neighborhood. He was to support and restoke the evil natured that had flamed out and now needed help or renewal. His destiny drove him to spread the ease and pleasures of evil as enticements across the community. He established himself as the sanctuary for those of deflated or beaten evil natures and the source of extraordinary strength to renew them. He was to bring decay and destruction to the civilization, especially to good natures. He was very influential and crafty. He made evil appear very desirable. He organized, coordinated, and led the efforts of his evil following in such ways as to fortify and focus their impact and effect on the community. He was infamous.

His destiny was to promote the things that fed the evil nature and that corrupted and degraded the good natures, such as drugs, alcohol, immorality, and crime. His destiny was to spread his poisons and his decadence throughout his community. He was to be recognized, to be a part of the headlines, to be seen as influential, powerful, and in command. He was to epitomize success at the lowest levels of the civilization. He was to train many in his ways, to recruit and entice others into his circle of disciples and followers, to grow the numbers that would spread and promote evil ways and evil-natured influences.

As he began to experience success, it then became important to ensure the longevity of his programs and campaigns. His longer-term destiny became one to develop a protégé who could one day continue his work as his successor. In this protégé, he would share all that he knew and the technique to perpetuate his influence over the community. His destiny was to shelter, protect, and nurture this protégé until it, too, was ready to be released on the community's many targets and victims where it, too, would spread its evil-natured powers and bounty on the community. Brenda Doran was his choice as his protégé. He could see the potential in her to grow her nature and her evil powers to his level.

This destiny to develop a successor was much like Becky Turner's. What was fortunate in Mr. Arthur's case and unlike that with Becky Turner was that both his spirits and his other bodily components knew his successor. Brenda Doran had been drawn to Mr. Arthur five years previous. She came to him as being of a weaker pure evil domain looking to be developed.

The relationship between them was symbiotic. Mr. Arthur benefited from her persuasive and pure powers over the mixed domains. She was very talented at recruiting followers and creating a loyal and growing market for Mr. Arthur's products. He also benefited from her special gift that only a weaker pure domain can offer, clairvoyance. On the other hand, Brenda benefited from Mr. Arthur's strength, especially from his stores of knowledge and experience. She benefited from his empire and his private marketplace and playground. It was an evil paradise.

Mr. Arthur and Brenda were an excellent combination. Only Becky stood in the way of perfection, an evil perfection. Both hated her. Both hated goodness. Brenda was the closest thing that Mr. Arthur would have to a sharing or nurturing relationship. As it was, neither he or Brenda was bound or committed to each other; rather, they were parasites of each other. This made them close. They extracted from each other all that could be taken. It made them both stronger. They were cut from the same mold. Mr. Arthur would leave Brenda well prepared to continue his work and to honor his legacy. Her development was one of his primary destinies.

Mr. Arthur's destinies include practicing different approaches from those practiced by most of his equals to achieve his evil ends. Many of his tactics were laced with risk. His destiny, as well as his nature, was to stretch the legal and moral limits of the community and test the tolerances of authority and its governing bodies. He practiced more unacceptable evils and used more extreme tactics than others. He experimented with how much an evil domain could do and get away with, to test how far it could manipulate the system and how totally it could intimidate or influence support for its needs and destinies. He would daringly and openly practice these tactics in all his dealings and appearances. He would practice evil directly under the noses of those who opposed it or those who were to regulate and had jurisdiction over it. He marveled at how he could avoid retribution or penalty. He was not only achieving his destiny but he also became a master over it. He was truly an evil mogul, a seasoned criminal, and a master manipulator of the community. His evil was pure. He worked hard to keep it so.

To do this, he avoided the effects of friendships, any sharing relationship, and carefully screened all outside influence or hindrance. He felt that friendship and sharing diluted his spirits' purity and drained him of his evil superiority. Dilution from sharing needed to be avoided if he was to maintain the highest level of his evil nature which was his destiny. Thus, he was to be a loner. His only trusted friend was to be evil. This isolated him from most of the world. It made him appear as an unhappy, unfriendly, and very dark-natured and sinister man. Appearances in this case were not deceiving. They were entirely accurate. Yet he was not entirely devoid of happiness. His happiness came in vile and odd forms. Crime, acts of immorality, hate, and abuses made him happy. He smiled as he read the daily newspaper or watched the newscast on television. He found them filled with sensational stories of evil and pain. He loved it all except the sections like the comic sections, which he abhorred for their goodness. Instead, he buried himself in the front page or lead stories. It was so rare to see anything of good in these sections. They were so safe to expose himself and his nature to. He often thought about owning a paper. It would contain only sensational front-page news.

He recognized that his destiny placed him in a position as the trailblazer for those who would follow. He was a member of a special and select breed. He represented a refined version of the pure evil domain. He intended to train lesser evil domains in how to reach their maximum potential. He would be their model. It was his destiny to be the ultimate role model. Yet this was in conflict to his guard against diluting the purity of his nature. He couldn't get too close. This is where and why he brought Brenda into the picture. He used her as his buffer and conduit. This would allow him to avoid most of the direct contact. It would ensure against mixing with less pure domains and dilution of his own. Dealing with Brenda as an intermediary would allow him to deal only with the pure evil element. It would allow him to maintain and even elevate the perception of his higher level of evil, his persona as someone very special. It would permit him his destiny to raise evil to the highest strata.

Mr. Arthur's destiny included actions aimed at assuring that the influences of the good-natured domains, particularly those of pure good-natured domains, would not supersede those of the evil nature. This was where much of his energy and focus had been directed, especially since Becky Turner arrived in the community. Mr. Arthur was driven by his destiny to deal with this special adversary before the full effect and before the powerful and change-affecting product of her pure good nature could be absorbed by the community. Becky's influences and her successes were beginning to touch, even overshadow, Mr. Arthur's claimed territories. Goodness was gaining a larger share of the neighborhood. Mr. Arthur denied the evidence, dismissed the possibilities, and snarled at the thought that he was losing ground to Becky, but he was. She was winning over a larger and larger contingency to her offerings of care and goodness. Mr. Arthur didn't understand her appeal, but it was forcing him to take personal interest and make personal contacts to confront the pure good-natured nemesis. It angered him to be required to expose his pure evil power to this challenge. It spurned the level of his ire to a point where the full extent of his advantage and his powers was being called on to address the problem. It had to be so. It was what his destiny had defined for him to do, what he'd been securing his evil purity and undiluted power for. It would be his defining moment on the earth both for his domain and his being. This would secure his legacy, his moment of grand impact. It would secure his place in the memories of those of the neighborhood. It would reverse this rare aberration and erase the embarrassment of the current moment where good was actually triumphing over evil.

It was all the result of two special domains, one good and the other Mr. Arthur's. Good-natured spirits were now achieving their destinies and changing the community for the better. It was becoming evident to all that Becky Turner-McDouglas was the greater and more effective influence. She was winning support and changing the prevalent and dominant nature of the neighborhood from evil to good. In evil's eyes, this had to stop. Mr. Arthur would see to it that Becky, through sacrifice of his own purity and to whatever degree was required, would be contained and the ensuing advantage returned to the side of the evil natured.

It had been over seven years since he'd first met Becky face-to-face. It was seven years since he'd had his first conversation with her at the apartment complex where they both lived. It was a short exchange. And even though she did not seem the threat she was today, he warned her then that she was not welcome.

He wondered why he'd never really followed up on this threat. She'd been a nemesis before today, but her impact through much of the period had been tolerable, perhaps just never drawing his immediate attention. It was now that he was realizing that her impact was significant and threatening his place in history. He'd allowed her far too much uncontested latitude. It was clear that he'd relied too heavily on Brenda's abilities to inform him of vulnerabilities and in Brenda's powers to keep Becky and her effect in check. It had been some time since there had been such a strong, pure good-natured domain in the neighborhood to contend with. He'd underestimated her influence and threat to his positions and his territories.

It was that brief moment seven years ago that he should have realized that she was to play a key part in his destiny. It was clearest today, but rather, it was then that she'd become the enemy. He should have taken action earlier. It made the here and now more crucial and the stakes much higher. She needed to be stopped. He stepped up his focus and attention on this assignment and the personal involvement necessary to begin hindering her every endeavor. She and he were competing for the same market, the same recruits of the neighborhood. Her strengths and support had grown to sufficient force to truly challenge him. The lines were drawn. There would be no lines of demarcation between the two fronts. There would be no truce. It was all or nothing now. But Becky continued to win battle after battle. Her confidence was great. This would need to be changed. As reluctant as he was to confront her directly, he acknowledged the need and the actions required to see that this changed. As Mr. Arthur viewed it, there could only be one clear winner and loser in this confrontation. The loser was not going to be him.

He was destined to win the ultimate war, even if at extreme cost. Within his destiny's allowances was the tolerance and willingness to prescribe more drastic measures to remove the irritant. It was time for these extreme measures. Becky Turner-McDouglas had evolved. She was too strong for Brenda Doran to confront. Becky had tested Brenda and he to the maximum. There was now need for strong reaction to her actions. But all the same, like a wild animal stalking its prey, he remained very careful, very patient, never allowing Becky to know or to have much advantage, especially not the advantage of knowing what he was thinking and scheming or how much he would become personally involved. There was too much at stake in this critical climax to their confrontations. Surprise was on his side. The tactics of evil would change under his direct involvement. It was now time to act differently. It was his destiny, one that he could not allow to fail. Yet he was failing.

It was far too important to both him and his kind that he turn the tables, that he changed these current trends from goodness to evil. He waited for the time when she would be most vulnerable and he most advantaged. He waited until she was burdened with an unborn child. His original plans called for only the destruction of the one pure good-natured domain, but Mr. Arthur was also one to deviate from plans and rules as he saw advantage and as it served his preference and nature, rather to go to the extremes when advantage was totally his to be used. He was not beyond doing more than the constraints of his original destiny.

Love, in particular, made Mr. Arthur's stomach turn. He hated the sight of it. It weakened him. It represented a power that he would never harness. It was his Achilles' heel. He especially hated looking from his balcony and seeing it grow in the relationship of Becky and Tom. He knew it was a powerful and infectious tonic. When protected by it, it weakened his power over those whom he would target for his influence and torment. In the case of Becky and Tom, it grew their powers, especially in her domain, the domain that he despised and directly contended against for the loyalty of the community's inhabitants. It was through Becky that good had the power to alter the balance between the natures in the neighborhood. Her influence and effect on the community was now even greater from her alliances with pure and perfect love. It was the one advantage that Mr. Arthur could not defend against.

Becky's edge over Brenda and him seemed to escalate even more after she married her soul mate, Tom. Even Tom turned out to be quite an ambassador for good as well. This expanded Mr. Arthur's effort and original plans. His destinies now needed to include a plan to destroy the bond that gave Becky and Tom such strength and advantage over him. He planned to destroy the love of Becky and Tom in hope of weakening their strength and position overall in the community. To do this, he would need to destroy their trust and, if this was not enough, then their beings. He might need to destroy the future influence, the future genealogy of Becky's pure good domain, to be sure that the pure line would end with Becky. In the crosshairs of Mr. Arthur's plans were now not only Becky but also perhaps Tom and her unborn. In the end, there could be three who would fall victim to the evil acts of Mr. Arthur's destiny.

The innocence of the victims was not a consideration or even of any concern to him or to his evil destiny. Only fulfilling this destiny was of paramount attention. It would make his domain's missions complete. It would grow his pure power and tip the balance back toward the evil-natured side again. It would be the most significant victory in his battles with the good natured of his lifetime. With this act, he, too, would be prepared to be sacrificed in the aftermath of things, but now it would be more a homage and testament to his greatness than punishment for crimes.

Tom McDouglas' spirit-common destinies were much the same as any other mixed domain. They centered on contending for favor in the balance of the natures and positioning the spirit and their natures with greater influence and power. His spirit-specific destinies were several. From the evil-natured spirit of his domain, there was a destiny to bring advancement and invention to the civilization and to replace simplicity and goodness with complexity and new and worldly sources of power. This destiny was generally common among mind-dominant beings of mixed domains. In this quadrant of life's circle, it was an especially common destiny, making it fairly easy to find and attract others with a similar makeup and focus.

Bonding with these other mind dominants enhanced the chances for achievement of this destiny. Tom was well bonded. It fed his evil-natured spirit's strength. It seemed natural; the setting within the office and the aptitudes of all that he worked with primed him to partner and interact daily with these mind-dominated beings, their spirit's destinies, and to creating synergies between them. Sharing of thoughts and ideas, experimentation, risk, and their creativity are the impetus for their discovery and invention. Tom's evil-natured spirit fed off these elements of his workmates in the laboratory. Their minds were gorged with thoughts and ideas from the stimuli that they would generate together and from one another. The pull from his own domain's stores, combined with those of his workmates, made discovery, thus this destiny, routinely achievable and allowed for forward and small incremental movement around the circular path of life. Neither he nor his spirit produced anything specifically that changed the world, but his influence and addition to the pool of knowledge was his significant contribution. His practice and support of science added to the nonspirit component's strength and stranglehold over magic. It eventually would add to the mind's dominance of the being and the lost position of the spirit within the being.

Tom perfectly exemplified the mind-dominant being. This introduced a new element to consider in the assessment of his purpose and being. His tendency was to introduce new discovery, science, structure, and process. Spirit-driven influences are suppressed by these things. It left him with an internal struggle between his reliance on science and the hard disciplines, the servants of his strong mind component and those of his domain such as love and emotions. There was little room in his being for magic except that which kept Becky and him attracted. He many times felt uncomfortable in this composition. His spirit's destinies were to influence the mind component and provide it with stored information from his domain as a trigger for new thought and mind advancement, even at the peril of his own domain. The destiny of his evil spirit was to bring movement around the life circle. It would contribute to the deterioration of the civilization but fortunately only to the limits that his other two spirits would allow it.

Another of the spirit-specific destinies driving Tom's lone evil-natured spirit was to bring conflict between Becky and Mr. Arthur. It was to plant the seed that would eventually trigger major confrontation between these two. It was to encourage and feed the competition between their two pure drivers. Tom would be the pawn played by both of their influence. The battle for Tom would not be the deciding factor in who would win the overall war but would be a significant indicator of their strength and their position in the community as a whole. This one spirit's destiny would be the impetus toward moving the two to their final confrontation.

The destiny of Tom's good-natured spirits' destiny was to protect and enhance Becky's goodness and impact on the world. The stronger one was to provide her with a partner, a special partner called a soul mate. This indeed was a very special and sacred destiny allowed to many but achieved by only a few. This same spirit was destined to create a son with Becky, and to contribute a good-natured portion to the new baby's domain. This contribution, along with that from Becky, would ensure that the new domain would be made up of no fewer than two strong and dominant good-natured spirits. It would assure a positive contribution to the portions of goodness in the world. It was this destiny that overshadowed and controlled the destinies of Tom's evil side of the domain. It was where Tom's strongest attributes and influences would form.

The destiny of Tom's other good-natured spirit was quite important and appropriate for Tom's spirit mix as well. It was to suppress invention. It was to hinder Tom's evil-natured spirit from contributing significantly to the world's advancement, both scientifically and technologically. It could not suppress the sharing of information from his domain stores with others like him, those with like domains of equally strong and well-developed mind components, but it could hinder its being's tendency and desire to create from his genius. It was to discourage Tom from being the source of the finished products that advanced movement around the circular pathway of life. His good-natured ones were destined to prohibit him the glory of his ideas. They would limit his potential to unleash the powers of his inventive and advanced thinking and ability to create mechanical solutions. Its arsenal would include distraction and diversion of his time to other things. Becky, her being, would serve this spirit and this destiny's needs well.

Tom's preoccupations with Becky and other diversions and uses of his time were examples of why some achieve what are seemingly great things during their allotted time on the earth, and others do not. It could be and generally is not an issue of ability or access to knowledge and know-how. Rather, it's more likely just a conflict in destinies between the good- and evil-natured spirits in their mix. We are all capable of advanced creations, of tremendous creativity and the unlocking of the secrets of nature and unknowns but simply not destined by our domain's makeup. Tom's constitution was ripe for a breakthrough, to introduce great new advancements, but his dominant side was good natured. It hindered his opportunity. It held him short of creating and achieving fame and reward for his ideas, thoughts, and contributions to the time's advancement. He remained always in the background yet proud and with some ownership in the final results of his thoughts, ideas, and inspiration. It was the evil from within him that would feel the pain of others taking his brilliance to fruition and fame.

Brenda's goals were blended into a few shared and focused destinies as was the case with most pure domains. They were clear and powerful. She was to take over for Mr. Arthur when the time would come. Until then, she was to learn from the master. She was to support him. She was to gain strength as his understudy. Over time, it became difficult for her natures to remain in the understudy role. This was because she was ambitious and aggressive as all pure evil-natured domains are. She had thoughts of removing Mr. Arthur herself to allow her to achieve her destiny immediately. But removing Mr. Arthur was not in her calling. Others would have this as their destiny. Rather, she was to remove obstacles for these other spirits to achieve this destiny. She was to subtly and methodically expose him to his doom. All the while, her ultimate destiny was to be ready to step in when the time came. She would then be in command and shepherd the evil-natured flock of the area. This was her destiny. It would be hers in due time if she simply played her role until the right time came.

In the meantime, Brenda served her spirit-common and pure evil-natured destiny to deceive the good natured of the community. Hers was to come from the trenches, the grassroots levels, as opposed to the tactics and strategies of Mr. Arthur. It formed a two-pronged, two-vantage attack on the community. She would select and focus on her good-natured prey and then connive ways to lead them astray. She used many devices and poisons to ensnare them. She would snuff out good natures and manipulate them as if her playthings. She took pleasure in their agony and decay. Usually, she would set herself up as a friend, only to betray her victim later for her own enjoyment and entertainment. She was a truly evil being. She was a cold and hardened being behind the alluring, pretty face and bright smile. She herself was a poison to all she came into contact, all but to Mr. Arthur.

Was she actually more dangerous than Mr. Arthur? In many ways and to the segments of the population that she targeted and interacted with; she was. She especially reached those and provided an identity for those younger than she was. It was in this segment that she was particularly effective with her evil repertoire. She left a swath of victims and converts through the ranks and breadth of her territory. Her missions, her targets, were calculated and planned. They were anything but random. Her method and maneuvers were effective and sure. Her devastation of the good natures, of those within her jurisdiction, was often and nearly complete. She had appeal. She sold it well. She used her position in Mr. Arthur's shadows as an advantage.

Her reputation had not yet preceded her. Much of the damage she caused was perceived to be Mr. Arthur's. And although this frustrated her ego and the credits due her and generated by her destiny, it kept her safe and sheltered while she learned, while she established herself and her loyal contingent, and while she, too, established her political markers and insurances. Hers was to be a formidable nemesis of the good nature. She was indeed that, but for now, in her apprenticeship, it was Mr. Arthur that received the acclaim. Her evil nature still craved and would need to earn his stature and his reputation over the community. Her destiny was to be great in time, greater than Mr. Arthur. It was a struggle to serve him, to wait for his demise. But it was her destiny to do so. Her spirits stayed the course and internally wished the worse for him; all the while, she smiled and served him loyally and obediently.

As she grew older, wiser, and stronger in spirit powers, her destiny also grew to be a more forceful driver within her. Her desire for fame and dominance was growing. It wore on her that others did not see her efforts as her own, but rather the effect of Mr. Arthur's commands. Hers was the handiwork that transformed good-natured beings to evil dominant. It served the evil position and common destiny of her kind. Mr. Arthur, on the other hand, had been avoiding her types of activities for years. He was growing older and less involved in the hands-on detail. He spent much of his time now simply accentuating those who were already evil in nature to be eviler. He did not affect the numbers or the balance on the scale of the natures, not so much. What Brenda was doing had greater impact on these areas and the positioning around the circular model of life.

Her nature gnawed at her to push for what was due her. It grew impatient with her and urged her to position herself as her calling prescribed. It was time. It was growing difficult to resist. But for the spirit to move against its destinies' road map and timelines was most uncommon. Brenda simply buried herself in her work of evil deeds. She looked for every opportunity to help the one with destiny to remove her obstacle from her. Her mental state and internal turmoil made her all the more lethal and dangerous to the good natured of the community. Her destiny to grow evil was nearly unsatiable.

Every mixed domain has proximity and access to a pure domain of its natures. It assures the spirits help as they need it. Pure domains are there to serve and, as they can, add advantage or support to the spirits of their kind. Becky, Mr. Arthur, and Brenda were all blessed with pure and advantaged domains. They could transfer to mixed-natured domains. They could transfuse strength to the other spirits of their nature. They could influence the balance of power in these mixed domains. The benefit of these actions come from their effect on destinies. With shifts in dominance and spirit strength come shifts in the domain's focus on their spirit-common and spirit-specific destinies. Pure domains can influence the actions of mixed domain's spirits and their position as dominant in conflicted, weaker, and vulnerable domains. They can influence which spirits hold dominance over the domain and, in turn, manipulate which destinies are given primary focus. The pure domain's envoys to these weaker mixed domains can also work with their like kind within these domains to plan and develop strategies to offset, weaken, or even sabotage the efforts of "unlike" spirits toward achieving their destinies. These actions result in a weakening or dilution of the effect of both involved spirits. Both spirits loose something in these trade-offs and dilutions, yet many times, both also win from what is salvaged or not achieved.

Daniel was fifteen years old and had a mixed domain containing two evil-natured spirits and one good natured. As his dominant evil nature would suggest, he was always in and out of trouble at West Crawford High School. His crimes were mostly minor offenses. He didn't quite seem to have what it took to be hardened in evil or really effective as a true criminal. His problem was his conscience. This was the countering offset offered by the influence of his one good natured spirit of his being and the counterinfluence to that of his strong evil natures. It was his good-natured spirit's destiny to provide this counterinfluence.

In a way, Daniel was lucky. He was constantly in and out of the school counselor's office at West Crawford. His counselor was Becky Turner-McDouglas. Each time he left her office, his conscience was strengthened and his evil placed under stronger restraints of this good-centered conscience. Conscience was the envoy of his good-natured spirit. It was this good-natured spirit's destiny to limit the evil that would be created by the domain. It was its destiny to feed the being with a counter direction and sense of guilt for deeds generated from the evil influences, the thoughts and ideas that would pass through its nonspirit components. It provided the counterintelligence to the mind and body to limit the actions that the evil ones compelled it to take. Daniel's good nature was kept recharged and strong by its periodic visits to Becky and her spirit transfers to his domain. The minor offenses that his being carried out while in school were insignificant yet enough to allow his evil-natured spirits to serve and achieve their destinies. At the same time, offenses brought consequences enough to warrant frequent trips to the counselor's office where his good-natured spirit could recharge with his mentor of pure domain and again exert its limits and control on the evil that the being would do. The overall result was that all the spirits' destinies were being served. It was dilution at its most effective.

Daniel's good-natured spirit conscience eventually grew in strength where it no longer needed Becky's support to remain strong and charged. Although Daniel would continue to play pranks and have many evil thoughts in his life, he would never gain the power over his good conscience to ever do anything too significantly evil in the future and certainly not criminal. He would simply be one of the many everyday people of the world with relatively insignificant moments of bad and good but fitting in to the norm with everyone else.

In the same neighborhood lived Gilbert Solkin. Gilbert was a young man of sixteen. His domain consisted in two good-natured spirits and one evil-natured spirit. He was liked by almost everyone of a good-natured mix. For the most part, he was the perfect gentleman. He was caring and giving. It was his destiny to support and strengthen a longtime friendship and to protect his friend from being enticed into a life of evil.

The other young man's name was Ted. Ted's domain was made up of one very strong good-natured spirit, one very weak good-natured spirit, and one very strong evil-natured spirit. Ted was very popular with everyone at school due to his partial celebrity status. He was the high school quarterback. This allowed his acquaintances to be from all walks of life, not just those who attracted Gilbert. In fact, Ted fit nicely into groups dominated by both good- and evil-natured people. The reason was that Ted's domain was relatively balanced -natured and highly vulnerable and attracted to both good and evil because of his domain's unusual balance. This was primarily attributable to the weakness of his one spirit. It allowed Ted to be influenced and to enter into relationships with almost anyone.

One of Gilbert's destinies was to provide Ted with advice and direction and to give him a trusted friend and good-natured influence to keep his domain protected and dominated by his good-natured spirits. Primarily, Gilbert's destiny involved protecting his friend from the temptations and influences of one particularly influential and dangerous evil domain belonging to Robert Zeil. Robert was influenced by an evil center. Ted had recently been befriended by Robert and was offered a place in his special clique of friends. Gilbert's purpose was now to use his lifelong friendship to keep Ted from being too drawn in and changed by Robert's offer, thus being added to Robert's current bevy of victims.

Gilbert's evil-natured spirit, on the other hand, had a counter interest in Ted. Its spirit-common destiny was to grow evil. It was destined to sabotage the plans of Gilbert's good-natured destiny. The chessboard was now set up to play. Ted was the king piece on the board yet oblivious to the plays being taken on all sides of him.

Ted was always happy to see his old friend Gilbert. They'd known each other for over ten years. They knew each other's every inclination and idiosyncrasies. Ted enjoyed Gilbert's company and his influence on his life. Gilbert kept him centered, especially now that he was growing into a special and physically gifted being. He was accepted by more and different people as his athletic endeavors and accomplishments had blossomed over the last few years. He was also a handsome youngster and becoming more popular with the girls. Gilbert's life was not moving in the same direction as Ted's, but still, he formed the trusted center from which Ted drew his advice and guidance. Gilbert had always been there for him as his true friend. He was one he could trust for wisdom and honesty and one he could confide in. It was this bond of trust that held them together strongly as friends. Trust is the lynchpin of goodness. It was the one element that Ted never doubted in his and Gilbert's relationship.

Any plan to thwart or dilute a good nature's endeavor to fully achieve its destiny must involve attacking its foundation, this being trust. Pure evil domains know this well. Brenda Doran knew this better than any. If Robert was to win Ted's allegiance, he would need to destroy the bond of trust between Ted and Gilbert. He would need Brenda's help to sever this line of trust. Every time Robert believed that he was making progress in luring Ted under his influence, Gilbert would come back into the picture and reset him to the original position toward good. After much frustration, Robert realized that he needed to work on Gilbert instead of Ted. This task would be difficult for Robert. He and Gilbert simply didn't get along. Their two domains strongly repelled each other. Robert found it a real challenge just to approach him. He needed help from someone more powerful and advantaged. He called on his mentor, Brenda Doran, for advice and help. She gladly and willingly accepted the challenge.

One day when mingling with Robert's group of acquaintances, Brenda found Ted and asked him to introduce her to his friend Gilbert. She let on that the interest was one of a girl's interest in a boy. It surprised Ted that Gilbert would interest her, but he was also glad for his friend. He said, "Sure, I'll introduce you. Gilbert is really a great guy." It was Ted's opportunity to finally do something good for his friend Gilbert.

Later that same day, Ted met Gilbert after class and shared with him, "Hey, Gilbert, it seems you're quite a hot commodity in the neighborhood." He slapped his friend on the back and laughed heartily. "I met this girl today, and she asked me to introduce you to her. She is really quite the prize, if you know what I mean." Then he playfully coaxed him to respond by backpedaling in front of him to maintain a face-to-face read of his expression.

Gilbert was surprised by Ted's message. He stuttered, "Who is this girl? Do I know her?" He rubbed his forehead to help it all sink in.

Ted responded, "I don't know, Gilbert, but she wants to meet you." He smiled. "Come on, Gilbert, she's interested in you. You should give her a chance."

Gilbert smiled as well. The flattery of it finally struck him. It was nice to be singled out as of interest to the female gender. He was now excited. Gilbert asked, "Describe her to me, Ted. Is she attractive? Is she in any of my classes? Is she nice?"

Ted laughed and responded, "I think so . . . to all of the above. But come on, I'll introduce you to her. You can determine for yourself." Ted took Gilbert to the commons and pointed out the girl who had asked to meet him. Gilbert was as surprised as anyone that this girl, one whom he'd never met or seen before, was interested in him. It made him feel very uncomfortable not knowing anything about her, yet she was so beautiful. His hormones took over his better judgment. It was the girl of his dreams. He couldn't believe she was asking about him. Ted continued to coax him forward. He was anxious to introduce him to this goddess. Life at that moment was very good for this sixteen-year-old boy. He anxiously agreed to go through with it.

He strode forward toward her, all the while trying to look less nerdy and more confident with each stride. Soon they were within feet of each other. She turned to him and Ted and smiled. Ted then addressed Brenda. "Brenda, this is Gilbert Solkin, my friend." Then he looked to Gilbert and said, "Gilbert, this is Brenda Doran. We have only met twice, but she asked me to introduce you to her."

Both Brenda and Gilbert looked into each other's eyes and smiled. At first eye contact, Gilbert's world turned to slow motion. She entranced him. Brenda had transferred one of her spirits to his domain. It was possible because, as she suspected, he was of a mixed-natured domain. She immediately put Gilbert's domain at ease. The two of them began conversation; while within Gilbert's domain, she connected with the evil-natured one. Without so much as an initial debriefing, the evil-natured spirits, one transferred from Brenda and one of the permanent residents of Gilbert's domain, began plotting against the good influences and bonds of trust between Gilbert and Ted's domains. Destroying this trust was the focal point of their sharing. It was to be their joint pact to work together. When it was done, Brenda's spirit transferred back without Gilbert's external knowing what had been plotted against him and his good-natured spirits. His evil spirit had set its trap through his desire for this girl. She simply smiled and giggled and made it so easy for him to want to fall within her influence.

Brenda and Gilbert made plans to go out on Saturday night after the game. They would invite Ted if he wanted to go and if he could arrange a date. It was all set for Saturday night.

Ted had no troubles with arranging a date for Saturday. In fact, Robert helped him with the final arrangements. She was a cheerleader, one from Robert's group of acquaintances. Her name was Stephanie Clarke. She was not as beautiful as Brenda, but Ted thought her nice. After the game, they all gathered at the open gate leading to the field. Brenda suggested that they go to her place. It was an apartment that she said she and her mother shared. It would be quiet there, and they could talk undisturbed. They all agreed to this plan.

They took Gilbert's car, and within minutes, they were there. The apartment was downtown in a high-rise. Gilbert, Ted, and Stephanie were all surprised that this was where Brenda lived. Gilbert asked Brenda, "Are your parents wealthy?"

Brenda laughed and replied, "Just enough so to pay the rent."

Then Gilbert asked, "If you live here, why do you attend West Crawford?"

Brenda wrinkled her mouth a bit and retorted, "I go to West Crawford High because I like the school and the students. They are not so judgmental of me." Gilbert felt bad for asking. He apologized for his quick judgment. Brenda grabbed his arm and showed him through the lobby and to the elevators. It was a new experience for three of them.

When they reached the apartment and walked through the outer door, their mouths fell open. The place was absolutely beautiful. Gilbert expected a maid or a butler to enter to greet them at any moment, but none came. Gilbert asked, "Is your mother here?"

Brenda smiled and said, "No, she works very late. I don't expect her back until after 3:00 a.m." It was a good lie. There was no mother. Brenda was a big girl and on her own, even though her youthful looks could fool most anyone about her age and into thinking that she was just a schoolgirl.

Gilbert then asked, "Will your mother mind us being here unsupervised?"

Brenda, Ted, and Stephanie were now getting annoyed by Gilbert's many questions; but instead of getting angry, they simply laughed in unison at the thought. Brenda replied, "We'll supervise one another. Now don't worry, Gilbert. Sit down and enjoy yourself."

One from Brenda's domain transferred to Gilbert's soon after they all sat down around the big screen TV with a bowl of snacks and sodas strategically positioned about them. With Brenda's spirit inside, Gilbert's questions turned to more comfortable and interesting conversation. The four talked for hours about relatively insignificant yet friendly things. They were having fun. On the internal, Brenda's focus was on how to erode the bond of trust between Gilbert and Ted. She needed the help of Gilbert's evil nature to do this. This spirit was pivotal in the plans to counter the influences and destinies of the two good natures in Gilbert's domain. Brenda and Gilbert's evil spirits needed a plot and a secret that they could use to betray Ted's trust in his friend Gilbert. It had to be significant to both of their lives. It had to be something that only Gilbert and Ted, perhaps only a few others, would know. Brenda could supply this. Tonight, she would create the secret that would put her plans and that of Gilbert's evil-natured spirit into motion, diluting his good-natured spirits' destiny, thus freeing Ted to fall victim to evil.

Midway through the evening, Brenda suggested that they take their party to the balcony. They were all in awe of the vista of their city. The thousand tiny lights in the distance were mesmerizing. As the two boys leaned against the outer rail, Brenda and Stephanie positioned themselves together by the balcony's opening. Brenda handed Stephanie a package and whispered in her ear, "Get Ted to indulge with you. I will do the same with Gilbert." Stephanie unbuttoned the top buttons of her blouse and then moved to the outer rail to nestle up to Ted's side. She kissed Ted and asked him to join her at one of the furthermost ends of the balcony, just the two of them. Ted followed her lead. When there, they kissed.

Brenda came to Gilbert's side as the other two were leaving. She gently coaxed Gilbert to the other side of the huge balcony and put her lips to his. Gilbert had only a very limited experience with kissing a girl and felt nervous yet very excited about it as well. He welcomed the experience. Brenda seemed very experienced, far more so than he had expected, and he let her guide and teach him in this matter. She was glad to do so. All the while, she positioned him such that when his eyes were opened, he could catch glimpses of Stephanie and Ted and all they were doing. Gilbert's curiosity at the urgings of Brenda's transferred spirit and his own evil-natured spirit kept the other two in his line of sight most of the time. Gilbert's senses were charged by Brenda's affections. He was now vulnerable yet not to the degree that Ted had become.

As Brenda nuzzled his neck, he turned toward Stephanie and Ted. Stephanie was removing a handmade cigarette from her pocket and lighting it. After taking a few hits, she handed it to Ted. He put up weak resistance to her urgings and then gave in. He inhaled several times, put his arms across his chest, and then coughed. It brought the attentions of all on the balcony toward him. Brenda and Stephanie laughed aloud. Gilbert was shocked that his friend would try marijuana. Ted was recovering from his inhalation and let out a laugh as well, more from embarrassment than from humor. The drug was affecting him now, and he took the joint again to his lips and inhaled. The result was much the same, but the increased dosage of the drug made it more bearable. Brenda took the joint from Ted and offered it to Gilbert, saying, "Do you want some of this?"

Gilbert took it between his fingers, examined it, smelled it, and then handed it back to Brenda, saying, "No thanks. I can't do this."

Brenda smiled and said, "Me neither." She handed the joint back to Stephanie. "I assume that this is yours? Please don't take it inside the apartment. It leaves such a nasty smell." She then led Gilbert back to the other side of the balcony where they resumed to hold each other, talk, and kiss.

Gilbert was happy that Brenda, too, chose not to experiment with the drug. It made him feel more comfortable and open to her. She was special. Gilbert immersed himself in his feelings of good fortune and attraction to this girl. Yet on the perimeter of his thoughts this evening, he worried about his friend. Ted had surprised him. They would need to have a friend-to-friend discussion later. Brenda could only gloat on the inside at how well her plan had unfolded. Gilbert was an easy victim of her seductive power. The secret had been established and the scene now complete. Only she, Stephanie, and Gilbert knew of Ted's indulgence in the forbidden drug. It was now up to Gilbert's evil-natured one to work it into a betrayal. Everything was going according to plan. The main mission of the evening was now complete. Brenda's mind turned to ways to end this evening and get these teenyboppers to leave her apartment. She had much still to do in serving her destinies.

At around twelve thirty, Stephanie got the signal from Brenda that it was time to urge Ted to take her home. Shortly thereafter, Stephanie, Ted, and Gilbert said their goodbyes to Brenda and left downtown for their less sophisticated neighborhood. It was a night to remember for Gilbert. It left him with such rich feelings, mostly of how sweet a relationship with a girl could be but also of surprise and wonderment of how little he knew his friend. Ted had obviously changed. There were things about him that he apparently didn't know. He was concerned that some of these things might hurt him. He felt a real need to protect him from these things as a friend driven by his good spirit's destiny. But the issue was how to do this without coming off as superior or endangering their trust and friendship with each other. Gilbert thought about it all the way back to the neighborhood.

The first stop was Stephanie's. Ted walked her to the door but was back quickly. Her parents were waiting at the door as if expecting her home much earlier than it now was. Ted, when back in the car, gave Gilbert a grin and a quick look of relief that Stephanie's parents didn't make a scene. By now, all the effects of the marijuana had passed from his system. Only the telltale stench of the weed remained on Ted's clothes. Gilbert felt compelled to tell Ted about it before his mother discovered it on him or in the laundry. She would surely ask him questions. He said to Ted, "Hey, what's up with you doing drugs? You know you could get kicked out of school or off the team for getting caught with that stuff."

Ted seemed surprised to be scolded by his friend but took it as concern for his well-being. He replied, "It was a moment of weakness, Gilbert. Honestly, it was my first time."

Gilbert looked over to him with a serious stare and then burst into laughter, saying, "Yes, I believe it was your first time. You nearly choked to death." Ted joined him in laughing about it.

Gilbert then added, "But seriously, Ted, you need to stay away from that stuff."

He let the message sink in before adding in jest, "No matter how alluring the girl is."

They both chuckled a moment before Ted replied, "I know that, Gilbert. And thanks for the reminder." They both touched knuckles of their inside hands and let it drop, all but one last comment from Gilbert before they turned into Ted's driveway.

Gilbert added, "Ted, you need to do something with those clothes. They smell of marijuana. Your mom will surely find them."

Ted replied, "I'll take care of it, Gilbert. Thanks. Goodbye. I'll see you this weekend."

Gilbert backed out into the street and redirected the car toward his home. He couldn't help but wonder if he'd really gotten through to Ted. He wondered how he could help him. The thoughts from his internal would simply not go away.

The next day, Stephanie and Ted drove by Gilbert at the video store. They parked next to Gilbert's car and said, "Hey, Gilbert, want to come over to Stephanie's and watch videos tonight?" Stephanie suggested he call Brenda to join in. The smell of marijuana smoke escaped from the window as Gilbert bent down to address them. It was strong and recent. Gilbert nearly coughed.

He had originally wanted to accept their offer, but after being faced with the reality of what they had planned, he said to them, "No, I have other plans for this evening. You two have a good time without me."

He looked at Ted and said in a low tone, "You remember what we talked about last night. See you later."

Ted looked down in embarrassment and frustration as Gilbert was moving himself farther away from the car. He waved and said, "See you later, Gilbert."

Gilbert's good-natured spirits were having their destiny sabotaged. His evil-natured spirit was achieving its destiny in spite of the good-natured ones efforts. It left Gilbert's internal thoughts in turmoil. It left him turned upside down. He was looking for help but couldn't share his secret and jeopardize the bond of trust he had with Ted.

Later that afternoon, Gilbert could no longer deal with the problem on his own. He wanted to share it with someone. In the past, it would have been Ted whom he'd turn to; but in this instance, this option didn't exist. He decided to call Brenda to talk about it. He thought of her as a bright and caring person. She would be one who could offer him options and advice on what to do.

Brenda heard the phone ring. She wasn't surprised to hear that it was Gilbert on the other end of the line. She greeted him, "Hello, Gilbert. It's nice to hear from you. I was hoping that you might call me." She had Robert in her apartment at the moment, and she motioned for him to remain perfectly silent.

Gilbert naively formed a vision in his head that she had been waiting by the phone for his call. He took pleasure in her perceived delight that he finally called. He said to her, "Brenda, I'd like to spend some more time together. Are you free this evening?"

Brenda put on like she was excited. She giggled into the phone and spoke. "I'd like very much to see you this evening, but my mother will be home tonight. Should I stop by your place?"

Gilbert didn't anticipate this response but thought it a good alternative and said, "That would be great. Would you rather I pick you up and we can go somewhere?"

Brenda responded, "No, I will already be in the neighborhood of the school this afternoon. If you want, I can pick you up, and then we can go somewhere from there. Can you give me direction to your house?" There was method to Brenda's desire to know and visit where Gilbert lived. It was important to the next phase of her plan. Gilbert gave her directions and set the date for seven.

Brenda finished, "I'll see you then. Bye."

Gilbert felt excited and important again. He was confident that she would help him make the situation with Ted go away. Meanwhile, Robert got up from the sofa in Brenda's living room and said, "That was disgusting. How much longer until you free young Ted from the bonds of friendship with this geek?"

Brenda looked angrily at Robert and said, "You were a geek once, not so much unlike Gilbert. Perhaps you forget."

Robert knew he'd gotten out of line. He replied, "But you do such nice work with geeks. I'm living proof, aren't I?" She smiled and brushed off his brashness. He was right. She had made him. She liked how he'd turned out. He was her toy. He was her pawn. She liked the power she had over him. Soon Gilbert would be her pawn as well.

At exactly seven, Brenda pulled into the driveway of Gilbert's house in a silver BMW convertible. Gilbert was surprised to see her in such an expensive car. He said, "Nice wheels. Is it yours?"

Brenda laughed and said, "No, it's my mother's. She lets me drive it when she's home. Do you want to take it out for a spin? I'll let you drive."

Gilbert was hesitant at first, but the allure was too great. He said, "I'll let my parents know I'm leaving. I'll be right back."

While he was gone, Brenda moved over into the passenger seat. When Gilbert reappeared, she held the keys in the air and dangled them as bait to his desire. Gilbert positioned himself into the driver's seat and snatched the keys from her fingers, saying, "Are you sure it would be OK with your mother to let me drive her car?"

Brenda responded, "What she doesn't know wouldn't bring her concern." This didn't bring Gilbert any relief. Brenda could read it in his face. "Come on. If anything happens, we'll switch seats. I'll protect you."

Gilbert smiled and asked, "Where do you want to go then?" He'd almost forgotten what he intended to talk to her about. He was too caught up in the excitement of taking out the powerful new toy. But he'd get to it later.

Brenda suggested, "Why don't we go to the lake and find a nice quiet, out-of-the-way place to snuggle and talk?" That fit Gilbert's intentions for this evening to a tee. The lake was only a few minutes away. They were off in a moment.

At the lake, they lay down on the blanket that Brenda brought. They spread it beneath a shady tree and held each other for a while. Gilbert finally broke the silence by sharing with Brenda his concerns about Ted. He didn't intend to come across as a busybody. He respected Ted and Stephanie's privacy and decisions to choose, but Ted was his best friend. Gilbert felt that it was sometimes easier to see mistakes from a distance rather than up close. He asked Brenda, "What approach do you think I should take with Ted? Should I remain passive and have faith that he'll work his way through this without need of my involvement, or should I take action that will force him to see the consequences of what he is doing with marijuana?"

Brenda raised her knees to her chin and directed her gaze out over the water. She didn't have a response right away. It required a bit of thought, but finally, she suggested, "If it were me in your situation, I would take a more active approach to get my friend straightened out before his problem becomes too large."

Gilbert put his arm around her and asked, "What exactly would you do?"

Brenda turned her head toward him by propping it on her contracted knees and said, "I might start with a mild threat to go to his coach if he doesn't stop with the drugs or even a counselor at the school. That could wake him up a bit."

Gilbert thought about it and then responded, "I could threaten but could never actually snitch on Ted to anyone with control over his permanent records and his future. It could be devastating for him."

Brenda smiled and quietly whispered to herself, *Indeed, it could be.*

Then she said to him, "Perhaps the threat would be all that is needed."

Gilbert thought about it. His two good-natured spirits saw value in her suggestions and the consistency with their destiny to protect Ted from evil influence. His evil-natured one saw the suggestion fitting perfectly in line with the plan it developed with Brenda's envoy spirit. All of Gilbert's domain, his spirits, their natures, and their destinies seemed to be comfortable with this approach. The issue was then removed from Gilbert's immediate concern and attentions. Companionship with Brenda would now fill the remaining time.

They talked for about an hour. They comforted each other. Gilbert thought Brenda made him stronger. In fact, she did make his one spirit much stronger. This boost made him feel charged. It was, however, not a good thing for his good-natured spirits. For them, she provided only deception. For them, she was simply feeding coercion between her good-natured spirits and the evil spirit of his domain. This supported the dilution of the domain and the destinies within. Regardless of the spirit influence and effect, Gilbert was strongly attracted physically and mentally to Brenda. It exposed his spirit domain to many challenges. Her hold on his external masked the warnings and signals that should have been coming from inside his domain.

On Monday, Gilbert called Ted aside after school. He asked him, "Hey, Ted, what do you have planned for the evening?" He wanted to get together with him and talk.

Ted was glad to hear that his friend was still talking to him, but he'd already made plans for the evening. He responded, "Sorry, Gilbert, not tonight. I've already committed to see Stephanie tonight. How about tomorrow?"

Gilbert burst out venomously, "Are you going over to Stephanie's to smoke dope?" Gilbert drew back in his frustration. He wished he hadn't said that. He felt shame that he'd shown so little tact.

Ted was understandably taken aback by his friend's accusation. He was offended and hurt. Even though it was a true statement, he didn't like hearing it from Gilbert. He didn't like to be judged, and he didn't like his affairs to be questioned or brought out into the open. He fired back, "Maybe. It's not really any of your business, Gilbert. When did you become my keeper?"

Gilbert swallowed hard and replied, "You are my lifelong friend, Ted. Your business is my business. Many people see us as much the same. I don't want to be associated with marijuana just because I am thought of as your friend. It's my responsibility to help you, Ted, as your friend."

Ted shook his head and looked him directly in the eyes. "I don't need any help, Gilbert, not from you or anyone. I'm able to handle my own affairs. I'm in control. I'm going to Stephanie's for companionship. I just like the girl's company. That is all." He held his focus on Gilbert and Gilbert on him. He could tell that Gilbert was still struggling with the marijuana issue. He tried to soften Gilbert's opinion of the relationship he was having with Stephanie. "Stephanie does have a few bad habits, Gilbert. You know which ones I'm talking about. But we don't just sit around and smoke dope together. We have fun. We do fun things. In fact, it's rare that we smoke." He was saying this solely for

Gilbert's sake and perhaps to ease his own conscience. He was feeling the guilt of his lies. He and Stephanie had actually smoked weed every time they'd gotten together. They did little else. The drug had become the mainstay of their relationship. Gilbert's message to him was beginning to hit home. It left him wondering what he was doing, what he saw in this girl.

While he was in thought, Gilbert asked Ted, "What if I were to go to your coach? Will that make you stop with the drug?"

Ted looked shocked to hear this coming from his friend. It was a threat. He'd just told him that he rarely smoked the stuff. Didn't he believe him? Ted replied, "Gilbert, you wouldn't. I just told you I don't do it often, only on a rare occasion."

After looking to the ground several times in disbelief of the conversation he and Gilbert were engaged in, he said, "Gilbert, I'll take care of it. Trust me. Give me some time."

Gilbert put his arm around his friend and said, "OK, I trust you, Ted. But do something about this problem now while you can control it on your own."

Ted replied, "Thanks, Gilbert, for being concerned. I know you won't do anything rash, like talking to anyone else about this, right?"

They shared a laugh and Gilbert said, "No, I won't tell a soul." They turned and went on to other things.

As they were leaving, Ted turned back to Gilbert and asked, "Hey, Gilbert, how's Brenda? Things still OK between you two?"

Gilbert responded, "They're great. That girl really gives me a lift. She is special."

Ted replied, "I'm glad to hear it, Gilbert. You deserve the best. Let's double up this weekend, if you want."

Gilbert fired back, "Sounds great. I'll ask her." He waved and was off.

That Wednesday, Coach Andrews walked into English class and asked Mrs. Baker, the English teacher, if Ted might be excused for a few minutes to talk to him in private. Mrs. Baker seemed disturbed by the interruption and asked the coach if he had a permission slip from the office. Coach Baker whispered something in Mrs. Baker's ear. Her eyebrows rose to show surprise. The whole class was spellbound on what was happening. The suspense was thick enough to cut with a knife. Ted could only wonder why the coach was asking for him and why the theatrics. He wondered if Gilbert had something to do with this. He had promised to take no rash actions in their earlier conversation. Ted had trusted him. He could only wonder if he'd been betrayed by his closest and most trusted friend.

Mrs. Baker motioned for Ted to come to the front of the class. He complied. When he reached Mrs. Baker and Coach Baker, he asked, "What's this all about?"

The coach responded, "Ted, I need to speak to you in my office." Then he motioned him toward the door.

Ted replied, "OK, do you want me to go now or after class?"

Mrs. Baker chimed in, "It's best that you go with Coach Baker now." Ted was partially frightened but mostly angered by the way this incident was playing out. It was embarrassing to be pulled out of class. He could just imagine the rumors that would be started. It made it sound very serious.

Gilbert sat in the back of the class, taking it all in, as did Stephanie. Both showed expressions of surprise for what was going on before them. Ted left the room just behind Coach Baker. On his way out, he looked back toward Gilbert with an angry scowl. It gave Gilbert a strange feeling.

After they entered Coach Baker's office, the coach closed the door. He'd said nothing to Ted all the way there. He motioned for Ted to sit and then took up his usual position behind the huge out-of-date wooden desk. The first words that he spoke were, "I'm very disappointed with you, son. You've placed both of us in a very difficult position."

Ted responded, "I'm not sure I understand what you're referring to, sir."

The coach then leaned forward into the desk and pounded it with his fist while shouting, "I'm talking about drugs, Ted! You and drugs!"

It was as Ted had feared. Gilbert must have made good on his threat. He'd been betrayed. All he could do now was to deny it. It would be his word against Gilbert's. The coach had no proof. He returned, "I don't know what you're referring to, Coach. I don't take drugs."

The coach's face turned to red. He fired back, "Don't lie to me, son. I'm here to help you as much as I can. I don't want this thing to be blown out of proportion any more than you do. Right?"

Ted asked, "Why do you think I'm lying, Coach? Who's told you that I'm using drugs? Is it Gilbert Solkin? He's made the whole thing up as a prank."

With that, the coach appeared to be surprised for a moment and then renewed his assault on Ted's guilt by saying, "Someone did come to me yesterday with information and proof. They said you'd been smoking marijuana quite regularly. I couldn't believe them at first, but then they told me to search your locker."

He hesitated briefly and then commenced, "I opened your locker, son. I found exactly what I was told I would. There's a cache of clothes, all reeking of marijuana smoke, and one small bag of leafy stuff that I presume to be marijuana."

Ted's mouth fell open. This certainly didn't help the argument that he was innocent. He knew the clothes were there. He'd put them in his locker to hide them from his parents until he could take them to the Laundromat. But the bag of weed that was with them, he hadn't hidden that. It must have been planted. He wondered how Gilbert could have pulled that off. Now he was really confused. Yet he was certain that he now had a problem. The coach had caught him. It no longer made any sense denying what he'd done. He confessed to his coach.

Ted was suspended for one game for what was classified as "unspecified reasons." The coach reserved the right to add to the punishment after additional facts could be gathered. Ted asked his coach, "tell me now. Who snitched on me?"

The coach's only comment was, "Someone who cares asked me to help you." That was all the coach would offer. It left Ted to come to his own conclusions on the matter.

Under his breath, Ted mumbled, "Goddamn that Gilbert Solkin."

It was actually Stephanie who had visited the coach the day before and told him that Ted had a problem that required the coach's immediate attention. She told the coach that Ted's personality and attitude was changing and that she was deeply concerned for him. The day before, she had helped Ted hide his clothes in his locker. She added the small bag of marijuana just to be sure his crimes were affirmed. She knew where to tell Coach Andrews to look for the evidence that would seal the deal, but in exchange for her confiding in him, she made coach Baker promise never to tell Ted that it was she who gave him the information. The coach agreed. Stephanie's role in the plot was now complete. It was the finishing piece in the plan that she, Brenda, and Robert had crafted with the help of Gilbert's evil spirit. It would aid the destiny of Gilbert's evil-natured spirit to weaken the bonds of trust that supported Ted and Gilbert's friendship. It would hinder the destiny of Gilbert's good-natured spirit to protect Ted from evil. Ted would surely think it was Gilbert who talked to the coach, especially after he'd threatened to do so the day before at the urging and influence of Brenda's evil-natured spirits.

The coach intended to protect his star player as much as he could. He made no report to the principal or counselors. What he told Mrs. Baker when he whispered into her ear was that Ted referred to the faculty as his puppets. They seemed to him to be willing to let him do anything he wanted to keep him, their star quarterback, in the game. This provoked Mrs. Baker's anger. She cared little about football or athletics. She didn't care that Ted was a star on the football field and especially didn't like being referred to as a puppet. Of course, Coach Baker lied. He was the one guilty of doing special things for Ted to keep this star athlete in the game. He suspended Ted for one football game, long enough to allow time to assess if anyone else knew of Ted's misguided indulgences or if anything else would surface from this problem. His objective was to affect Ted, his program, and the perfect season he was enjoying as little as absolutely possible while still appearing to address Ted's problems and well-being.

Gilbert heard that Ted was telling people that it was his fault that he'd been suspended. It was all the more hurtful because people knew that it was the reason why West Crawford had suffered its first loss of the season that Friday night. As if it couldn't get worse, the loss was to the weakest team in the district. Gilbert was getting the cold shoulder from everyone, everyone except Brenda. She was the only one he could still turn to for advice. Brenda told him when he called her that afternoon, "Gilbert, he's been your lifelong friend. Call him out. Confront him on his turf. You know you're in the right." It seemed to be good advice. Communication between he and Ted needed to be reestablished and done so immediately before any more damage was done.

Gilbert got in his car and drove to Stephanie's house, thinking that Ted would be there. He knocked on the door and was greeted by Stephanie's father. Gilbert asked, "Mr. Clarke, can I speak to Stephanie for a few minutes?" Mr. Clarke told Gilbert that Stephanie had gone out for the evening and wasn't expected home until after ten.

Gilbert then asked, "Did she say where she might be going, sir?"

Mr. Clarke responded, "She went out with an old boyfriend. You might know him. I believe his name was Robert Zeil." He paused for a moment to see if Gilbert might respond. "They said they were going to a party downtown at the Doran girl's residence. I can't say that I'm unhappy that she's through with that quarterback. I think he's stoned most of the time. I didn't like him seeing my daughter." It was more information than he bargained for. But it all came as a big surprise. He mulled it all over in his mind as he redirected his destination to Ted's house. Fortunately, he found Ted home.

As he expected, Ted was very cold toward him. Gilbert said, "Ted, we've got to talk. I think you've got this whole thing very wrong."

Ted replied, "Gilbert, I think you've already talked enough and to the wrong people. What do you have to say that I want to listen to?"

Gilbert retorted, "See, that's where you have it all wrong. I've said nothing. Tell me what the coach said to you. Why were you suspended?"

Ted's mother joined them in the foyer to assess what the loud exchanges were all about. She was relieved to see that it was only Gilbert and Ted. She returned to the family room. Ted motioned to Gilbert to move to his bedroom. He didn't want his mother involved in this affair.

In his room, he confessed, "I was suspended last week for using marijuana." He then pointed his finger at Gilbert. "You went to the coach and told him about me and Stephanie."

Gilbert then asked him, "Why would the coach believe me?"

Ted then responded angrily, "Because you gave him proof. I don't understand how you could have been so mean as to plant that bag of marijuana in my locker, Gilbert. That was dastardly."

Gilbert was caught completely by surprise. He defended himself, "Ted, what are you talking about? Please start over from the beginning. What proof did Coach Baker have, and where did he get it?"

Ted shook his head and waved his hand at the air, saying, "Come on, Gilbert. Stop putting on the show. You know what you told him, what and where to search for the proof, even where you planted the weed."

Gilbert was getting frustrated. He replied, "OK, Ted, you're so sure I'm guilty. How did I know where to tell Coach Baker to search, and just where do you think I came upon a bag of weed?" Gilbert's face flared in anger. "All I offered was to help, not to destroy you. I said nothing to Coach Baker." Gilbert then redirected his response. "And what's the deal with you and your girlfriend? Maybe you should suspect her of telling the coach. I hear she's now going out with Robert Zeil instead of you. Both she and Zeil have the access to drugs."

This hit a nerve with Ted. Gilbert should have left this card unplayed. Ted fired back, "Don't deflect your guilt on her. She didn't threaten to go to my coach a day before he suspends me." Then he calmed a little and considered the coincidence of the timing of their breakup and his suspension.

He grumbled at Gilbert, "Stephanie and I are not a couple anymore. What's it of business to you?"

Gilbert couldn't resist. It made his case complete. He reiterated the point that Ted had been thinking. "The timing of her leaving you is kind of coincidental, don't you think, or didn't you think that there might be someone else who could have set you up?" Both were at the pitch of anger. Both were ready to say meaner and nastier things to each other.

Ted actually took the higher road and just asked Gilbert, "Please leave me alone. You've caused me enough grief for one week. I need to think through all this on my own. Please just leave, Gilbert."

Gilbert stood before Ted, angry that he wouldn't listen to his reasoning. Ted belligerently continued to hold him accountable as the one who told the coach about the marijuana incident. In his anger and before he left the room, Gilbert took a gold medallion from Ted's dresser, one that he'd always cherished. He knew he shouldn't, but something within him urged him to do it. It was his evil-natured spirit's influence. Long ago, when they were much younger and just boys, one was given to Ted and another to Gilbert by their fathers. It was the year that they were champions of their Little League. Together, their fathers coached the team. It was the one team that they'd both been selected to participate on together. Gilbert, at the time, didn't hold his medallion so dear as Ted did. He lost his long ago. It now made Ted's all the more desirable. Both had since lost their fathers. It was the only real treasure Gilbert had earned as an athlete, certainly not like his friend who had a room filled with trophies, banners, and ribbons of glory. It reminded Gilbert of his father and how proud he had been of him; how proud he was to present him with his medallion. He cherished that moment so much more now that he was older. Since it looked like he and Ted might have a permanent falling out, he snatched up this reminder as his own. Ted, with all his other memorabilia and honors, would surely not miss this one piece. The theft would be covered over by all the many larger and more glorious-looking trinkets that filled the room.

Later on, Ted thought about what Gilbert had said to him. The truth was that it would have been highly unlikely that Gilbert would have known that he'd stashed his smoke-saturated clothes in his locker. It was even more unlikely he would have known how or had the courage and money to purchase the bag of marijuana. The more pieces to the puzzle that were fit together, the more Gilbert seemed innocent of the crime. Stephanie now seemed the most likely snitch. Ted could only wonder why she would have set him up. His conscience told him that he owed his friend an apology. He planned to stop over to see him later that evening to do so.

Gilbert's mother greeted Ted at the door and invited him in by saying, "It's good to see you around here again, Theodore." She chuckled at his grimace. It was her routine to call him by his formal name whenever there were troubles between Gilbert and him, even though she knew he hated it. "Gilbert is in his room. I'm sure he'll be glad to see you."

Ted knew the way. He scampered up the stairs and to the right. Gilbert's room was at the end of the hall. The door was half open. Ted could see Gilbert inside, working on his computer. He knocked on the door frame and said, "Hey Gilbert, I thought about what you said this earlier afternoon." He paused to get his attention. "I think I owe you an apology. It seems that maybe Stephanie had it in for me."

Gilbert showed an expression of relief and said, "Ted, I knew you'd see things more clearly in time. It seems we've both been played by our previous girlfriends."

Ted expressed surprise. "What do you mean, Gilbert? Have you and Brenda broken up too?"

Gilbert responded, "No, not officially, but Stephanie, Robert Zeil, and Brenda are all at her house tonight. My guess is that Brenda's with a new mark tonight as well." Gilbert looked at Ted. "It seems they might have been in on this together."

Ted asked, "But why would they do that, Gilbert? What would be the purpose? Just to damage my reputation and character?"

Gilbert rubbed his chin and then hypothesized, "What if it was to damage our friendship, to set us against each other?" Gilbert didn't have it completely figured out yet but was getting many thoughts from his internal. His domain knew the truth and was parsing it out in small dosages.

Ted was still very much in the dark. He could only question, "But why would they want us to be at odds with each other? It doesn't make sense."

Gilbert replied, "Maybe not, but maybe it's you and your influence they want. Maybe I'm in the way."

Then Gilbert looked down shamefully and asked Ted, "Don't you think it odd that someone as beautiful as Brenda would pick me out of the crowd as the one, she was interested in?" He looked up. "And don't you think it odd that Robert fixed you up with Stephanie? All three are together tonight. It may be that they're celebrating their victory over us or plotting their next score."

Ted thought it all a bit far-fetched, but the facts lined up in such a way as to allow it a possibility. Ted said, "So you think it's a plot?" Then he scrunched his face in anguish. "Does it matter?"

Gilbert responded, "I don't know, but I've been thinking about ways to find out."

Ted asked, "And what have you come up with?"

Gilbert laughed and shared, "I've got nothing, nothing but to confront them directly."

Ted then agreed, "OK, let's go. We know where they are. Let's go downtown and get to the bottom of this once and for all."

Gilbert looked frightened. It was too bold a plan for him alone. But with Ted, it was more appealing. He grabbed his jacket and his keys and said, "Let's go."

They arrived at the downtown high rise building and parked the car. Fortunately, the doorman remembered them from the previous night and allowed them in, saying, "Here for Miss Doran's party, I presume?" They both nodded yes and moved quickly to the elevators. They pushed the button for the twenty-second floor and stood quietly until the door closed. They were the only ones in the elevator's car.

Gilbert spoke. "It's strange that we were not invited, Ted. Perhaps their use for us is now complete?"

Ted chuckled and said, "For my sake, I sure hope so." They both grinned and prepared to exit the elevator on twenty-two. Brenda's room was number 2209. They knocked on the door and waited out of view of the peephole from inside the door. No one asked who was at the door. It simply swung wide open. The partiers were much older than Gilbert and Ted. Most were drunk or drugged.

Gilbert caught sight of Robert in the corner of the room. As they moved toward him, he noticed them as well. He had a surprised look to see them. He asked, "What are you doing here? You weren't on the guest list."

Gilbert responded, "We're here to see Stephanie, to straighten out this mess involving Ted once and for all."

Ted noticed the many bags of marijuana lying on every table. They looked identical to the one found in his locker. It was the confirmation that Stephanie, Brenda, and Robert had been involved in setting him up. Ted asked Robert, "Where are they, Robert?"

Robert laughed and pointed to the doors along the east wall of the apartment and said, "Do you want door no. 1, door no. 2, or door no. 3? The choice is yours." Robert was very high and laughing hysterically the whole time.

Gilbert responded, "It's not very funny, Robert, what you did to Ted."

Robert just continued to laugh and replied, "Ted did it to himself. Stephanie just helped him fall." Both Gilbert and Ted moved away from Robert and toward the doors. Robert didn't budge. He continued in his indulgences and his indifference to the two.

Gilbert knocked on the first door, but no one responded. He opened it a crack to see inside. Several young girls were with older men. Gilbert was shocked at what he saw. He now wondered about the occupation of Brenda's mother. In the next room, they found Stephanie. She, too, was engaged with older men, much the same as those in the first room. Everybody was high, or drunk. Stephanie seemed in no condition to talk to either of them. She looked at them at the door but made no sign that she recognized either of them. For Ted, he'd had proof enough. It was time to go.

As they made their way to the door, Brenda's voice pierced them. "Leaving so soon, boys? Don't you want to stay and join the party?" Gilbert was surprised when he turned to face her. She seemed much older than she had in their last encounter. She was dressed skimpily but not as one of the entertainments. She was clearly running the party. She said to Gilbert, "What, you don't want me to give you a little advice?"

She allowed her jab a full measure of effect before continuing, "If you did, I'd tell you to loosen up and stay." She laughed like Robert had. He was now at her side, supporting her. Gilbert suspected that Brenda was part of the plot against him, but it hurt all the same to confirm it as truth. He turned and hastily made his way to the door. Ted was in close pursuit. It seemed to take forever for the elevator to arrive. Both expected that Brenda or Robert might come through the door of 2209 any minute to further torment them. It didn't happen though. They escaped to their car and drove back to Gilbert's.

Ted planned to stay the night at Gilbert's. In the morning, they would put the final pieces to this puzzle together. As for Gilbert, he now was feeling the pain of rejection and of having been used emotionally by Brenda. Ted was just surprised by it all.

That night at Gilbert's house, after Gilbert had fallen asleep, Ted stayed up, thinking about the events of the past weeks. He paced around the room, looking for things to amuse himself with while his mind kept him awake. He found the gold medallion that was given to him by his father. The inscription on the back confirmed that it was his. It was a very special piece to him. It was special for two reasons. First, it was the last thing he'd received from his father before he left his mother and him; and second, it was the medal he'd won alongside his friend as part of the same team, the only one that they'd shared. It made Ted furious that Gilbert had taken it from his room without asking. He wondered if the disappointments of the week would ever end. This one hurt. It cut deep into his psyche, worse than the other disappointments that were mainly superficial types of damage. It proved betrayal from the person he'd just reinstated his trust in. He was weary; he was not thinking straight at this hour of the night, but still, this was a disappointment that sent his mind racing and his anger over the edge. He'd had enough of everybody he currently trusted and relied on, especially Gilbert, whom he called his best friend. He arrived at the conclusion that he needed to change his company.

Once again, he found himself wondering how much he could trust Gilbert. Gilbert's facade of goodness and innocence was wearing thin on Ted. He questioned whether he and his old friend were still alike and compatible people. Both were changing, a lot it seems, over the past weeks and months. It was time for change. Gilbert was obviously developing an evil and unpredictable side. Ted, on the other hand, had learned some lessons from the recent past. He was moving in the opposite direction of Gilbert, more toward good. He didn't need the betrayal and the pain that came with the evil influence. Trust was at issue now. Their relationship changed this night. Ted no longer held Gilbert above others as he had at one time. He questioned if Gilbert was one he could now trust. He stuffed the medallion in his pocket and decided to never mention that he'd found it.

Ted took partial responsibility for the changes in his friend. He'd introduced Gilbert to the wrong people. He introduced him to Brenda. The evil influences from Robert's group, like Stephanie, possibly affected Gilbert as well. He considered himself as part of the source of the problem. With his experimenting with marijuana and alcohol, these might have acted to erode the goodness and trust between them. Ted held the proof of the damage done from evil in his pocket. It hurt him to downgrade a friendship. It felt worse to be betrayed.

The many occurrences of pain that had been brought on him over the past weeks had awakened and strengthened his weaker good spirit. Hardship and pain are often an opportunity to wake the good spirits from inside a person. This renewal drove him away from Robert, Stephanie, and Brenda's influences and back toward better-natured relationships. He redirected his energies toward another. Her domain was of two good-natured spirits and a weak evil spirit. Her name was Tiffany. She'd come from a poorer family but was filled with goodness. It was what he dearly needed. He could trust her. There was a very strong bond between them, in fact that of the soul mate variety. She represented a break from his problems and a tonic to cure his hurt.

Even in his failures, Gilbert's good-natured spirits had achieved their destiny of keeping Ted from Robert's influences. What he'd lost in the process, however, was a friendship and the trust of a longtime friend. This was the gain of Gilbert's evil spirit. It served its destiny. This was a victory for dilution and the counter struggles of mixed-domain destinies. Gilbert was left in bad shape from his losses. He never really got over how Brenda and her partners had taken advantage of him or what he'd lost in the past month. His reputation at school was damaged.

Robert took every opportunity to capitalize on Gilbert's condition. Even Brenda would show up now and then and act as if she never knew him. He could not let her go in his mind. In his imaginary view, he thought of her as the best thing that had happened to him. His evil-natured spirit was left unstable as well. The sudden abandonment of his evil support and the ensuing emotional hurt that was created by the abandonments fed his need for vengeance. This was the only cure to his evil nature's ailments. Eventually, it dominated and eroded his goodness. He became much like Robert and Stephanie. His evil nature became strong, and his good natures became much lesser factors in his choices and actions. His instabilities surfaced through his external, and he became even more dangerous both from his domain and the other components of his being. He was noticeably changed to all who knew him. He cared little for anyone around him or the consequences of his actions. His action became evil and hurtful.

They were small time compared with Brenda's and Robert's, but Brenda especially avoided him all the same. There were few whom she paid caution, but Gilbert was one she did. She'd made him, and she'd made him evil. She'd nurtured his domain, so she knew his potential. He would destroy others' goodness as well as his own. She watched, knowing the source and the fuel of his anger. She had influenced his evil spirit well. Although it represented a direct danger to her, he was doing her work. His evil nature was achieving its common destiny. He was mad and beyond reason. He'd lost his regard for being. He drowned himself at age seventeen and a half.

Ted was surprised to see Brenda, Stephanie, and Robert at the funeral. They now made him feel very uncomfortable. He knew them for what they were. He saw the changes they'd all contributed in Gilbert. Ted was the only one with remorse. It would reside in his conscience for some time. It was healthy for a good-natured one to feel the hurt of a loss and to be able to relate from conscience. Gilbert's destinies were complete. The spirits from within his domain were released.

The key factors for achieving destinies involving others are many times different for good-natured spirits versus evil-natured ones. With the good-nature-dominated mixed domain, it's a matter of trust. Establishing and maintaining trust with the target of the destiny is key to achieving delivery of the destiny. With the evil-natured mixed domain, the key success factor in achieving its destinies is defending against conscience, guarding against the good conscience of the good-natured spirits of the mixed domain. As the keys to success are so different and counter to the influences of the opposite nature residing in the domain, most destinies never reach a pure and fully attainable state. Dilution in the degree to which these destinies are attained is the norm. The influences or obstacles created by the other spirits in the domain space weaken the purity of all things and create disappointing, unintended, negative, and lessened movements around the circle of life. It's natural and as planned. Significant destinies in their truest and fullest form are difficult to deliver from a mixed domain. Mainly, these destinies are assigned to the pure or strongest of the mixed spirits.

So, what, then, is the impact of the destinies that get diluted or that do not get fulfilled? Each domain has multiple destinies specifically assigned to its resident spirits. Conflicts arise between the destinies of each spirit of the domain. The thing is few destinies assigned to the mixed domains can be achieved by a single spirit alone or by the single mixed domain. Spirits and domains must work together with one another in their space to be successful, even if this means that they must find common ground and share with other domain resources. There may be information and partially constructed destinies stored within their own histories or other domains that are required to fit together as the pieces to form the answer to the questions and mysteries, allowing the achievement of one spirit's destiny. Destinies are steps that provide the materials to build and produce multifaceted, complex, and grander deliverables and results.

As with many things, destinies require collaboration and relationships. Even with these things, however, not all destinies can be achieved and rarely simply so. Some fall to the many circumstances and happenstance of changing conditions of life or, as time goes by, conflicts of many types. This creates an aggressive nature in society as all spirits strive to have their destiny achieved with greatest urgency while conditions favor and match the assignment. It doesn't matter what the destiny's priority is in the overall order of importance or its benefit to the world; missed destinies influence the balance of power between good and evil. Missed destinies affect movement along the circular path of life. Spirits are individually accountable to their natures to achieve their destinies in the span of their assigned being's lifetime.

When a spirit does not achieve its destiny, a hole is left in the domain's stores of experiences and knowledge. This omission to the domain's stores will create a weakness. It will one day leave the domain unable to answer the call from the mind and the body for answers and direction to a situation or stimulus. It will create doubt in the domain by the other components as an infallible source of solutions by the other components. These other components will then question their prudence of being totally reliant on spirit guidance. It will smudge the record of success and reliability of the domain for support in their time of calling. It will open the door for the other components to be more assertive and venture out on their own for answers, answers that will come from other willing, less reliable external sources, mainly the world these other components interface with constantly. This will represent the first closure, the movement into the fourth quadrant of life's circle. As the body and mind's confidence grows in making decisions and taking action without the influence and impetus of the spirit domain, the spirit domain will be slowly relegated to a lesser position of strength and influence. The movement down this path to the end of civilization will be accelerated, all this because of missed destinies, missed opportunities to gather needed information, experiences, or influences. This is the importance of spirits constantly achieving their destinies in spite of hardship, conflicts, and challenges.

It's the cumulative effect of missed destinies in all the domains and the holes of information and experience within their domains that leads to the closure of the circle of life. When all beings disconnect in part or in whole from primary reliance on the spirit domain, the circle will close. The spirits will be released, and the beings will be no more. In the case of Evan Filmond addressed previously above, his evil-natured spirit achieved its destiny; yet in doing so, he killed the being. His domain's other evil-natured spirit and good-natured spirits were released to the unassigned pool of spirits before reaching their assignment's destinies. There was no working together between the spirits within this domain. As a result, two significant holes were created within the domain's stores for the next recipients of the two unfortunate spirits assigned forward from Evan's domain. This would create vulnerability and will eventually catch up to these spirits in future generations of assignments. It will move the point on the circle one small notch closer to closure.

Anita's destiny was to be a friend to Becky and to support her. Her domain was mixed; therefore, her destinies were also mixed. Becky provided help and strength to the ones of Anita's domain that were of a good nature. This reciprocated itself because these same spirits' destinies were to help Becky and her causes as an accomplice and friend. But the destiny of her evil nature was beyond Becky's jurisdiction. Actually, Anita's evil-natured destiny was to provide challenges to Becky. In total, Anita's mix of destinies was almost entirely focused on Becky and would provide her with a leveling, a common yet friendly specimen to model and practice her approaches and influences with before rolling these out on a larger scale to the community of primarily mixed domains and mixed destinies.

Anita's significant destinies will reveal themselves as this story further develops.

Robert Zeil's destiny was to recruit new domains to evil, to convert good to evil ways. He was to work with the younger people of the school and lure them to the evils of Mr. Arthur and Brenda Doran. His was to serve as a peer and appear as a friend to the vulnerable, luring them to his evil. He was to be the bait to attract and pull them to environments where Mr. Arthur and Brenda could influence them. First, his destiny was to earn Mr. Arthur and Brenda Doran's trust. This was most difficult for an evil nature, especially as it applied to Mr. Arthur. Mr. Arthur trusted very few, especially few without a pure evil domain.

Many of Robert's destinies were linked to Brenda's. Finding each other made them better able to achieve these destinies. The synergies of their efforts made them a more powerful team, much more so than working on these apart. It especially gave strength to Robert's efforts. Theirs was not as powerful as, say, a soul mate relationship, but their creativity and dedication to their evil natures made them bond strongly and compatibly toward common goals and objectives. Robert helped Brenda grow stronger in her pure evil ways. He gave her creative method and access to targets that gave her advantage, on occasion even over Mr. Arthur.

The destiny of his one badly suppressed good-natured spirit was the most surprising of all. It was to bring Mr. Arthur to his end. Its final plan would be flawless but would not be achieved to its fullest measure. It would fail only in its timing and thus require the involvement of others to complete. However, it would mark the beginning of the end for Mr. Arthur.

Dewaun Burkes was an evil one. His primary destiny was simply to spread evil and to be a force in the distribution of evil and evil influence. He was brash and self-confident. His destiny was to challenge Mr. Arthur's chosen one, Brenda, for position. His destiny was to force Brenda to defend her position and commit to actions to justify and embody it. It was confirmation of sorts. Dewaun was to antagonize and coax out these actions.

Dewaun was destined to present a strong and brash evil on the earth. He felt destined to add new rules, challenge old ways, and develop his own circles of evil. He was not a team player but rather saw himself as the captain. All those around him were to answer his call and heed to his direction. His destiny did not fit well into Mr. Arthur or Brenda's established plans or methods. His destiny was to overcome this and to rise to become influential. His destiny, and his dream was to become the second strongest influence in Millborough, only behind that of Mr. Arthur. His evil nature didn't realize that it would be Brenda who represented the stronger evil, that actions toward attaining this destiny would only contribute to the growth of Brenda's powers through test. His destiny was finally to die as his final act of evil.

The destiny of Dewaun's good-natured spirit was embedded in his evil-natured spirit's destinies. It was to infiltrate Mr. Arthur's evil network. This destiny needed to be cloaked completely by Dewaun's other destinies; to defy authority to get the attention of the top of Mr. Arthur's organization. He was actually placed in the community undercover. His good nature's destiny was to remove Mr. Arthur from all influence in the community. He was to make a case against him that would stand up in court in spite of the judges and politicians on his payroll. He was handpicked for the assignment because he proved to be a top-notch FBI agent. Unfortunately, one good nature was not enough. The FBI picked the wrong guy and the wrong domain makeup to serve the need. His evil dominance made it too easy to turn on his duty and mission and to become part of what he was to put an end to. It was his undoing. As it appeared in the aftermath, he'd gone too far. Neither Brenda, Mr. Arthur, nor the FBI knew who he was really representing. All thought he'd turned on them. No one would claim responsibility for his actions or the authorization that led to his demise. He was viewed as an undercover agent gone AWOL. It was a destiny unachieved. Dewaun's legacy was one of leaving nothing to the good side of the ledger of life.

Bringing the Past to the Future

Spirits have access to many gifts. An example of one previously mentioned is magic. Yet another that they bring into this earth is of equal, maybe even greater value than magic. It is vision. It is vision that allows the domains to predict and provide a near- or longer-term picture of the future.

There are many degrees of vision, so many that to address them all would be impossible. But four that are most notable and known to beings. They are clairvoyance, telepathy, déjà vu, and insight. The greatest of these is the ability to see and predict what is to come in the long term. This is clairvoyance and is made possible to only a few special domains. It involves gaining access and then the ability to decipher another domain's accumulation of scripted information and experience as they are integrated into their destinies. It's made up partially of history, that which a domain knows, and destiny, what a domain will strive for. These form the base ingredients for creating vision into the future. Clairvoyance is the most exclusive, and most difficult to master, and thus at the highest level of the vision's hierarchy. It's the most well-known and bizarre of the visions.

At the opposite end of the spectrum, at the lowest level of vision's hierarchy is insight. All domains, if they choose, have the gift of insight. Insight is practiced to many degrees; the level of insight is dependent on the strength of the creating domain and its developed skills and capabilities. Insight is often a warning or a gentle influence to do or not to do something. It's often taken for granted, not considered a form of vision by most external beings. It's the most widespread of the gifts. It is easiest to master and call out. There is little restriction to the spirits to its access.

Residing at the midlevel of vision's hierarchical forms is telepathy and the instances of déjà vu. Telepathy, like clairvoyance, is limited, in its stronger forms, to only the pure domains. It includes a spirit's metaphysical transfer to another's domain. In its milder forms, it is also sharing between auras of two or more domains. Finally, déjà vu is altogether different from the other three forms of vision and can be affected by any type or mix of domain. It is therefore lower on the hierarchical chain than telepathy because it is less restrictive. Unlike the other forms, it is not initiated or controlled by the spirits of a domain. It is beyond and deeply internal to the spirit from the domain storages. With déjà vu, the spirits act as a conduit under the control of déjà vu. It is a device to externally trigger releases of memories and events from the depth of the domain itself.

All these types and levels of vision are important and prevalent in the spirit realm. Regardless of their level, frequency of use, or type, they are all gifts of the spirits. None is perfected without a qualified spirit's involvement nor are their occurrences without clear reason and purpose. They are produced for the spirit's reason and purpose, to be shared with the beings. They are the product of the spirit's mystery and mystic. They are gifts, and as such, they are primarily delivered for special reasons and from special calling. This is especially true as the level of difficulty and the unique attributes required to produce the type of vision increase.

The differences between the spirits that render the highest forms of vision and those at the lowest levels of the hierarchy are inherent to the spirit domain's makeup and attributes. There are indeed vast differences that allow a domain the ability to read another's future as opposed to that of allowing one to recognize their own insights. There is less difference as you compare types residing further down in vision's hierarchy. An aptitude to read one's own insights and short-term visions is inherent and common to all spirit domains but requires practice and care. It allows domains to plan and act on their own destinies. It is a basic tenet of a domain, a price of admission, so to speak. It acts as a guide through which the near-term scripts of the domain can be enacted.

At the other extreme, mastery over a domain's intermediate and long-term future, even those of its own control, is a talent that is unique and gifted to only a very few domains with specific attributes. The first criteria to achieving clairvoyance is that the reader must be a pure domain to support transfer. Included in the necessary specifics is that the pure domain must lack dominance, strength, and assertiveness of its residing spirits' natures. This ensures a unique spirit unity and likeness within the domain, and open perspective and special domain discipline. This is a combination unique to only a few special pure domains. It allows a totally committed, concentrated, and synchronized focus by three highly coordinated and noncontentious spirits of a domain. It allows them to be less intrusive guests to their host and to achieve capture and to gain extractive license over the host domain's internal blueprints and plans. It requires special and unique skill to navigate through and isolate only the information destined to the domain as its current life's scripted strand of future intents.

In this case of clairvoyance, a special type of transfer from the reader's domain is required. It requires that all the spirits from the reader's domain transfer, acting as one, into the targeted subject's domain. It requires a synchronized, nonjudgmental, and nonintrusive visitation, as well as an unbiased indifference to the condition and plans of the domain receiving a reading. There can be no intervention, no offering of help, no support, and no residual change left behind within the domain of the subject to the reading. It is this unbiased, nonintrusive position on the part of each of the transferring and reading spirits that allows them unhindered and unlimited access to zero in, to move freely about the layers of the domain stores, and to extract a precise slice of subconscious intent and history.

Most of the pure domains are not capable of clairvoyance. Their primary roles are to help, to grow, and to influence the common domains. This is their destiny. They get distracted on the very first situation or the segments of their intent that they feel need to be helped, influenced, changed, or supported. They can pass no further into the reading. The stronger the pure domain is, the more incapable they are of clairvoyance. This is where the unique lack of strength, even though pure of domain, comes into play.

Clairvoyance is a gift that all spirits strive to command, if only for a brief moment. For those other than the special few, it's only an allure, the unattainable goal. It's like a carrot dangling just beyond the reach of a hungry mule to tempt and to keep it moving forward, trying to attain it. Attempts, even those so limited as to create a vision of one domain's own future or intents, fall futile. Failure is inevitable. It's not about the will or desire of the domain giving it a try; instead, it's tightly interwoven into the attributes and the domain's makeup. Even though success is improbable, even impossible, the allure to a spirit to overcome this impossibility is great. The unqualified will still try. Try they do in primarily two ways. First, they try to extract a reading from their own domain, that which they believe should be under their control. Second is to try and extract clairvoyance from another's aura. Sharing from the auras is known to them. Testing its extent seems a reasonable approach toward clairvoyance.

As for those who try the first approach and are not of the special few, they most frequently find themselves disappointed from the effort. The results are only products of blurred images or undecipherable fragments from their domain's periphery. There is no real vision. Rather, the end product is mostly unstable. These images are the result of false readings of intermixed and primarily majority portions of influences from the conflicting, many contending, and often divergent intents and destinies of their natures. These provide little clarity and no long-term vision. Their attempts deliver a view that is grossly distorted and out of focus. These results are of no use to any spirit or anyone.

Attempts by the ungifted to venture beyond their own domain, to try to read a future from another's aura, produces still greater failure. As intriguing and as sound as this may seem to a common domain to try, it is simply not a plausible way to create a vision of a future. First is the fact that between any two domains, there exists a vast array of knowledge, thoughts, and outcomes to sort through to derive a single and focused clarity and meaning. To a common domain, the focus and synergies with and between the domain partners is not consistently unified or single threaded enough to avoid contamination, divergence, or noise from the exchange, nor is it strong enough to establish depth. Depth is a second reason for failure of this approach. Depth is particularly important to obtaining a vision. The details and scripts of one's future are not often stored on the periphery of the domain where the aura draws its charge. The periphery is where common domains may connect but not the intricacies and complexity of visions. Therefore, extracting a vision of the future from another's aura, although frequently tried, is impossible.

Common spirits relentlessly try anyway, even though clairvoyance is limited to only a few with special attributes. It challenges the ungifted. It draws and creates persistence and drive. And on occasion, their efforts are rewarded by the one glimpse, perhaps a perceived snippet, an exception to the rule. It's this one instance that keeps them forever trying. It's only a small prize for their efforts. It's like the consolation prize. It's not clairvoyance. In these prized instances, the domain is allowed a short and occasional glimpse of a vision and only of a near-term variety. Theirs is limited to a rare and momentary snapshot involving only their own being's near-term future. These are only slightly greater forms of vision than insight, but they are the pinnacle of what the common spirit can achieve.

On the sporadic occasions when the spirits and natures of the mixed domain work cohesively and unified within the domain, it is only then that a self-vision might momentarily come into focus and provide a peek into their near future. It is in these moments of insight that personal direction and aspiration is set. Only in these times of total domain harmony are the spirits of a mixed domain allowed a self-view where they might be going, what is possible for them. Personal goals, plans, and attainable visions result. These infrequent snapshots from the inner periphery of their personal futures lay the groundwork for delivery of their destinies. It's only enough to keep the domain forward sighted and directed. It's not clairvoyance; it's a derivative of insight. These are a milder version of vision's level of value. Yet they provide critical purpose. They provide direction and hope.

Working simultaneously with the aforementioned challenges, it's also often a significant challenge for the common and mixed domain just to sort through the current possibilities and destinies within their own domain and those under their own control. This is reflected through beings who think they understand where they are going with their lives but often find themselves unknowing or surprised by the turns of events that occur in their immediacy. They simply miss the insights that can help direct them on nature's course. Within their own domain, the gift of personal insight needs to be a primary focus in the quest for creating vision instead of clairvoyance, which represents an aim that is often off target and rarely rewarded. It's in perfecting insights where their return and value are greatest. Even with success, these personal and protracted insights usually don't provide farsighted, predictive value for the owner; rather, each step comes into focus just shortly after completing the previous and only moments before the next. As a result, common spirits do not often acknowledge these insights as visionary at all but rather just thoughts and reactions from stimuli. They believe only the highest forms of the gift to be a true vision. This is their mistake. This is why clairvoyance, even to those unable to attain it, is frequently coveted. Those who achieve insight often don't acknowledge it as special or from a gift. They simply take their power for granted. Not acknowledging this oversight and failing to achieve higher-level visions, they may even doubt that visions to the future really exist. But the pure domains know and recognize all visions, in all forms and degrees, to be the special spirit gift that they truly are. It is the pure domains, and only the chosen few among the pure domains, that master and perfect the highest levels of looking into the future of another domain.

Perfecting insight and short-term visions are important for every domain. They come from power over that which is on the periphery of the domain. It is a reading of what will surface next. It is predicting a situation and matching it to the what and the reaction that will come from the outer periphery of the domain's stores. It is reading the information and experiences that are most readily available, those that will surface first to address the next event. It's knowing what will happen at the urging and influence of a stimulus. All of life's major, and even its most minor, events are scripted and logged by nature's devices. They are within the domain stores to guide us. They are there for the skilled and gifted to read and draw from. Predicting events and one's corresponding actions from these scripts is easy for those who are practiced. The difficult part thus becomes the development of the skill to extract the precise insight from the working periphery of one's domain. Those with skill easily isolate these.

Nature's internal scripts support all types of visions, not just insight. They are nature's guide to the being for addressing reaction and response to life's situations and events. They contain the triggers that draw out both externally and internally provoked stored knowledge, thoughts, stored destinies, and the pieces of plans put away for safekeeping in one generation until needed in a following one. These are the portions of destinies stored from previous assignments of the spirit throughout its history and intended for a future time. All these add to the future that can be predicted and read. The being will act on these scripts. It is their conditioned path. In practice, the reader of the script may change it to small degrees, perhaps so much as changing a word or two, perhaps a slight change in the form of delivery, but the final enactment and result is always the same. It's scripted and always quite predictable.

To those who have mastery of the gift of clairvoyance, they will read the path of one's domain and destinies as they are guided by the scripts. They will decode the script from the other intertwined information and stores within the deep inner confines of the domain. These few can extract the future enactments long before the script is due to be played out. Visions of a distant future are dependent on the same components as those of the short-term vision's variety, but extracting the details to the longer-term future events and their effects requires delving deeper into the depths of the subject's domain stores, well past the periphery. It is a significantly more challenging process because it requires a larger, more unified, and more coordinated effort and a transfer on the part of all the reading spirits of a unique domain. This is the case to bring the details together into conformity and view as a vision. It is the reason why these powers are not common among most domains. For a mixed domain, the type most prevalent in beings, it is never one of total spirit unity or conformity. Contention and inconsistent focus within the mixed domain's spirits preclude clairvoyance.

So, what about these special few among the spirit ranks with the common focus within their domains to give them the power, the cohesiveness, and the access to others, as well as to the control and use of vision's gift to the fullest? It's not an all-inclusive group of the pure domains. Clairvoyance, in part, comes from weakness or, better stated, their lack of strength. This may seem like a contradiction, to be both a pure and weak domain. But it's not. It's a gift that is bestowed on the weaker-spirited pure domains to give them unique advantage and a special strength over the more powerful, more prevalent pure domains. Only a very small percentage of pure spirit domains are gifted with the ability of clairvoyance. It manifests itself within the weaker pure spirit's passiveness and willing nature to accept, absorb, and learn rather than to direct or affect change. It allows for unbiased and unfiltered readings. The future reveals itself to them in full through these attentive, receptive, and finely tuned mediums.

The weaker pure domains usually mentor under a stronger one. They provide clairvoyant visions to them and help them steer a clear course to the future. It's an advantage that these weaker pure domains hold in the relationship. It's their strength, even though it's through their weakness as a pure domain that it is afforded. This relationship between the powerful and weak pure domains thus allows the powerful ones to know their futures through their weaker apprentices. The weak ones give up themselves in this act. They are, in fact, unconscious throughout the activity. It is not a painful or strenuous activity. It is their special offering and show of support to the powerful and pure domains. In return, the strong domains teach and mentor the weaker pure domains in the ways of domain strength and responsibility.

When the weaker ones grow from this mentorship, when they, too, grow stronger in their pure nature's planned destinies and purpose, they will lose their gift and ability to tell futures. This will be their sign that they are stronger and ready. It will be the sign of transformation. It's the rite of passage, the gauge of readiness of a pure domain for its own stand-alone assignments as a powerful pure domain. The last vision of those who transform is one of their own destinies. It will guide them to what and where they are to be and what they are to achieve. But while weaker and pure, they are clairvoyant.

Brenda, for the early part of her tenure under Mr. Arthur's tutelage, was one with the gift. This is one of the reasons why Mr. Arthur took her in. The reading she eventually received of her own future was why she was willing to wait in the wings of Mr. Arthur. She knew her day to control and dominate would come. She'd seen it at the time of her transformation from a weaker to a stronger pure domain.

Not all pure domains start out as weak. Most are brought directly into the world as strong domains. In many cases, there is immediacy for their powers, their purposes, and their influences. These are the ones who are dispatched to the earth with an immediate and significant impact or cause to be carried out from their inception. It is unfortunate, but these domains are never able to experience reading the future of another domain. It is only with help of the weaker pure ones that their future will be laid open to them through the sharing of a clairvoyant's vision. Yet the odds of one finding a weaker pure domain grow worse as the civilization moves around the circle of life. It's a time when clear course into the future is most needed, but the seeker is often left searching for what will not be found.

How can it be? How can these weak pure domains see into the future of another domain? The simple answer is that it's in nature's mysteries and the world's master plans for balance. It is in the weak pure domain's purity and openness that allows it. In their weaker form, they are nonintrusive. They are undistracted by mission or responsibility, like the stronger pure domains, or by inconsistencies between the spirits, like the spirits in mixed domains. As pure spirits, they are focused and cohesive. Their destinies are strong and clear. They have powers to transfer and to share with other's domains. Yet their power in this regard is unique. Because they are weak, they have the special ability to transfer three spirits as if one to the subject's domain. It takes the power of three specially gifted spirits to draw out a reading from deep within a domain. Their window into the domains of others has few limits; it has no shades or window dressings of preconceived ideas or influences to shield or hinder them from seeing clearly through each pane. They see all the pieces of the puzzle and how they will fit together. This is the special value that these pure spirits will provide through their time, a time until ready to be a stronger and dominant influence to the community.

Through this stage in their development, they are still naive and innocent. They do not assume package or create their own interpretation. Their spirits do not set direction, nor do they yet dictate. They simply provide vision. They can still let things materialize around them without contamination of their contribution or influence. It is through removal of their importance and the absence of a perception of themselves as necessary, special, and powerful that allows them unrestricted and unfiltered passage into others' unknowns. This is how they support both their stronger mentors and weaker mixed domains. They fit nowhere yet everywhere. They are caught up in searching. They find the places and things no one else will find. They allow these findings to form on their own accord.

The final form is a vision, a reading of the future. Soon they, too, will grow to be more seasoned and stronger, too seasoned and strong to avoid influence and input. With this transformation and growth, they will lose their clairvoyance. It will be then that they will be used for a more specific destiny and purpose and will then make futures instead of reading them. The progression through the weaker stages will benefit them in their future.

To a lesser degree, all have some tendencies, even some abilities, to create visions at some level. The levels of capability between clairvoyance and insight are innumerable and range from the purest to least pure of domains. Yet the gift of vision is present in all spirits and all domains. Unfortunately, it's not the full tool set or makeup that they carry. In almost all cases, it is not the ability to read another's future. But also, at times, a lesser-level version of the power might surface in our times of passiveness, vulnerability, or dependences. It comes from our spirits and their ventures through our domain stores. It is evidenced by special instances, such as when we have a bad feeling or good feeling about someone or something, when we have a hunch, when we stop short of doing something or saying something and are later glad we didn't and don't know exactly why we didn't. It's in the spirits, their interactions between domains, their connecting to one another's outermost blueprints or through auras. It's more than insight. It's far less than clairvoyance. It's in one of the many middle levels of vision's hierarchical span, these numerous midlevel categories of vision. Two of these will be addressed in the following.

Telepathy is a special midlevel form of vision. It's an exclusive form of the gift. All pure domains, and only the pure domains, are gifted with telepathy. Thus, it is higher on the hierarchy of visions than most types. This type allows one to transfer to another less pure domain to read their current or past thoughts and to share the value and wealth stored within their domain stores. The pure domain can read, but more often, they deliver guidance and information to and from their domain. Most of the time, telepathy is used primarily to influence rather than read. It is practiced by the pure domain and governed under a strict code of conduct and limits. Pure spirits are self-governed on how they can and will use these powers. If the unwritten, but understood, rules of nature are not adhered to, these pure domains will lose their telepathic ability in the current or future frames of existence.

Spirits use telepathy primarily to support other spirits, not to directly coerce them or their being. Its primary use is to build and strengthen a spirit or nature that has lost potential and effectiveness. Pure domains provide strength to needy spirits through transfer, but the strength that is provided is more of a replenishment. Rarely is it given in excess of the receiving spirit's original portion of strength or dominance. It simply rejuvenates what was once there and raises their potential to original standards, not necessarily new ones. It does not give participating spirits the ability to see into the long-term future, primarily only the past, the current, and the planned near horizon.

Déjà vu is another midlevel variation of vision. It is a midlower level of vision's hierarchy compared with telepathy. It is somewhat higher than insight. It is a reawakening of the domain to its past experiences from prior assignments and prior beings. It occurs when a current event or situation brings attention to a specific and previous experience stored in the domain. This experience then triggers a spirit history, a memory from the domain stores, or a stored message, perhaps a link to previous portions of destinies that will support the current generation's destiny. Every spirit has a history. Every spirit carries its history and wealth of knowledge forward. It's the triggers to this history and information that take us by surprise and enact déjà vu. Déjà vu is the event passageway to our spirit's previous times.

When you remember something that you can't quite put your finger on or have a memory with no reference from this life's experiences or when an event feels frightfully familiar to you for no apparent reason or explanation, it's the spirit's work. There are explanations for these events, but they all lie within and from within the spirit domain. They come from dredging up information and links to history within the domain's storage. It can be simply an excerpt from the spirit stores of past life's history and experiences that rise to the surface, brought there by a similar and triggering event in the present. It could be a correlation to a place or proximity to a spirit within another current-day person who was present when the past-life item was created and stored. It could be almost anything that acts as the trigger or conduit to the past.

It is natural to remember these previous contributions and experiences of the spirit's past lives. These help the spirit remember and the being recreate the important and significant events intended for them to recall from the spirit's past. It helps the current being benefit and build from its hidden history. It forms the foundation for further evolution and development of the being. It's a mind twist in that the spirit allows the current being to believe it had experienced the event of the previous time when, in fact, it was only the spirit that experienced the event in the past while within a different being from a different generation or cycle of time. The mind and body must be persuaded to adopt the experiences as part of their own and for its benefit.

The way it works is that each spirit can mark memories and history that it wishes to be brought back by a trigger in future life. It is up to the current or future life to trigger the déjà vu and then to uncover the significance of it. It is with the help of the spirit, of course. Most events go unnoticed or unattended with nary a second thought, but there is real treasure, special value, or special reward to exploring and unraveling the mystery and significance of why the being and event were chosen, why it was tagged by the spirit in its past for the future spirits or being to find. For those that allow their being to find the special artifact and to find the lost secret, it allows them the building blocks to support a current destiny, to piece together the foundation of previous contributions that form significance. Whether it is to finalize or simply to add another stage to develop an unfinished destiny from a past generation, there is great reward in it for the current spirit and the current being and to life's master plan.

Stanley Boston was destined to help someone dear to him, to keep her from harm. He was also destined to ease her pain and torment from an event that happened long ago. He would be aided by an occurrence of déjà vu from his domain stores.

He lived with his wife in Des Moines, Iowa, where he'd spent his entire life of forty-two years, aside from eight or nine weeks that he'd spent on several sporadic vacations of distance, one to the Rockies and one trip to the West Coast. This year, he and his wife were trying something different. Stanley and his wife, Belinda, decided to take three weeks and travel to the northeastern parts of the country into the New England states. They'd seen a few brochures and talked to a few friends who had previously traveled this region. They'd listened intently as their friends shared their experiences of its beauty and mystic. Stanley thought it would be a welcomed adventure and change from his and Belinda's norm. They made a few reservations but, for the most part, decided to plan the trip on the fly. They started their adventure. They especially liked the small out-of-the-way towns and back roads that took them away from civilization. The northeast was a beautiful part of the country, and they were thoroughly enjoying their vacation.

One and a half weeks into their adventure, they came upon a small Vermont town named Belleville. Stanley had strange feelings as if he knew this town. Memories of time spent roaming its streets, details of its buildings, and its people flooded his memory from the stores of his domain. He had no explanation for it, but he could swear he'd been in this town before. It was so familiar.

He shared his experience with his wife. She listened in disbelief. Quite frankly, she didn't know what to think of it. She questioned,

"Stanley, are you sure you have never in your life been to this town before, perhaps as a child?"

Stanley replied, "No, honey. You've known me most of my life. My parents never took us out of the state. This is quite strange. It's like an episode of déjà vu." He couldn't believe he was admitting to something from the supernatural realm but had nothing else to offer. "I could swear I've been here before. Maybe it was in a previous life." He looked to the passenger next to him in the car and smiled after just introducing a second seemingly bizarre and unaccepted theory, this being reincarnation. He was not a believer in it either. He suspected that his wife wasn't appreciating his episodes into the unknown. She looked puzzled, even afraid.

Stanley looked in wonderment of his visions. He seemed quite intrigued by it all, and he asked her, "Would you be willing to stay here tonight? I want to further explore this phenomenon I'm caught up in." He chuckled in an attempt to break the growing anxieties. "If I'm right, I could show you around the town just like I was a longtime resident."

Belinda was not as anxious to explore her husband's unknowns. The whole series of events filled her with discomfort and skepticism. She even questioned that her husband might be playing a joke on her. Yet as they drove through the town, he surprisingly knew Belleville's streets, even its alleys. He knew its buildings. He knew them in much detail as if he'd architected or perhaps built them. He told her what was inside each as they drove by. It quickly became clear that he was not playing a game with her. The longer it went on, the more precise his knowledge of this place, matched perfectly with reality; She began to believe in his unexplained episodes of deja vu. It was very mysterious. She wondered what would happen next. It added to their adventure.

They found a bed and breakfast at what Stanley told her used to be the old Stewart mansion. Interestingly enough, it was owned by Dorothy Paige. Dorothy's maiden name was Stewart. There was a brochure in the foyer explaining how Benjamin Stewart built the house in 1938. Mr. Stewart was a state senator from the region. He had a wife and two children, a boy and a girl. Only the daughter was still alive. The house had been passed down to her. It was a huge house for one person to live in; thus, Dorothy turned it into a bed and breakfast.

Before they entered it, Stanley described the inside of the house to Belinda in great detail. Sure enough, when they walked inside, she was shocked to find it exactly as he explained it to be, except for the colors and wallpaper on some of the walls. Stanley assumed that these had been changed by the owner but asked her, "Didn't these walls used to be blue, and wasn't there striped wallpaper in the room with the fireplace?"

Dorothy Stewart was quite surprised and said, "Well, yes. But it's been years since I've redecorated. How did you know that? Have you been to the house before?"

Stanley didn't know what to say. He just replied, "Years ago as a young boy." His wife reacted in surprise of this response but remained quiet.

Dorothy Stewart responded, "I don't recall you. Did we meet? Perhaps we played together."

Stanley replied, "I think we might have. It's been such a long time ago."

Dorothy then asked, "Since you remember the house, is there a particular room you'd like to stay in?"

This intrigued Stanley. His mind was flooded with memories of an upstairs room at the center of the house facing the west side. As it turned out, Stanley's precise description of the room allowed Dorothy to pinpoint it as her brother's room. She replied, "You must have been here previously to see my brother, John. The room you describe was his." Belinda took it all in and said nothing. It was so amazing.

Dorothy then asked, "Did you work for the builder, old Mr. Johnson, like John did? Perhaps this is how you know us."

Stanley rubbed his chin and thought before he replied, "I've always enjoyed working with my hands." He left it very vague on purpose. He honestly didn't know how or why these visions of déjà vu were coming to him. He was allowing the scene to play out as he went.

Dorothy showed Stanley and Belinda to their room and offered to help them bring their luggage up. Stanley asked, "Do you live here with your husband?"

Dorothy's smile disappeared for a moment. She shared, "My husband, Joe, passed away only months after we were married. I've been very unfortunate with those I've loved."

She then added as if Stanley would know, "He worked in a very dangerous trade, steeple restoration." She paused in reflection and then restarted with a comment. "It's big business in these parts, you know. He fell from the steeple at St. Anthony's in Wellburg." Her eyes showed signs of moisture. "He only lived a few days after the fall. We buried him with the rest of my family. I'm now the only one left."

Stanley replied sympathetically, "That is sorrowful news, Dorothy. Joe Paige was a good man. He was a friend when we were young." The words spilled from his mouth involuntarily. It was as if he'd known the man. In his subconscious, he did. In his being, he did not. Belinda was bewildered by her husband's seeming insensitive lies of familiarity with Dorothy's husband. Dorothy, on the other hand, seemed charged by his concern and sorrow. She felt comfortable and familiar with Stanley. She was convinced that he was an old friend of the family.

Stanley finished by saying, "About your offer to help with the luggage, thank you, but we can manage. It's a very nice place you have here."

Dorothy smiled and offered, "If there is anything you need, just call me. I'll be just down the hall or somewhere about the house."

Belinda added, "It's nice to meet you, Dorothy. I'm sure we'll be very comfortable here."

Dorothy left the room and closed the door behind her. On her way out, she said over her shoulder, "Don't forget, dinner is at six. We're having baked chicken tonight. I'm told that it's my best dish."

Before going downstairs for the luggage, Stanley moved about the room as if searching for something. He finally stopped in the middle of the floor and tapped the toe of his shoe to the varnished wooden floorboards several times in succession before finally pulling up a loose board and extracting an old box from within. He opened it to find it filled with things from Dorothy and John's parents. There were jewelry, pictures, and things that they'd apparently given to their children. There was a beautiful necklace and a locket within. It seemed that these might be things that Dorothy might have treasured rather than John, even though it was clear that this was John's treasure stash.

It filled Belinda's thoughts as well; these were strange things to be in a boy's secret box. It didn't fit. She wished she could know why. Perhaps it would play out in time. There were also some gold pieces, a money clip, a jade miniature, and several keys. Stanley held up one key and said, "Belinda, I think this is what we are here to deliver." Stanley didn't know why the key was important at that moment, but he would later realize that it was the key that freed a young boy's conscience. John's spirit was participating, and that which it stored within Stanley's domain would be the medium through which this mystery would be revealed.

John had been a mischievous one as a younger being. This mischief had carried forward and now captured and lured Stanley into this spirit's plans. It transcended to its new assignment as one within Stanley's domain mix. When it was part of young John's domain, it encouraged its being to pilfer and collect other people's things for fun. John was a very accomplished thief. He never intended to keep any of the things he stole. He didn't need to. His family and correspondingly he was financially quite comfortable. He'd stolen things as a game, a preoccupation, and a challenge.

He'd, for years before his being's death, been afraid to confess he had taken these things; thus, he was in his teens before he gained the courage to confront his parents with his concern over his strange obsession. It was then that he desired to make amends. It weighed very heavily on his conscience and mental well-being. He never had the opportunity to fully carry out his intentions. There were reasons, many of them, but none so restrictive as his complete breakdown. He would pay dearly for not tending to his crime in earlier times. His good natures would be lost, swept away by his guilt and loss of his destiny. He went insane, not directly from his crimes but as a result of them and what they drove him to. He was confined in the state's care for a period before he died. None of this was yet revealed to Stanley. It lay at the periphery of his domain though.

Stanley said to Belinda, "Before we leave tomorrow, I must find a way to deliver this box to Dorothy without her thinking that I was the one who stole these things long ago as a boy."

Belinda then asked him, "How did you know where to find these things? Are you sure that it wasn't you who took them? Perhaps in this or a previous lifetime?"

Stanley couldn't believe that his wife considered the possibility of this situation involving a previous life. She had never allowed him a clue that she could entertain such possibilities. Stanley himself had blurred vision in this realm of thinking. He could only reply, "I don't know, Belinda. I honestly don't know. Perhaps it was me in a previous lifetime." At that point, he was willing to consider any reasonable explanation. It had been exciting to play this game to this juncture, but now he was becoming concerned with where it might lead. He was growing tired of not knowing, of being left in the dark of its intents and use of his being.

As they slept that night, he remembered the comfort of this bed from a previous time. He experienced a dream. It distressed him greatly. His own perspiration soaked his pajamas, and eventually, the damp and cold woke him from sleep. He recalled a vision of a boy of teenage years. In the first frame, the boy's parents were visibly upset. They were angrily discussing a problem involving the boy. The mother was crying. The father was yelling. He said, "Our son has a problem. He takes things without cause. He's a thief."

The mother responded, "But, Ben, it's a sickness. He can't help it. He confided in us. He's asking for our help." They both were exploring the possibilities of what to do. Finally, they both agreed that they should send the boy away for help. They should send their son, John, to private school. It was to be a southern military academy. The school's program based on discipline would surely break him of this problem. The father said he would look into it in the upcoming week. This frame ended.

The next frame had young John thoroughly upset with the news that his parents wanted to send him away for the school year. The plan was to send him to a private school in Georgia. John thought this would not do for him. John skipped school that day and snuck back into the house. Both of his parents had taken the day off to make plans for their son's transfer of schools. However, after getting the kids off to school, they decided to go back to bed and sleep late. After all the stress of the recent situation, they were both exhausted.

John found his parents asleep in their room, and in his anger, he killed them. He stabbed them repeatedly with a stiletto while they lay in bed. When he regained control, he left the room and locked the door behind him with the key he'd taken from his sister's room. He returned the key to where he found it and then took the bloody stiletto and placed it in a paper bag. He left the house for a few hours to settle himself, long enough to go to the local bank and place the murder weapon in his own safe-deposit box. He removed the stiletto from the bag before letting it fall into the box. He discarded the bag in the trash basket. This whole sequence of events left him quite disturbed and on the brink of insanity.

Later that afternoon, Dorothy came home from school and looked for her parents. She found John asleep on his bed. She found her parents' room locked. When she called to them and asked that they please open the door, there was no answer. She became concerned. She went to her room to get the key to their room. It was the only one she knew that existed other than the ones in her parents' possession. She went inside and immediately screamed at the gruesome sight inside. She became hysterical from the horror of it. Her reaction was loud and horrid enough to wake John and also to bring the neighbors to their door. All that Dorothy could do was to shriek and cry.

John was frantic as well but reacted differently. He curled up on the floor. He hid his face and said nothing from that day until shortly before he died. His sister's shock and pain from finding her parents dead was so severe that it triggered his crossing beyond the final threshold into insanity. He was lost to this world's reality. Before his death, he would venture back from time to time but for only short instances.

Both Dorothy and John were taken initially to the local hospital to be treated for shock. After several weeks in the community hospital, Dorothy had responded to treatment and was making steady progress toward recovery, but John had gotten no better. He was later sent to the state psychiatric hospital. He died one year later. All he said over the entire time he was institutionalized was, "Dorothy, I'm sorry," over and over again. The message never left the state hospital. It died with John, secured within the padding on the walls and the many secrets of the insane.

The case of Mr. and Mrs. Stewart's murder was never solved. Some thought Dorothy had something to do with it. Some thought that was why she didn't wind up like her brother. They thought that perhaps the pain and shock wasn't as great since she knew what happened. Nothing could ever be proved one way or another. The murder weapon and motive were never discovered. Dorothy had been living with the pain and the mystery that took her family from her for almost sixty years now. It was further hardened by the loss of a husband many years previous as well.

That night, another guest in the bed and breakfast went to sleep while smoking a cigarette. He slipped into unconsciousness before putting the cigarette out. The sheets of the bed caught on fire, and from there, the fire spread quickly to other parts of the room. Soon half the house was ablaze. Stanley was fortunate to have awaken in his cold sweat. He smelled the smoke. When he opened the door to his room, he was met with roaring flames and heat. The west wing of the house was engulfed with fire. He woke his wife and guided her to the connecting entry of the room of John's sister. Before he left, he grabbed the box from beneath the floorboard and tucked it under his arm.

Dorothy still slept in the same room she had as a girl. Stanley and Belinda found her asleep in her bed and woke her. She was groggy and dazed with the cobwebs of sleep, but even so, Stanley managed to hustle her and his wife to the next room in the series, the master suite. It had not been used by anyone since the murder of Dorothy and John's parents. To Belinda and Dorothy's surprise, Stanley went directly to the built-in bookcases and initiated the trigger to open a secret passageway that led to the main floor and then out of the house.

By now, the fire had been reported by the neighbors. Fire trucks surrounded the home and were dousing it with water and foam. It seemed it was of little use. The fire had taken over most of the house. It was an easy victim of the hungry blaze. Dorothy looked on in fear and sorrow. All her memories were going up in flames and smoke. She was sobbing and pulling away from any attempt to comfort her. Stanley's wife put her hand to her husband's face and said, "You saved Dorothy and me. You are a hero, Stanley. You are my hero. How did you know that the passageway existed from the upstairs master bedroom?" She stared into his eyes and gave him a serious look as if to confess that she was now a believer. "Was it more of the déjà vu?"

Her husband answered her, "I think I've been inside this house before. And I think there's more to me being called here than that which is under my control."

Belinda then asked him, "What do you think it means, this calling? You don't think saving us from the fire was the purpose of your calling?"

Stanley shrugged as if to imply he didn't know but then said, "I think I'm here to carry a message from a past life. I think it's John Stewart who sent me."

Overhearing the two, Dorothy came out of her trance and looked around to Stanley in concern and disbelief. She looked to him and said, "What are you saying, Mr. Boston? Are you saying that my dead brother, John, has possessed you?"

Stanley then told her the dream that he'd had just before waking to the fire. While Dorothy was reliving the events and revelations of new facts relating to her brother's involvement in her parents' murders, Stanley offered her the box, especially the key. He said to her, "I believe that this was intended for you to find much earlier in your life. When you couldn't, I believe John encouraged me to help you."

Dorothy moved toward it, afraid to accept it. The contents from within would either open old wounds or provide the answers to allow them to heal. Stanley and Belinda coaxed her to open the box by saying, "It's one box of salvaged memories. There are things inside from each of your loved ones."

Stanley added, "It was put together for you by your brother as if he knew you would need these one day."

It made Dorothy so happy, as happy as one could have been in the instance of such great loss. She opened the box and carefully and caringly sorted through the treasures. Every once in a while, she looked up to show her surprise at what she was finding and to whisper, "Thank you." They all made refuge on the nearby hillside and waited and watched as the fire continued to burn.

Early the next morning, when the fire was finally out and most of the smoke subsided, Stanley and Belinda went back inside the partially burned-out structure in hope of salvaging any of their possessions. In one of the soot-coated rooms, Stanley pulled a small picture from the wall and dusted the ash and debris from it. He saw himself in the picture. His wife saw another man from an earlier time. It was a picture of John Stewart. Stanley put it back on the wall and marveled that his wife didn't see what he did. Nonetheless, before they left, she turned back to the small picture and said, "Thank you," under her breath. It didn't matter to her how it happened. She was just glad that he and her husband worked together to save their lives.

Stanley and Belinda went with Dorothy to the bank the next morning. The possessions of the safe-deposit box had since been bagged and turned over to the state. They went to several state offices involving matters of escheat until finally recovering the contents of the box. They decided it best to open the package in the presence of the sheriff based on Stanley's vision of the prior evening. When it was opened, the stiletto rolled out and onto the floor. It still had dried blood on the blade. The contents within also had remnants of dried human blood on them. It appeared that the weapon was placed in the box with the other contents in haste. It was sent to the crime lab to verify that it was the weapon that killed Dorothy's parents. Through the marvels of modern science, it was confirmed as so.

It was a sad yet relief-filled experience for Dorothy. She had suspected her brother soon after the murders but didn't want it to be so. She was now free of guilt, innocent of the accusations and the suspicions of others. John Stewart, her brother, was the only person who could have accessed the box from the bank's vault and stashed the stiletto within. It was clear that he was the guilty party in her parents' murders. Dorothy thanked Stanley for all his help. Stanley could only say, "I think it was your brother working through me who wanted to set the record straight. I can't help but think that some of him is now a part of me."

Then he chuckled and finished, "Isn't it strange? It's like déjà vu."

Becky hadn't experienced episodes of déjà vu. Nor could she see into others' futures. Yet she could see telepathically into the likely events or hidden experiences and activities of her students. She did so using her gift of spirit transfer. She could plant and nurture the seeds of influence and goodness telepathically but could not see how they would sprout or if they would flourish. It was trust and hope that she would need to rely on. She did not possess the gift of clairvoyance.

Becky's richest source of information about Mr. Arthur's activities and methods of influence came from her transfers and from her sharing within the domains of the troubled students whom she counseled. She gathered details of Mr. Arthur's true nature and the strength of his domain. She gathered enough information to begin to understand him, to allow herself to begin to predict his actions and his tendencies, and to isolate what few vulnerabilities he might have. The opportunity to explore these channels left few secrets between their pure domains. It was not clairvoyance but telepathy played at its best.

Becky also learned of Mr. Arthur's destiny to destroy her good and the good of all the good-natured spirits of the community. From her work with the mixed domains, she learned of Mr. Arthur's evil deeds, his temperament, and his legions of loyal followers. She learned much about Mr. Arthur's followers and his hold on them, especially from Robert's domain, from her direct work with him. She learned a number of truths about the common evil nature, also, and mostly through these encounters with Robert. He became her personal laboratory for research. She discovered that you can change the tendencies of the domain only so much. These are driven by the destinies, the purposes, and the natures of the spirits. Rather, it is best to influence activities and decisions of the mind and body. It is here that focus and motivation can be most easily altered.

Mr. Arthur also had the power of telepathy. Becky's secrets, tendencies, and vulnerabilities were just as much an open book to Mr. Arthur as his were to Becky. Again, the mixed domains were their deliverers. There were no real advantages between them.

Tom and Becky had made plans to attend the amusement park one weekend. Becky asked Tom if it would be all right to bring Anita along with them. She was feeling lonely now, with Becky spending so much of her free time with Tom. Anita wanted to become a friend to both of them. She wanted to get to know Tom much better than she did. It seemed a good idea.

The day came, and all three were having fun, riding the rides, and playing games. They'd covered nearly the entire park, leaving little unattended and untried. Finally, they came to a smaller tent with a sign on the outside that read, "Clairvoyant." Anita lifted the flap to the tent and motioned the other two to come inside with her. Becky was the most hesitant and, as a result, delayed Tom in his advance. He pleaded to her, "Come on, Becky, we haven't tried this attraction yet."

Then he followed with, "Come on, it might be fun."

But something held Becky back. She wasn't usually so tentative to try something seemingly harmless. But in this case, it was a feeling deep within her that warned her to be cautious. She moved forward toward the tent but was still hesitant. She finally said, "Why don't you two go in? Let me know what you find."

But there was no easy reprieve allowed her by her friends. Anita and Tom implored her, "Oh come on, Becky," they chimed. "It's not nearly as fun without all of us getting involved." They seemed insistent to try out the attraction.

Becky finally gave in. She would enter the attraction but only for the benefit of her friends. She informed them, "I'll go in, but I will not participate in any mind-reading hocus-pocus." She gave them each a look of surrender and joined them.

As they entered, Anita touched her arm and asked, "Becky, what is it that causes you concern about this place?"

Becky responded quickly, "I don't know exactly. It just gives me the creeps. Something is not right about it." She then glanced down in embarrassment.

Anita followed by saying, "Gee, Becky, you're scaring me." Then she turned her serious look into a laugh. "I have nothing to fear from Madame Extrovia. I have no secrets that anyone would care to know about." But she did. She just didn't know it yet. She didn't heed Becky's warnings or give it another thought.

Anita pulled Becky close, and they walked together into the inner sanctum of the tent. Inside was a lavish display of tapestry and velvet-covered tables. The traditional crystal ball stood positioned at the center table, with two chairs anchoring it on either side. On one side of the open space were additional chairs. They assumed that they were put there to accommodate those who waited their turn before the crystal ball. The decor was intended to promote the mystique of the event. It made their wait more exciting.

Suddenly, they heard an explosion. There was a purple puff of smoke coming from an opening to their right. Through the smoke entered an older woman. She was in her fifties. Her hair was jet black. Her lips stood out behind thick ruby red lipstick. She had moles on either side of her nose. Her eyes were dark and frightening. She could easily pose as a witch, but from the way she was dressed, she was playing the gypsy woman today. She announced, "I am Madame Extrovia. You are in my quarters." She sent a piercing, frightening stare toward the three. "Do you intend to have your futures revealed through me?"

Now the other two began to feel the hesitancy that Becky had shown from the start. They wondered if Becky had known what they had just experienced, perhaps her intuition, or memory from a previous encounter with one so frightening. Words would not come from Tom's mouth. He was not good in these types of situations. After waiting a moment for Tom to reply and when no one else responded, Anita took the lead and replied, "What is involved in having my future revealed?"

Madame Extrovia walked toward her and looked at her with a serious, seemingly angry scowl. She said, "It is a very serious act." She compressed the sides of her lips into a fish mouth. "Once I've read your future, I cannot take it back. It's out there for all to know and use."

She paused before adding in the most mysterious voice, "Are you sure you want to risk a reading?"

Anita was not intimidated whatsoever. To her, this was an attraction at the amusement park. It was for fun. She thought this actor quite good yet also quite amusing. She asked, "Is there a cost?"

Madame Extrovia was taken aback by her lack of heed. She answered, "Only to you, my child. The cost may be quite great should I reveal something you might not want to hear." She scrunched the wrinkles in her forehead to accentuate them all the more. "And if you like, I do accept tips." This confirmed for Anita, and now Tom, that it was all in fun. Both were now willing to take their place before the madame to have their futures told.

Anita went first. She walked up to the table and sat directly in front of Madame Extrovia. The crystal ball blocked her view of that portion of madame's face beneath her eyes. But it was the eyes that mesmerized her. They captured her line of sight and held it in check throughout the entire session. Anita thought it odd that she could not recall blinking even once through the entire reading. She lost her thoughts in the big ball and the gaze of Madame Extrovia. She could recall nothing of the experience except when it was done. Madame Extrovia released her from her gaze. She was looking down when Anita regained her senses.

The madame spoke. "How much, my dear, do you want me to share?" She looked up with a more soothing gaze now.

Anita asked, "Is there good in my future?"

The madame replied, "There is some good."

Madame Extrovia hesitated but then added, "It is short lived and affected by a decision that you will make." She hesitated for effect.

Anita coaxed her, "Go on, please. I want to hear more. Is there more that you can tell me?"

The madame complied with more of her reading. "There is an act that will change your life significantly thereafter."

Anita was puzzled. She asked, "What is this decision you refer to? What is this act that will change my life?"

Madame Extrovia looked away. She mumbled in a very low voice, "I can only tell you so much, my child. You will know it when the time comes. Your decision will change your life. That is all."

Anita was left dumbstruck. *What did this mumbo jumbo mean?* she thought. She was left unsatisfied, uninformed. She asked one final question of the madame. "Can you tell me if I will find love in this lifetime?"

The madame looked her in the eyes with sorrow and replied, "No, my child, not in this lifetime. Another lifetime will be kinder to you."

Anita was sobered by the whole experience. She thought that this experience was to be fun. It left her upset. It left her wondering to herself. How could anyone be so mean? She no longer wanted any part of Madame Extrovia and her nasty game. She left no tip. She was ready to leave when Tom stood forward to take his place at the table with the crystal ball.

Madame Extrovia was surprised that he, too, would take a chance before her. The readings had been cruel to his friend. She did not think him brave enough, at her first impression, to come forward for a reading of his own. She motioned for him to sit and look into her eyes. Anita, by now, had taken a seat beside Becky. She was still upset and whispering insults about the madame into Becky's ear, then suddenly the madame stood and addressed her, saying, "Do not hold me in too much ill will, my child. I only read what is before me." She sat back down. "Please forgive me."

Then she refocused on Tom's gaze across the crystal sphere. She had him fully mesmerized in her capture as she pulled from his domain his inner secrets. Her lower jaw dropped, and her chest let out a conceived gasp. Tom could not see her reaction, but Becky caught it all.

Anita was still in total shock of the madame's awareness of her earlier sharing, in secret, with her friend. *How could she know I was insulting her?* she thought. *My comments to Becky were completely concealed in a most silent whisper.* She was now in a state a fright. This was the best sideshow she'd ever attended; either that or it was real. The latter held her in fear.

Madame Extrovia also seemed in the grip of surprise. She held her control of Tom's gaze, but her body reacted to each bit of information that she seemed to unveil. Finally, she released him. Tom, too, wondered what had happened in the past few minutes. He had no recollection of the time under the madame's control. Becky observed it all in wonderment. Something extraordinary seemed to be happening in these exchanges. It was stimulating her curiosity about this woman. Could it be that the old woman could be a true clairvoyant? Could she be pure and good natured? Becky, too, was now ready to cast her lot and partake in this adventure. But first, the madame was to address Tom about what she saw.

She looked to him for permission to excuse herself from this revelation. She asked him, "How much, my dear, do you want me to share with you?" She looked up with a more soothing gaze now.

Tom asked, just as Anita had, "Is there good in my future?" He looked confidently at Madame Extrovia.

The madame replied, "There is some good." She then hesitated. "It is short lived by a decision that you will make out of love. There is an act that will change your life significantly thereafter."

Tom was left questioning. It seemed that he had heard similar words only moments earlier when she tended to Anita. Anita also perked up. It was very much like what she had heard regarding her future. It made her feel relieved. As it now seemed to her, it was just a scripted game. Becky was left still mesmerized. She was still not so sure it was only a game. Finally, Tom broke the moment by asking, just as Anita had, and also now sure that it was just a game, "What is this decision? What is this act that will change my life?"

Madame Extrovia looked away. She mumbled in a low voice, "I can only tell you so much, child. You will know it when the time comes. Your decision will change your life. That is all."

Tom laughed aloud and was about to walk away. Then he remembered the lines from Anita that he had forgotten to recite. He turned to ask one final question of the madame. "Can you tell me if I will find love in this lifetime?" He looked briefly back to Becky.

The madame looked him in his eyes again with sorrow and replied, "Yes, my child, in this lifetime and the next. You have found love in this lifetime already but will lose it. The next lifetime will be kinder to you."

Tom placed $10 in the madame's bowl and said to her, "You are very good. It has been fun." Then he walked back to his place on the side of the canvas-enclosed room to share the experience. Tom and Anita now recognized the show for what it was. Yet Becky still had many doubts. Her instincts were telling her that there was truth and reality in it. She was compelled to take her turn before the madame.

As Tom was repositioning himself at the side of the reading room, Madame Extrovia asked Becky, "Do you wish a reading as well, my dear?"

Both Anita and Tom coaxed her to join in on the fun. She was encouraged to do so. Becky rose from her seat and stepped up to the gypsy fortune-teller's table for her reading. She sat in the designated chair and looked across the table and above the crystalline ball to connect with the mysterious dark eyes of the madame. Madame Extrovia's mouth opened, and a silence filled the room. It was not the usual chant or routine from her that she'd repeated for Anita or Tom. It seemed strange to them, but they presumed it was all part of the show. The fortune-teller was shocked to learn that Becky was one like herself but much,

much stronger. Becky was able to transfer her spirit into the gypsy woman's domain, but Madame Extrovia was not able to reciprocate. As such, she was not able to recite Becky's future. But she was able to provide it. She was very useful in allowing Becky to read directly from the domain of the gypsy woman. All communication was internal to their domains. Madame Extrovia's services were fully rendered.

What appeared to the observing audience of Anita and Tom was that something went wrong in the madame's attempts to draw a reading from Becky. The appearance was that Madame Extrovia was repelled by the stronger domain of Becky. It appeared that there would be no reading for Becky to share with her friends from the madame's attempts in this instance. The madame rubbed her forehead in an outward show of frustration and said, "I am sorry. I am not able to pick up anything in our reading. It is rare, but it happens."

She and Becky both knew what had happened. Her response was more for the benefit of Anita and Tom than for Becky. Internally, between the spirits, Becky's spirits had extracted the reading from the madame's domain. Her future was revealed and secured at the spirit level. Only a pure domain can read or render a reading to another pure domain and only if of the same type of nature. On the exterior, Becky and the madame exchanged surprise over what neither Becky nor the old woman could explain. The madame had experienced this only once in her lifetime. The other one she'd encountered and shared this experience was truly a good person. Her spirits, but not the being, knew then, as she knew now, that the spirits of the being sitting across from her on the other side of the crystal ball had obtained a reading from her. It was a reading in which she was not privy to. Her being could only express at the end of the session that she could get no reading. This was only partially true and one-sided.

Becky's external was disappointed that she could not be part of the fun as Anita and Tom had been but left the old woman $10 for her efforts. Becky turned and said, "Thank you," as she and her two accomplices left through the front of the tent. Becky was still caught in her thoughts. These thoughts were sourced from her spirits and from the reading. Her external components wondered how much of the past events had meaning. They wondered if any of it had been truth.

The old gypsy clairvoyant couldn't reach Becky's domain because every spirit in it was much stronger than the clairvoyant's, even though both had a pure good-natured domain. Rather, only Becky could transfer to her. Only the stronger domain can establish an intraspirit sharing encounter. In this case, as with all those involving a strong and a weak pure domain, the sharing was one sided. The clairvoyant provided Becky with a vision of her destiny, one of her future and instances where they linked. It made things clearer. It was like looking into a magic mirror. What Becky saw was part of the script of her life.

All the great ones are allowed to read from their script. They are allowed to know their destinies and clearly see the target and what is in store for them. It is part of the gift of being a powerful and dominant pure domain. They all before her had been allowed to find one like them but not quite as strong natured, and that allowed them to read their future. All the really great ones' lives are scripted to be read, at least all the major points and milestones. The details, of course, are different and get more developed along the way. This is why they are not afraid to face their destinies, even though the outcomes are sometimes certain death or defeat. They know what to expect upfront and know the value, purpose, and effects that lie beyond. They know they cannot affect or change their future. They know the honor of their role and purpose. They are most grateful to their weaker clairvoyant domain for clarifying their course and revealing their obstacles. Becky knew she owed Madame Extrovia much thanks.

In the old clairvoyant's spirit domain, Becky's spirits saw her future. She saw that Tom was indeed her soul mate. Their love was true. She saw happy times with Tom but short-lived times. She saw that she would die. It would involve Mr. Arthur. It was through her destiny that her students and the community would eventually be freed of him. It would free good-natured spirits of his demands and his influence. She also learned of her destiny to establish a successor. She didn't discover who this being would be. She learned that there was a destiny, a set plan to support this successor. The plan, as it related to her, involved those whom she would need to talk to and form relationships with and to plant the messages, the information, and the triggers that would pass the know-how and experiences from her that her successor would need. These special relationships would serve as the messengers and conduit of exchange between Becky and the successor. It was spirit work. The being would be left unaware. These efforts and her successor would continue her goodness and her legacy into the future.

Becky returned to the old clairvoyant several days later without Tom or Anita. She wanted to talk to her. She wanted to thank her. She wanted to make her feel more comfortable than she had left her after their first encounter. She had much to explain.

They would become friends. She never understood why she had hesitancy to meet her at the onset of their first encounter. She could only assume that it was an intuition about the bad news that she was destined to obtain from her, or the disappointing news that Anita and Tom had received.

Mr. Arthur also experienced the gift, just as Becky had received it. His clairvoyant was Brenda. She had the power to provide this gift as a pure domain of evil nature and one of lesser power. These were the qualities that allowed her to provide Mr. Arthur with his future. Mr. Arthur learned his destiny. He would kill Becky and remove a strong good from the world. He also learned that he would die. He learned that Brenda would surpass him in power and spirit strength. He would return the favor of clairvoyance to her as her second-tier disciple before he dies.

Sherry Cower was a young girl. She resided with her parents in a moderately sized town four to five hours west of Millborough. Her parents were not rich but were comfortable. Sherry had been well cared for. Her parents loved her. She was a very happy girl. Her domain was made up of three strong good-natured spirits. This made her domain special and pure. It also made her domain vulnerable. She often experienced episodes of déjà vu. It raised many questions of her heritage, of the secrets that had been kept from her. Her heritage, as it turned out, was quite essential and critical to her destiny. Her visions and memories would be the paths that would lead her back to her heritage.

Sherry grew up in a protected environment. There was no reason to believe that things were different from what she perceived them to be. Expanding on reason, however, would allow all from her orderly world to be shaken. She was in for a surprise, in fact an awakening, just because, one day, the circus came to her town.

She and her friends decided to visit the big tops. One of the feature attractions was a gypsy fortune-teller named Madame Extrovia. It seemed a harmless adventure to have her fortune read by the gypsy woman. She entered the tent and encountered the old woman face-to-face. It was through her first look into those smoldering dark eyes that Sherry was presented with a vision of her future. It was made clear to her who she was and what her destinies were.

Madame Extrovia was aware that Sherry was of a pure good domain and stronger than she was. She also knew that this was the chosen successor to one she had encountered earlier in her life. When she was certain that this child had extracted the full portion of her reading directly from her domain, she asked her to sit before her in front of the crystal ball. It was all for show at this point. Through her incantations and chants, her hocus pocus, Madame Extrovia was unable to extract a reading. She knew she wouldn't be able to tell her anything specific. She did not share her results verbally with the crowd who had gathered to watch the show. Rather, she whispered in Sherry's ear that she had done a reading for one very much like her in spiritual strength and of pure good nature a number of years previous. She was certain that they were connected by a strong and common destiny. Madame Extrovia gave her a business card with her cell phone number engraved on it and told her to call her if she should ever need help or support from her.

The vision that Sherry saw within the old lady's domain was very clear. It was a focus that Madame Extrovia was not allowed. It was one that was filled with people other than those

Sherry knew and felt comfortable with. It frightened her, yet she couldn't stop thinking about it. It contained her destiny. It revealed her identity. It set her directions. And even though she was still very young, what she learned was very different from how she charted her course and fortified her foundations to this point. This encounter would be the catalyst to all her subsequent changes and the realignment with her destiny and purpose. It would give her new insight and perspective on her being and value.

Sherry didn't know at first just how to take all that she had experienced with the old clairvoyant. It was all very frightening on one hand but very exciting and enlightening on the other. In her innermost thoughts, she knew the reading was accurate and true. Her domain stores were being opened up to her. Episodes of déjà vu, especially those linked to times earlier in her life, became commonplace. Her innermost self was revealing her history and destinies to her through many forms of visions. She knew she could not escape now that she'd had a first glimpse through the old clairvoyant's eyes.

Relationships

Relationships are like gambling. You assess your chances of a winning combination before you make your decisions. You win when the odds and the numbers are in your favor. You lose when they are not. In the game of life, it is spirits and natures that determine the odds that you play instead of played cards, dice, or numbered color wheels.

Relationships, or lack thereof, are the result of favorable spirit attractions or unfavorable repulsions. They are the by-product of natural pairing of the spirit natures residing in two different beings' domains. When spirit pairs are of like nature, they produce an attracting charge. When they are of different natures, they produce a repelling charge. The tally and effect from the nine possible paired combinations of the three spirits within each of the two domains and with the attention paid to the number of attracting and repulsing charges created by these spirit pairings determines the compatibility and likelihood that a relationship will form. The pair in the majority will determine the interpersonal attraction or repulsion between the two beings.

Regardless of whether it's an overall attraction or repulsion, inherent in this process is the fact that few relationships are perfect. This is as nature designed and intended it to be. In most cases, there are both attracting and repulsing pairings and contending charges between the spirits of the two domains of the beings. It allows for difference and diversity in the relationships. And although the overall likelihood that a relationship will form between two beings depends only on the tally of their spirit pairings being a majority of like pairs, at the level of the nine specific-spirit pairings, each continues to individually vie for dominance over the domain of their pair's core natures, good or evil, their attributes, and their destinies. Encouragement of this comes from their unyielding makeup and drivers. The charge of each pair is still fed by their good and evil virtue's internal drivers instead of the outcome of the majority attraction or repulsion between their domains assessing compatibility.

Behavior comes from a much more complex set of determinants. Therefore, even though the relationship, in general, will be held together based on the majority pairings determined at the onset of two beings' meeting, there is allowance for deviations, complexities, and inconsistencies at the behavior level throughout the relationship as influenced by each spirit nature's one of nine pairings and their uniqueness, characteristics, and specific destinies working within the pairs. This is attributable to the effect that each of the nine separate spirit pairings elicits as each is given its time of dominance within the domain. The pair in dominance dictates the current behavior, even when the pair given dominance over the domain's natures are not consistent with those of the majority good or evil pairs determining compatibility for the relationship. This creates diversity and character. Only in the case where two pure domains of like natures might interact would there not be this opportunity for deviation and inconsistency in the intermittent behaviors of those of the relationship. All pairings in this case would be of like natures and emit only a like charge and a like set of drivers. This is rare. In the majority of cases, the spirit pairings that are formed and evaluated in determining relationship compatibility are mixed and subject to deviation and difference and some unpredictability in the behaviors within the relationship, no matter how strong or compatible the relationship between mixed domains might be founded.

Relationships versus behaviors within the relationships, the drivers, and the differences are indeed complex and at times confusing. The difference is in the aggregate versus each specific and individual pairing. The aggregate, or majority effect of all pairings, determines the relationship compatibility. Each of the nine pairings individually and separately determines different variations, even igniting different behavior within the relationship based on their pair's nature, good or evil, and position of dominance in the domain. Behavior, thus, is not subservient to the relationship. But it is not altogether independent either. They both are the same pairing of natures, one in aggregate and the other as separate pairings.

Contributing to the degree and variability in the behavior, particularly in the strength of moods and emotional swings within relationships, is the third attribute of the spirit makeup. First is the nature, good or evil. A pairing can be either good or evil, can be like or unlike. Second, there is its status and position of domain dominance. Dominance determines which spirit holds control of the domain at a point. Third, is the strength of the spirit nature. A spirit's nature can be strong or weak. This is a measure of the influence that the spirit nature will exert when allowed a position of dominance within a pair or the domain. The strength or weakness of a spirit nature is different from its dominance. When a spirit is placed in the role of dominance, the measure of strength or weakness of the nature will determine the impact that the nature will have on the domain, all pairs of the domain. Dominance allows weak natures, as well as strong ones, to influence the actions and thoughts of their being. Strength or weakness allows variations in one's actions. It allows for the being to have strong opinions or weak ones, strong actions or those more subtle. It allows passion versus preference. From this constitution of the spirit and the spirit domain emerges the complete range and repertoire of spirit influence on the being and its relationships with others.

As some examples of the effect of the spirit attributes, one strong and dominant evil-natured spirit in a domain mix of two good- and one evil-natured spirit can often offset or counter the two good-natured spirits in the domain when gaining dominance and influence over it. For its time in dominance, it can evoke intense influence and action from the being. It can form the most impressionable personality traits and characteristics in the opinions of others relating to, and interacting with this being. It can make a being appear counter to its domain's majority makeup. Likewise, this will occur for a strong, dominant, good-natured spirit in a domain with two lesser potent evil natured spirits. The truth, therefore, as it relates to one's personality is that it's not always about the number of good or evil natures that matter; rather, it's also very much about the strength of the spirit and which is dominant at the most critical times of influence.

One's mood, attitude, and personality are influenced by different factors and considerations from one's attractions and ability to form relationships. The totality within these differences nurtures the complexity that resides in human relationships. Both compatibility and behavior are driven by the constitution and attributes of all the spirits of two domains. Relationships are primarily determined on nature and number of like pairings of the spirit natures in these two domains. Behavior is dependent on the independent pairings between the two domains and most importantly which has dominance in the domain. but probabilities give the odds to the natures of like pairings determining compatibility. Strength of the spirit is only a secondary factor in determining relationships. One's personality, on the other hand, is primarily influenced by the nature's type and its strength to rise and establish position of dominance within the domain, as well as with the changing situations and stimuli affecting its stay in the position of dominance. It's all unique and magical. It's almost entirely of the spirit and of nature's design. It's one of life's natural offerings. Life is a gift from the spirits. It all fits naturally.

The most common result of an encounter between two beings is indifference, this being an insignificant or primarily neutralizing set of charges between the two. These are the everyday encounters we have with the beings we pass on the sidewalk or shop among at the mall. We neither affect nor are affected significantly by others' domain natures or charges. On the other hand, there are also those instances when another catches our attention or sends an unexplainable sense of fear, apprehension, or perhaps, and to the contrary, a feeling of interest, comfort, or ease. These are the significant interactions of our lives. These are spirit based, brought on by the connections between the spirit natures in our domains. These result from strong or majority attracting or repulsing charges between paired spirits of two domains. These attracting or repulsing charges can't be altered. They can't be changed. They can be challenged and suppressed by the mind and body, but at the spirit level, they are permanent and pure. They grow and dictate our life's meaningful relationships, as allowed.

How do spirit-based relationships form? I'll present three basic examples. The first involves two beings, their domains each containing two good-natured spirits and one evil-natured one. The paired combinations of their domains total nine. The distribution of the spirit pairings breaks down like this. Starting with the first good-natured spirit of the first being, it connects with each of the three spirits from the second being's domain, creating three pairings; two pairings are of like good-natured spirits, and the third is of an unlike good-natured and evil-natured pairing. The second good-natured spirit of the first being's domain is also paired likewise to the three spirits of the second being's domain. This creates the same results. The current tally is thus four like good-to- good natured pairings and two unlike good to evil pairings. Finally, the third spirit of the first being's domain is an evil-natured spirit. It connects with each of the three spirits of the second being's domain, creating two unlike good-natured and evil-natured pairings and one like evil-natured pairing. The final tally of all the pairings between the two beings' domains is four like good-natured pairings, four unlike good- to evil-natured pairings, and one like evil-natured pairing.

The relationship is determined by the five pairings where like natures result. Each of these pairings creates a strong attracting charge. These attractions counter the repulsing charges of the four pairings of unlike natures. The aggregate effect is thus an attracting basis for a relationship and one of predominantly good natures. The like pairings are in the majority. The criteria required to support compatibility and for forming the relationship is met. The number more than a majority is inconsequential. It is, however, still up to the being to establish a relationship from the compatibility test. The mind and physical components of the being not overrule these results and must initiate action to take advantage of spirit compatibility.

No matter which combination of spirits holds dominance within the domains of the two beings of this example, and the majority charge between them, the subsequent and resultant relationship will always an attraction. The relationship does not change based on the compatibility of any one spirit combination or that of the pair that holds dominance within the two beings' domain. There is a higher order of influence between the two beings' compatibility as a result of this majority overriding aggregate and holistic effect of all pairings. This is the case even though a mixed pair of spirits within the domains (being a good-natured spirit in one and an evil-natured spirit in the other) will at times holds dominance and will create a repulsing effect within their time in station of dominance. In this example, the effect on the compatibility (unlike that on behaviors) of these two unlike and paired spirits in dominance will be one of neutralization rather than repulsion.

As it relates to compatibility, relationships allow for tempering of the paired natures that are in the minority. This can help explain why beings can be better or eviler or less good or less evil in a relationship than they are on their own. It can help explain how relationships can affect and seem to change a participant's general nature, why people can mellow in loving relationships and turn dastardly or radical in relationships founded on a majority of evil pairings.

In an attracting relationship, the strongest influences come from the significant pairings and majority. There is an accentuated and magnified influence and synergy from like pairings when dominant. There is controlled blending of unlike pairings, especially when they are allowed time in a position of dominance. This is similar to what happens between the spirits in the mixed domain of a being yet now extended across and affecting two domains. The majority nature often controls time in dominance and "masks" those in the minority. Relationships simply add to and accentuate this effect. Thus, the spirits of the beings we interact with and befriend have a great influence over us as do our own spirits over those we befriend.

The relationship of the two beings of this example primarily emits good-natured influences. Good-natured actions and positive relationships should result when four out of the nine pairings of the spirits are elevated by the domain for dominance. In another four of the nine pairings of spirits chosen for dominance, the relationship will be neutral. These are the four unlike pairings between the two. Although the relationship compatibility attributes will not be affected, the good or evil actions or behaviors coming from the two beings may be different. In one of the nine possible pairings of the spirits that might happen when like evil natures are paired, the effect while in dominance will be an evil-natured influence. The relationship will always be strong. The nature's influence will, at times, be mixed but primarily good-natured and in rare instances be from like evil. Beings with domains of mixed natures can do things contrary to their individual natures or in greater effect when paired in relationships, depending on the spirit pairings of the relationship and the pair holding dominance.

The second example involves two domains, each containing two evil-natured spirits and one good-natured spirit. The three spirits of the first being pair with each of the three spirits from the second being's domain. The resulting combination of like and unlike pairs is exactly the inverse in our first example. A strong relationship between the beings is trending, but will predominantly be an evil-natured one. Allowing the other two spirits from the first spirits to pair with the second's the tally will be the same as in the first example; only with the majority of the like pairings to be evil natured. The evil effect of each being while in the relationship will be accentuated and magnified while like evil pairs of spirits are in the dominant positions within the domain. Goodness will come from the relationship when in one of the nine pairings, being when the like good-natured pairing is in dominance. All that held true in the first example relating to a majority of like good-natured spirits now hold true in the inverse nature in this relationship with a majority of like evil-natured pairs.

Our third example involves different combinations of good-and evil-natured spirits between two beings' domains. The first being has a domain of two good-natured spirits and one evil-natured spirit. The second being's domain contains two evil-natured spirits and one good-natured spirit. In this case, the pairings result in two like good-natured pairs, two like evil-natured pairs, and five unlike good-natured to evil-natured pairs. In this example, like natured pairs, the ones that support a relationship, are in the minority to the unlike natured pairs. In this scenario, it is highly unlikely that a relationship can occur between these two beings. The significant charge emitted from this encounter is one of repulsion. The same holds true for the other scenarios of unlike mixed domains in this example. The two beings will most likely not like each other. They may indeed grow to hate each other depending on how much they are forced to be in contact with each other or to contend for destinies and influences. In any regard, this combination of spirits and natures will not likely result in these two beings connecting in friendship.

This brings us to the next set of considerations that influence the forming of relationships. These represent the exceptions to the set of rules.

The strength of the spirits in each pair must also be considered in the assessment of what forms attractions and repulsions between beings. Strength or weakness of the spirit can influence the extent and effect of the charge emitted by the pair. It can be a factor in determining whether compatibility, thus a relationship of tolerance, forms. Although strength of the nature is only a secondary factor in the assessment compared with the primary factor of good or evil type, it weighs in. The nature's strength or weakness will only be a factor when two criteria are met.

First, the pairings must result in a majority of unlike pairs and second, there must be an equal number of like good-natured pairings to like evil-natured pairings in the like pair minority. This is the scenario created in the third example addressed previously. When these conditions are met, a special type of relationship can occur based on consideration of the strength of one being's natures and consequent influence over another. This is somewhat different from the relationship formed from a majority of like-natured pairings and where both domains contribute equally to the standing of the relationship. Reconstructing the example from before, this exception will evolve from a being with a domain containing two good-natured spirits and one evil-natured spirit. The second being's domain will contain two evil-natured spirits and one good-natured spirit. Without strength of the spirits being considered, the relationship will not form. The outcome will be a neutral or a repulsing encounter, and no significant basis for a relationship will develop.

Now with these spirits' strengths taken into consideration, this can cause the final effect to be different. For example, assume the evil-natured spirits of the second being are strong natures, and the two good-natured spirits of the first being are weaker-natured spirits, the other spirit natures in both domains are neither strong nor weak. The new pairing is represented as two like good-natured pairs, one spirit in the pair being weak and the other being of average strength, two like evil-natured pairs, one spirit in the pair being strong and the other being of average strength, five good-to-evil pairs, four having one weak good-natured spirit and one strong evil-natured spirit and one pair having a good-to-evil-natured spirit of equally average strength natures. The aggregate effect of the nine pairings in the encounter, as represented and without concern for strength of the natures, now shifts. The unlike pairings are less neutral, and the repulsing charge is weakened as a result. A fragile and often temporary relationship of tolerance can form from this, favoring toward the stronger-natured charge within the unlike pairs. Strength of spirit allows the unlike pairs to now appear as more tolerant, less repulsed by the like-natured pair's charge.

Now instead of equal offsets of the nature's attracting or repulsing charge from the unlike pairs, there is an advantaged spirit in the pair that favors a good or evil nature's charge much like what is coming from the like-natured pairs partners. It is a matter of degree and a lesser degree than that of equally strong like-natured pairings. It changes the pair's contribution to the overall charge emitted by the encounter. It can be enough to change repulsion to neutral or even from repulsion to a weak attraction. The strength of the spirit can thus be an influential and important factor, in addition to and supplementing the spirit's nature type. It can allow beings of different nature's type domain mixes and with different strength of their natures to attract and form temporary and usually one-sided relationships of need or influence. The key component of these relationships is that one being is of weak spirits, and the other is of stronger spirits. It becomes a relationship of domination, and it's short lived.

Relationships formed on strength usually occur in times of change or upheaval in the lesser being's life or from times of uncertainty. They are usually based on one being's needs or insecurities. They are commonly characterized as being one sided in terms of influence and highly manipulative. One legitimate reason why such a relationship might form will be to support a destiny of the stronger-natured spirit. There are many lesser legitimate reasons for these, but they may come from the needs of the other components of the being. The other components might benefit from these types of pairings of the spirit natures to allow advantage to a stronger being. A weaker being might draw strength, reassurance, or a sense of identity from a being of stronger influence. This might provide temporary feeling of protection or self-identity and search, although it usually isn't well founded or entirely healthy. This exception is one of the few that allow the other components of the being to use the spirit for serving their specific external needs.

Strength of the natures also creates an interesting paradox. This occurs in an attracting relationship, one with the favor and majority in the like pairings. In this case, an exception can occur in the overall nature of the beings in this relationship when the unfavored like pairings of natures (for instance, like good-natured pairs in an evil-favored, evil-majority mix) are so strong and dominant that their strength places them in position of dominance quite often. Likewise, the same will hold when very strong like evil-natured pairings are part of the combinations in a good-nature, favored relationship. This can tend to create confusion on the part of the expected overall result and effect on the relationship. It can make two beings act uncharacteristically and inconsistently. A good-natured person can act eviler when paired in the relationship than when they are apart. An evil-natured person can likewise act better in a relationship than when apart. It can contribute to an apparent paradox in their characteristics, attitudes, and personalities as a pair from those they exhibit as single. A very strong nature in unlike (good to evil) pairs can stand out and create a significant effect to these types of relationships as well but only with limited and temporary effect.

Another and actually the strongest exception to the rules of relationships occurs when the domains of two beings house spirits that are destined to be naturally paired. These spirits are soul mates. When these two spirits encounter one another, all other rules and considerations relating to pairings are negated.

There is no stronger factor in relationships than the joining of beings with soul mate spirits. No matter the overall charge of the pairings, no matter the strength of the spirits, the two beings will find love. The two soul mate spirits will form that overriding, overbearing, strong attracting relationship that takes precedence over all else. The domain as a whole will transform to good natured.

In this instance, the soul mate spirits rise to greatest power, greatest dominance, and special status over the others. Soul mate spirits take on and dictate authority and dominance, allowing them to step in and out of dominance as they wish or feel the need. This keeps all other paired combinations, when taking roles of dominance, in check. Soul mate pairings, and thus the relationships formed by them, are always good-natured. True love brings out the best in beings and the spirits. This is at least true as it relates to the one pairing within the domain. In the matter of soul mates, it's the one and the *only* case when a spirit will change its nature. This, too, is rare but is provided for a spirit. It occurs when an evil-natured spirit chooses, or happens to find, its soul mate. If the beings accept the soul mate match, any evil nature of the soul mates will transform to good. It is love that is the magic. Love is the storehouse and origin of good. It is very strong. In this case, it can change the evilest natured to good. It happens less frequently than life's master plans would have hoped.

Love was to have been the counterinfluence to the world's tendency toward evil. Yet nature misjudged the power and tendencies of the evil spirit. In life's original and master planning, love's infectious appeal was the hope for retaining equal balance of power between good and evil. It was actually to have tipped the balance toward the good-natured. Love was to be the greatest force in life's creation. But there were unexpected deviants from the expected. There was a flaw. There was a variant in the original design or maybe just miscommunication sourced from wishful thinking.

Two factors came into play to thwart this plan. The first was that nature overestimated the tendencies that evil natures would be willing or motivated to search out their soul mates. It was against their natures to look for that which would bring them goodness. It didn't happen nearly as often as it was projected or hoped to occur. Evil natures simply don't understand the need of a soul mate. It doesn't drive or motivate them. It doesn't occur to them unless they unintentionally happen upon it. In reality, love is rarely chosen by evil natured spirits over the strength and allures of evil.

Second, the physical and mental components of the being have much effect in the selection of a mate. Over time, their influence has many times overridden the influences and attractions of the spirit. The joining and binding of the soul mate pairings has been prevented or severed in many instances, not allowing a relationship to develop as a result of the non-spirit components' preferences in the physical or superficial characteristics of a mate.

These factors have significantly affected the success rate of soul mate pairing in our world. It has significantly affected the instance of true love. The lack of true love, in turn, upsets the balance between good and evil. It has given preference to the evil natures. This has initiated movement along the circle of life and the inevitable movement toward closure.

Love is available to every being. Omissions are usually by our own fault. Every spirit has a soul mate. Every spirit has the potential and promise of a strong and perfect pairing. As pairings are missed, as connections are missed, and as time has passed, soul mate pairs have come out of sync with each other either in their timing on the earth or their spacing and locale. They have become harder to find, adding further to the tailing frequency by which they occur. Although these are the strongest pairings of spirits, the strongest bond, and the most absolute factor in a relationship, they've become most difficult to achieve. This qualifies these relationships to the category of an exception to the norm or standard rather than placing them as the norm and standard. Had love become as life's master plans had intended it, all other factors and criteria for forming relationships would never have been so important. Love and good natures would rule all. But this just didn't happen.

In the absence of love, the next greatest relationship between beings involves those with a pure domain. The relationship formed with one of the pure domains will always result in a strong attraction between the domain's spirits. A being with a mixed domain will always benefit from the relationship. The pure domain will provide it strength and influence to its like natured spirits in the domain, be their two or only one. A very, very rare occurrence is when two pure domains of the same type of nature encounter each other. In this case, the attraction is absolute. It is pure. It is most powerful. Much good or evil will come from these relationships. These relationships will leave their significant and lasting mark and influence on the world. Incrementally, these affect the society most significantly from each single encounter or effect. More prevalent, however, is the connection between the pure domain and a mixed domain.

These are the encounters that, because of their numbers and frequency, in aggregate, make larger overall effect, even though their separate and combined incremental effects are smaller their instances are much greater.

A third possibility is when two opposite-natured pure domains meet. In this case, the relationship is pure repulsion. It is also a very powerful encounter. These send beings running. These two can leave their mark on the world but primarily of conflict or spectacle. These result in the clash of titans. These often affect the innocent and uninvolved bystanders caught in the path. The impact is usually identified by the lack of containment and control; and by the damage.

Regardless of the type, relationships with the pure domains are special. They are most special for the mixed domains, because these relationships are a gift. Pure domains give the like spirits of the mixed domain special power and strength. Pure domains fill the mixed domains stores with knowledge and experience and give favor to the spirits and natures of its type. Pure domains tender the weaker ones of its type. They shift the advantage of strength and dominance within the mixed domain.

Another phenomenon of the pure domain and mixed domain relationship is that in a mixed domain's encounter with a pure domain, the pure domain can mask the effect of attractions or repulsions of other factors in the domain. This is done only through transfer of a spirit from the pure domain to the mixed. By becoming a part of the mixed domain through transfer and creating the strong direct connection with the like spirit(s) of the mixed domain, a pure domain assures a favorable temporary relationship. In this scenario, even a predominantly good-natured mixed domain can have a relationship with a pure evil-natured domain. It explains why some people can seemingly get along with anyone.

The last exception that I will address involves groups. Groups are a special yet least impactful relationship. In a group setting, the many encounters and pairings of the spirit natures of the beings can create an aggregate assessment. Two beings that might repel each other in a one-on-one encounter can stand neutral in the masses where the aggregate effect of all pairings from the group as a whole is a mix of both attracting and repulsing charges. These charges offset at the group level. The overall effect is then neutral. This phenomenon allows one within the group to form a relationship, yet only as part of the group. It is a weak relationship. It is the weakest of all relationships overall. This relationship certainly won't stand up alone between individuals outside of the group but will allow for temporary exception. Generally, these allow beings with opposite-natured domains to focus on a task, a common mission, or a purpose. Spirits refer to these as destinies. It's just another aspect of relationships that the spirits support through the mixing and pairings of their good and evil natures and attributes. It allows common pursuit and achievement of destinies.

In summary, encounters with others can form a number of situations and interactive pairings of the spirits from beings' domains. The greatest good and the strongest of all relationships is love. It occurs when soul mate spirits form the basis of a relationship between two beings. Soul mate love is always the product of this relationship. It is nature's perfect gift to all beings that search and patiently allow it to find them. Yet it is a relationship that occurs far too infrequently. The reasons are unfortunately many. The second strongest relationship is formed by the interaction of domains where at least one is pure. This relationship will be primarily supported by the strengths and special powers of the pure domain. The third scenario of a strong relationship occurs when interactions between two beings' domains result in a majority of like paired and matching natures. When this is the case, a strong relationship will form from the attracting charges of the like pairings. The relationship as a whole will be characterized by and generally serving the nature of the majority pairs. Behaviors in this relationship will most times follow the lead of the majority pairings. This is the most common of the three favorable scenarios supporting a strong relationship.

A relationship is built on the foundation that a spirit's nature can never change. An attraction is always an attraction. These attracting spirits and their drive and zeal to form relationships will be permanent. We refer to these relationships as friendships. This isn't to say that friendships cannot end or cannot turn. The domain is made up of three spirits. Each spirit's influence within the domain can change with its dominance and its strength. Combinations and pairings in control will change. As dominance can change, a single isolated spirit pairing can take temporary dominance and influence in the domain and can change the moment's charge from attraction to something less. This allows relationships to take on many different looks and feels. It allows for love/hate swings, shaky relationships, and shifts of mood and behaviors. The characteristics of the relationship and odds of compatibility and favorable behaviors are usually in favor of the pairings with the greatest number of like pairings. Mixed relationships are frequent, mirroring the makeup of their domains. The intensity or even the actions of the beings in the relationship can change with time. It will soon change back again when a new pairing takes dominance. But the overall attraction and foundation supporting the relationship will not change. It will keep the participants working to make the relationship work, even through times when pairing of unlike spirits or those with aversions are in a dominant position of the domain. It eventually will work out as each spirit and each paired combination takes its part in the domain's position of dominance. The laws of probability will dictate this as so. Just as stated in the opening paragraph of this chapter, relationships are much like gambling. It's all based on the odds.

Let's look at how these scenarios work in real-life examples. Tom and Becky's relationship grow from the very start. This is because it was one of the strongest types, made up of the soul mate variety. Immediately after meeting each other, much was happening in the spirit domains of Becky and Tom. Both had one special spirit in their domain. They were paired from the beginning of time by nature itself. They were soul mate spirits. In this case, they were both good-natured.

In many cases, the preferences of the being's physical or mental components become barriers to allowing the spirits to pair. In some cases, the girl might not be pretty enough, or the boy might not be strong or athletic enough. The external factors and other components of the being might exile the spirits from one another. In this case with Becky and Tom, all components worked together to allow the attraction of the spirits. The two destined spirits found one another out of all the combinations of proximity and time. Theirs was a powerful and dominant relationship, one that would last their beings' lifetime. Theirs was true love, not the type that most beings mistakenly identify as such from a lesser form of a relationship; theirs was from the strongest bond of commitment and friendship, from fulfillment of special destiny, and from natural and magical forces gifted from life's master source. It's as it was intended before becoming endangered and diluted by life and the spirit's many obstacles placed in its way.

Every spirit has a special partner. These partners travel through time from being to being, hoping to find one another in each generation. Many times, the sequence, the timing, is not in line to support the pairing of the two. Love is not about the stars needing to be in alignment or the winds shifting in a certain way. It is about the spirit soul mates existing in beings of comparable age and like locale. Nature does its best to deposit spirit soul mates in such a way as to find each other. But it is not always possible, nor is it possible to ensure that they will find each other when they do exist in time and proximity. It takes effort and diligence on the part of the spirit. Here again, the other components of the beings often determine success by their willingness and receptiveness to allow and entertain all the possibilities through which the soul mate might reside. Each domain has three chances to find its mate, one chance from each of its domain's spirit. Once partnered, the benefits are true and bountiful. This doesn't guarantee total compatibility though. It doesn't completely downplay or restrict the other spirits of the being from dominance or from pursuing their destinies, from exerting the influences of their natures. Rather, it assures a very strong and mostly overriding and dominant attraction and commitment between two spirits and their beings. Successful marriages and partnerships are founded on this binding in love of the spirit soul mates. Becky and Tom have been blessed with goodness and a strong relationship to build on. Most are not so lucky.

A gift and product of the goodness of love is children of good natures. Children of a soul mate relationship are always good-natured. A contribution from each of the soul mate spirits is passed to the new embryo at conception. Matched soul mates are always good-natured spirits. This is a gift from nature for their success in finding one another. There are no exceptions. The contribution of a spirit from the two to the new domain ensures a majority of good-natured spirits in the new domain. This adds goodness to the world.

After dating for two years, Tom was ready for more in his relationship with Becky. He asked Becky to dinner at the Italian eatery where they enjoyed their first date. Tom thought it an appropriate place to revisit for this special occasion. Becky naturally said yes to his offer to return there for a date. They left their apartments at six thirty and walked hand in hand to the restaurant just like they had on that first date. It was special to both of them, certainly more comfortable for Tom this time than it was the first. Still, he was nervous. Not because of any uncertainties of how to act around Becky like on their first date, but for another reason.

When they reached the restaurant, Tom pulled the maître'd aside and asked if they might sit at the same table that they shared two years previous. Fortunately, it was available. Becky was thrilled by the thought and planning that Tom had put into this night. It was so romantic. It was a bit out of character for him. Service was just as slow as it had been on that first date, yet even now, after years had passed, the time was still easy to fill with plenty to share and discuss about their days and their plans. Becky noticed that Tom seemed a bit distracted this night. She asked him, "Tom, is everything OK with you tonight?"

Tom quickly responded with a chuckle, "Everything is really fine tonight, Becky. Why do you ask?"

Becky returned a smile in relief and said, "Well, it seems you're a bit distracted. Anything you'd like to talk about?"

Tom thought it the perfect prompt. He leaned in toward Becky and reached into his jacket pocket. He began, "There is something I'd very much like to discuss tonight."

He hesitated a moment to calm his nerves. He thought, *I can do this. I want to do this.* Then he spoke to Becky. "Becky, I've been thinking about our future and how I want to spend my life with you." He stalled on the last word. He looked into her eyes for the coaxing and strength that he needed. He was never good in these situations. He especially wanted this one time to be special.

Becky prodded, "Yes, go on. I want to hear what you've been thinking."

Tom then proceeded, "Becky, I'd like us to be together forever. I'd like for you and I to be married as man and wife." He pulled the ring to the table and offered it to her as a symbol of his commitment to marry. "Would you marry me, Becky?"

There was no hesitation from Becky with an answer to his question. She loved him. She gushed, "Yes, Tom, I would be so very happy to be your wife." She reached out her left hand so that he could slip the ring on her finger. She looked at it closely. It was beautiful. Normally, Becky would not get caught up in material and expensive items, but she gasped in surprise. "Tom, this ring is so beautiful. The diamond is so large. You didn't need to impress me with anything so expensive. But I absolutely love it. It makes me so very happy." She then squirmed and fluttered like a bird the rest of the evening, so anxious to share this moment with everyone. Tom knew that he had done well. He, too, was excited.

She asked him, "Can we tell all our friends?"

Tom replied, "I hoped that you would be this excited. Let's not wait long to schedule the wedding."

Becky laughed. She was so filled with joy and thoughts of the planning. She asked Tom, "Where would you like to get married? Here in the city or in one of our hometowns?"

Tom hadn't given this much thought. He shrugged and said, "What would you like?"

She couldn't answer. Then she said to him, "You have never met my family. We must tell them in person. They must meet you." She looked for him to agree.

He replied, "I'd like that. Will you set something up, soon?"

She responded, "Absolutely. It's been months since I've been back home. I'll set something up soon."

The night's special event prompted the topics that filled the rest of the evening's conversation. It was a special date, a special event for both of them. It was mostly for the physical and mind component's benefit. The spirit soul mates had been committed to each other for two years. It was time to get the whole beings in sync. Becky and Tom went home that night excited and happy.

Tomorrow would be the first full day of their engagement. They had many people to share their excitement with.

The ring was indeed quite impressive and expensive. Tom had happened upon a really special deal. He purchased it from a downtown jeweler. It cost Tom $2,500, while others like it cost well over $4,000 and more. Tom asked the jeweler why he was offering it to him at such a reasonable price. The jeweler told Tom that he'd purchased it from a mortician who wanted to raise money for a shelter to help troubled young women. The jeweler said it bothered him to resell the ring at full value. As such, it was available to Tom for under market value if he was willing to pay the $2,500. Tom was agreeable. He thought that Becky would look very good in the ring. Indeed, she did love the ring. There was something about it that brought her memories of someone close to her, not only of Tom but of another as well. She could not quite put her finger on what it was. It was truly a special ring.

Before she was able to schedule a date to return home, Becky got a notice in the mail that her high school was planning a reunion picnic. Becky thought how wonderful it might be to attend this as well while she was home. She wanted to show Tom off to all her old friends from her hometown. This would be a perfect opportunity. She mentioned it to Tom, hoping that he might not mind. He was agreeable, even though on the inside he had reservations about meeting so many people whom he'd never met before. But these were people who were important to Becky. He wanted her to be happy in this moment. The weekend for visiting Becky's home was set. On that Friday, they would arrive at her parents' home and share dinner with her family.

On Saturday, they would picnic with Becky's hometown friends and acquaintances.

Both Becky and Tom took that Friday off from work. It would be a ten-hour drive to Becky's hometown. They would need to arrive in time for dinner. By six thirty in the morning, they were on the road for the little rural town of Councilville, where Becky had been born and spent her pre-adult years. It was barely a blip on the map. Its greatest significance was its people. As Tom saw it, its best contribution was Becky. He was glad to have the opportunity to experience firsthand the origin of her past, to learn more of it from those who knew her and experienced it with her. It would add new perspective and depth. The trip was not just being made for her. He, too, would come back home with a better understanding of who she was and who she had been. He wondered as he drove if she had always been such a good and caring person.

Becky spent the first four hours of the trip curled up in the front seat, catching up on her sleep. Tom enjoyed watching her. She looked so peaceful and happy. He wondered if she always smiled in her sleep. He wondered what was going through her dreams. At that moment, it seemed important to know these things. It was all he had to keep him awake and keeping the car pointed toward its destination. It was nearly time to stop for lunch when Becky finally woke up. It was the first opportunity that Tom had to hear another's voice since leaving the city. He was bored and ready to talk. After Becky readjusted herself in the seat, he asked her, "Did you have a good sleep? You were quiet as a mouse."

She replied, "As good as can be expected in the car. It's such a beautiful day for a drive, don't you think?"

Tom chuckled at how she always seemed to see the good in everything. He asked her, "Do you know you smile in your sleep? Is it every time or only when you're with me?"

Becky returned a chuckle and playfully asked, "Do I really smile? I didn't know that, but I'm sure the smile is because I'm out of the city or because I'm taking a day off work. It wouldn't have anything to do with you, Tom."

Tom responded, "I know better." Then he aimed a smile at her. "It's me. I know it."

Becky just smiled. It had been Tom that had filled her dream. She was getting married. She was marrying a man who was her spirit soul mate. It made her smile continuously.

Finally, Tom asked, "Would you like to stop for lunch soon?"

Becky nodded yes. She suggested, "Tom, let's pick something up in the next little town and take it to a spot in the nearby countryside to eat. Surely, it wouldn't delay us too much to leave the interstate for a few miles. We can have our own private picnic."

Tom thought it was a great idea. He wanted to get some fresh air and stretch his legs. He didn't relish the idea of fast food or sharing his lunch among a bevy of truckers and vacationers. Off on the side of a country road would be perfect. He acknowledged, "There's a town just two miles ahead. We'll get groceries there and then look for something outside its limits. I have this vision of a stream with trees lining its banks."

Becky and Tom found a perfect spot outside the little town. Sure enough, there was a river. It had a covered bridge across it. At the covered bridge were large oaks filling the area with shade. Tom pulled a blanket from within the trunk and spread it on a flat area with a full view of the water flowing over stones and pebbles under the bridge that stretched across the river. It was mesmerizing to watch the water. Meanwhile, Becky began to prepare sandwiches. She was about to hand Tom one when he asked, "So, Becky, this picnic tomorrow . . . what should I expect?"

Before she could answer, he added, "What do I need to know? What shouldn't I do? What shouldn't I say or think?" It was the first time since their planning for this trip that Tom had expressed any concern or apprehension.

Becky responded, "I don't know of anything, Tom. Just be you. If they don't like you for who you are, it won't change my opinions. I've been away from most of these people for so long I don't know most of them very well anymore, probably not much more than you will."

Tom then asked her, "Are you anxious to see them?"

Becky replied, "Very much so. They are a big part of my past. I'd like to think that they can be a part of our future as well." She then snuggled up against Tom. "They're good people, Tom. You will like them."

They spent a few minutes after lunch down by the water's edge. Becky took off her shoes and dipped her toes in the cool, flowing water. She finally braved wading into the shallow parts of the stream. Tom preferred to skip stones across it. On occasion, he'd get one to hit next to her and create a splash on her. She'd jump and dance. Tom would laugh loudly and apologize. Yet within a few moments, he'd return to his pranks. The setting and the atmosphere brought out the kid in both of them. Had it not been for the tight schedule, they could have stayed there all day. But their appointment for dinner soon had them on the road again.

Becky and Tom arrived at her parents' house just as planned. The house was not large, not as large as Tom had envisioned it to be. Becky's family was of modest means. After the house, Tom's second vision was of roughly thirty people spilling out from a porch that was meant to handle fifteen. Every one of the people was smiling and talking at the same time. It was difficult to isolate any one conversation or zero in on any one speaker. But the buzz intensified as soon as they heard one voice shriek, "They're here!" Immediately, a stream of additional people flowed from the front door. The parade started to extend toward Becky and Tom as they stood outside the car. Everyone wanted a hug, especially from Becky, yet none of them treated Tom as if he was a stranger. Rather, each introduced themselves and treated him as if they knew him, as if he'd been a part of the family for years. The more members of the family who joined the throng, the more Becky and Tom were separated. The swarm of people was like a splitting wedge moving them in two different directions. Tom had hoped for some help from Becky with the introductions, but getting back to her through the crowd was not in the making. There was too much excitement and too much activity around her. Tom was made to feel welcomed yet not entirely at ease.

Dinner was served in the backyard on picnic and card tables. It was the only way to accommodate all the family and close friends who showed up to greet them. Tom was finally reunited with Becky at their place of honor at one of the forward tables. She was detoured from him several times by women wanting to see her ring and congratulate her. Tom had heard more shriek and shrill squeals than he'd heard in a lifetime. The return of Becky, the ring, and the news of her engagement were the primary sources of the party's excitement.

Finally, Becky was back at Tom's side to help him deflect some of his uneasiness. It was a challenge for Tom to take in and absorb it all in the first full hour of the gathering. Tom couldn't remember many of the first names of the relatives whom he met. He couldn't fully recalibrate his bearings to the many differences from what he was familiar with. He had hoped that he would have been better able to adapt and fit in. But it was all new and different. Becky came from a very large and close family. He did not. These people were so open and friendly. His family was not so much. It was a different world. It would take some time to get used to it, to adapt to it. Yet he continued to smile and nod to each person he met as if he was enjoying it.

His spirits were besieged by a great many new and continuous encounters, one right after another. Each encounter created the internal and involuntary spirit pairings and resultant assessment of attracting or repulsing charges flowing through his domain and being. His spirit position toward each person he met was constantly being registered and catalogued for future reference. This generated a general feeling of anxiety and discomfort within his being to be in such internal flux and turmoil from the variations and diversity of his feelings for those he was meeting. But it was natural for the situation. Unlike the case with Becky, who already knew where her attractions would occur and where her repulsions were as well, Tom was left to discover his likes and dislikes from these first meetings. He was directly exposed to those Becky would naturally avoid. It was a struggle for him in the immediacy but would help him in the future. The number, the influence, the levels and variation of the natures and strengths of the natures in this family amazed Tom's spirit center. It seemed that Becky's family was represented by the greatest number of possible combinations that a group of domains could have.

Finally, Becky's mother and father came up to greet Tom. Mr. Turner was first to speak. He extended his hand to Tom and said, "Welcome to the family, Tom. We've heard so much about you over the past year from the phone conversations we've had with our daughter."

Mrs. Turner broke in and added, "You've been so good to our Becky. I'm so happy for you two."

Mrs. Turner said to Becky, "This is so exciting. Have you introduced Tom to everyone?"

Tom replied, "Most of the family introduced themselves to me. Everyone is so friendly, Mrs. Turner."

Mrs. Turner quickly corrected him by saying, "Please call me Mom. You'll be like a son now."

It made Tom feel uncomfortable to do so, but he replied, "Very good, Mom."

Becky beamed a smile. She took both her mother and her father into her gaze and said, "Does this mean that Tom has officially passed the test?"

Mr. Turner replied for both him and his wife, "There was never a doubt, Becky. If he is good enough for my daughter, he is more than good enough for us." Then he draped his arm around Tom and the other around Becky and proclaimed his joy. "You two will make us all very happy. It's as we would want it."

Within Tom's domain, he felt an attraction to both his new mom and dad. They seemed to have similar natures and spirit mixes. They were much like his own. They were predominantly good. Together, in this nucleus, there were many good natures and domain attractions. It made Tom feel more at ease. It made Tom's domain feel stronger and complete. But one thing surprised Tom's domain. From the sharing through the auras offered from the relationship, it was evident that Mr. and Mrs. Turner were not joined by soul mate spirits. Their relationship was strong and was bound by many common elements, but it was not perfectly forged. It was not one of perfect love. It was then that Tom's domain realized that Becky and his relationship was different from her parents'. It was stronger and more perfect. His and Becky's was of perfect union. It was then that he realized that Becky and he were truly something special. They were soul mates. It was evident as well to both Mr. and Mrs. Turner's domains. Their daughter had found a special partner. It influenced and encouraged them to provide their total support of Becky and Tom's engagement.

Mr. Turner made a shrill whistle with his fingers and his mouth. It startled Becky and Tom. It drew the crowd quiet. It indicated to everyone that Mr. Turner had something to say.

He then announced to them all, "As most of you already know, my daughter Becky has recently become engaged to marry a wonderful man from the city. None of you know Tom well. Nor do I. But I know Becky. And only a very special man could capture the heart of one so pure, one of the most wonderful creatures of this earth, my Becky."

He wiped a tear from his eye and caught his breath. He continued, "Becky's mother and I welcome Tom into our family, soon to be my son-in-law. Please treat him, as I know you will, as a Turner and as my son."

He then directed the attention to Becky's mother by saying, "Mother, do you have anything to add?"

Mrs. Turner seemed anxious to add her thoughts. She addressed the group. "This is such a special time. I hope everyone can celebrate our joy. I expect everyone to be at the wedding as well, to celebrate the joyous union. You all know that you are invited and welcome." Then she chuckled and added, "And I expect everyone to bring a nice gift to help get these two started." She followed it with an admission. "I'm just kidding about the gift, you know." But it was an escape of the evil-natured spirit within her. Her materialistic side got the better of her for just an instant.

Mr. Turner then motioned to Tom. He offered, "Tom, it's often hard to get a word in edgewise with this family. This is a rare opportunity for you. Would you like to share a few words?"

Panic rushed into Tom's consciousness like a swollen river over its banks. His timid nature was under attack. Yet he knew that this was a defining moment. He needed to win these people over and to make them feel comfortable with him. Offering a few remarks would help. He took his cue, stood up, and took a few steps from the table while speaking. "For those of you, especially those whom I haven't met yet, if there are any, my name is Tom McDouglas."

He paused to measure his courage, and then he went on, "I come from a much different environment. My family is much smaller and certainly not as outgoing and friendly as this one. I'm very happy to meet all of you and thrilled that you have come out to greet Becky and me today, especially for your acceptance of me as part of your family."

He spaced his pauses to allow himself to assess the audience's response. They seemed receptive so far. He went on, "I'm here because of one person who is very special to me. I believe that she and I were meant to be together forever."

He cleared his throat and then confirmed while looking at Becky and said, "And of course, I'm referring to Becky as that special person whom I want to spend my forever with." He held her gaze and watched her smile. "I suspect that you people know what I see in her. You know that she is an angel of goodness." He then smiled back at her. "Why she loves someone like me is a mystery, but I know that I am truly blessed. I'm honored to be among those who nurtured and developed her. I'm honored and thankful to become a part of this family."

He then redirected his focus on the masses at the tables and assured them, "I will take good care of her. I will honor my commitments to her, her parents, and all of you. I hope to live up to the expectations that you have of me. From what I've taken in since arriving, You're a good family to be a part of."

Some of the women were getting emotional. The men were smiling. Others began to clamor, talk, and laugh again. The speeches were good, but now they were over. The party began again. Becky's mother and father were hugging. Becky was crying. It was an emotional and powerful moment. It was a perfect speech at a perfect time. Becky knew how hard it was for Tom to stand in front of her family and spill his heart out. He'd won the whole family over to him. He was accepted. He had won Becky over long ago but won over her emotions this night. She was charged by his words. She knew from where the words came. They were initiated from his spirits. They were pure and true. It confirmed their love. It was going to be a wonderful weekend. From that moment forward, it got better for Tom as well.

So what is marriage without a soul mate bond? Can it be a marriage bound in love? If it's not the soul mate spirits, then what is it that marks the difference between love and friendship?

The answer lies in the development of strong relationships between women and men. Many women and men never find their soul mates. This isn't to say that they will not marry and find happiness and strength in their marriage. Marriage is an act of the mind and body. It is not of the spirit. Marriage can confirm and commit what the spirits feel. In the case of soul mates, it's a commitment of love. True love only comes from the joining of soul mates. Without soul mate spirits, there is no true love. But still, there can be marriage. There can be a successful joining.

There is a level between friendship and true love. It is called infatuation. Infatuation is often thought of in a negative context, but this is just distortion. Infatuation is a good thing, a heightened sense of friendship. Infatuation is the strongest of friendships and a weaker form of love. Its strength comes from commitment, respect, and sacrifice. It can make a marriage strong and powerful. It is not as easy as soul mates' true love, but good is not easy. Infatuation reflects the attributes of goodness and love. It feeds and grows these attributes. The domains of Becky's mother and father were of a good-natured mix, although not pure like their daughter's but blessed with the components to make infatuation work through their marriage. There's was one filled with challenges, but a good and happy one.

Becky's domain makeup came two-thirds from her parents. She was lucky. They were not pure domains. They were not a soul mate couple. Yet she received a good spirit from each. It could have just as easily turned out differently.

In the absence of a soul mate spirit pair, physical relationships are in the best case from infatuation. In the worst case, from lust. There are many degrees in between. The insignificance in the difference between the highest form of infatuation and lowest form of love makes it difficult to differentiate between the two. This is especially true without consideration of time. Infatuation is much more fragile and most times shorter cycled than true love. It requires effort and progressively more of it to keep its intensity and level of commitment and dedication sustained as time goes by. This isn't to say it can't be or doesn't happen. It isn't to imply that a relationship based without soul mates is not stable or without the prognosis of longevity. Many such relationships without the soul mate spirit ingredient, are strong, healthy, and lasting. But unlike those of a soul mate relationship, there are no guarantees. It's up to the spirits and the being. It's up to the effort and the work that they put into the relationship that will determine if it will survive the challenges of time. It's not automatic like most times with soul mate spirit relationships.

Second and unlike the soul-mate-based pairing, there aren't any guarantees that good-natured spirits will be passed by the couple to their children. With non-soul-mate relationships, there is much opportunity for randomness and chance. Any of the three spirits of the parent domain can be chosen to contribute its contributing spirit to the new domain of the offspring. It can be a good or evil-natured spirit. Good-natured spirits pass from love, but love is not a guaranteed part of a non-soul-mate partnership. The nature that is passed from these relationships is determined by which spirit and nature is least diluted and, if equal, which is in the position of dominance at the moment of inception. The contributing spirit is called the advocate. This allows for spirits who are incapable of love or for a nature not suited to love, (mostly of the evil nature), to pass its spirit contribution to the child's domain. It allows for manipulation and growth in numbers of the nature's type. It's often an act of advantage, sometimes deception. It can also be from goodness. It all depends which spirit is the advocate donor.

The partnership of Becky's parents was still strong after many years. Theirs started as a strong attraction between the spirits within their two different domains. Their bond grew to be quite intense, intense enough to simulate love. Yet it was not, and their spirits were not soul mates. They had much in common. They had several spirits within their domains that paired to produce strong attracting charges and influences. Each was very consistent in cause and makeup with those of the other's domain, yet they were not soul mates. The spirits knew this. Outside of the spirit level, however, their attraction and desire for each other resembled soul mate status. To fortify this relationship, the mental and physical components must also support, attract, and bond to each other.

It's strange that the nonspirit components of the being will work hard to grow and nurture non-soul-mate spirits' infatuations, yet these same nonspirit components can be the cause for turning away soul mates from joining in a true love relationship. The mind and body obviously crave love and affection. It's that they are not well versed in loving relationships. Their emphasis is not on the spirits. Their emphasis and focus are more superficial. Their role is critical in the selection of a mate yet misguided and many times harmful. Until love was introduced by the spirits, they knew not of its gift or its goodness. Only through the spirits is love granted. Yet only through the nonspirit components are the spirits granted freedom to find soul mates and love. The mind and body want to be involved in the selection of a mate, yet it's when they give freedom to the spirits that soul mates and love are achieved. It's sort of a hole in the design which allows for glitches

In reality, often the soul mate spirits are not allowed freedom to connect because of antiselection at the physical and mental level. When partners are rejected by the mind and physical components of the being and therefore the chance for love discarded, infatuation becomes the best that components of the being can hope for. Relationships and marriages of infatuation have evolved to be the norm in marriage relationships. Becky's parents are a prime example. There are many. It didn't need to be this way. It wasn't intended to be this way.

Becky's father and her mother's best friend, Janice, each housed soul mate spirits within their domains. When they were younger and in high school, the younger Turner was a very handsome young man. He was a star athlete and very popular. He drew the attention of all the young ladies. His two favorite interests were Becky's mother, before they were married, and Janice. The attraction to Janice surprised most of his classmates. She was a very plain girl. She was not so popular, nor did she stand out in any way. Yet young Turner felt strongly attracted to her. She made him feel comfortable and strangely complete. Her magic on his inner being was strong. Yet her appeal to his physical and mental components was not so strong. His mental heard and evaluated the opinions and questions of his peers and those he trusted. They'd ask, "Why would did he consider Janice for his attentions?"

Alternatively, was the young girl who was the envy of every male in the school. She was a beauty and the sweetest, nicest girl by the assessment of most. She was a cheerleader and active in most of the interests that were consistent and compatible with young Turner's. From the physical and mental components' perspective, these two were the perfect pair. Yet from the spirit perspective, it was ordained that young Turner and Janice would be granted truest love. It didn't happen. Young Turner chose Becky's mother. The physical and mental components of his being made it so. They worked hard to support and maintain the high levels of infatuation between the couple since dating, through marriage, and now into their later years. Clearly, this is an example of a success arising from failure to find the most successful solution.

As for Janice, she was very much the victim in this case. She knew what she lost in this sequence of life possibilities. She never found either of her other two soul-mate possibilities, though she tried. Her physical and mental components tried to find a mate of their preferences. She married twice from strong attractions to others. In both cases, the attractions were infatuation at first but with time diminished to lower forms. As these diminished, the support from the physical and mental components of both parties lessened. Janice suffered through two divorces. She now has two children, one from each failed marriage. She remained close to her friend Mrs. Turner. She would never wish ill will or mishap on her friend's marriage, but her match to that within Mr. Turner's domain lay in wait for a chance. Her friendship to Mrs. Turner allowed it to remain in proximity and informed on opportunity. Spirits do not sabotage other spirits or situations for their gain, not even for love. In Janice's case, it was simply a game of waiting, and maybe someday better judgment from Mr. Turner's physical and mental components would allow a perfect match to occur.

This example marks the pressures on marriages and relationships formed from non-soul-mate relationships. Soul mates will not intentionally interfere with these marriages and relationships, but they will be there, and when they find their match, they'll be there in proximity and in contact as they can arrange it. They wait and remain ready for corrections by the physical and mental of their earlier mistakes.

Becky was one of three children born to Mrs. and Mr. Turner. Her sister, Ella, and her brother, Randall, were both quite different from Becky. In fact, they were all quite different from one another. Becky was the lucky one. Her two advocate spirits were good natured. Ella's advocates were a good-natured spirit from her mother and the evil-natured spirit from her father. Each contributed their portion to Ella's domain. The third spirit added to her mix from the unassigned pool of spirits was an evil-natured spirit. This made Ella an overall evil-natured domain. The spirit from her mother's advocate was identical to that filling Becky's domain. This created a permanent and special bond between Ella and Becky. This bond along with Becky's pure mix superseded all other considerations. This placed this spirit in a position of special strength and dominance when in her presence. Yet because their domain's mix and the aggregate result of their pairing was a repulsing charge, they still disagreed and quarreled. It drove their parents crazy. It was definitely an unpredictable sibling relationship.

Becky's brother, Randall, was altogether different. His advocates were the evil-natured spirit from the mother and the good-natured spirit from the father that was other than the advocate to Becky's domain. His third spirit from the unassigned pool was a good-natured spirit. This made Randall an overall good-natured domain. Randall shared no common advocate with either of the other two siblings. As a result, there was no superseding bond to either of his siblings. His domain's mix created an attracting charge with Becky's domain but a repulsing charge with Ella's domain. This was evident in how each got along as they grew up together. Randall and Becky were close. Ella and Randall could just never get along. They seemed to be family by name only.

Just as a connection was created between Becky and Ella resulted from a common advocate spirit, the same held true between the donor parent and child. The common spirit in both creates this special link between the common spirits within their domains. It was much stronger between Randall and his parents than for the one between Ella and her parents because in Ella's case the remaining mix of their domains resulted in repulsing charges, and in Randall's case an attracting charge. Still, the bonds of family were strongly in place and overriding in all cases. The only exception was that between Ella and Randall. The one significant hole in the fabric of family was created as a product of the parents not being soul mates, that between Ella and Randall. The many lesser significant flaws represented by pairings eliciting repulsing charges were also the result of the non-soul-mate parents. Becky's family was not a perfect one, not even close, yet each of the members' domains tried hard, most of the time, to make the best with what they were given to work with. The family pulled together in time of need and in time of celebration. There was strength in this occasion.

It was set by the pairing of their spirit natures that Tom and Ella would not find a strong relationship between them. There was nothing overriding the normal rules for determining relationships in their meeting. Their domain mix was not compatible. From the first introduction, Tom felt uncomfortable with her. On the other hand, Tom felt very comfortable around Becky's brother, Randall. Randall's domain mix was favorable. Tom would never be a welcomed addition to the family as Ella saw it. He would need to accept this and deal with it.

When the dinner part of the celebration was over, Tom asked Becky if she'd like to take a walk with him. He had a number of things he wanted to talk to her about, all arising from the evening's events. He was most disturbed about his feeling of uneasiness with her sister, Ella. He confessed to Becky, "Becky,

I don't think I hit it off very well with your sister tonight. I feel badly about this."

Becky knew that there might be an issue here. Ella had the same effect on most of Becky's friends. She understood his frustration. She assured him, "Tom, my sister is a hard one to win over. She has always been the different one in the family. I wouldn't worry about your first encounter with her."

Tom responded, "I really wanted your whole family to accept me. I think I have failed in this regard."

They walked hand in hand for a block or two before Becky stopped and faced Tom. She kissed him on impulse and then said, "You were accepted by my whole family tonight, Tom. Don't let Ella leave you with questions regarding this. She acts the way she does purposefully. It's her nature."

It struck Tom as odd the way she was referring to her sister. It struck Tom that there seemed to be a rift or old scars between them. Tom questioned, "What do you mean it's her nature? She is your sister. Isn't she much like you?"

This brought on a flurry of arm motion and a quick explanation, "Oh Nooo! My sister and I are not at all alike. We love each other as sisters, but we are as opposite as day and night."

Tom injected, "Specifically in what ways do you differ so greatly?"

Becky motioned toward a short wall made of stacked, flat rocks and suggested that they sit. She proceeded to explain, "Let me share with you a few stories involving my sister. I have not shared these for a long time." She then confirmed that she had Tom's full attention and interest. Tom was locked in and curious.

Becky began, "From the time we were small, Ella always had a devilish streak. She was the child who demanded attention. She would disregard every rule and request. She would throw a tantrum when she didn't get her way. She was a difficult and unruly child."

Becky stopped only to take an occasional breath. She went on, "She often embarrassed us all. She was the type of child who, while at the store, would slip a package of gum in her pocket without paying. She was the child who couldn't get along or share with the others. She was the girl who would set others up to get into trouble and then laugh as they were punished. As her nature and her actions began to be better known, we all started to be hesitant to take her with us when we went out."

Tom interrupted, "Can you share any specifics? She sounds like she was a little hellion."

Becky responded with an example. "One day when I was ten, we were at the five-and-dime. Ella slipped a watch that she wanted in my bag. As my mother, Ella, and I were walking out of the store, the alarm at the exit sounded. Security rushed to assess the reason for the alarm. My mother and I were shocked to find that it was from a watch in my bag. My mother's knowing glance was first toward Ella. She knew her nature." Becky let out a gasp of frustration. The memory was still painful.

She went on, "As we were questioned about the watch, Ella finally admitted to her deed almost proudly. She didn't intend to harm anyone, but if anyone was to be caught, she didn't want it to be her."

Becky shrugged and admitted, "I had difficulty trusting her after that incident. I was truly afraid and embarrassed at that moment. I was afraid that someone I knew might have seen us, might have asked questions and assumed that I stole that watch."

Tom asked, "What did store security do to her?"

Becky responded, "Nothing. They didn't charge her. They could see the anger in my mother's face. They assumed that Ella would get punishment enough when she got home. They didn't keep us long. They could see my fright and dismay. They released Ella and me to my mother's custody and asked that we not shop in that store ever again. We were no longer welcome there. Before that, it was my favorite place to shop."

Tom continued to question, "Did she apologize or assure you that she wouldn't do it again?"

Becky looked to the sky and paused. She finally answered, "No, I don't think she did. She was defiant, even at this age. She took her punishment from my parents without any show of remorse. I think she thought it was my fault for getting caught. I ruined everything for her. She would say this to me often."

Tom's curiosity was piqued. "This can't be the only reason that you find your sister difficult. Is it?"

Becky responded quickly, "Oh, certainly not. My whole life has been the target of her pranks and evil deeds, this or in avoidance of the effects." She took off the figurative gloves and readied to tell the really good stuff. Her voice lowered. She leaned in closer and proceeded with the next story. "I don't make this common knowledge, but Ella has spent time in reform school. In fact, she's been there twice." She looked to the ground in shame. It was as if it had been her who had served the time. It was the proverbial skeleton in the Turner family closet.

Becky explained, "I found her overdosed in her room when she was only fifteen. I was sixteen and a half. I didn't know what was going on but called the ambulance. She told me that she hated me for calling them, but she would have died without them. Reform school and a rehabilitation program was required by the courts. Before this, she apparently had robbed a gas station in another town with her friends. They were all wanted by the law. Their faces were caught during the robbery on surveillance cameras. Even if it hadn't been for the overdose, it was only a matter of time until she would have been identified and caught for the robbery."

Becky paused for a moment to again catch a breath. The memories had again stirred her anger, but she went on, "To serve her sentence, Ella spent three months in rehab at the state hospital and three months in reform school." Becky went silent.

After a moment of silence, Tom asked, "So what happened then?" His interests were really sparked. For him, it was the most intriguing part of the evening.

Becky wrung her hands as if to remove the residue of the memories. She continued, "Well, needless to say, Ella held me partly responsible for the humiliation of getting caught and punished. I was a handy scapegoat for her problems. She wanted to get back at me." Becky mysteriously left the discussion hanging.

Tom didn't know whether to pursue it further, but his curiosity urged him on. He asked, "Did she pursue revenge?"

Becky looked straight forward. Sharing these memories was more difficult than she had planned. But Tom needed to know. He needed to understand why she and her sister were not close and why he might be having natural reservations about Ella. It was for the best that she proceeded. "Ella came back home after being released from reform school and indeed got her revenge. It was on all of us." She took Tom's hand and looked into his eyes for comfort.

Tom was growing impatient. From his impatience, he let slip, "How? What did she do?"

Becky then confessed, "Well, I have not had many boyfriends in my life, Tom, but I must admit you were not my first." Both she and Tom chuckled over her embarrassment.

Tom asked, "Did she steal your boyfriend?"

Becky chuckled some and then said, "She certainly did. She became pregnant soon thereafter, and they were married."

Tom seemed surprised by this. He gushed, "Your sister is married? I wasn't aware of this."

Becky secured a smile. She responded, "No, she is not currently married. The two of them were so different and incompatible. Their natures were complete opposites. The only reason she did this was to get back at me. She didn't realize that the boy and I were just friends. She was constantly doing things to mess up her own life and others around her. They divorced within three months of being married. I believe it was called an annulment."

Tom then asked, "So what about the baby? Do you have a niece or nephew?"

Becky replied, "Somewhere. I'm not sure which it is. Ella never said. She put the baby up for adoption. She left home soon after the divorce. Where she went no one knows but Ella."

Becky shook her head in disgust and then continued, "She could not support the baby on her own. One day my parents got a call that Ella was in the hospital. She had been beaten and had not eaten in some time. She'd been moving about from city to city and living in the streets. Mom and Dad went to get her. She, too, was a wanted woman again. Again, it was a number of robberies and scams. She was not eighteen at the time. As a condition of her release, she was to serve another period in reform."

Tom couldn't believe Ella's history. Becky was surprised by his curiosity and his laughter. "This was serious. She returned to reform school and survived a second sentence. She's been home ever since then."

Tom was compelled to ask, "Did this straighten her out? Has she done anything illegal since?"

Becky responded, "Mom and Dad say she's better. I can't tell you. By the time she returned home, I'd moved out and was in college. She and I never reconciled her affair with my boyfriend, not that it's important."

Tom then asked her playfully, "So I got you on the rebound, right?"

Becky laughed and said, "Absolutely! And you can thank my sister for that."

Tom replied, "I think I will."

Becky squealed and playfully patted him on the shoulder, saying, "You better not. Not a word of this to anyone, do you hear me?" Then she took his hand and pulled him from the wall. "We'd better be getting back now. I think I've shared enough family secrets for one night."

Tom laughed and did his best look of surprise. He asked, "Do you mean to tell me that this isn't the only skeleton in the closet? There are more?" He moved ahead of her and backpedaled. "Can we do this again tomorrow? I want to hear all the family dirt, especially now that I'm a part of this family."

Becky played along. She asked Tom, "Can we start with some from your family first?"

Tom returned, "Yes, but it's not nearly as interesting as your family's. I might bore you."

Becky replied, "I'll take that chance." They stopped to hug and to remind each other that they loved each other, before returning to the house. Becky's mother had been concerned for them. They had been gone for nearly an hour and a half. Tom thought to himself, *It was nice to be missed.*

Ella had indeed been married, but actually, it had been two times before. There was one marriage by the justice of the peace from another town that not even her family knew of. It was in exchange for shelter, food, and vices. It was a marriage of convenience. Her choices in men were always influenced by the physical. A good-looker or a high roller was always attractive to her. Her nature was evil. It got in the way of finding love. But it almost happened once. Her soul mate spirit had found him.

He was an orderly at the hospital where she had been recuperating the second time, where Ella's parents came to retrieve her after her long disappearance. His name was Anthony. He took special interest in her. He expected nothing in return for his caring. He made her feel special. He helped her in her recovery not only of her health but also of her self-worth and dignity. He called her after her release from the second sentence in reform school, even after being separated and out of range of their spirit's attracting charge.

Ella's physical and mental components felt that Anthony was too plain. He was too poor. He was not exciting enough. He simply didn't measure up. It was not enough that he made her feel good and whole. These feelings would not provide her the things her nature craved or would not put food on their table. All the factors and influences of her being, except the soul mate spirit within her, convinced her to pass on the opportunity of true love. It all came down to the fact that what was best and long lasting for her was to be passed over because the being containing her matching soul mate was not handsome or wealthy or evil enough. He didn't have a respectable enough job or lots of nice things.

Ella was now an office administrator in a furniture company and moving up in her career. Anthony would just hold her back, even though she always felt very connected to him when he was near her. Anthony was heartbroken, yet it was from his spirit, not his heart. He continued to try to win her approval. He visited and looked for opportunities for their paths to cross. He was even at this night's gathering. But it was another futile attempt to win her over.

Becky had heard stories of the man who wooed her sister. These came from conversations with her mother. Her mother thought it was romantic. She liked Anthony. Becky finally met him lurking on the outskirts of the guest circles. She knew it was the same man of her mother's stories as they introduced themselves to each other. She transferred to his domain out of curiosity of his intent and persistence. It was clear from her transfer that Anthony would be special for Ella. He was her soul mate. Spirits know. From their meeting, Becky's being was compelled to help Anthony. But because it was Becky, it only pushed Ella farther away from both her and Anthony.

Becky so wanted to transfer to the domain of her sister. She wanted to draw from her domain stores the reasons for so many of her actions. She wanted to help her soul mate find the strength to influence the body and allow Anthony to be a part of her life. There was so much opportunity to set this confused and wayward life straight again. If only she could get inside her domain. But she couldn't. It was a law of nature. It was an interesting phenomenon that restricted a pure domain sibling from transferring to the domain of her other siblings. Spirits from a shared origin cannot reside in the same domain at once. Both shared a spirit from the same advocate spirit of their parent. Therefore, the abilities of Becky's pure domain were useless to her in this case. It was such a shame. Ella was on her own.

Becky could only help Anthony not give up his persistence. She was sure that he would eventually win Ella over.

Becky's brother, Randall, lived a very normal and low-key life, seemingly always in the background of his sisters' higher-drama filled life. He was a good athlete. He'd been an average student but not cut out for college. He liked to work with his hands. He was very social and wanted to be around people. He was friendly, and most people liked him. They were usually willing to help him whenever he needed it.

All things considered and without consideration of the spirit makeup of the three siblings, one would surely have predicted that Randall might be the one who would do something significant in his life. As it often happens, it didn't turn out this way. As Randall moved five years beyond high school and well into adulthood, he moved out on his own. He spent quite a bit of time in a nearby town called Ricklan. He was attracted to this town because of a woman. She was the daughter of its most prominent family. The domains of Randall and the woman, Estelle, attracted. His physical component was most strongly attracted to her. They thought they were in love, but rather, it was infatuation.

Randall and Estelle were married several years later. It was a very big affair. Randall's family, even as large as it was, felt very much in the minority at the wedding. They were in awe of the extravagances of the reception. The couple started out very well. Estelle's father gave the couple a house to live in as a wedding present. It made the gifts of cookware and dishes given by the Turners look very inadequate. Estelle's last name had been Ricklan. Her father owned and ran the biggest plant in the town. A job was created for Randall. It was perfectly nontechnical and undemanding. It also paid a premium wage compared with others with similar responsibilities.

Both Estelle and Randall were good natured but not soul mates. Their differences were many, especially their backgrounds and the social circles that they were accustomed to. Randall was not very refined. His executive potential was limited. He did not pursue college. He was not cut from the mold that Estelle's father had been. Estelle had thoughts that he might someday aspire and magically transform to the level. But Randall was a line worker at heart. He was happiest in the factory as opposed to the front office. His limited level of responsibility and authority suited him just fine and made him comfortable and happy. Estelle, on the other hand, had loftier dreams and visions yet not the motivation to get there on her own. She dabbled in college, going part-time for six years before their marriage. She continued to take courses sporadically·even after they married. She went to her family whenever she needed or wanted anything beyond the means that Randall could provide.

This frustrated Randall. It played badly on his ego and pride. For this reason, and others, Randall didn't feel comfortable around his wife's parents or the rest of the family. He felt that they always looked down on him. It played on his self-worth. It began to affect his relationship with his wife. It seemed that she often went to her father and mother for answers to their issues. Randall resented this and finally put his foot down. He resented their means to resolve the issues that Estelle and he should have resolved together. It was a structural flaw in their marriage, one that Randall could not seem to fix, but he decided it was time to try. Estelle preferred the quick remedy. She was not willing to sacrifice anything of her pampered life or to change in any way. She'd always relied on Daddy in financial matters. She couldn't understand what the fuss was about when she went to her father for money. Money was part of their familial bond, a big part actually.

Over the next three years, Randall and Estelle had two children together. One was a boy, Alex, and the other was a girl, Patty. Just as Randall was not particularly fortunate in his relationships, neither he nor Estelle were particular lucky in their random selection of advocates from their domains. With both children, the evil-natured spirit within Randall's domain acted as the advocate. In the case of the boy, his mother's advocate was a good-natured spirit. But in the case of the girl, her mother's contribution to her domain was filled from the evil-natured advocate. Both children drew an evil-natured spirit from the unassigned pool. Randall's children were both evil natured. Patty's domain was pure evil. They were ideally suited to the lifestyle fostered by the mother, and although she was good-natured, she constantly fed the child's evil nature with the indulgences and status provided by her family.

The mother's evil nature became dominantly strong. It opened the door for her children to feed from its influence and encouragement toward its evil indulgences as well. Randall became a prisoner of his wife's nurtured nature and his children's preferences and domain makeup. It drove him out. He was divorced after seven years of marriage. It was a crushing blow to him. His meager salary was further reduced by child support and alimony to his wife. He became emotionally closed off to just about everyone. He went to work, came home, and confined his life within the walls of his very small apartment.

He would occasionally call his sister, Becky. She was the only one, it seemed, who could give him comfort. Although he would visit with his children, they never seemed to respect him. He died from a boating accident on a pond within the town's park. He was with the children. He had apparently hit his head on something and fell into the water. It was only seven years after his divorce. The children, it seemed were powerless to help him. Yet to this day, how he died still raises questions. Patty didn't seem nearly as distraught as Alex had been over the accident. Neither had talked about it since it happened. The town thought it was such a misfortune. No one showed up at the funeral but his sister Ella, her husband, and a girl named Sherry. His ex-wife and children had all but abandoned and forgotten him.

Randall's daughter had not been the first pure evil domain produced by the Turner family. There was one at the dinner party where Becky and Tom confirmed to the family their plans to marry. Old uncle Ned, the brother of Becky's mother, was quite different from Becky's mother. It was as if he was from a different family. Ned and Becky could never get along but always tolerated each other at family gatherings, mostly by avoiding each other.

Ned loved his ale. He was a crude man. He was the town drunk. He was an accomplished thief. He headed a band of thieves who stole cars from the towns in the vicinity. Uncle Ned's garage was really a chop shop. He bragged of his success. He tried to place himself on a pedestal within the family. He had money. He had material things. Those he surrounded himself with respected him. Yet most of the family knew him for what he was, a small-time thief. They gave him little acclaim as the family's wealthiest member. He resented this and carried a chip on his shoulder because of it.

Becky's mother and Ned's parents must have been a non-soulmate pair. This must have been the situation to have created such opposites in their offspring. It's a common trait of marriages founded on infatuation. Becky warned Tom to steer clear of old uncle Ned before they arrived in Councilville. Tom did his best to do so.

The first full day back in Councilville was a long one. Both Becky and Tom slept soundly and well into the morning. The new day would bring on a whole new set of challenges. Today would be the reunion picnic.

Becky showed her first signs of nerves since they'd arrived. She was frantic that they'd slept in too late. She was overly concerned that the dress she intended to wear had become wrinkled. Finally, she was in a fret over what to take to the picnic. It was all for naught though. They had plenty of time to get ready. The dress was ironed. It only took minutes, and Becky's mother had prepared the picnic earlier in the morning.

These things were not the real reasons for her nervousness. She was nervous because she didn't know whether her schoolmates would remember her and how they might react to her and Tom. She remembered some very lively characters from her class. She remembered some who were good friends. She remembered some who made her younger years more difficult. She had not been the most popular girl in school. She certainly had not been the prettiest or most talented girl. She was anxious to see her old classmates and where their lives had taken them, but she was not anxious for her own life to be on display and dissected before them. She was hoping that Tom might deflect some of the attention from her and onto himself instead. He would protect her.

Becky and Tom left the house at eleven thirty. The picnic was to begin at the same time. Since the town park was only a few minutes' walk from the house, this would put them there as fashionably late. The closer they got to the park, the more nervous Becky became. She began to chatter warnings to Tom about who not to sit next to and what not to ask certain people. Tom knew that he would not remember any of these warnings. He asked Becky, "Are you nervous about today?"

Becky looked surprised. She responded, "Yes, I am. Why do you ask? Does it show?"

Tom replied, "It does. You've been fluttering around and chirping like a sparrow all morning." Tom's attempt at a country-style analogy made Becky laugh for the first time today.

She responded to Tom, "Where did you pick up the homespun antidote? It is so unlike you. You've been in the country for only a day, and it's growing on you. I like it. It is the medicine I need."

Tom smiled at her. He was a bit embarrassed at her reaction yet glad to have helped. He said to her, "I could fit into this environment. I should have been a small-town man." They both laughed. They both knew that Tom had probably used most of his small-town repertoire in the one previous sentence. He was no small-town man.

At the entrance to the park, there were several greeters, name tags stretched across a table, and a stack of bulletins that contained bios of the class. The bios contained details of what each class member was now doing, who they had married, how many children they now have, and where they were living. Tom was surprised to see how many from Becky's class remained in Councilville. He was more surprised to see how many had married others from the class or those from the classes before and after. He counted seventy-seven members of her class. Only seven had attended college. Four had received Bachelor's degrees. Only one of those earning a bachelor's degree went on to get a masters. That one was Becky. Another became a doctor and resided in the town. One of the two others was a programmer at the plant in Ricklan. The other became a teacher, like Becky, but in Councilville. Most of the others became farmers, shopkeepers, laborers, civil service workers or were now unemployed. At least eight of the men had not held jobs in several years. The mix surprised Tom greatly.

Becky recognized each of the greeters and immediately jumped into a conversation with them. There were a lot of excited chatter and occasional gushes of laughter. Tom was soon beckoned over to meet each of them. Becky introduced him. "Sarah and Ellen, this is Tom, my husband-to-be. He came home to Councilville with me to meet the family. Since his arrival, however, he has had opportunity to meet most of the townspeople as well."

Tom quipped in, "I believe I can address many of them by name now." They all chuckled over this.

Sarah returned, "It's a good thing that we are a small town, Tom."

Then Ellen jumped in by asking, "What do you do for a living, Tom?"

Tom responded, "I work in a university research center. I am a physicist."

Both women were surprised. They had never met a physicist before. They were few and far between in Councilville and the surrounding areas. In fact, there were none at all. Sarah responded, "Well, we'll definitely have to add you to our class records for the next reunion." Then she chuckled. "It's very nice to meet you." In the back of her mind, she was jealous that her schoolmate had landed such a catch. Sarah was a mixed domain but of evil nature majority. She was trying hard to put a number on Tom's earnings. She would keep an eye on him and flirt with him when she could. Tom, on the other hand, felt uncomfortable around her. He thought she was a bit snooty.

Ellen, he thought, was the nicer of the two. She seemed more genuine and good. Ellen indeed was "more good. She was also a mixed domain but primarily of good natures. It was an interesting pair that was chosen for greeters. Neither of the two felt comfortable with the other, but there was a compatible one for each person whom they greeted, whether of good nature or evil. Both Becky and Tom migrated more toward Ellen.

Finally, Tom said to Ellen and Sarah, "It says in the bios that you both have husbands." He looked up at Ellen. "Ellen, you have two children, a boy of seven and a girl, five. I'll bet they keep you very active and busy."

Ellen smiled that this outsider would take such an interest in her. She shared, "Yes, they are such joys in my life."

Then she asked Becky and Tom, "I hope you don't think this too forward, but have you two talked about children?"

Becky blushed but responded, "We both hope for them someday." They all gushed with joy at the thought.

Not to exclude Sarah from the conversation, Becky asked her, "What about you, Sarah? Do you and your husband plan to have children someday?"

Ellen cringed at the question. She knew more about Sarah's marriage than Becky or Tom. It was a sore topic with Sarah. Sarah responded, "I haven't seen my husband in six months. He left me for another woman." She then gave them a defiant grin. "I'm just waiting for the divorce papers to catch up to him so that I can finally rid myself of that problem."

Tom, in particular, felt badly for her. He responded, "That's too bad, Sarah." Then he looked to Becky. "I hope that someday you can find someone as special as I have in Becky."

Ellen then chimed in and added, "And as special as my Jim." Both Tom and Ellen had found their soul mates. Their special relationships were secure.

Sarah smirked and said with sarcasm, "Yeah, right. My Prince Charming probably rode out of this town years ago." The bitterness was definitely not attractive. It simply fed her evil side. Becky and Tom enjoyed their conversation with Ellen. The one with Sarah was somewhat disturbing. It was time to move on.

They both placed their name tags on their tops and moved inward toward the heart of the gathering. As they left, they said, "Goodbye. I'm sure we'll see more of one another throughout the day."

Sarah responded to Tom, "I will make a point of it."

Becky nudged on Tom's sleeve and whispered out the side of her mouth, "Tom, stay away from that woman. I think she has a thing for you."

Tom laughed and replied, "I will gladly do that." Becky smiled and led him forward to the next couple.

At the picnic, Becky and Tom were surrounded by relationships of all types. Sixty of the classmates were now married. Most of the singles had been divorced. Of those who were now married, fifteen had been previously divorced and now remarried. Of the forty-five others who hadn't been divorced, eight of them were soul mate couples. The others were primarily strong like-natured relationships. It was fairly easy to tell the good-natured from the evil-natured couples. They tended to mingle among the others of like natures. Becky and Tom tended to migrate toward the good natures. Yet Becky made it a point to talk to everyone. She knew from her high school days which were the good natured and which were evil natured. A spirit usually never changes its nature. Some surprised her, however. Some of the evil natured had found a soul mate.

Becky heard a voice from behind her. "Becky Turner, is that you?" Becky turned around to an older version of Ed Harman. Ed was probably the most handsome and charismatic boy she had known. He was also the epitome of stuck-up and conceited. He used to tease her and make her life difficult. He had been a mixed, two evil-natured domain. His personality and attributes fit his nature to a tee.

Becky responded, "Why, Ed Harman, how are you?" It was a defensive hello.

In fact, she didn't even introduce Tom to him until Ed asked, "It's been a long time. I hear you're getting married. Is this the lucky guy?"

Becky responded, "I'm sorry, Ed. Yes, this is Tom. We plan to marry in a few months."

Tom extended a hand in greeting. He asked, "You are Ed Harman? It says in the bio that you are the mayor of this fine town. How does one aspire to such a high position?"

Ed responded, "Well, I guess no one else wanted the job, so they gave it to the first fool who would take it." Tom and Ed both laughed heartily. Becky joined in with a token chuckle but remained apprehensive. Ed could tell she was still cold toward him. He knew why. The whole intent of approaching her was to apologize for the past. He was a changed man. He'd found his soul mate and married. It changed his nature. He just wanted her to know that he'd changed and that now he felt bad for all the grief and hardship he'd caused her. He finally just came out with it. "You know, Becky, I was not always a friend to you in high school. In fact, I could be a real idiot at times." He looked for her reaction. It was now an expression of amazement. The eye contact revealed the truth to Becky. It allowed her spirit to transfer. Ed was sincere. He'd really changed. His nature was now good. What a transformation.

Ed continued, "Becky, I want you to know I've changed, and I'm sorry for the pranks and antics of the past." Becky was still unable to speak.

Ed finished by saying, "That's really what I've been wanting to tell you."

Becky smiled and finally sputtered, "Thank you, Ed. It means a lot to me."

Then she asked but already knew the answer, "What caused the big change?"

Ed extended a smile and said, "Come with me. I'll introduce you to her."

He took Becky and Tom to a table on the fringe of the gathering and motioned to a woman. When she came near to them, he said, "Becky, do you remember April?" April was another of the snobs of her class. Becky remembered her as one was above all the other girls. She would degrade almost everything and everyone, and talk behind the backs of her classmates to maneuver herself in a position of favor or to gain advances from the most popular males in the class. She had apparently caught one. April always had stunning beauty. Her family was wealthier than all the others from the town. These were the qualities that fed her evil disposition when she was younger. Fortunately, however, they were also the qualities that first lured Ed to her. Ed and April, without knowing it, had soul mate spirits. Their paring changed them both dramatically. Everyone who was still around after high school would vouch for this. Both their evil natures were transformed to good. It was their love.

Becky responded to Ed's question, "Yes, of course, I remember April. How are you?"

April responded, "Embarrassed." Then she showed her model's smile and pose. "I'm embarrassed to see you after all these years and how you must remember me."

She gave a nervous laugh and continued, "I really was a snotty brat in high school, wasn't I?"

Becky responded, "Well, we all change with a bit of age."

April then said, "Thank God that is true. I hear you have a big day coming. Are you excited?"

Becky transferred to April's domain just to verify that she, too, had transformed to a good nature. The soul mate was present. Her domain was now predominantly good natured. Her remaining evil nature, as was also true with Ed, was still strong but mostly controlled. Regardless, it was now safe and comfortable to talk to her as a former classmate and potential friend. She shared, "I am very excited yet a bit afraid that I wouldn't remember everything that must be done."

April comforted her and said, "Don't let things worry you, Becky. Make it a special day emotionally. The other things will take care of themselves."

Then she finished by saying, "Look at Ed and me. If 'hellcats' like us can hitch and turn for the better, marriage is a wonderful magic." She was right. Yet Becky's domain knew that there was much more that April was talking about than just marriage. It was a soul mate relationship. It took two evil-natured people and made them good-natured. It created a new life.

Ed and April had a daughter. She was a naturally good-natured child. Her two advocate spirits were her parents' soul mate spirits. These two good-natured spirits were joined in her domain by a mild evil-natured one from the unassigned pool. Abby Harmon was truly a sweet and loving child. She was also a strong influence of goodness on her parents. She, too, would find soul mate love like her parents had. Goodness was surrounding the Harmon family. It changed their lives. Remnants of the old life still remained, however, yet in much less proportion or dominance within each than it had been before. Both were involved in the governing of the town. Ed was mayor, and April was a councilwoman. They still needed to stand out and stand above. They still carried with them many of their preferences of their previous evil-influenced lives, even though their natures were now good. There goodness was still fairly new and being learned and matured. Their history had been constructed under different influences and over twice as many years. They still cherished beauty. They both still needed money and nice things. They were slowly transitioning into a new and more good-natured style of life, but it was slow and gradual. Their evil nature was fighting for its last hold on them. Their daughter was altogether different and remained the best influence.

Becky wondered if Abby could use some help. When she transferred to Ed and April, she gave each of the two domains the strength and influence to combat their evil nature's influence. She hoped she could stick around to see her influence work to fruition through them. But it was time to move on. April wished Becky and Tom, "Good luck with your wedding, and may your marriage be as happy as Ed and mine."

Becky said, "Thank you."

Tom assured her, "If we can be as happy as you two, it will be wonderful." They wandered back into the mix to find the next encounter. Becky hoped for more positive encounters like this one with April and Ed. It was nice to experience such a wonderful and good-filled transformation.

Unfortunately, Ed and April's case was the exception. Most of the evil-natured ones from Becky's high school days were still evil-natured. Most of them married non-soul-mates. It was the natural attractive charge between spirits of the evil-natured domains and not from a soul mate pairing to, follow the preferences of the physical and mind's influences leading them to their marriage partner. In most cases, it was lust that was feeding their bonds of their marriages. These tend to be quite fragile over the long term.

Becky recognized Tonya Smith Everson among the crowd. Tonya had been a friend of hers. It had been many years since she'd seen her. Becky and Tonya had much in common. They both had been shy and quiet. They both were liked by most of the class, but neither was considered of significance. Both received good grades. They both wanted to be teachers when they were young and would role-play. They made a pact to study to be teachers together and then get a job in the same school.

Tonya was not a pure domain like Becky, however. She had an evil-natured spirit residing in her domain that over the years sidetracked some of her dreams, particularly the one involving being a teacher. She married very young. In fact, she was married near the midpoint of her senior year in high school. She was with child. Her husband was also a classmate. His name was Bill. Theirs was a relationship of like-natured pairings. Both had mixed domains of two good-natured spirits and one evil-natured one. They were not soul mates, but their domains were bound together in infatuation for each other.

On an evening earlier in their lives, both had given dominance to their lone evil natures. It had resulted in many changes to their future. The child that was conceived was from two evil-natured advocates. The baby's third spirit, from the unassigned pool was good natured, making the domain mixed. The child was bound to the parents through the advocates, but its different nature made the relationship stressed and challenged, especially as the child grew older and more independent. The boy was always in trouble. This caused Tonya and Bill embarrassment. They avoided public scrutiny of their squabbles and stress points as much as possible. Their mistake had taken its toll on them many times over. Their marriage survived only on the strength of their good natures.

Becky touched Tonya on the back to get her attention and said, "Hello, old friend. Do you remember me?"

Tonya recognized her immediately and gave her a hug. Tonya said to her, "It's so nice to see you again, Becky. You are looking well."

Becky reciprocated, "And you too. How's the family?"

Tonya responded, "They're all fine." But internally, she wanted to share with her friend the troubles and challenges that she was dealing with. She thought how nice it might be to talk to Becky like they used to when they were younger. Becky read every signal and message. She'd transferred to Tonya's domain.

She wanted to get a better read of what was going on in her old friend's life, as well as to give her good-natured spirits assurances and strength. What she learned was that Tonya had many challenges and disappointments, mostly brought on her by her son. She was desperate for a friend to confide in. Her spirits needed Becky's strength and encouragement. Her situation was really wearing on her.

When Becky's spirit left Tonya's, it left the good-natured spirits of the domain energized and with greater confidence that she was doing the right things. Tonya added to the conversation, "Just seeing you, Becky, has given me a lift, just like it was when we hung out together in high school. I heard you became a teacher like we'd both planned." It made Tonya sad that she had not honored the promise they made so long ago, not like Becky had.

Becky replied, "Yes, I teach in the city. It is everything we thought it might be. It truly fulfills me."

Tonya asked, "And what's this I hear about you getting married? Is this your future husband?"

Tom had been there, silently soaking in the conversations around him. He injected, "Yes, it is. I am he. I'm Tom McDouglas."

Becky apologized, "I'm sorry to both of you. I was so excited to see you, Tonya, that I neglected to introduce you to Tom. I am truly so sorry."

They all exchanged background and pleasantries. Finally, Becky asked, "Where's Bill? Is he here at the picnic?"

Tonya replied, "He was here but had to leave for a few minutes. Our son had an appointment that Bill needed to run him to."

Becky knew from her connection to Tonya that the appointment involved detention at the school for setting off the fire alarms. Becky said, "Well, maybe I'll see him later. Everything is OK, isn't it?" Even without her powers of telepathy she could tell it was not.

Tonya closed by saying, "I'd like to get together with you over lunch someday. We have a lot to catch up on."

Becky replied, "I'd like that a lot. You'll be at my wedding, won't you?"

Tonya responded, "I would very much like that. You are special to me. Sometimes late at night when I can't sleep, I still think about our plans to teach together. It makes me smile."

To the same degree that the first encounter with Ed and April gave her added hope, this one with Tonya gave her concern. It was clear that the relationships and the choices we make regarding these relationships of our lives play so very important a role in our happiness and futures. A few mistakes or a few off-plan choices can really change a life. Becky said to Tonya before they parted, "I'll be back in town next week to work with my parents on confirming reservations for the wedding. I'll call you, and we can set up lunch that Saturday. Will that be all right?"

Tonya replied, "I'll make sure it's all right." It left her with a feeling of goodness. Becky's strength gave her the renewal that she needed.

They both said, "See you later." And they went in opposite directions.

The next to greet Becky and Tom was Emily Turnbull. She and Becky had been very good friends for most of their early lives. She had been Becky's best friend before moving to the city. It was exciting for Becky to see her at the reunion. Emily was also glad to see Becky and ecstatic over the news of her upcoming wedding. She burst in excitement at their first sighting of each other. Emily was first to speak. She exclaimed, "There she is! It's Becky Turner." Everybody around her turned to see one of the few who got away from Councilville. Becky was met by a myriad of greetings but zeroed in on her old friend. Emily looked and sounded great, she thought. She had always been upbeat and optimistic. It was so good to see her again.

As Becky was able to single her out from the crowd, she asked, "How is Chip and the family?" Becky always thought that Emily was a lucky one. She and Chip had been two peas in a pod since they met in junior high. Becky knew that they were soul mates then. They'd been in love forever. They had three perfect and good-natured children. None were pure domains, but each was hardworking and happy. It was a model family the majority of the time.

Emily smiled and responded, "Life couldn't be any better than it is." Then she gave Becky a hug and a kiss. "I've heard through the grapevine that there's a wedding on the horizon. You're not going to forget your old friend, are you?"

Becky laughed at the notion and said, "Absolutely not. I want you to be in my wedding party, if you will."

Emily squealed in delight. She said, "Oh, it's been a while since I've been invited to be a part in a wedding party. This is so exciting. How can I help?"

Becky told her, "Maybe you can stay in the city with me for a few days and help me plan." Becky's eyebrows rose in question. "I'd like to get started in the next several weeks. Can you get away?"

Emily replied, "I'll check with Chip, but I think it will be OK."

Then they both looked around to find their mates. Interestingly enough, Tom was talking to Chip. They were talking about shortwave radios. It seemed that both had an interest in them. They both seemed very happy. Becky tugged on Emily and said, "Come on, I'll introduce you to Tom." Then she pointed to where Tom and Chip stood. "It appears that Chip and Tom have already gotten to know each other."

Emily thought it funny. She said, "Well, Tom will fit in very nicely to our group." They made their way over to the guys. Becky, Emily, Chip, and Tom picnicked together. The women talked about the wedding. Tom and Chip covered many topics but never seemed to run out of things to say or laugh about. It was a very comfortable lunch for all. At last, Tom was really having fun.

After lunch, Emily and Chip needed to leave to get back to the kids. Their lives these days were filled with dance lessons, Little League, and scouting. Emily mention to Chip that she'd like to take a few days to go to the city and help Becky with wedding plans. Tom suggested that Chip and the kids come as well. He said, "While you two are caught up in the bridesmaid planning,

Chip, the kids and I can go to the zoo or a ballgame. Between our two apartments, we could accommodate everyone. It would be fun."

Chip added, "I could take a couple of days off work. It might be good to get away from the small-town quiet."

Emily looked at Becky. It seemed like a good plan. She said, "I'm OK with it if you are, Becky."

Becky smiled. She was happy. She thought it great that Tom and Chip had hit it off so well. She said, "It would be wonderful."

Emily then concluded, "Well, Chip and I will see when he can get off, and I'll call you when you get home, probably Monday or Tuesday after 7:00 p.m." They all looked forward to it. Becky and Tom walked Emily and Chip to their car. It was as if they'd been friends forever. Of course, this was pretty much true as it related to the three of them. Tom was a natural and comfortable addition.

On the way back to the picnic, Todd Jamison ran into Tom as he was chasing down a Frisbee. As Todd picked himself up from the ground, he said to a still dazed Tom, "Hey, buddy, can't you see we're trying to play a game here?"

Tom was amazed at his attitude. This man had just pushed him over, and now he expected an apology. Tom responded, "I except your apology, buddy."

Todd grunted and just looked down on Tom, now beginning to collect himself from the ground. Todd considered his next move. Todd had been a bully since fifth. It was then that he realized that he'd grown bigger and stronger than the rest of the class. He was the prototypical evil-natured neanderthal. Tom, without his knowing, was probably face-to-face with the nastiest of the lot from Becky's class.

Becky saw what was happening and jumped in, stating, "Todd, this is no place to make a scene."

Todd tried to place her from high school. Finally, he remembered. "Oh, it's Miss Goody Two-shoes, college girl Becky Turner. Have you come home with your boyfriend to show us all how much better you are than us?"

Tom was now upset. He was about to respond when Becky grabbed his arm and responded. But before she made a move, she looked into his glaring, hateful eyes and transferred to his domain. There, she called upon the one good-natured spirit within him to take up dominance in his domain. Through this one spirit, she could reason with his domain and in turn his being. She then said, "Todd, I'm not here to show you anything. I'm here for the reunion, just like you." Her spirit returned to her. "Now let's all get back to what we were doing before this incident."

Tom noticed a calming change come over Todd. He was still a bully, but he gave in. Becky and Tom moved on to the other side of the park to avoid Todd for the rest of the day. Here, they sat down beneath a tree to enjoy the shade from the hot sun. The woman who sat next to them looked familiar to Becky. She was there with her three children. She was the first to speak. "You did a nice job of handling my husband's temper." She chuckled, knowing that Becky and Tom had settled to their current spot to be far away from him. "He's not the horrible man you might think he is."

Becky then asked her, "You look familiar to me. Were you a member of this high school class?"

The woman replied, "No, I was one year younger than you and Todd. I was Ramona Tiant back then. Now I'm Ramona Jamison. These are my children, Allison, Timmy, and Susie." Becky remembered Ramona Tiant. Back then, she ran with a rough crowd. She had actually been a member of what could have been considered the only neighborhood gang in Councilville. She was tough and evil natured. Becky had never previously transferred into her domain to size up Ramona Tiant, but it only required one to observe. Now she was curious. She wondered how much being a mother might have changed her. She wondered what attracted Todd and Ramona to each other.

She approached the woman to start a conversation. Yet what her domain craved was information, the kind of information she could only get by transferring to her domain. When she was face-to-face with her, she looked deep into her dark eyes and transferred. She learned that Ramona was of a mixed domain. Her nature was of the evil virtue. Her attraction to Todd was not brought on by a soul mate pairing; rather, it was a relationship that was charged by attracting like-natured pairings of their domains.

Two of their three children were much like her and her husband. Each of the spirits coming from the advocates in these two were evil. In the youngest, however, one of the advocates had been good natured. All three of the children were of mixed domains; two were evil natured and one was good natured. The good-natured one was very quiet and introverted. She was the one who didn't seem to fit in with this family but was as much a part as any of the others. Because of her goodness and her age, she was often an easy target for the others' antics and actions. She often took the brunt of frustrations and the anger of the other four evil-natured ones in the family. Ramona often felt for her child in these situations yet often did little about it. It was the conscience and emotion from the one good-natured spirit of her domain that brought out her feelings for her daughter's plight. It had been her good-natured spirit that played advocate to her daughter's creation. This was also the spirit that Becky connected with and gave strength and support.

Ramona and Becky talked for a while, even after Becky's spirit had returned to her domain. Ramona was more open and less cynical of her after the transfer, yet still, the two were uncomfortable around each other. Their spirit pairings were not favorable. The result was a repelling charge, just as Susie's was to the rest of her family. The bond between advocate and offspring was all that Susie had to bind her to her mother and family. Her good nature kept her willing to make this work and to keep her strong.

Becky met with the daughter who played nearby. It seemed magical, but they immediately formed a strong bond, the type of bond the little girl had wished to transpire from any of her family's members. Becky transferred to the little girl's domain. She was quite surprised in her goodness. She had already been through so much at such a young age, and it only strengthened her goodness. Becky gave the domain of the girl encouragement and strength. She was only six years old.

The girl saw Becky as someone very special. She was still young enough to believe in the magic and mystique of the world. Susie really inspired Becky. One incident in particular involved her brother, who was seven at the time, now eight. He was quite troublesome even at this early age. He'd followed in his mother's footsteps in life and hung out with tougher older street kids. He'd already run astray from the law. He was sent to reform school for three months in an attempt to scare him straight. Susie was distraught for her bother, even though he had caused her much suffering and discomfort throughout her life. They shared no common advocate. They shared little in common other than a name, yet she felt for him. It was just the goodness of the little girl that came through.

This incident touched Becky deeply. Becky didn't know why, but she was compelled to look after the little one. She felt it was in her destiny to help her. She decided to ask if the girl could be a flower girl at her wedding. She wanted an opportunity to spend more time with her, to get to know her and her story better. She struck Becky as someone very strong and special. Ramona thought the request quite bizarre and unusual, and it was. It seemingly came completely out of the blue. She was apprehensive at first, but her daughter begged her to reconsider. Susie tugged at her and begged, "Mommy, it would be fun. Other girls at my school have done it. I want to be a flower girl . . . please!" The strengthening of Ramona's good nature and the presence of Becky and Susie allowed it to gain dominance within the domain.

Ramona was weakening to the suggestion. It was beginning to seem a harmless act. She bargained with Becky, "I'll consider it for the sake of my daughter if the wedding is in town and if you will pay for the dress and shoes." It seemed to Ramona to be an opportunity for free gifts and free babysitting.

Tom just sat back and absorbed the whole situation in amazement. This whole thing had come out of left field for him. A moment earlier, he'd assumed that Becky and Ramona were not on friendly terms. It made no sense to him, but he trusted Becky and her judgments. As long as he wouldn't have to confront Susie's father too often, he was OK with anything else. Susie did seem a very good-natured, bright, and mature girl for a six-year-old. Tom liked her as well. He would back Becky's plan whatever it would be.

As a result of this, the wedding location was now confirmed. They had suggested it, but this confirmed it. The wedding would be in Councilville. Tom would need to inform his parents and family. Becky looked at him and asked, "You don't mind, do you?" She always melted him.

He said, "No, this is a nice town. The people are nice people. Councilville will be a good place to marry." It was settled. Susie would play her part.

It was finally time to go home. Both Becky and Tom were exhausted. On the way out, however, Becky spotted another old friend from her class. It was another of the classmates whom Becky so wanted to see at the picnic. She yelled to her, hoping to get her attention before she moved farther away. It worked. She turned. Becky said to Tom, "Come on, let's run. I want to introduce you to another of my dearest high school friends. I want to ask her to be in our wedding party."

Jane Deystus was the daughter of the meanest, most dominant teacher at Councilville Elementary. Jane was also the nicest and best natured of Becky's previous schoolmates. Next to Emily, and now Anita, she was one of Becky's closest friends. She gave Becky strength. She knew why Jane's goodness shown so strongly and evidently. It had to, in order to counter the strong evil influences of growing up in a predominantly evil-natured family environment. Her hardships and challenges made her stronger; they accentuated her goodness. Her goodness was tempered through trial.

When Becky caught up to her, a huge smile covered her face. It was clear that even though years had passed, the relationship had not changed. They hugged and shared their happiness to see each other again. This time, Becky remembered Tom and introduced him, saying, "Jane, this is Tom, my soon-to-be husband." It felt good to Becky every time she referred to him as a husband.

Jane held out her hand to him and responded, "Tom, it's very nice to meet you. I've heard from others at the picnic what a nice man you seem to be."

Tom responded, "Thank you, Jane. It's nice to get a positive review now and then." Then he chuckled to make sure everyone understood it as a joke. Jane smiled but didn't break a chuckle.

Becky sensed that something might be wrong. She looked into Jane's eyes and asked, "Is everything OK?" While asking, though, she transferred to her friend's domain. The answer lay very shallow on the surface.

Jane carried a torment around with her that Becky's situation only irritated. Jane was still single. She still lived at home, even though it was uncomfortable because of her different nature from those of her mother and father. She had many suitors in the past, but none was right for her. She was looking for her soul mate. Many thought that she was just too choosy, but she understood the importance of this decision on her life. She was just looking for the magical one who would make her feel special and right. The magic had not hit her yet.

Becky understood her loneliness and frustration. Only a few years ago, she was feeling similar frustrations. It seemed a common plight. Becky was glad to find that it was only this problem that Jane was dealing with. She was strong. She would find her soul mate eventually. Becky hugged her again and whispered in her ear, "I waited for my special one and he eventually came." She backed off her embrace. "It will happen for all of us. Aren't you happy for me?"

It seemed to break her out of her melancholy and again brought out her smile. She looked at the two before her and hoped to share their joy. She asked them, "Tell me how all this happened. How did you two find each other? When did you decide to marry?" She could have asked a million questions, but she knew that Becky would answer most of them at the appropriate time and fill her in on the details of her romance. Becky was always one to share. She was always good with the details.

Becky and Jane made their way to a table to sit and talk. Tom excused himself and decided to take a little walk around the park. He took his time doing so to allow Becky and Jane time to catch up on lost years. It was half an hour before he made it back to the table. By then, Becky and Jane were both laughing and motioning their hands demonstratively. They both seemed totally connected to each other. Tom questioned whether he should interrupt their fun but was growing tired. As he stepped in, he heard Becky ask Jane to be her fifth bridesmaid; the other four were her sister, Tom's sister, Anita and Emily. There was a shriek of excitement; it was clear that the answer would be yes. It was.

Becky reacknowledged Tom by saying, "Oh, Tom, my bridesmaids are complete. I'm so happy that we came home this weekend." Then she hugged him.

Tom felt renewed again but asked, "Did you want to leave now? If you like, we can walk Jane home with us."

Becky and Jane both laughed. It made Tom feel silly until Becky pointed to a white house only yards in front of them and said, "This big white house in front of us is where Jane lives. We've been sitting in her backyard all the while."

Tom chuckled and said, "Well, I guess the joke's on me. How wonderful it must be to live beside this beautiful park."

Jane smiled. "I have made this park my own. It's been a truly wonderful sanctuary for me."

Becky knew that Tom was getting anxious. She had imposed on him all day. He'd been supportive and patient. But she could see the limits and the stress of the day wearing on his face and through the fidgeting that now began to be quite noticeable. She looked at Jane and said in closing, "Jane, I'll call you to set up a time to get together with the others and select the dresses.

I'll make sure that you're paired up with Tom's cutest and most eligible friend." Then they giggled, and Tom laughed.

He parted by saying, "Now I understand where the discussions were focused while I was gone. You've been plotting." It continued their laughter. It all seemed so good at that moment. Much of Becky's anxiety with whether her old friends would share in her moment of joy was now gone. Her friendships were strong and had survived the test of time. It was a comfort to her.

Becky and Tom returned to the small house at the outskirts of town. There was a note on the table that said that Mrs. Turner was working concession at the school basketball game. Mr. Turner was at the fire station with the volunteer patrol. The last statement read, "Stop by and see us when you're done."

Tom followed the aroma to the oven. It was on. Inside was a turkey roasting for dinner. Tom said to Becky, "I hope you learned how to cook from your mother."

Becky replied, "If you want my mother's cooking, we'll need to visit here often." Then she assured him that she had picked up a few skills in the kitchen over the years and then shooed him off. They left the house, walking hand in hand toward the fire station. It was on the way to the school.

Becky and Tom stopped in to see her dad. He was working at the fire station as a volunteer preparing the equipment for when, and if, it might ever be needed. With him were three others, the chief, the deputy chief, and another. The chief was barking continuously. He wasn't happy when Mr. Turner pulled away to visit with Becky and Tom. He yelled, "Hey, Turner, we got to get this done today! Can't you socialize afterward?"

Mr. Turner looked back at him and responded, "I'll be with you in a minute. This is my daughter. She's only home occasionally."

The chief started out toward them, but the deputy said something and he stopped. Mr. Turner redirected his attentions back to Becky and Tom. He said to them, "Don't pay too much attention to old Ike. He takes this job way too seriously."

Becky was always interested in people and what made them the way they were. She asked her father, "Why is that, Dad? Why shouldn't we pay attention to his meanness?"

Mr. Turner rubbed his chin, moved his whole open hand from the point of his chin to the point of his nose, and said, "Ike has lived his life at this station. It has consumed him. He's had two families, but they haven't seemed to satisfy him much. Just his work."

He looked back to see Ike. As he expected, he was eying him. Mr. Turner went on, "He doesn't value our strong family relationship at all. He doesn't know what we feel for one another. His job has pushed out all his softer side."

Becky had seen this occur often with parents of the students she counseled, parents who allowed their work to push out everything else in their lives. The power of their jobs and the status consumed them. Their evil sides craved it. Becky said to her dad, "How can you work with him? He treats you like a servant."

Mr. Turner replied, "I'm not here for Ike. I'm here to ensure we can help if there's a fire." He smiled and felt the goodness of his daughter's concern for him. "We all pull together in a crisis.

It's a good team that we have. Ike's assertiveness is well served when we are faced with a fire."

Becky saw the value of each nature in crisis. She knew and understood the unique and mysterious dynamics of the group relationship. This was clearly an example of when it worked for a common and good cause. She was glad that her father was flexible and giving enough to allow it to work. The job dictated a relationship that otherwise would certainly not have existed between Ike and her father. She was assured that it was good. Both men, although quite different, would cover each other and their other fellow firemen in time of crisis.

Becky wanted to approach Ike and probe his spirit for the answers to what made him the way he was. She thought that he might be an interesting case study. Her father nudged her toward the school, knowing that Ike was already in a rather foul mood today. He said to her, "Now leave Ike alone today. He's not having a good day. I'll deal with him." Then he motioned toward the school. It was within sight from the fire station. He brushed Becky on the back with his hand. "Your mother will want to see you."

He mentioned to Tom, "There's a pretty good game going on. The Councilville Hornets are playing their rivals from Johnstown. Both teams are tops in the region." It wasn't that he wanted them to leave, but he had work to do and partners who were running low on patience.

Becky turned to him and kissed him before saying, "Goodbye. I'll see you at supper."

Mr. Turner replied, "You should save those for Tom. Wasting them on me will just get Ike all worked up again." Then he laughed, said goodbye to both, and returned to the jeers of his fellow volunteer firemen. He didn't mind much. He felt the joys of his family. This joy far outweighed the satisfaction of his other activities. It left him charged and renewed. He felt sorry that Ike could not experience the same contentment.

It only took fifteen minutes to walk to the school from the firehouse. There was plenty of excitement at the school. Several yellow buses with "Johnstown Local Schools" printed in black filed along the curb in front of the school. Becky and Tom weaved between them and then up the concrete stairs to the front doors. Inside was a lady at a folding table selling tickets and stamping people's wrists. She asked, "Two adults?"

Becky responded, "No, we're not here for the game. We're here to see my mother, Mrs. Turner."

The lady looked closer at Becky and said in surprise, "Well, hello. You're Becky Turner, aren't you?"

Becky looked a bit embarrassed. She recognized the lady as well. She was a friend of her mother's. They'd been friends forever. Becky remembered that she had been at the house even when she was a little girl. She replied, "Yes, Mrs. Thompson, it is me. It's very nice to see you again."

Mrs. Thompson told her, "Well, you won't need to pay since you're just here to see your mother."

But Tom held out $6 and said, "I might take in some of the game while Becky and her mother talk. I haven't seen a live game in quite a while."

Mrs. Thompson took his money and gave him two tickets. She pointed down one of the halls to the left and said, "Your mother is running the visitor's concession stand today. Isn't it a shame?" Then she chuckled and waved a small Councilville pennant. She ushered for Tom to enter the gymnasium. "The home team is to the right. You'll find it friendlier on that side." They all said their thank-you's and goodbyes.

Becky kissed Tom on the cheek and told him, "I'll see you in a little while." Tom went into the gymnasium to watch the game. It was now nearing the end of the first quarter with the home team down by three points.

Becky started down the hall toward the visitor's concession when Mrs. Thompson asked, "Becky, I hear you're getting married." Then she paused a moment. "Congratulations." Becky said "thank you" again and then proceeded toward her mother.

It got noisier and busier the closer she got to the concession area. Becky caught up with her mom and jumped right in to the work that she was doing. It allowed them time to talk, which they did at a rapid pace. Ms. Turner was curious how the day went and who she met. Finally, she asked, "Where's Tom?"

Becky informed her, "He is watching the game. I think he just wanted some time to relax without being the showcase event."

Mrs. Turner smiled and said, "I'm sure it's not been easy meeting all these new people. He is such a nice person. He is a lot like you, Becky." She surprised her daughter with a kiss. "I feel strongly that you two are a special couple. I'm so proud of you."

Becky began to well up in tears of happiness. She said to her mother, "I'm so glad you feel this way. It means a great deal to me." They hugged.

Mrs. Turner whispered in her ear, "Your father feels the same way too. He really likes Tom." The hug tightened, and then they let go.

Mrs. Turner pushed her hand toward the door and then said, "We have plenty of help in here. Go now and find your fiancé." She smiled. "He'd rather be sitting next to you than all those strangers he's been surrounded by since he got here. I'll see you at home for supper."

Becky responded, "Thanks, Mom. I'll see you at home." She then left to find Tom in the mass of people who were there for the game. He wasn't easy to spot at first, so she hovered along the first few rows for a while. She couldn't help but hear the coach of the home team ranting and swearing at the referees and his players. It offended Becky. She couldn't understand why he carried on so in front of his team and the fans. It was embarrassing to her to hear his exchanges. She stopped to see just who this madman was. When he finally turned his face enough for Becky to recognize him the final whistle for the half had just blown. Councilville was up one point at the half.

Jan Tullis turned completely around to the stands before directing his squad to the dressing room. He couldn't help but recognize the lady in the second row who seemed frozen with her mouth open. He recognized her right away as the sister of his old best friend, Randall. Jan yelled up to her, "Hi, Becky! How have you been?" He stepped up the bleachers to greet her.

Becky couldn't believe the change in his attitude and tone from only a few minutes earlier. Now he was friendly and calm. She greeted Jan and talked to him for several minutes at the intermission. She transferred to his domain. It was filled with the static of competition. It clouded much of his goodness. She could tell that he was generally very good natured. It was his dominant virtue. Yet competition drew out his evil nature. When he was involved in the game and the competition, it brought out his evil side. He was like a Jekyll and Hyde personality on the court and off. Fortunately, his two good-natured spirits could control the evil one when not in the frenzy of the game. She thought the situation odd.

They talked for a few minutes longer, and then Jan said, "Well, I need to get back to the team now. It was really nice to see you while you're in town. I'm sorry I didn't get to meet your fiancé."

Becky replied, "It is too bad. I wish you luck in the game."

Jan started down the bleachers but continued to turn back to Becky. He said to her, "We might need that luck. We're not at our best today." Then he reached the court level and waved. "See ya."

Becky waved as well and looked around for Tom. Within a few minutes, he reentered the gym with a hot dog, a bag of popcorn, and a soft drink. Becky yelled to him, "Hey, Tom! What did you get for me?"

Tom looked up from his first bite of the hot dog and held it into the air to suggest that he would share. Becky and Tom found a seat together just as the teams had reentered the gym. Becky took ownership of the popcorn. Tom didn't mind. It wasn't long before the whistle blew to begin the third quarter of the game.

Becky noticed that the coach from the other school acted much like Jan was when in competition. She concluded that it was competition that had consumed them. Their evil natures were very close to the surface at these moments. It frightened Becky to see someone like Jan taken over by it. He would not seem the type outside the gym. She immediately thought of other instances of this same phenomenon. Men and women at work act much the same when a job or an opportunity opens up. It appeared that competition was not good for the good-natured spirit. It made her nervous.

Tom could see her fidgeting. He asked her, "Do you want to leave? I don't need to see the end."

Becky hadn't wanted to ask. Tom seemed to be enjoying it. It was good that he was so tuned in to her feelings and nonverbal cues. He surely cared for her. Becky responded, "Yes, I would like to leave, if you don't mind." They both got up and shimmied their way to the main aisle. Once there, it was a straight shot to the floor level and to the exit. Becky felt better the instant she left the gym. The competition was left inside. Goodness could again take charge.

Tom walked Becky home. It had been a busy day. Both of them were ready for a quiet, unplanned evening. They started by peeling potatoes together. Mrs. Turner would be pleasantly surprised to see the accompanying dishes to the turkey started when she came home. Becky and Tom wanted to surprise her.

Strong, dominant spirits gather more from each other's company and have the advantage in relationships. Less dominant spirits grow more incrementally from each contact. It allows the domains to share from other domains' stores. Each sharing makes their domain stores more knowledgeable and fills these stores within the domain's bank with information. The more relationships that one forms, the better and more comfortable one becomes in these relationships.

Spirit soul mate connections are forever and unchanging, even when suppressed by the other components of the body. This may create conflict within the being and mixed reactions toward another when inhibited by the other components. The physical and mental components of the being might encourage the being to entertain a relationship the spirits warn it against or to disregard a relationship even though there is a strong spirit attraction and impetus to nurture and befriend. Social pressures and directives from outside the being, endorsed or adopted by the being play havoc with the guidance and influences of the domain toward or against a relationship. It upsets the balance. It occasionally steals one from love and companionship. It results in failed commitments and promises. A relationship of the physical or mental components is often short term and fickle. The lucky ones are those who trust their natural forces, the spirit connections. The especially lucky ones are those who might not, at first glance, appear to be the ultimate choice from a superficial standpoint; those with patience and who are not restricted by their superficial desires.

Becky and Tom sat on the porch that night. They said little. They sat side by side, Tom's arm over Becky's shoulder. The connection was intense. It fused them together as one. It grew more spiritually strong by the moment. It filled them with comfort and joy. It healed the day's wounds. There was no stronger tonic or cure. It came from only one source, the spirit domain. Their beings allowed it, and it was good.

The next day, Becky and Tom returned to their apartments in the city. It had been a successful trip to Councilville. Next on the list was the trip to the town of Saint George to meet Tom's parents. It was planned for the following Thursday. Fortunately, Saint George was only an hour and a half drive from the city. It would not require an overnight stay. Nor was Tom's family large or close. Only his mother, father, and sister would be there to greet Becky.

Tom's mother and father were soul mates; his father's domain had been one of an evil nature before converting to good through the power of love for his wife. The two soul mate spirits had been good-natured ones. Tom's sister contained the same makeup as Tom. Tom and Teresa, his sister, shared common advocates from the parents. The advocates were the soul mate spirits of their parents. It was a good-natured family. It made the encounter with them pleasant and reasonably comfortable. There was a natural attraction between them all. This meeting went off without flaw.

What is love?

Love happens because of soul mates. This doesn't explain it entirely though. It's actually very hard to explain. But here's an example.

Saundra and Larry have been married for twenty-eight years. Valentine's Day is just around the corner. Each year Larry is just as motivated as he was early in their courtship to find that perfect Valentine's Day gift for his wife. It's not that he only buys her things on holidays or birthdays, but Valentine's Day and their Anniversary are extra special opportunities to show his love for her. Weeks before this Valentine's Day, as is the case for every year, both Saundra and Larry vow not to spend money on each other for presents. Saundra makes it especially clear that she doesn't want sweets or flowers that will wither away in a few days or weeks or add ounces to her figure. These restrictions leave Larry with a challenge to be more creative this year. His forty-nine years of experience and creativity leave him well suited and up to this challenge.

On Valentine's Day, the delivery truck pulls up to the curb at Saundra and Larry's house. The delivery girl makes her way up the walk with a package in hand. She rings the doorbell. Saundra responds and opens the door. She's surprised to see that there's a truck in front and suspects there's a package. The delivery girl states, "Hello. Are you Mrs. Holstrom?"

Saundra nods to confirm and then says, "Yes, I am."

The girl smiles from knowing that she's about to deliver a surprise. She says, "I have a package for you, ma'am." First, she holds out her clipboard. "All I'll need from you is your signature on line four, next to your name."

Saundra takes the clipboard and pen from the girl and complies with her request. She is now anxious to see what is in the box. She suspects that the sender is her husband. She smiles knowing that he has not honored their pact of several weeks' prior. She's glad he hasn't. It's nice to be surprised and by someone she knows and loves so well.

Once inside, in the privacy of her living room, Saundra admires the strange box. It's different from the traditional Valentine's packaging. She then remembers her words. "No candy and no cut flowers." It looks to be neither of these. She smiles again. She dragged out the suspense from the moment long enough. Now she's really curious. She says to herself, *what could it be?* It takes only moments before she's carefully opened the top of the package. Her anticipation is further heightened as nothing becomes clear from what she can see so far. It's very strange. She works her way into the center of the contents and squeezes down on a furry object within. She pulls it from its confines. It's truly different from anything she might have expected from her husband. It's a custom teddy bear. It brings a full laugh, a full quiver of her abdominal muscles. It's perfect.

"What an idea," she whispers to herself. "What a husband." She places it in front of her to admire the dark brown fur. There's a red velvet pillow across its chest that says, "I love you." This is the heartfelt message from the sender. Its left paw holds out a bouquet of tiny cloth roses. Its eyes are bright and shiny, and its little mouth is curved upward in a smile. It's muzzle, its face, and its teddy bear ears are adorable. The detail is remarkable. It makes her moment special.

Larry has caught it all from the upstairs catwalk. He's been quiet not to disturb or influence the show. By now, he's confident that he's done well. It's safe to venture downstairs. He looks forward to his reward. His emotions are now heightened a bit in the moment as well. As he walks into the room, Saundra looks up and smiles. "We promised not to give presents this year, you old bear. You shouldn't have." She giggles.

He plays with her. "How do you know that it's from me? It could be from a secret admirer." Then he chuckles and asks, "How about a hug for an old bear?"

She gets up and opens her arms for him. This is a special sharing of their love. Saundra and Larry are soul mates. But their love is more. It consumes them daily. It carries forward. It is not the gift or the joy in getting the gift; it is so much more. It's what carries forward.

Almost a month passes, and Saundra finds herself sorting through the bills of the household. It's time to pay the credit card company. Saundra peruses the detail just to verify that no charges seem out of the ordinary. She spots a charge to a vendor that sells specialty teddy bears. Her eyebrows rise, and her temper flares. The charge is for over $100. Saundra explodes. It's fortunate that Larry finds himself at work at that moment. It allows Saundra to cool a bit before he steps through their front doorway later in the day.

As soon as she hears him enter, Saundra tracks him step for step into the kitchen. He can feel that she's not happy with him but says nothing and allows her first to state his crime. This is not the first time he's been in this situation. He has the routine pretty well down pat by now. She finally asks him, "Have you seen the credit card bill this month?" She knows he hasn't. He never pays attention to these things. "How could you spend $100 on a stuffed animal?" It is said with plenty of inflection and feeling of disappointment.

He is well aware of her displeasure and first thinks that he might try to explain it partially as shipping costs. But he knows this will not make his case any more palatable for her. He then dredges back deep into his defenses. He searches for the reasons he's made the purchase in the first place. This seems a good place to start. He offers his hands out to her and opens with a soft voice, "Do you remember the day that the bear came? If you could have seen the look when you first opened the top of the box." He pauses to allow her to remember the moment. He follows with what seems a turn of direction. "You often ask me why I love you, and I rarely answer you with any one thing that specifically answers the question. Well, on the day that you opened your bear, I got something as well."

He smiles and shares, "I've got the answer to your question."

Saundra doesn't know what to think at this moment. She is expecting the traditional apology for his frivolous spending, maybe just lack of concern, but he is really searching for an answer to her question. She is sure that it is something other than the one she poses regarding the charge on the bill. She is interested.

Larry begins to speak again. "The reason I love you became so clear as I watched you that day from the catwalk without you knowing." He looks into her being through her eyes and says, "It's the look that you give me or that you share when I've pleased you. It's the spark I felt when you were truly pleased with me. It gives me worth and value. It charges me. It's that electricity that you pass through me that pinpoints why I love you. Those moments help me understand love. They are priceless."

Saundra's anger has now melted completely. She is so surprised at her husband's perfect presentation and defense. He is indeed innocent of all crimes. She realizes that most of her anger is just to make a point anyway. All that is left to the moment is the final and closing admission by Larry. He says to her, "That is how and why I could spend $100 on a bear. It was not only for the bear but also for that moment, for the look on your face and the feeling of our effect on each other."

Saundra is near tears. Again, the twinges in her stomach are about to force her to spill her emotions. It is one of the most heartfelt sharing of love she's ever heard from him. The $100 expenditure will be paid without further thought or question. It has turned out to be worth every penny spent, not for the bear but for this moment. Instead of anger and rage as she's met him at the door earlier, he receives another full hug and the feeling of her heart against his, racing in unison. This is what made him love her, why he loves her. It is still hard to explain. It is not physical or mental. It is truly of the emotions, the memories, and the special moments. It is of the spirits. It is soul mate love.

If there were more love, good would be the dominant force on the earth. This, unfortunately, is not the case. The world moves naturally toward balance. To achieve balance between the virtues of good and evil, love is not always made easy to find. Soul mate spirits are not always brought together in contact at the preferred time or place. They are not always easy to find. It's the mystic of love. It forces one to be vigilant, open, and patient. And we are not. It's not our nature. Once the possibility of it arises, it then forces time and test to bring confirmation from the mental, physical, and spirit components. This is what represents the human's search for love and perfect lifelong companionship. Many will never find it. Some will be satisfied with something less because they lack the patience or faith. Some beings' soul mates are out of sequence of time or locale. Some spirits will never find their true mate. Some domains will never find more than like-natured friendships, but all will have at least one encounter with another being containing their soul mate match. It may be a missed opportunity. It may be thwarted by other factors. It may be nurtured. It's the burden of us humans and the spirits that are assigned. There are no guarantees. The lucky ones will find their soul mate.

Lust is the substitute of love. It is purely physical. It is easier to achieve and many times paints a convincing facade of love. It is temporarily satisfying. Lust is an important factor in retaining the balance between good spirit domains and evil-natured domains. It supports the evil side of the scales. It only requires an attraction between like spirits from two domains. It is a strong relationship yet is the opposite of love in most all respects. In the long run, it is a poor substitute. The effects of missed opportunity for soul mate love are what is long term. It scars the civilization and emotions of mankind from its failure to sustain and to satisfy as love can and does.

Tom and Becky are lucky ones. Their spirits are now assured. They are soul mates. The bond is strong and reinforced in goodness.

Over the next three months, there were many trips between the soon-to-be in-laws and the city. Emily, Chip, and the kids visited Becky and Tom in the city. Anita made several trips with Becky and Tom to Councilville. Becky's mother came to stay with her for several weeks during the period. Tom's mother would also drive in from Saint George to join in on the planning whenever asked. It was such a hectic time. It made Tom's head spin. There was so much to do, plan, and arrange. His checkbook and charge card balances were moving in the opposite and least desired directions. Becky did most of the coordinating, purchasing, and physical planning. Tom went where he was asked to and did what he was asked to do. It was all so new to him. He never knew just where to begin without Becky's guidance. He placed total faith in Becky.

By the time the date was near, he knew the drive to Councilville like the back of his hand. He could tell you the number of patterns in the living room wallpaper of Becky's mother and father. He could impersonate the village pastor to a tee. He now knew most of the people in town. He could fluently speak on the gossip. None of this amused Becky much. She was getting more frazzled by the pressure and the continual number of small inconveniences that kept arising. Tom understood her anxiety and gave her plenty of space and support when it was needed. It was amazing what she was able to do. He marveled at her abilities more and more every day that he was around her. In his mind, there was nothing she couldn't fix, prepare, or do.

Several weeks before the big day, Becky asked Tom to accompany her in taking Susie Jamison shopping. She would need a pretty and colorful dress and shoes to match. Becky suspected that Ramona might bargain for more. Becky had visited Ramona and Susie each time she was in Councilville. Each time, she joined with Susie's spirit domain. It was getting stronger. Susie's spirits were growing and strengthening her personality and nature. She was a very pleasant and bright young lady. She was very fond of Becky. She looked forward to her visits. They gave her comfort and escape from her environment.

Becky could tell that this was beginning to bother Ramona. Ramona knew that this child was different and needed something that Becky could give her but that she could not. Only a mother's love for her child allowed the relationship between Susie and

Becky to continue. It was very difficult for her nature. It tore at her internals. Becky hoped that it would not create conflict and certainly not until after the wedding.

Becky knocked on the door of the Jamison's' small and unkempt house. She had called earlier in the week and again when she got into town to let Mrs. Jamison know that she would be coming. Becky had her mother's friend Mrs. Andrews, who worked at the local dress shop, hold a few dresses back for Susie to try on. They would start there. Mrs. Jamison answered the door and immediately called for Susie. "Susie, Miss Turner is here to take you shopping for a dress."

Becky asked her, "Are you sure you won't join us?"

Ramona replied, "I have so much to do here at home. I would like to, but I can't."

Becky then asked, "Would you like me to bring back what we find for you to choose?"

Ramona responded, "Oh, no, you two pick it out. The decision is yours."

Becky was glad to hear this and said, "Thank you, Ramona. I know what an inconvenience I'm putting you through."

Ramona then asked, "Does the flower girl or the parents traditionally get a gift from the wedding party?"

Becky was surprised by the question at that moment but expected a surprise from her eventually. Becky responded, "Well, in this case, it might be in order. What did you have in mind?"

Becky expected her to ask for money or something for herself. Instead, she was pleasantly surprised when she asked, "Could I get a picture of Susie dressed for the wedding? I'd like to have it on my wall."

Becky responded, "I'll be sure that you get this, Ramona. Again, I thank you for allowing Susie to be my flower girl."

About that time, Susie popped into the picture. She was excited to see Becky and ready to go. Ramona blew her a kiss and shut the door behind them. Susie was wound tight. She was giggling and full of chatter. When she arrived at the car, she saw Tom and immediately said, "Hi, Tom. Are you going to buy a dress with Becky and me?"

Tom replied, "Do you think I'd look good in a dress?" Then he held a straight face while Susie and Becky began to laugh.

Susie said to him, "No! We're not buying a dress for you. It's for me!"

Tom then brushed his hand across his forehead and said, "Phew! What a relief. You and Becky will look so much better in a dress than me."

Susie giggled some more. She thought Tom was funny. She liked him almost as much as Becky. She was at her best with these two. Today would be fun. It would not take long to purchase the dress, the shoes, the slip, and a doll from the shop. Becky knew what Susie would like. They were connected.

After shopping, the three ate lunch together and then visited the ice cream parlor. When they took Susie home, Ramona was not at home. Her husband was in the living room, watching TV and paying no attention to anything else. Becky asked of Susie, "Show these to your mother to be sure she likes them."

Susie responded, "She will. But I'll show her."

Becky shooed her inside and finished by telling Susie, "Tell your mother that I'll call her later today for her final say."

Susie responded, "OK." Then she disappeared to her room with her new treasures. Susie felt bad. Her friends were leaving. It had been such a special day. Susie had not had many like it. She held it safe inside for memories when she might need it. She lay down on her bed and fell asleep.

Becky called Ramona later that day, and as expected, everything was fine. She finalized the details and timing for the arrivals at the church. She assured Ramona that the picture would be taken of Susie. It was set. The agreement to allow Susie to be a part of the ceremony seemed the one detail that Becky worried over the most. It seemed what she had least control over.

The bridesmaid's dresses were purchased and fitted. Becky bought her dress as well. It was a special event that brought Becky's mother, her soon-to-be mother-in-law, and all her friends together. They had lunch and planned the final details. The final wedding shower was done. Each of her friends had held a shower for her. Tom was in awe of all the nice things that people were giving them. He never imagined how many friends and well-wishers Becky knew. He liked to tease Becky about the stash of gifts. He'd say, "We certainly better go through with the wedding now. If we change our minds, it would take a year to return all these gifts to the givers."

Becky knew he was teasing. She'd play along and say, "Even so, if I changed my mind now, couldn't we keep just a few of these things?" They laughed a lot during this period. Becky would have a cry now and then from the pressure or a miscalculated plan. It was difficult to maintain her energy with her teaching, her commitment to Tom, and the wedding all bearing down on her. For the most part, she juggled them all very well. But there were times.

The week before the wedding, both Becky and Tom took off from work. Tom saw to it that tuxedos were fitted and picked up. He made sure that the church was in order and that the pastor was ready. He and Becky made final arrangements with the florist for delivery and setup. Tom and Becky's father confirmed the reception hall and the band. Becky confirmed that the bakery would deliver the cake. The final call was to Ramona Jamison. Susie was still committed to be available, but it still worried Becky.

Finally, Becky and Tom needed to decide how to pair up the bridesmaids and ushers. Chip was asked by Tom to join the wedding party. He therefore was matched with Emily. Next to be paired was Jane Deystus. Becky remembered her commitment to her from the picnic. Becky suggested that Jane be paired up with Tom's most eligible friend, Dennis Mathany. It took a lot of convincing before Tom agreed to pair them up in the procession. He argued, "Becky, you know Dennis. He has a reputation of being a womanizer. Jane is so nice and innocent. Their natures seem so completely opposite."

It was true. Tom was right on all accounts. Jane was good natured. She was relatively inexperienced in relationships and, in fact, a bit of a prude. Dennis was very skilled with establishing the hopes in a woman of full commitment, but as soon as he had them thinking of marriage, he'd break off the relationship. It seemed a game he would play to most, and he wasn't above talking about his exploits. He was of an evil mixed-natured domain. He was immoral and unfeeling toward those whom he left along the wayside. He had established a rather ugly reputation that would now precede him wherever he went. He did seem a rather unlikely match for Jane.

Yet Becky knew more. She saw the one spirit in both Jane and Dennis that yearned for each other. She knew that the "love of the conquest" characteristics that Dennis exhibited with most every woman he met would remove obstacles of the two getting to know each other and allowing compatible spirits to connect. Becky believed the two spirits to be soul mates. It seemed improbable, but it was true. Spirits know these things. Becky needed to convince Tom that this pairing was right. She knew the soul mates would take it from there. Jane would be safe from Dennis's old ways. If all worked out as anticipated, Dennis would be changing his ways. If they possessed soul mates, his domain would be transformed to good. She responded to Tom, "You have to trust me, Tom. Jane will be the best influence on Dennis that he has ever known. You've heard about woman's intuition, haven't you?"

Tom shook his head and replied, "Becky, I have every faith in you, but this one leaves me feeling uncomfortable. Will you at least warn Jane?"

Becky snuggled up to him and assured him, "There will be no need. If it looks like there is reason, I will raise the issue with Jane. She is my friend. I would not do anything to hurt her."

Then she looked into his worried face and smiled. "Maybe it's Dennis that needs to be warned."

This brought a smile from Tom. He replied, "Not hardly."

Then Becky added, "You never know." And she left the thought open. She was sure that the effects of this pairing would leave many surprised. It appeared that Tom might be at the top of this list.

The day of the ceremony was upon them. Becky and Tom were married. It was a beautiful ceremony. Tom froze in his tracks at the first sight of the white-laden beauty that approached him with her father in her arm. He nearly cried to think how fortunate he was to be marrying this special woman. He was totally committed to her by spirit, by mind, and by body. It was the same for Becky. Her emotions were overflowing. It was the day; it was the husband whom she'd searched for. Everything was so right.

Even Susie was waiting on her doorstep to be picked up. She performed her role to perfection. She sat quietly with Becky's parents, taking in all the beauty and magic of the wedding vows. The bridesmaids quivered and cried. Both mothers wiped their eyes on occasion. Both fathers looked on proudly. It was a perfect ceremony. When the vows were spoken, the rings blessed and exchanged, and the final exit completed, the McDouglas' started their joined life together. It couldn't have been more perfect.

Pictures were next on the agenda. Becky made sure that everyone would get pictures but took special care to have several of Susie Jamison. She really enjoyed the attention. She looked forward to getting her picture back. She asked Becky, "Can I have a picture of you and me? You look so pretty in your wedding dress. I hope to someday look as beautiful as you."

Becky hugged the little girl. It made her so happy. She whispered in her ear, "I hope you will be as happy as I am one day. You will be a very beautiful bride indeed."

Tom injected, "I, too, think my new wife is the most beautiful bride ever. Let's take a picture of the three of us, two princesses and a beast." They laughed and made their request of the photographer. He was more than willing to accommodate them. He took shots of just Becky, then just Tom, then finally of the bride and groom together. Becky's parents had ordered a full portrait of Becky as a special present for Tom. It would be a gift that was most treasured by him.

After photos, it was off to the reception. The party was in full swing when the bride and groom arrived. Everyone was happy, eating, and talking. The band was playing. There were people of all ages and backgrounds. It was as if they were all one family. It was a time to celebrate, and they did. Becky and Tom led off the dancing but were quickly joined by others, especially Jane and Dennis. They had really hit it off in the few days prior and now at the wedding. Tom thought it wonderful how gentlemanly and respectful Dennis seemed to act around Jane. He treated her as special. He opened doors, pulled out her chair, and made sure that she was comfortable and first in everything. He seemed smitten by her as opposed to the other way around. It was amazing. It was as if they were made for each other. Tom whispered in his new bride's ear, "Have you noticed how well Dennis treats Jane? It's as if he's been overtaken by some strange force."

Becky chuckled and replied, "He has. It's the same force that we share. I told you to trust me. Now you'll know never to doubt me."

Tom chuckled and gave her a kiss to the clanging of spoons on the glasses. It started expectations for the rest of the evening.

Anita found someone at the reception as well. It was one of Tom's friends, Peter Brennen. He was a good-natured man. Anita and Peter connected physically, mentally, and spiritually. They' were soul mates in their domains. The two spent the entire evening together. They talked, they danced, and they laughed together.

Near the end of the reception, long after Becky and Tom had left, Peter confessed to Anita that he was married. He had not been patient in his search for a mate and married too soon. He was in a troubled marriage. Unfortunately, there was a child involved, a little girl. It was this daughter who kept Peter and his wife together as a couple. Peter wanted to continue to see Anita. She made him feel complete. She allowed him to feel love for the first time. Anita was upset. She, too, had felt something special. She was confused about what to do. She thought, *Oh, what a time for Becky to be off and away.* She needed her friend to talk to.

Before leaving the reception, Peter left Anita his work phone number and asked her to call him. Anita was reluctant to take it but did. Their fun for the night had ended. Peter left the reception ashamed. Anita left disappointed. He seemed like such a nice person. She felt something special about him, but it was wrong. It left her with a heavy burden to work through. It ruined a perfect afternoon.

Two weeks later, after Becky had recovered from most of the wedding hysteria, Anita invited Becky over for an afternoon chat. Before that and about a week after the wedding, she called Peter. They had met twice since. It was strictly dinner and talk. Anita's conscience was weighing very heavily on her. Yet there was something very special about the time she spent with Peter. Anita couldn't fight it. She couldn't let it go. It was the first time she'd experienced these strong, perfect feelings. She needed Becky's advice. She struggled with how she would present her dilemma to her friend. She wanted Becky to tell her that what she was doing was right.

Becky arrived at Anita's right after school. She was anxious to spend some time with her. It seemed to Becky that with so much to do before and after the wedding, she was neglecting her friends. Anita was a true friend. Anita had made tea and cookies. They sat in her living room as they usually did. Anita coaxed all the details of the honeymoon from her. She wanted to know all about Becky's transition to married life.

Becky had much to share. For the most part, it was all wonderful. There were a few flaws in Tom that she would need to fix, but she said this mostly in jest. Becky then redirected the conversation to Anita. She asked, "How have you been? Any new loves in your life?"

Anita looked stunned. It was as if Becky was clairvoyant. Becky also noticed Anita's surprise. It puzzled her. She hadn't intended the question to be difficult. Becky suspected that something was wrong. This was why Anita had wanted to meet and talk. It must have been about someone she met. To be sure that she didn't misinterpret or miss anything, her spirit transferred to Anita's domain. Anita recovered quickly. She began to speak. "Becky,

I need your advice on something. It's something I'd not like to get out to anyone else just yet."

Becky took her hand and said to her friend, "It sounds serious, Anita. I'll do whatever I can. You know that I can keep a secret, if that's what you want."

Anita replied, "That's just it. I don't know what I want. That's why I need your help." She looked like she was about to cry.

Becky could feel her pain and moved close to her to hold her friend. Her spirit was already aware of Anita's dilemma from sharing with her domain. It had transferred back and sent signals of concern to Becky's being. Becky sensed that whatever was troubling Anita would not be an easy fix. They held each other for several minutes without a word before Anita released Becky and said, "Are you ready?"

Becky offered a smile and said, "Sure."

Anita rubbed below her eyes to remove any moisture before proceeding, "I've made a bit of a mess that I need to work through."

Becky didn't know if she should interject or just let Anita talk, but she seemed to be struggling. She decided to help. She asked, "How's that, Anita? You're such a help to everyone."

Anita then smiled from her friend's kindness and said, "Not this time. I think I've done something bad but can't help it." Then she looked into Becky's eyes. "I've fallen in love with a married man."

There was a silence as Becky began to consider the many possible responses. Each response differed based on which of the three components of her being would be offering the response and the factors of the married man's relationship. The spirit domain was first to try to address some of these factors. It posed the question to the being. Becky asked, "Are you sure it's love?" It was important to determine if soul mates were involved. If they' were, the attraction was permanent. There would never be a clean break between the two.

The worst possible answer was returned. "Becky, I have never felt the way I do for this man. I believe he feels the same about me."

The obvious question came next from Becky's mind component. "Who is this man? Is it anyone that I know?"

Anita dreaded this question most. She looked down toward the floor and mumbled, "It's Peter Brennen, one of Tom's friends. We met at the reception."

Becky didn't want to show her disapproval but involuntarily put her hand to her mouth to cover her expression. It was a man whom Tom liked. Becky had met his wife. She had met their three-year-old daughter. The family seemed very happy. All three had good-natured domains. She remembered that they were not a soul mate couple, but there was a strong like-natured attraction between Mr. and Mrs. Brennen. The daughter was strongly tied to both through a good-natured advocate from both sides. The unassigned pool had given her a weak evil nature, making her a mixed domain. Becky's external being couldn't understand how it could happen, why it would happen, especially to her friend Anita. She was no home-wrecker. She was basically a good person.

On the other hand, her spirit domain knew that Anita had little to do with it. The blame belonged on Peter and his impatient and premature choice in a mate. It was Anita whom he belonged with spiritually. They were soul mates. Anita couldn't resist the attraction. It was natural. But now it was misfortunate. There were factors. There was a commitment to two other ladies that should not be broken. Peter in his impatience and either infatuation or lust had created a nightmare that now was enacted by the pull of Anita's and his soul mate spirits. Becky considered all these factors over and over in her domain and her mind. What to advise Anita was oh so very complex. She delayed her response. Time helped her sort out some of the facts but did not resolve the conflicting answers to this problem.

Becky felt the extreme fulfillment and joy of a soul mate relationship. Part of her spirit domain and her physical component pushed her to advise Anita to continue and grow the relationship. On the other hand, was the commitment that was made by Peter to his wife and their daughter, the damage it would surely do to both, and the revenge that would be granted to the daughter's advocate spirit should he decide to leave the marriage needed to be strongly considered. All these justified a response against encouraging Anita to continue to see Peter. The just part of the good-natured spirit domain and the mental components of Becky pushed for telling Anita that what she was doing was wrong and harmful. This was the alternative that Becky decided was the position most consistent with her nature. She touched her friend's shoulder and said to her. "You know that they have a little girl?"

Anita could sense that Becky was pointing out the obvious. The daughter and wife were innocent. She would hurt them greatly. Anita replied, "Yes, I am aware."

Anita began to cry again. She buried her head in Becky's shoulder. She sputtered between sobs, "You're going to tell me what I already know is the right thing to do. But it's such a very hard thing to give up."

Becky put her arms around her to comfort her. She said to her, "Yes, I was going to suggest that you not pursue this relationship further for the sake of the wife and daughter. But I can't tell you what is right." She lifted Anita's head to look at her directly. "You are the real victim here. People who were made for each other should be together. Peter made mistakes." She stroked her hair and let her head again rest on her shoulders. "He is the one who should suffer. Neither you or his wife and daughter deserve to pay for these mistakes."

Anita sat up and, looking sad and defeated, said to Becky, "I know what I must do. I am strong enough to deal with it." Becky wasn't sure, but she had done all she could.

The love between Anita and Peter would always lure them together. It was not over, even if Anita stopped seeing him. It was now temptation that would pull at them both. They would both need to be strong and separated to allow the relationship with the wife to survive. Becky wondered where this would lead long term. She would need to help Anita. From where Peter would get help was still an issue. It remained a dangerous situation that played with so many people's emotions. It would result in heartbreak no matter which way it fell. *Heartbreak* is such a misunderstood term. It's not the heart that breaks at all.

It's the spirits. It's most devastating when its soul mate spirits that are involved. In this situation, there was destined to be much heartbreak.

Within three years after the wedding, a number of instances of good news materialized. First, Becky had learned that she and Tom had conceived a child, and it was growing within her. It was a baby of their love. Becky was totally fulfilled and happy to hear the news from her doctor. When Tom heard the news, he was ecstatic. It was the most perfect gift he had ever received. It was even better than the portrait of Becky in her wedding gown that her parents had given him and was now showcased in their bedroom. It filled them both with emotion and thankfulness. The call to the families brought on special joy. The first trips home after the news again brought everyone to greet them. Becky was uncomfortable being the center of attention but felt good to be able to spread such joy. She was truly happy.

Tom sheltered and protected Becky in all she did. Becky would shoo him off and tell him she was fine. It didn't matter. Tom still took on most of her duties, carried everything no matter how light, and scolded her when she would exert herself. It would make Becky mad. She would send him off on meaningless errands just to be out from under his protective concern. She loved his ridiculous behavior and basked in his caring but drowned in the restrictions and help he provided. It all made her smile and chuckle to herself. He would need to get a grip soon, or he would drive her crazy. He needed to reenter reality before the baby came. He would be such a doting father. He would be a perfect father, just like he was the perfect husband. She knew that he would find center again. Becky and Tom spent much of their time now looking at baby furniture, baby clothes, and debating names for a girl and for a boy. It was a very good time. It seemed nothing could disturb their happiness.

The second instance involved Ella and Anthony. They had started to date. Within the previous six-month period, the two became nearly inseparable. It was a truly welcomed gift. Becky's mother told her that the change in Ella was so complete that it was frighteningly delightful. Her wild side had disappeared completely. Ella was getting along with her and her father marvelously. They finally had a more normal relationship. They talked. They shared thoughts. It was wonderful.

In the spirit domain, the transformation had started. Now that the two soul mates were joined in a relationship, the influence and resistance to Anthony that had come from the body and mind no longer was primary. The strength of the bond between them and their love would keep them together forever. Ella's evil-natured soul mate spirit was turned to good. It converted her whole domain from one of evil to good natured. She was now much more compatible with the domains of her mother, her father, and both of her siblings. It made their family so much closer. It made them complete. The wayward sheep had come back into the fold.

Becky couldn't help but wonder on the details of the change. She wondered if it was something from within her that was awakened by the wedding. Perhaps her resistance to Anthony had softened by the emotional beauty of a wedding. She hoped it to have been something so romantic. But it was not. It was Anthony, a bit of ingenuity, and a risk on this part that won her over, not a wedding.

Anthony's new plan to win Ella worked to perfection. It was a plan crafted together through a partnership of the spirits of his domain. His good-natured soul mate spirit was in agony. It called for help. It employed the others of the domain for their contribution and creativity. It was willing to take whatever measures might be necessary, even those most drastic and out of nature. It came down to solving what was necessary to persuade Ella's outer components to allow him a chance with her. Being nice, caring, and civil was obviously not working. Instead, the old plans needed overhauling. The new plan called for giving Ella and her strongest influences what they wanted. His evil-natured spirit was promoted to dominance to lure Ella's interest. The domain knew that even though their primary natures were different, if they could remove or satisfy the primary obstacle, being the physical influence, the soul mate connection could work behind the scenes and would eventually fuse them together. Neither the difference in their natures nor the preferences of the other components would then matter once the soul mates were allowed to join and their power and allure to grow. Allowing his evil nature dominance, it made Anthony more assertive, more compatible to Ella's current being's liking. It made him more fun.

He spent hours at the store handpicking his new clothes to look more the evil part. He met her in her favorite bar. He drank a couple of beers and offered the same to Ella. After the alcohol set in, Ella's physical resistance weakened. They played pool and drank until well into the night. All the while, Anthony was gaining acceptance as a potential suitor. In spite of what was happening on the external levels, the soul mates were also connecting. Their influence was growing. The external influences were being barraged with positive signals from the internal domain. Anthony, all of a sudden, didn't seem so plain and boring anymore, no less so than most of those Ella had been seeing. There was less need to repel Anthony's good-natured advances. He was not the threat he'd seemed to be before.

The opportunity was now available. It wouldn't be long before the soul mate bond between them would be the dominant influence driving them and would change them both toward the ways of good. Love would grow and push out the evil. The whole thing had been a risk taken by Anthony, one of great creativity and ingenuity. It was also one very much adverse to his nature and far outside his range of comfort, but he felt something special about Ella. For the sake of love, he was willing to take great risk. It would change both of their futures for the better. Goodness would be added to their lives and all those associated with them. The unconditional support of Ella's parents of her would return dividends to them in the long run. Faith in a child is a wonderful thing.

Becky, from her vantage, was most pleased and happy for her sister. She knew that soon there would be another wedding in the family. She looked forward to that day.

The third instance involved Jane and Tom's friend Dennis. They announced to their families that they were engaged to be married. As Becky knew it would turn out, they were indeed soul mates. It was one of Becky's secondary destinies to pair these two up. This destiny would soon become complete. Tom couldn't believe it. Most of all, he couldn't believe the incredible change in Dennis. He was much better than he had ever been before. There was a goodness to him. He honored and adored Jane. He was completely faithful and committed to their relationship. He was also a better friend because of all the changes in him. The self-center had melted away. He had learned to care, as well as to be the great mind and partner that Tom needed in their work. This was incredible news.

Tom heard of the engagement directly from Dennis. Dennis asked Tom to be his best man. Tom was honored. "Most definitely. I will be glad to." Then he confided in him, "You know, Dennis, I was really concerned when Becky suggested matching you two up in our wedding party."

Dennis responded, "I can understand why, Tom, but I'm sure glad you listened to Becky's wisdom."

Tom said, "I am too. She certainly saw something in you two that I missed." He paused for a breath and a thought. "I was really concerned for Jane. You had a reputation."

Dennis hung his head in shame and confided in Tom, "I wish all my past could be swept away. I am not proud of it." He looked directly at Tom. "I made mistakes, but now I have what I need. The games and the search are over. I have found what makes me whole and good." He was sincere. He was truly a changed being. It was love's magic, love's tonic.

Tom was left convinced that Dennis was truly changed and committed to Jane. He was certain that he liked the new Dennis much better than the old. His past relationships were formed on the physical. Although he thought them strong, they were really ones of mutual physical need, not ones of spirit. This was now changed.

Both Becky and Tom were completely supportive and happy for their friends. Becky and Tom had been asked to participate in the wedding, Becky as maid of honor and Tom as best man. A special dress would be needed for Becky. By the date of the wedding, she would be seven months pregnant.

The odds will continue to be tabulated in the chance and types of relationships being formed. Spirits will continue to be paired, either attracting or repelling the energies released. Beings will come together in relationships. In many cases, it's beyond our control. These relationships will be destined to grow or fail. It is the way of nature. It is an important element to existence and being. It is the product of influence and the magic of the spirit realm. It is what makes us social and gives us a belonging. They also give us hate and deceit. Relationships are an important component gifted to our being. The strong relationships are of the spirit and spirit natures.

Book Summary

This is a story of the often-overlooked component of every Being; the spirit domain, and why it is such a necessary component of all Beings. The spirit domain is important for many reasons. It orchestrates and coordinates the internal workings, communications and influences to and from the mind component. It provides the mind with materials from its stores of knowledge and experience since the beginning of time. Unlike the other components of a Being, spirits never die. They are reassigned to a new-born. retaining all they have gathered through time to support past, present and future Beings. Spirits, from their domain, also influence motion and movement from the Being's physical component. This gives the Being fuller flexibility, dexterity and movement capabilities. Most important of all, it's in the spirit domain that life itself for each Being is centered and originates. This story tells of how the spirit domain interacts with, and influences through and with, the other components of a Being. The spirit domain contributes a great deal to determining who we are, how we act and why we behave the way we do. It will explain how a spirit influences a Being through its life's pathways.

The spirit domain of a human being contains three spirits. Each spirit has a nature, either good or evil. The strength of the spirits nature ranges from strong to weak. The domains combinations of the three spirit's natures and the different strengths of each spirit nature makes every spirit, and each domain, uniquely different. It is the three spirits within the domain contributing as one, yet contending and conflicting between the three that forms our differences, our actions and the personalities of each Being. Most of all, however, it is the spirits that give the Being life itself.

The inner spirit and domain influences are at work through many of the primary staples of our existence. Referring to a few are a Being's goodness or evil, love and all emotions and feelings, how and why we form relationships with other and those we don't. They enable us to achieve our destinies and purpose, and reasons why not. They support foresight, insight and intuition, a conscience, the forming of our personality and reason for changing moods and disposition. Miracles, magic and the mystical come from spirits and the domain; as do curses. There is so much more that will be addressed in the stories that follow.

These stories will explain how the spirit domain works in partnership with and influences the other components of the Being. The spirits provide history, knowledge, and experience to the Being and future generations. The longevity of the current civilization is based on the aggregate condition and strength of spirit domains.

About the Author

Racq grew up in rural mid-America. He is much travelled and has had many experiences and adventures helping him to develop his unique and alternate explanation on how things might be; even that hidden beneath established accepted views of our realities. He is highly creative and imaginative, and as such able to develop thoughts and ideas from different angles and perspectives. He tends to like to take risks in his stories and rethink the things presented as the established truths and presently established worldly perceptions. These will be challenged within his imagination and are drawn out in his stories. His ability is as a storyteller, and to give challenge and original material to our minds through his stories This allows consideration and proposals of new, possibly better, explanations of how things might be and might have transpired with time. He is willing to present the improbable and magical to appear as possible, sometimes even likely. Now retired from 47 years in many business roles, Racq is finding time to transform and share many of his thoughts and ideas into publishable stories.

PGIL2021USA